P9-CDY-204

Praise for Bestselling Author
CHEYENNE McCRAY

MOVING TARGET

"The sex sizzles and the danger crackles in McCray's hot new tale. Staying one step ahead is the name of the game in this dynamic story that races cross-country and tests the loyalty and character of all involved. No matter what the genre, McCray is hot!"

—*Romantic Times BOOKreviews* (4½ stars)

"A riveting tale that brings the reader to the edge of their seat. It will definitely take you on a ride that leaves you breathless and wanting more. Once again, Ms. McCray has written a winner!" —*Fallen Angel Reviews*

"A captivating tale that will keep readers on the edge of their seats." —*Romance Reviews Today*

"A hot romantic thriller that ratchets up the sexual heat and suspense." —*Fresh Fiction*

CHOSEN PREY

"Bestseller McCray takes her blistering-hot writing style into a new arena with her first romantic thriller. McCray's versatility and talent make her a star in any genre she chooses." —*Romantic Times BOOKreviews* (4½ stars)

"Sexy, sinful and a rollercoaster ride of emotions make *Chosen Prey* a must-read for all romantic suspense fans. Readers will be enthralled from the very first page. Ms. McCray is truly a genius who knows exactly which elements work best together." —*Dark Angel Reviews*

"Rip-roaring romantic suspense from start to finish."

—*Fresh Fiction*

MORE...

WICKED MAGIC

"Blistering sex and riveting battles are plentiful as this series continues building toward its climax."

—*Romantic Times BOOKreviews* (4 stars)

"Cheyenne McCray shows the best work between good and evil in *Wicked Magic*. The characters are molded perfectly...sure to delight and captivate with each turn of the page."

—*Night Owl Romance*

"A sinfully engaging read." —*A Romance Review*

SEDUCED BY MAGIC

"Blistering passion and erotic sensuality are major McCray hallmarks, in addition to a deft and exciting storyline. This magical series continues to develop its increasing cast of characters and complex plotline; the result is erotic paranormal romance liberally laced with adventure and thrills."

—*Romantic Times BOOKreviews* (4 1/2 stars Top Pick)

"The slices of humor, the glimpses of the characters' world through fantastic descriptions, not to mention fascinating characters landed this book on...[the] keeper shelf."

—*Romance Divas*

"Witches, drool-worthy warriors, and hot passion that will have readers reaching for a cool drink. Cheyenne McCray has created a fantastic and magical world where both the hero and heroine are strong and are willing to fight the darkness that threatens their worlds." —*A Romance Review*

FORBIDDEN MAGIC

"McCray will thrill and entrance you!"

—Sabrina Jeffries, *New York Times* bestselling author

"A yummy hot fudge sundae of a book!"

—MaryJanice Davidson,
New York Times bestselling author

"*Charmed* meets Kim Harrison's witch series, but with a heavy dose of erotica on top!"

—Lynsay Sands, *New York Times* bestselling author

"Wildly erotic and dangerously sensual, this explosive paranormal thriller sizzles. McCray erupts on the scene with one of the sexiest stories of the year. Her darkly dramatic world is one readers won't mind visiting again.... McCray knows how to make a reader sweat—either from spine-tingling suspense or soul-singeing sex...."

—*Romantic Times BOOKreviews*

"McCray's paranormal masterpiece is not for the fainthearted. The battle between good and evil is brought to the reader in vivid and riveting detail to the point where the reader is drawn into the pages of this bewitching and seductive fantasy that delivers plenty of action-packed sequences and arousing love scenes."

—*Rendezvous*

"*Forbidden Magic* is a spellbinding, sexy, superbly written dark fantasy. I couldn't put it down, and you won't want to either...[a] fabulous plot.... Longtime fans and newbies alike will be enchanted and swept away by this enduring tale of courage, love, passion, and magic."

—*A Romance Review*

"If one were going to make a comparison to Cheyenne McCray with another writer of the supernatural/sensuality genre, it would have to be Laurell K. Hamilton.... *Forbidden Magic* definitely puts McCray in the same league as Hamilton."

—*Shelf Life*

"Cheyenne McCray's *Forbidden Magic* is an intoxicating blend of luscious eroticism and spine-tingling action that will have you squirming on the edge of your seat."

—Angela Knight, *USA Today* bestselling author

"Cheyenne McCray has written a sexy adventure spiced with adventurous sex."

—Charlaine Harris, *New York Times* bestselling author

"Erotic with a great big capital E. Cheyenne McCray is my new favorite author!"

—Bertrice Small, *New York Times* bestselling author

"*Forbidden Magic* is a fabulous faery tale. The writing is sharp; the story hot!"

—Virginia Henley, *New York Times* bestselling author

"Cheyenne McCray has crafted a novel that takes the imagination on an exciting flight. Full of fantasy, with a touch of darkness, a great read for anyone who loves to get lost in a book that stretches the boundaries!" —Heather Graham, *New York Times* bestselling author

"Explosive, erotic, and un-put-downable. Cheyenne McCray more than delivers!"

—L.A. Banks, bestselling author of The Vampire Huntress Legend series

"Magical mayhem, sexy shapeshifters, wondrous witches and warlocks...in *Forbidden Magic*, Cheyenne McCray has created a fabulous new world. You won't be able to get enough!" —Lori Handeland, *USA Today* bestselling author

"Fans of dark paranormal fantasy will enjoy the fast-paced, spine-tingling twists and turns of Cheyenne McCray's *Forbidden Magic*." —Toni Blake, author of *In Your Wildest Dreams*

"Cheyenne McCray's *Forbidden Magic* is a rich mix of witches, demons, and fae in an epic tapestry full of conflict and desire." —Robin Owens, author of *Heart Choice*

"Chock-full of emotion and action, Cheyenne McCray's *Forbidden Magic* will find a spot on the keeper shelf of every reader who enjoys a touch of the paranormal along with her erotic romance. I highly recommend it!"

—Ann Jacobs, author of *A Mutual Favor*

"Cheyenne McCray has written a tempting, exciting novel rich in magic and pleasure."

—Lora Leigh, author of *The Breed Next Door*

"McCray's knowledge of Fae, Fomorii, elves and ancient Irish magics shines in this book of witches, warriors and dangerous desires."

—Linnea Sinclair, author of *Gabriel's Ghost*

"Cheyenne McCray delivers a scorching tale of modern witches and ancient Fae, a winner rich with lore, fantasy, gritty action, and heart-gripping romance."

—Annie Windsor,
award-winning author of *Sailmaster's Woman*

"This modern-day tale meets ancient-world paranormal isn't just a book, it's an event. The elements all come together in this paranormal romance. You start reading for the story and end up reading for the characters. You're left at the edge of your seat needing more until the very last satisfying word. You won't be able to put it down once you start reading!"

—Sheila English,
CEO of Circle of Seven Productions

Other St. Martin's Paperbacks titles by

CHEYENNE McCRAY

Paranormal Romance

Dark Magic

Shadow Magic

Wicked Magic

Seduced by Magic

Forbidden Magic

Romantic Suspense

Moving Target

Chosen Prey

Anthologies

No Rest for the Witches

3 1526 03627783 5

THE FIRST SIN

WITHDRAWN

Cheyenne McCray

HARFORD COUNTY
PUBLIC LIBRARY
100 E. Pennsylvania Avenue
Bel Air, MD 21014

St. Martin's Paperbacks

NOTE: If you purchased this book without a cover you should be aware that this book is stolen property. It was reported as "unsold and destroyed" to the publisher, and neither the author nor the publisher has received any payment for this "stripped book."

This is a work of fiction. All of the characters, organizations and events portrayed in this novel are either products of the author's imagination or are used fictitiously.

THE FIRST SIN

Copyright © 2009 by Cheyenne McCray.
Excerpt from *Demons Not Included* copyright © 2009 by Cheyenne McCray.

Cover photo © Royalty Free Image/Veer.

All rights reserved.

For information address St. Martin's Press, 175 Fifth Avenue, New York, NY 10010.

ISBN: 0-312-94644-9
EAN: 978-0-312-94644-9

Printed in the United States of America

St. Martin's Paperbacks edition / February 2009

St. Martin's Paperbacks are published by St. Martin's Press, 175 Fifth Avenue, New York, NY 10010.

10 9 8 7 6 5 4 3 2 1

To the world's best agent, Nancy Yost.
May there be many more sinful adventures ahead.

ACKNOWLEDGMENTS

After a few research trips to Boston, it has officially become one of my adopted cities. I love the people, the atmosphere, the history, the lay of the land. (Which I traversed on foot from Back Bay to Southie and everywhere in between and around. What a blast!)

I have so many special thanks to give. NUMBER ONE is Officer T.J. Leonard, patrolman with the Boston Transit Police Department. Wow, what an incredible, tremendous help he has been throughout writing *The First Sin*. I cannot begin to thank him enough. Even the most inane questions he answered—possibly with amusement—but he helped me in more ways than I can thank him.

Chris Vanderslice, you are awesome. You were my first official Boston tour guide and you are the best. Thanks for everything, including giving Lexi and Nick good homes.

Lauren Vitale, it was a pleasure and thank you. Armani it is!

Thank you so much to Boston Police Department Sergeant Detective Kelley O'Connell of the Family Justice Center Human Trafficking Task Force. I greatly appreciated her time and the information she provided on human trafficking for this persistent author. This book is a long way (a long, long, long way) from what we talked about, but I have a much greater understanding of the overall picture relating to HT.

Much appreciation to Suzanna Jones for your support of the Arizona Literacy Foundation.

A huge thank-you to Rani Ogitani for your support of Brenda Novak's fourth annual online Auction for Diabetes Research.

Anna Windsor, Tee O'Fallon, Patrice Michelle, and Nelissa Donovan—I love you, babes.

Thanks to everyone at St. Martin's involved in every step of every process in making this novel come to light, and to Monique Patterson for helping it to come alive.

To my three sons—your understanding of Mom's need to bury herself in this project means a lot to me.

And thank you, Dave Gilpin, for all of the smiles when I needed them most.

“Can’t shake the Devil’s hand and say you’re only kidding.”
They Might Be Giants, music artists

PROLOGUE

Kristin

March 15

Kristin Donovan looked around at all the flashing lights in the packed nightclub, jammed with lots of hot, sweaty bodies, and barely dressed barmaids walking around selling Jell-O shots and neon shooters. At least that's what Carlene and Tess called them.

Kristin shifted in her chair and tugged down on the dress that kept creeping up her thighs. "I can't believe you two dragged me down here."

"The Diamond Castle is one of the hottest Boston nightclubs." Carlene set down her Heineken. "It's Friday night. You can forget your stupid paper and take one day off with no guilt, Kristin."

Tess finished her cosmo. "You spend too much time studying and not enough time living."

Kristin shrugged. "I'll do my 'living' when I graduate."

"Yeah, right." Tess shook her dark hair. "Then you'll be wrapped up in whatever it takes to be a psychologist." She waved her hand. "In-service work or something?"

"Practicum. Internship. Fellowship. Or something." Kristin smiled as her body relaxed from her two rum and Cokes and she began to feel more than a little tipsy. "You're right. It's good to get out. I can spend Saturday and Sunday working on that paper."

The paper was for her graduate class in abnormal psych, one of her toughest subjects at Harvard, and she would get through it without help. Other than asking each of her professors questions from time to time.

The abnormal psych class was so difficult, though, that when she went to Professor Michaels's office to ask a question he'd offered to give her private tutoring, like some of her other teachers had. After he answered her question, she'd said thanks to his offer but she'd figure this thing out if it killed her.

It was a tough class, but she preferred to make her way through her classes on her own. Her professor had simply nodded his bald head and turned his attention back to grading the essays on his desk.

She should be studying for that class.

Nah. Screw it. As long as she didn't have a hangover on top of lack of enough sleep tomorrow, she'd be fine.

"Your turn to buy." Carlene waggled her Heineken from side to side.

"I could use a Smirnoff Ice." Tess had downed her cosmo. "I need something a little more refreshing." She glanced at Carlene. "Something that doesn't come in a black or green bottle."

"And you could use another rum and Coke." Carlene gestured to the glass that was only filled with melting ice now. "You need to mellow out a little more."

"I *am* mellow." Kristin stood as Tess rolled her eyes. "Okay, *one* more rum and Coke."

"Lightweight," Carlene said, and Kristin grinned as she turned away.

In her too-high heels, Kristin did her best to push her way through the mass of bodies in the nightclub. Deafeningly loud music throbbed in her head and the flashing, colored lights caused her to blink and see spots whenever she closed her eyes. Lots of dirty dancing was going on—really wasn't room for anything else.

The two rum and Cokes Kristin had downed gave her such a relaxed, tipsy feeling that she didn't care how many bodies pressed against her.

She wasn't much of a drinker. When was the last time she'd had alcohol?

Smells of sweat and too much cologne and perfume made her wrinkle her nose. The heat of so many people crowded together made her own body sticky with sweat.

Kristin winced, then grimaced as someone slammed into her from behind. She stumbled sideways and hit a man's chest with her shoulder, hard enough to force them both against the bar.

She blew out a huff of air which poofed her long blond hair out of her face. "Sorry," she shouted over the pounding beat of the music, as she looked into a pair of dark brown eyes.

Wow.

The man's grin was so sexy that she caught her breath while he steadied her before bending close and murmuring in her ear, "No problem at all."

Kristin shivered, a streak of desire shooting straight to her belly. The rum and Cokes, definitely working overtime.

"Dance?" he asked, his mouth still close to her ear.

When she looked at the incredibly gorgeous face, her body said, "Oh, yeah, I'm so there," but she just nodded without answering.

He settled his palm on her waist and guided her into the middle of the hot, gyrating bodies. When they came to a pause, he smiled and moved his other hand to her waist and pulled her close. Their bodies weren't quite touching, but they might as well have been. Kristin's entire being was aware of this man she didn't even know, and her body was screaming at her to get to know him better, a lot better.

She could just picture their naked bodies sliding together, his minty aftershave mingling with his male scent.

What's wrong with you, Kristin Donovan? You don't do one-nighters. Actually she hadn't "done" anyone since her first encounter with Steve, her freshman year, and that hadn't been nearly as exciting as the way this stranger made her feel.

"I'm Joe." He slid his hands a little farther down from her waist, his fingertips nearly touching her buttocks, and she gasped. "What's your name?"

She settled her hands on his shoulders. "Kristin."

He moved his mouth to her ear and she shivered while an arrow of desire traveled straight between her thighs. "I didn't hear you."

Joe's face was close enough to hers that she caught her breath, wanting to kiss this stranger. Feel his lips move over hers and taste him as his tongue explored her mouth.

Get a grip!

"Kristin." She swallowed when his stubble scraped her cheek as he moved his face closer to hers.

Joe said, "You're so sweet," just before he nipped her earlobe and she gasped. "Yeah, sweet."

Heat flushed from her neck to the roots of her hair as he drew her tight to him, his hands on her butt now and what was clearly a good-sized erection pressed into her belly.

What are you doing, Kristin? You don't do things like this.

The way he was holding her so close made it automatic to slip her arms around his neck. Blood rushed in her ears, muffling the sound of the pounding music and she had a hard time catching her breath. She moved her face away from his and laid her cheek over his heart. Its beat was steady, calm, comforting.

Joe rubbed her backside through her short dress and nuzzled her hair as they slowly rocked and turned in the same spot. He smelled so good. Kristin started trembling with need so great she wasn't sure she could control it.

She could picture this big man and his thick erection sliding into her in hard, deep thrusts. Her panties grew damp the more she pictured it.

Must be the rum and Cokes. Need to get out of here. It's too dangerous getting the hots for a stranger like this.

But maybe he'd want to see her again—with no sex. Yet. Maybe they could date a while.

But just dating this big package of sensuality wouldn't be enough. She'd want him more than she could probably control herself.

"What are you drinking?" The warmth of his breath and the light mint of his cologne pitched another thrill straight to her belly.

Kristin tipped her head back to look at him. "Rum and Coke."

He took her hand and she could just imagine that big hand skimming down her body.

Joe guided them to the bar and turned to speak to the bartender, whose boobs were half falling out of her skintight shirt. When Joe gave his order to the barmaid, it gave Kristin a chance to check out his firm backside and the way his T-shirt stretched across his back. He looked as delicious from behind as he did from the front.

Joe let go of her hand and at once she wanted him holding her again. While she waited, Kristin looked around the dance floor and tugged down the thigh-length blue dress Carlene had loaned her.

His smile sent crazy sensations through her body as he turned and handed her a glass that was light on the ice but cold in her hand.

She shivered from his nearness and more wild thrills stirred in her belly when she looked up into his handsome features. He had a square face, nice eyes, and short-cropped brown hair.

He clinked his bottle of Guinness against her glass and said what she thought was, "Here's to sexy blond women."

Her stomach flip-flopped and her hand trembled a little as she raised the glass to her lips. The rum and Coke tasted funny, but she'd always preferred her drinks out of a can over sodas dispensed from a machine.

The drink couldn't begin to quench the thirst that came on suddenly. Probably from the heat of all the bodies pressed against her. She drained her glass in moments before handing it back to Joe. He winked, and set his bottle and her glass on the bar.

The stuffiness of the room, the gyrating bodies, the loud music, and the stench of sweat became more pronounced. A sense of light-headedness caused her to list to the side, and Joe caught her by the shoulders.

"You okay?" he mouthed in her ear.

"I—I think I need some air." She barely managed to get

the words out as she struggled for breath. Hyperventilating. She was hyperventilating.

Joe anchored her by wrapping his arm around her shoulders and he kept her from tripping.

Her head spun even more as Joe guided her through the packed room. Vaguely she realized he was taking her to the back rather than the front entrance.

They walked through a fog-shrouded doorway and into a hallway where the noise seemed cut in half. Kristin stumbled but Joe kept a grip on her as he brought her down the long hallway, farther from the noise and heat and smells.

"Better?" he said in a low voice that was as sexy as his grin.

Better. Yes, this was better.

Her head lolled against Joe's chest and her knees gave out. He kept her from falling as he pushed open the back door.

Funny how the cold air wasn't making her shiver. She felt hot all over, like she had the flu.

Joe led her toward a maroon van. "I think you need to sit down, baby."

Sit. Yeah, she'd feel better once she had a chance to rest for a moment.

She frowned as the door opened and another man appeared from the inside of the van.

"The boss is waiting," the man said in what she thought was a Swedish accent.

Kristin felt like she was going to slide into a gelatinous puddle as she tried to register what he was saying and what was happening as they dragged her into the van and spread her out on the backseat.

Her dress hiked up to her waist, exposing her panties. She would have pulled it back down if her arms hadn't felt like stretched taffy. And if she had cared.

The other man disappeared and the van vibrated as the engine started. Joe stood outside, his hand on the door as he looked her over. "I'd sure like to fuck you right now. But rules are rules. Don't screw the merchandise."

He slid the van door shut.

CHAPTER 1

Shaking the devil's hand

March 27
Wednesday morning

The harshness of the heat presses down on me. Sweat slips from my forehead, drips over my brow, and into my eyes. Can't move to wipe the sweat away. Can't blow my cover. I don't even dare blink as I site my target through the scope of my M16. My spotter, Keets, remains as motionless as I do.

The mission is its own version of hell. Ever since we landed in Nigeria, a crawling sensation along my spine has told me that something's off about this whole setup. Something desperately wrong.

When I told Captain Williams, the bastard blew me off. He doesn't like the fact I'm one of the first women snipers in the history of the US Army. And I'm damned good at what I do—

Killing terrorists, saving American lives.

Captain Williams—what a dick. But a soldier follows orders.

My spotter, Keets, gives me the signal that I've got the best shot possible.

Target in my sights. I squeeze the trigger of my M16.

At the same time, Keets gets some chatter over his comm. He shouts, "Wait!"

But it's too late. I see the spurt, the telltale arc of blood from my target's forehead before he goes down.

One shot. One kill.

My heart thunders as I look at Keets, who says, "Oh, shit."

Something has gone horribly, horribly wrong.

I'm running.

Bars—I'm behind bars. Everything's so close. Tight. Damp. Pain riddles my body and I can barely keep consciousness. I've been beaten so badly I have a hard time grasping what's real and what's not. Was I captured? I was following orders. What happened to my team? What happened to Keets?

The pit of hell. How long have I been here? Why am I here?

The urge to claw my way out of the pit makes my arms and fingers ache as if I've already tried.

Oh, God, not again. The whip draws blood through my shredded camouflage and I try not to scream. The pain—I hold onto it, make it a part of me, pretend I want it. If I don't, they'll break me.

Fists slam into my face, my temples, my belly, even my breasts. I want to scream but I make my mind retreat into a private place where I embrace the pain.

Four men, maybe five surround me. Huge men. Their faces, so dark, so shadowed. Are they human? Their forms sway and distort.

One man steps forward, but I still can't make out his features.

Fear tears through me. Fear like I've never felt before. Fear worse than the agony threatening to cripple me. The man—he's the one. The one to introduce me to pain like I've never known.

I don't have the strength to recoil as he slides his palm down the side of my face, through the blood running down my cheek. What is he going to do to me now? Put a cloth sack over my head again, nearly smothering me? Then submerging my face in a water tank until I nearly drown? Shock me with electricity a second time while I'm soaking wet and feeling half dead already?

"Now will you?" he says in a tone that tells me he's ready to dose out every bit of torture all over again.

Can I survive any more of this?

"Will you?" *His voice is harsher, angrier, and I know I've lost.*

Tears flow down my cheeks, mixing with my blood as I force myself to say those horrible words.

"Yes. God, yes."

I woke with a hard jerk. Heat seared my chest. My heart was beating so hard it felt as if someone was kicking my ribcage from inside. Cloth bound my legs and wrapped my body like a giant python. The more I struggled the tighter it got.

I was back in hell. I would do anything to be free. Anything. My bindings grew tighter. My breathing became more frantic. I kicked and kicked while clawing at my bindings.

The taste of salt was on my lips and in my mouth from sweat dripping down my face. I scraped my own arm and felt the sting when my nails raked my skin.

I gasped. Arched my back. Opened my eyes.

Reality hit my consciousness. I was in my room. My own room. I wasn't tied with rope while being beaten in that dark cell. I wasn't attempting to force myself into that dark corner of my mind where I tried to pretend that pain was pleasure to escape the agony.

Cloth, soaked with perspiration, bound me. I was tangled in my own sheet. Sweat slicked my damp palms as I rubbed my face. I pushed back my chin-length dark hair that was plastered against my cheeks.

My face grew hot then cold. Over the years I'd been beaten, stabbed, and shot so often that I'd developed a coping mechanism that helped me focus—trying to turn pain to pleasure to escape what my body was going through. But having the shit beat out of me wasn't optimum for that kind of mental retreat.

Acid burned my throat as I held back the urge to throw up.

Moving air from the ceiling fan cools my sweating body as I kick the damp sheets the rest of the way off. I stared at the ceiling. It needed a new coat of paint. I'd have to let Marty, my super, know.

The nightmare was nothing new. The nightmare that would probably never leave me.

The mission gone wrong
My so-called court-martial.
The prison.
The beatings.
The ultimatum and later the killings.
Was it even possible to atone for my sins?

The nightmares, my past . . . No one at the Recovery Enforcement Division would believe that I wasn't nearly as strong on the inside as I am on the outside. The other RED agents think my last name suits me. Steele. All they know is that Lexi Steele can totally kick ass. As a Team Supervisor for the Human Trafficking and Sex Crimes Division of RED, I have to be tough. And that's not a problem. Not at all.

It's when I have to acknowledge the past and all of those nameless, faceless people I'd assassinated, that I unravel inside.

I wished Gary was here. He'd tuck me against his big, hard body, kiss me on the top of my head, and tell me to go back to sleep. It didn't chase away all of the bad things I'd done, but it was so much better than lying there, shivering in the dark.

I'd met Gary at a Red Sox game a couple of years ago, and I loved his big, hot muscular body and the way he held me, kissed me, made love to me. Gary was *wicked* hot.

He liked my petite frame and had said how amazed he was that dynamite came in a small, five-foot-four package. He always said how much he loved green eyes too, and would slip his fingers through the silkiness of my dark hair that I kept shoulder length. He always said I was beautiful and I told him he was delusional. Well, I'm not bad looking and I do have my moments.

Unfortunately, his bodybuilder competitions and my job as an undercover operative often kept us from spending time together.

It was so difficult not to tell Gary the truth—that I wasn't really a foreign language interpreter, although I do speak several languages.

Keeping my true career hidden from everyone in my big,

messy, Boston Irish family was probably the hardest. No one had any idea except for one of my five brothers, Zane, who was an undercover RED agent, too.

My friends and neighbors—of course they had no clue about what I really did.

Sometimes I didn't like it, didn't like it at all—having to lie to everyone but Zane because I had no choice. As a special agent for RED, a clandestine branch of the NSA, I lived a secret life.

RED was an offshoot of the National Security Agency (NSA) that only a short list of bureaucrats knew existed: RED's Director; the Deputy Director; a federal judge; a federal prosecutor; the head of the NSA; Senator Jeannette Shelton; and the President. Not even the VP or his cabinet members knew we existed.

And definitely no other branch of law enforcement or civilians had a clue we were protecting them, saving countless American lives.

But that hadn't been the case up until five years ago. Prior to that I'd been a killing machine. An assassin who didn't even know the names of her targets or why she was killing them.

Before I was an assassin, I'd been an overly confident but first-class sniper for the Army Special Forces. Then everything was blown to hell when I'd been court-martialed for a mistake I'd made. A mistake caused by following my captain's orders, but it all came down on me. I was the one who'd pulled the trigger.

It's not easy to break a Special Forces Officer, but "FAS" did a damned good job of it. I didn't even know the real name of the organization that had abducted me moments after my court-martial, so that's what I called them—Fucking Asshole Sonsofbitches. I do have even more choice, appropriate words for the bastards, but I'll leave it at that.

One of the men had distracted me while another managed to inject an animal tranquilizer with just one stab in my thigh. Next thing I knew I was sitting in front of the FAS. They talked about "saving me" if I did their dirty work.

Assassinate people.

I was half dead from all of the countless beatings and the whippings. Then they'd nearly drowned me before electrocuting me. It was when they started breaking fingers in my left hand that I knew I'd lost.

They'd broken me. Then programmed me.

It wasn't until one powerful woman took me out of hell that I had a life again. RED became everything to me. Only my family was more important than the organization that had saved me.

There's a lot of blood on my hands. But then I was given the opportunity to turn my life around. Only RED and my family kept me sane.

The sound of something vibrating against wood came from my nightstand. Box springs creaked as I rolled onto my side and I picked up one of two cell phones which I'd set to vibrate. When I flipped open the cell for RED, the caller identification screen said "Unknown." No big surprise there.

"Yeah?" The word came out in a croak, my voice still rough from sleep. What time was it?

"Steele." Karen Oxford's voice had me sitting straight up in bed and all trace of my sleepiness vanished. If the Assistant Special Agent in Charge was calling, then it had to be serious. My gut clenched as she said, "Get to HQ, immediately."

I glanced at the clock. Seven-fifteen. I normally got in around eight-thirty. And why would Oxford call me herself?

"What happened?" I asked as I swung my legs over the side of the bed and planted my feet on the worn carpeting before I stood.

"It's Randolph." Oxford's tone turned weary and the feeling in my gut notched up tenfold.

I'd made Team Supervisor six months ago and Stacy Randolph was one of my agents working on Operation Cinderella, a probe into a local-turned-international sex slave ring.

I went rigid as Oxford continued, "She was raped and murdered. Her body was found just after midnight in Boston Harbor."

Numbness crept over me as I tried to assimilate Oxford's statement and I closed my eyes.

Randolph had penetrated one of the inner circles of the organization that would ultimately bring us to whoever was responsible for auctioning off young women to the highest bidder.

And now she was dead. One of my team members had been murdered.

"You will notify the other TSs, then your individual teams once I brief you," Oxford said.

A burning sensation gripped my throat and I opened my eyes. This was supposed to be Special Agent Stacy Randolph's last op.

It had been her last op.

At twenty-five, tough, smart, and filled with enthusiasm for her job, Randolph had been one of our best. She'd also been just days from leaving RED to become a civilian to marry and start a family. She'd been so excited and almost always wore a smile when she was at HQ.

And now she was gone. The first agent I'd ever lost.

More blood on my hands. I knew I wasn't being fair to myself, but I felt like Stacy Randolph was yet another life that could be laid on the altar of my sins.

"Yes, ma'am." I tried to draw an even breath. "I'll take care of informing all TSs and agents."

"Our contact in the BPD is notifying next of kin." Oxford said. "I'll brief you in my office. The other TSs will be assembled in conference room one by the time we're done."

I gave a stiff nod even though she couldn't see me. "Yes, ma'am."

"Randolph's partner notified us," Oxford said. "Their backup never saw it happen."

"Deseronto is too deep to come in and the targets didn't know they were together." I gripped one hand into a fist. "I'll arrange for a new partner. And more backup."

"Fifteen minutes, my office." Oxford clicked off and I dropped to the edge of the bed, my chest aching from the blow of Randolph's death.

It was RED's standard protocol to provide the BPD with a fictitious story because no one could know what any of us really did.

Some stranger would be going to the Randolphs' home and lie to them about how their daughter had died.

Her family would never know their daughter was a hero and not just a victim.

I got back to my feet and headed for the shower.

CHAPTER 2

Nick

March 27
Wednesday morning

Nick studied the yellow triple-decker, or "trip" as the residents of Southie called this cookie-cutter style, three-story apartment house.

Alexi Steele lived in the third-floor apartment. Nick focused on the window on the top floor with its white curtains drawn together. He hadn't been watching her place long, but long enough that he'd seen lights come on behind those curtains ten minutes ago. They'd just clicked off.

A petite brunette, maybe five-three, five-four at most, shot through the front door of the trip, slammed the door behind her, then jogged down the steps.

Nick was surprised when he felt an unexpected stirring of desire. His attention sharpened on her, all senses becoming painfully alert as they focused on this one woman. Damn, she was hot. Alexi Steele was a small package, her features delicate, making him think of a fairy that should be tucked safely away somewhere. But her body ruined all pretense of delicate innocence. She had curves in all the right places, curves that drove him to imagine touching her, stroking her, feeling her. That short, chin-length hair looked so soft, ready to be caressed, to run his fingers through. He suddenly felt primal, like a wolf who had suddenly caught scent of his mate.

So this was his new partner. Damn, he'd never be able to keep his hands off of her.

Lucky for him, he wouldn't have to. He'd have his hands all over her within a couple of days.

He watched as she climbed into a black Jeep Cherokee parked at the curb and she started the vehicle. She barely glanced at the empty street before pulling out and gunning the engine. Her tires squealed as she spun the Jeep around and headed in the direction that would take her to the RED HQ.

Special Agent Lexi Steele, the head of *Operation Cinderella*. A supposedly tough, "kick-ass" agent, Lexi would have looked like a fragile doll—if it wasn't for the tight, angry expression that had been on her features when she'd come out of the apartment building and climbed into the Jeep.

Nick's work phone vibrated against his hip. He drew it out, checked the caller identification screen. "Slave Nandra," he said when he answered and at the same time glanced at the digital clock on his dashboard. "You're late. Looks like you've got yourself a punishment first thing tonight."

"I'm sorry, Master Dunning." Nandra's voice shook a little. "I couldn't help—"

"No excuses." Nick put a growl in his voice. "Ten o'clock tonight. Dungeon Room."

"Yes, Master Dunning." Then she hurried to add, "I won't be late."

"Make sure you're not," Nick said before he snapped his phone shut and stuffed it back into its belt clip.

"The goddamned hunt begins," he murmured as he started his Ford Explorer and headed on out.

CHAPTER 3

RED

March 27
Wednesday morning

By the time I got on the road in my Jeep Cherokee, a steady burn of fury had settled in, replacing some of the shock. It had been all I could do to keep from punching my speed to a hundred from Southie to Portland Street.

The guilt was still there, but whoever had taken out Randolph was going to pay. The bastard was as good as dead.

My personal cell phone vibrated in its clip at my waist as I pulled up to a stoplight. I drew the cell out and answered it without looking at the display. "Steele," I said, my voice unintentionally harsh.

A pause, then "Something's wrong, isn't it, pet," my mother stated in her strong Boston Irish accent.

"Mammy." I took a deep breath. "Everything's okay."

"It's not, but you'll tell me if you have a mind to." She hardly paused for breath. "You'll be here for Sunday dinner?"

Sunday. Dinner.

Talking with my mother—I could use a few moments of normalcy.

Every Wednesday morning she called to make sure I'd be there on Sunday because I couldn't always—sometimes work kept me away when I was undercover. Otherwise, I wouldn't miss a Sunday of getting together with the lot of us unless I didn't have a choice. The time I'd been in the Army and had to miss Sundays with my family was hard, but it was nothing compared to the nightmare my life had been as an assassin.

During those two years, being with my family and sharing every Sunday with them had been nothing but a dream. FAS barely allowed me enough leeway to contact my family to let them know I was alive. As far as they knew I was traveling throughout Europe in my new career as an interpreter after leaving the Army.

Yes, talking about normal things unrelated to the harsh realities of my career was what I needed right now. Like a day with my family.

"Dublin coddle?" I asked with a hopeful note in my voice. Mammy made such wicked good coddle.

I put my black Jeep Cherokee into gear and headed through the light after it turned green.

"And wild mushroom soup. Apple crumble for dessert." The pleasure in her voice was clear when she added, "Ryan will be home and I'll have to make enough for the lot of those boys."

I'd forgotten one of my four older brothers, Ryan, would be home on leave from the Marines. I also have a younger brother and sister. I couldn't help but smile. "And you'd better make enough for me. Don't worry about Rori. She doesn't eat, anyway."

"Lord above knows that girl needs to." Mammy gave an exasperated huff. "Is that boyfriend of yours coming? I'll need to make another lot for him. Eats as much as your brothers."

I guided the Cherokee through traffic, checking my rearview mirrors. "Gary eats even more than Sean."

Mammy laughed, knowing it was true, that my twelve-year-old brother could out eat my four big, brawny older brothers.

"Yeah, Gary will be there." Note to self: call Gary to remind him. "He won't want to miss your coddle or crumble."

"Are you sure, pet, that you don't want to tell me what's bothering you?" she asked.

I sighed, her question slamming me back to reality. "It's just starting out to be a rough day." Of course I couldn't tell her about Randolph. It was for my family's and my friends' safety that I kept up the illusion that I was an interpreter. Not only did RED require me to keep my career a secret, no way in hell was I going to endanger them.

The only exceptions to my friends and family who knew were one of my older brothers, Zane, and my best friend, Georgina, both of whom worked for RED, too.

Mammy was a no-nonsense mother who'd raised seven children and she always knew when something deeper was happening. "It's not good to keep as many secrets as you do."

"What secrets?" I tried really hard to put a smile in my voice. "How could anyone keep a secret from you?"

She humphed. "See you Sunday, pet."

"Dinner is already calling," I said before I told her I loved her and clicked the phone shut.

Fifteen minutes after Oxford's phone call, I guided the Jeep, my personal vehicle, into RED's parking garage. I stomped on my brakes harder than I should have and jerked back and forth in my seat as I took my space between my government-issue dark blue Trailblazer and the red Mercedes sports car.

The Trailblazer was registered in one of my undercover names, Alexi McGrath. The second I got into the dark blue Trailblazer, I'd carry my McGrath ID. I used it when I went undercover in a seedier environment.

When I climbed into the red Mercedes, I'd be Alexi Adams, a socialite with a hell of a lot of money and clout that I wouldn't mind really having.

I was going undercover soon as Adams in just three days. I'd be one of the elite young Bostonian crowd, a socialite who just happened to be into kink. I'd work my way into a small group of BDSM players who were suspected of kidnapping and selling young women.

The thought made every muscle in my body tighten even more than they already had been. Girls and women sold to the highest bidder.

After I'd jumped out and locked my Cherokee, my running shoes pounded concrete in the parking garage as I jogged the distance to the elevator. It would take me to the first floor of a five-story building that had an Interpreter Services Company sign outside—RED's cover.

My faded blue jeans were a little loose, and I was wearing a T-shirt and matching overshirt the same color of green as my eyes. Forest green.

After I got off the parking garage elevator, I went through a set of doors. I gave a nod to the receptionist of the "Interpreter Services Company" and hurried past her to the set of elevators that went up to RED's upper floors.

Working for RED was practically a dream job. Power with no red tape. After those years of operating under a group's iron fist, using *any means* necessary to perform and complete an operation was the kind of freedom that suited me. Hell, we didn't even have to do everything "by the books."

Once I passed the receptionist, I headed for the elevators that would take me from the lobby to the upper floors. I placed my hand on the fingerprint scanner and almost immediately the elevator doors opened.

Smells of generic air freshener met me on my way into the elevator and the door closed behind me.

What had gone so wrong? How could Randolph be dead? I watched the digital numbers flash by while I let the fingers of my left hand thump a steady beat-beat, beat-beat against my leg.

Second floor, narcotic and weapons trafficking, along with weapons of mass destruction. Third floor, technology theft. Fourth floor, terrorist activity and organized crime. And finally we reached my floor, human trafficking and sex crimes.

I stepped out of the elevator and onto a black-tiled catwalk above a chrome-and-glass control center. Immediately a wave of climate-controlled air blew away the generic air freshener and I was hit with smells of technology. That almost indefinable smell of plastic, wiring, electronics.

An overall blue glow from the countless screens and monitors in Command Central, below the catwalk, reflected off the shiny glass and chrome surfaces. In front of me, stairs led down to CC, an area designed with the highest technology available—and some technology no one outside of RED even knew existed. Within CC were multiple Team Centers for every operation currently in progress, including *Operation Cinderella.*

To my left the tile ran past the glass-walled offices for all the Team Supervisors. Not far down that line of glass and chrome was the very spacious office of our Assistant Special Agent in Charge, our ASAC, Karen Oxford.

The woman to whom I owed my life.

Special Agent in Charge Carter, the man who was ultimately responsible for every operation on every floor of RED, was probably playing solitaire on his computer on the administration floor behind those curtained glass walls. No kidding. Our SAC figured he was above us anyway, and let the ASAC of each department handle the "dirty work," while he sat on his ass taking kudos for our stats.

I glanced to my right, where a conference room door just about to close caught my eye. I'd only caught a glimpse, but a very tall man shut the door behind him. Definitely a back and a tight ass I'd never seen around here before.

We agents are trained to notice everything.

Along the same wall were the doors to several other private conference rooms. The doors broke the flow of smooth black granite. No glass walls there.

I swallowed. Conference room one would be filling with other TSs soon and I needed to be briefed by Oxford first.

Every step I took was like wading through some kind of surreal fog. The consistently cool air felt hot and burned my skin. I tried to figure out what had gone wrong with Randolph and the op as I walked past one glass-walled office after another, each office belonging to a Team Supervisor, a TS.

Lee's, Taylor's, mine, an empty office, Kartchner's, Martinez's, Armistead's, Blomstein's—

Oxford's.

Darlene, Oxford's too-serious assistant with the bad bowl haircut, glanced away from her computer monitor and looked over the top of her square black-rimmed plastic eyeglasses at me. I'd been in Oxford's office a few times for not following protocol, and Darlene had always made it obvious she didn't approve of me.

So, I'd made a couple of smart-ass remarks to Darlene in the past. Maybe that crack about her salad-bowl haircut making her look like John Lennon hadn't been a real hot idea. But did that make me such a bad guy?

Darlene gave me the same tight-faced look she always gave me and I doubted she knew about Randolph yet. Oxford would have me make the announcement to the agents first. Darlene had liked Randolph. Everyone had.

Darlene gestured to Oxford's door. "She wants you in right away," she said before going back to her computer, and back to pretending I didn't exist.

I slipped into the office and closed the door behind me. Her glass-walled office overlooked Command Central, where below her agents moved like worker bees in a hive. None of them aware an agent had been murdered.

Oxford's desk lamp cast a glow on her skin that was as smooth as bronze silk. Only the fine lines at the corners of her eyes gave away the fact that she wasn't in her thirties anymore and had the experience to go along with her forty-something years.

Usually I followed a certain protocol with my ASAC. I waited until she invited me to sit—she didn't always. And I'd let her speak first.

Not this time. I was pissed. Had been since I got her call.

I didn't wait for an invitation and sat in one of the low-backed chairs in front of her desk, my spine straight and stiff. It took me a moment to realize I was gripping the armrests so hard my fingers dug into the black leather.

"Tell me everything," I said.

Oxford's dark eyes met mine. Professional, emotionless eyes. "Your target organization caught on."

A sick feeling curdled in my belly and I wanted to hug my arms tight around my midsection. This was Randolph, one of my agents, we were talking about.

"Boston PD found her floating in the harbor early this morning," Oxford continued. "Randolph's undercover ID popped on our grid the moment a BPD officer relayed the information, and we stepped in. An expedited exam showed she was raped before her throat was slit."

I pinched the bridge of my nose with my thumb and forefinger. "Christ." I raised my head. "I shouldn't have let her do this last op."

"Never second-guess your decisions, Steele." Oxford held a pen in her left hand but, like usual, didn't make any agitated or nervous movements. A pad was on her desk with notes scribbled across it in handwriting worse than any doctor's.

"The other TSs should be waiting for you now. *Every* available resource is yours to catch Agent Randolph's murderers." Oxford's voice and eyes did turn hard now and I finally realized how angry she was. "Get the bastards and deal with them using any means necessary."

Any cop or soldier took it seriously when one of their own was taken out. Everyone on my team had just been given a hell of a lot of motivation to take these bastards down. And I would see to it personally.

Oxford went back to jotting down notes, and I knew she had as good as excused me. I pushed myself up from the chair and left Oxford's office.

When I reached Conference Room One, I restrained myself from jerking the door open. I entered and let the door slip behind me with an almost imperceptible swish.

I stood behind the chair at the head of the table and faced the other six TSs. The seventh TS had just moved to another RED HQ, in San Francisco.

It took everything I had to hold back my emotions. The only thing I let show was the fury burning inside me. I propped my hands on my hips, pushing aside the shirt that I wore over my T-shirt. I braced my right hand beside my Glock and my left hand next to my RED cell phone and my personal cell.

"Agent Stacy Randolph has been murdered." I met each one of their shocked gazes. "An op went bad and the killers raped her then slit her throat before dumping her in the harbor."

Randolph had been spunky, determined, friendly, and down-to-earth. I don't think she had a single enemy in our division. Anywhere in RED for that matter.

"We're going to get the fuckers and we're going to take them down," I said, a definite growl in my voice. "After we've neutered each and every son of a bitch in that operation."

When I was finished, my fellow supervisors expressed rage that almost matched mine. Then Martinez, Taylor, Blomstein, Kartchner, Lee, and Armistead all filed past me. Each wore expressions of anger and determination. You bet the SOBs who killed Randolph would be history.

The next part was harder, as we each went to our individual teams and told them the news.

After going down the stairs to CC, following the other TSs, I headed to the Team Center for *Operation Cinderella*. I had built OC from the bottom up.

The constant hum of voices and technology was usually white noise, but right now the sounds added to the buzz and haze of anger in my head.

I glanced around CC and saw the other TSs reach their teams about the same time I reached mine.

"Listen up," I said, raising my voice enough that everyone on my team could hear me. My three lead agents, David Takamoto, Rick Smithe, and Marti Jensen looked at me over their shoulders. They'd been studying a series of monitors on one giant flat screen. All of the agents on comms stopped what they were doing and gave me their full attention.

My skin prickled as the entire CC went silent at the same time. No white noise. Only the hum of technology. The air crackled as if every single one of them instantly knew something bad had gone down.

I stood next to my team leaders and met each team member's eyes as I spoke to the group. These men and women had worked closely with Randolph. A lot of them were her friends.

My throat worked as I swallowed. I couldn't completely act the cool, detached Team Supervisor. I was so angry I still almost couldn't see straight.

"Agent Stacy Randolph . . ." I swallowed hard again. ". . . was murdered while undercover."

The stunned silence in the CC lasted all of five seconds. Then it was like the entire CC burned with a hot wave of fury. Voices filled the center, voices filled with anger and promises of retribution.

Everyone would be out for blood to take down Randolph's killers.

All agents were professionals, but some of my people couldn't help the tears they wiped from their eyes and off of their cheeks, even as they tried to maintain composed expressions.

When my team calmed down a bit, I said, "We've been given as many resources from as many teams as we can use on this op to find Randolph's murderers. And to bring the slavers down at the same time."

I rubbed my hand over my head, no doubt making my dark hair a mess.

"Okay. Best thing to do is go at this with both barrels," I said. "Tear this thing apart."

The agents on comms went back to work and I sensed a new fervor to their work. The agents each utilized computer systems while monitoring activity on Internet chat rooms and message boards, e-mail, and phone lines.

Key words were programmed into servers, and as soon as a match popped up we'd get a copy, a recording, video, or a snapshot to review. Any combination of certain words, especially those with "sex" and "slave," would send the alert.

Slave. Sex slave. Auction. Boston. Nightclubs. Those were just a few of the words that we'd keyed in. We'd included specific nightclubs, and the first and last names of girls who'd been taken while at those establishments.

Usually it turned up nothing because most bad guys were smart enough not to use such obvious lingo, but sometimes we'd get a hit.

We already had Randolph's undercover name in the database, as well as Deseronto's, so we'd know if we got a hit there, too.

Takamoto caught my attention as he said, "We screwed up, Steele. The girls are gone."

"What?" The room nearly echoed with my shout. "They got away?"

Goddamnit! How the hell had we screwed up enough to miss the movement of the girls and not catch the bastards who were holding them?

A new burst of heat burned through me at the thought that we'd let the bastards slip away with the auctioned girls. We would have done *anything* to stop them if we'd just found their location fast enough. We'd been so damned close to nailing their positions.

Maybe we could even have saved Randolph.

I swore I would blow away every sonofabitch who kidnapped and auctioned off young girls as sex slaves. I glanced to the screen with the dozen or so monitors. "We had solid information. How could the slavers have just gotten away with over a dozen girls while under our watch?"

Smithe rubbed the back of his blond GQ haircut with an uncomfortable expression on his face. "Apparently our intel was bad. They were feeding Randolph the wrong info from the start, which ties in to what happened to her. Looks like she jumped in too fast."

Probably because she was ready to get out.

"Christ." I braced my hands on my hips and looked up for a moment at the white ceiling panels before I turned my gaze back to Takamoto, Jensen, and Smithe.

"I want you three to gather what information you can from your snitches." I turned to Takamoto. "Chancy Yeager is our best source. By this evening I want everything Yeager can give, and I want it on my desk no later than six."

Yeager was the one who'd gotten us two passes into the exclusive club where I was going undercover Saturday with Agent Perry.

Takamoto was good at schooling his expressions and his emotions. He gave a brief nod. "You've got it, Steele."

Takamoto headed out of the CC as I turned to Smithe. Of course, since I was six to seven inches shorter than him,

I had to look up to give him orders. Smithe was a jerk sometimes and I don't think he liked taking orders from me. But I had to admit he was a good agent.

I gestured to the agents on comms and computers. "Smithe, I want you and your team to expand your searches. Pull as many resources from other teams as you need."

Before I continued, I took a good look at the vid cams. "Photograph and video everyone coming and going from the clubs Randolph worked. Identify *every single one* of the patrons. I don't care if they have a criminal background or not. We're going deep."

I hardened my gaze. "I want financial records for the clubs. Find out who owns every damn one of them, annual income, tax records. Just get someone in each club. We've got our blanket warrant, so get me all of the info on their hard drives. Whatever it takes."

Other agencies had to get warrants for every damn thing. Like I said, we could get away with a hell of a lot.

Smithe nodded and turned away without a word.

Jensen was only a couple of inches taller than me when she wasn't wearing heels. I told her, "I'm going to need help reviewing all of Randolph's reports, taped conversations, photographs, videos she made while undercover. Get me the intel on who Randolph suspected and what the hierarchy was that Randolph was investigating. Pull whatever resources you need."

Jensen gave a brief nod. "Done."

I blew out my breath. "I'll be in my office."

CHAPTER 4

Exit Hell

March 27
Wednesday late morning

I barely kept from slamming my office door shut behind me. The blue lighting from the CC poured into the room through the glass wall.

The blinds were opened all the way now, but I needed privacy. I pressed a button on my desk and the blinds whirred as they ran along the track, until they closed and blocked out everything.

I'd brought my punching bag to HQ and into my office when I was promoted to Senior Agent and Team Supervisor six months ago. Everyone knew I worked off my stress with the punching bag, and many times other agents had used it.

Now was a good time to let the bag have it.

I jerked off my overshirt and tossed it in a corner, leaving me only in my T-shirt. Bare-handed, I slammed my fist into the bag.

I hit the bag harder and harder, faster and faster. I felt no ache, no pain, just numbness and anger.

Had Randolph stumbled across something vital? It was common for a RED agent to encounter critical evidence that could easily disappear if not seized immediately. She could have been trying to download information from a hard drive or take pictures of important documents.

Sweat started beading on my forehead as I continued to hit the bag.

When RED agents were in we couldn't just extract ourselves from a location and get back in after obtaining a warrant. I wondered if that's what had happened to Randolph. If she'd been caught grabbing evidence.

I slammed my fist into the bag again, feeling the blow burn all the way to my shoulder.

Fist to the bag. Again. Again.

For a second I could see the faces of the men who'd beaten the shit out of me in that Cuban jail, unusually corrupt members of the Policía Nacional Revolucionaria, PNR, while they tried to get me to tell them who I worked for when I'd assassinated their leader.

I speak nine languages and I understood every word when they told me rape was next.

One of the four men had said I would bring good money, an American on the sex slave market. The man laughed and left the cell, after telling the other three men he'd be back soon.

Harder, harder, I hit the bag so hard pain started to shoot through my arms.

I could still smell the sweat of the three men, the stench of piss in the cell. I could still feel the hardness of the chair they'd shoved me onto before they'd started slamming their fists into my face and body. They'd bound my wrists behind me and hadn't let me catch my breath between each punch they landed.

The stink of the first man's breath was hot on my face as he leaned close to me and started to unzip his pants as he told the other three men to cut off my clothes. He grasped the top of the seat back, released his penis, and slowly stroked it while leering at me as the other men started toward me.

No. Fucking. Way.

I gripped the bottom edge of the seat with my bound hands.

The moment the bastard leaned close enough, I gripped the seat with my fingers for leverage. I swung my legs up and clenched his neck with my thighs. One quick squeeze and jerk, and the sonofabitch's neck snapped.

I twisted out of the chair, avoiding the now dead man's

body as he collapsed onto the wood so hard the chair shattered beneath his weight.

Before the other men had even realized what had happened, I was on the floor next to the body and jerking the dead man's gun out of his holster with my bound hands as I rolled away.

Shouts filled the cell. Shots echoed in the small space as I pulled the trigger and shot in the direction of the men, with my hands still bound behind me.

If I could create enough commotion to send them scattering, I'd have a chance to make a break for it.

I kept rolling, moving, shooting.

One of my wild shots made contact. It was the fattest man who screamed and dropped. Blood was already soaking his chest as I looked over my shoulder while scrambling to get to my feet.

A chilling clicking sound next to my head. I went completely still. The one remaining man in the cell pressed the barrel of a handgun just over my ear.

"You fucking bitch," the man said in English.

"Not in your lifetime," I growled right before I ducked and shot one of my feet out between his. He didn't have a chance to make a startled sound before I jerked his foot out from under him and he went down. Flat on his back.

My spine chilled as a bullet grazed my left ear when he shot at me from his position on the floor. His face was flushed dark red, sweat dripping down his face, and he raised his gun again.

I swung my leg out and kicked the gun from his hand. He shouted and grabbed for my ankle. I almost lost my balance because of the way my wrists were still bound behind me. I managed to square off on both feet on the concrete floor.

I raised one of my boots and jammed it with everything I had onto the man's larynx.

His cry rose up with a gurgle of blood and he looked at me as if staring death in the face.

He had been. One more smash of my boot and he instantly went quiet, his head twisted to an odd angle.

The man I'd shot was gasping and wheezing as the other two lay dead on the cell floor. I kept my eye on him as I knelt by the man I'd just killed. The gun clattered on the floor as I released it to use both hands to try to draw the dead man's knife sheathed on his belt.

I moved my gaze to the cell door. The fourth man—had he really left the jail like he said he would? I sure as hell hoped so.

My fingers fumbled and I became aware of the tremors in my limbs from the adrenaline rushing through me.

I kept part of my attention on the dying man across the room as I finally jerked the knife free. I watched him for any sign that he was going for a weapon at the same time I cut through my wrist bonds.

The rope fell away. I lunged to my feet and brought the weapon up with my now free arm. I flicked my wrist and released the knife. It flipped end over end exactly three times before the blade buried itself into the dying man's forehead.

He went slack, his glazed eyes staring at me, the knife protruding from just above his eyes.

Would the PNR officer who'd left be back soon?

Backpack. Where had they put my backpack? Everything I needed was in it, if it hadn't been looted.

My bid for freedom had amounted to maybe ten minutes, but with all the gunshots, shouts, screams and other noise, if anyone else had been in that small jail they would've been on me already.

I grabbed the last dead man's pistol and tucked it into the waistband of my cargo pants and pulled my shirt over it to hide it. In moments I'd jogged through the jail and in a crappy office found my backpack on the desk—the backpack intact, thank God, and it looked like the contents were secure. They probably hadn't had enough time to look. Apparently they'd been too busy with me.

I peeked out the front entrance and made sure everything was clear. No sign of the first man or any others in uniform. Then I stepped out of the stinking jail and into the welcome sunshine of that Cuban town.

Men and women, and even children stared at me as I dodged through a crowded street. I felt warmth on my face and I dragged the back of my hand over my cheek. Blood coated my skin when I looked at my hand.

Shit. I needed to get cleaned up and get the hell out of this town. I had a rental car waiting, but I'd be stopped for sure if anyone got a good look at me. Not to mention I'd be a bit conspicuous trying to get on a plane looking like this.

My jaw felt bruised and swollen, and it hurt when I clenched my teeth. My white shirt was ripped in places and filthy, my taupe cargo pants not a whole lot better. Just by being seen by civilians I was leaving a trail.

I ducked down one side street to another until I found a run-down hotel and checked in. The short man with graying black hair said nothing as I handed him what was probably double the usual rate. The suspicion in his eyes was keen as he reached for a key before handing it to me.

This wasn't going to work. He'd probably be notifying the PNR as soon as I walked away.

Still I took the key but hurried straight through the hotel, out the back, and into another side street.

It took two more hotels until I hit one with a kid manning the desk. Again I paid double the rate, only this time I went to the room I'd been given and rushed to clean up.

I kept a few first aid supplies in my backpack and I used them to clean up the gash above my eyebrow and the cut along the cheek. As fast as I could, I used antiseptic wipes to clean all of the cuts to keep them from becoming infected.

I'd just stripped out of my torn clothing when I heard my cell phone ring from inside from backpack. I froze. When I carried a phone on an assignment I kept it on silent or vibrate. This time it was ringing and I hadn't been the one to set it on ring.

For a moment I just stared at my backpack. The only people who had that number were my FAS handlers.

It stopped ringing. I hurried to my back and snatched the phone out and looked at the incoming caller display. *Unknown.*

That's what it always said when a FAS tried to get a hold of me. One of the Cubans must have screwed with my phone.

It rang again. And I stared at the display as it lit up. I didn't want to answer it. I didn't want to know what they were going to ask me to do next. I gritted my teeth and instantly regretted it as pain shot from my jaw to my temple.

FAS bastards.

I grabbed the phone. "Redbird," I said in a harsh snap.

"Alexi Steele," a female voice said, immediately sending a shock through me. None of my handlers were female, and no one *ever* called me by my real name. The woman continued, "If you don't want to be killed in that motel room, I suggest you leave within the next three minutes."

My bare skinned chilled. "Who is this?"

"If you make it out of there alive, I have a proposition for you."

"What—"

The woman gave me an address on Portland Street in Boston, not far from my Southie home. "I believe you have a minimum of two minutes left before you'll have company." She hung up before I had a chance to respond.

The part about "two minutes" clicked first as I snapped my cell phone closed.

I swore and tossed the phone into my backpack, jerked on a clean pair of cargo pants and a tank top, and jammed the "borrowed" pistol into my pack with my own weapons. I left my discarded clothing and the rest of my mess. No time to clean up.

After I hitched my backpack on my shoulders, I slipped out of my motel room. I headed out the rear then made my way around the side of the building where I could see the road. Still some distance away two PNR jeeps barreled down the dirt road.

"Shit." Must have been the fourth dickhead who'd tracked me down.

Being dark-haired like the locals—as well as too short to tower above anyone, even if I wore stilts—made it easier to slip into a crowd and avoid being spotted. Not being covered with blood was a big help.

As I walked through the crowded street, I kept myself on full alert, my senses automatically cataloguing everything including possible escape routes.

Who was that woman and how the *hell* had she known about what was going down, and how did she know anything about me?

The next day I walked into the building on Portland Street and was introduced to the world of RED by Karen Oxford.

My whole body was sweating now and my arms were like rubber. I leaned my head against the bag on my forearm.

Oxford had been just as stern and imposing then as she was now. Something about her made me feel as if I should come to attention. Like facing a superior when I was Special Forces in the Army. Before I'd fucked up.

I grabbed a towel from a shelf in a closet in the back of my office, near the corner where my shirt was lying. I always kept spare clothing in my office—casual and dressy, in case I needed either for undercover work, so I had plenty of extra things to wear.

I started dabbing my face, my neck, and beneath the hair at my nape with the towel.

The moment I met Oxford, every single nuance of it, was burned into my mind. "I've been observing you for some time now, always a RED agent following your trail," she'd said, and my skin had gone cold.

She tapped a folder that was lying on the table in front of her with her forefinger. "Sniper in Special Forces before you made one hell of a mistake and you were court-martialed.

"Then an organization you can't even name broke you. Trapped you into working for that organization, where you're required to assassinate anyone they tell you to.

"You are sent to country after country and you are never told why you are ordered to kill these men and women. There is no time limit and you have no way out. They continue to hold that same threat over you like a noose."

I'd sat, stunned, as she laid out my professional life on the table.

"I am prepared to offer you a way out, Alexi."

That's when Karen Oxford saved my life.

RED had been my ticket out of hell.

I walked to my desk and plopped into my chair. The wheels made bumping sounds as I rolled across the carpet in front of my desk. The cotton of the towel was soft as I continued to dry myself off.

A few framed photos of my brothers, sister, and parents were on my black-and-chrome desk next to a chrome reading lamp, a huge computer screen, and an open *Operation Cinderella* manila folder.

My bare office showed just how much time I'd had to make it the least bit "homey" since I'd been promoted.

I braced my elbows on the tabletop and rubbed my sweaty temples with my fingers.

Randolph hadn't gotten out. In fact her last moments had been nothing but hell. No matter what Oxford said, I couldn't feel that it wasn't my fault.

I braced the heels of my palms against my forehead.

Going undercover into the world Randolph had been immersed in was my next step.

A step I was more than willing to take to even the score for not only the auctioned women, but for Agent Stacy Randolph who hadn't deserved her fate.

CHAPTER 5

Nick

March 27
Wednesday evening

Nick studied the woman who knelt in a submissive position facing away from him. Her naked ass was high, her wrists tied behind her back and her face turned sideways against the dungeon's stone floor.

Tears trickled from Nandra's eyes, her mascara streaking her cheeks. She was biting down on the ball gag but moaning with pleasure.

Before he took another swing, he rubbed his palm over the warm skin as he examined his handiwork. Her flesh was bright pink everywhere he'd swatted her with the leather paddle.

Hard, like she always wanted. With Nandra, the more she was punished the more intense her climax.

She moaned again and pushed back so that her ass was even higher, which told him how close she was to orgasm. She wanted more and she wanted it now.

Nick swatted her hard on the left ass cheek.

Nandra's whole body rocked with her climax as she collapsed to the floor. No doubt the sound she was making behind the ball gag would have been a scream of intense pleasure while she squirmed on the dungeon's stone floor.

He moved to the dungeon's sink and washed his hands while Nandra whimpered behind the ball gag. When he looked over his shoulder she was staring at him with clear adoration.

She'd been a good sub, good experience for what he was about to do within a couple of days. Thanks to Master Richardson's tutelage over the past few weeks, Nick was now proficient with most forms of BDSM punishment, including becoming an expert with the whip.

It was time to let Nandra go. She wouldn't be happy, but he was going undercover.

And Nick would have the delectable Alexi Steele to keep him more than occupied.

CHAPTER 6

Nobody screws with me

March 27
Wednesday early evening

Their bodies moved together, sweaty, hot, sultry.

The muscles in his back flexed as he slowly slid his erection in and out of the woman. The blond's breasts were large, her nipples hard peaks. She moaned every time his chest grazed her breasts, and she gasped as he thrust into her and drew back out.

The smell of sex was strong and his gaze was focused entirely on the woman's face as she tipped her head back and moaned even louder.

It could have been a real turn-on to watch.

If it wasn't my boyfriend with another woman.

The pain in my chest and the flames flushing my body had nothing to do with the heat between Gary and the woman with her long legs wrapped around his hips.

"You sonofabitch."

Gary jerked his head up and the woman let out a scream nearly loud enough to shatter one of the lamps.

"Lexi." Gary's face flushed red straight up to his blond crew cut. He scrambled from the bed as he grabbed a sheet and wrapped it around his hips. "Oh, shit."

"You better believe 'Oh, shit.' " It wasn't far to the closet where he kept his baseball bat. Everything I touched seemed to burn my hand, from the closet's doorknob to the grip of the aluminum baseball bat.

"What the hell are you doing?" When he saw what I was

holding, Gary backed away so fast he tripped on the edge of the sheet he clutched.

My fingers ached from gripping the bat hard with one hand while slapping the thickest part against my palm.

"Uh, Lexi." Gary managed to keep on his feet. "Christ, I—I'm sorry."

"You're going to be a lot sorrier." I ground my teeth so hard I probably came close to cracking a molar as I headed for the kitchen, carrying the bat. The ache in my gut grew as his betrayal hit home.

The knife drawer squeaked when I jerked it open. *Perfect.* This one would do. I clenched the handle of a butcher knife in my free hand. Both weapons felt good and solid as blood pounded in my temples and I faced Gary.

His jaw dropped. "What the—"

A shriek cut off the rest of his sentence. The very tall blond he'd been in bed with stood in the bedroom doorway. Apparently he wanted a lay with longer legs to spread than me.

She was wearing his T-shirt.

When my overshirt fell open enough for her to get a good view of the Glock holstered at my side, I winced at her shriek. Oh, yeah, he'd gotten himself a real screamer.

I hefted the bat against my shoulder and Gary's eyes widened as I met his gaze. I didn't blink.

"Lexi—" His Adam's apple bobbed as he glanced to the bat and knife.

At that moment I could almost feel the satisfaction of hitting a grand slam with Gary's balls. I gave an evil smile and glanced at his nuts before looking back at his face, which had gone white. He knew exactly what I'd been thinking.

Forget that. I knew a better way to damage his manhood.

I jerked open the front door of his first-floor apartment hard enough to rattle the hinges, then strode to the front door of the triple-decker apartment building. Cool spring air smacked me in the face when I headed for the short flight of stairs leading to the concrete sidewalk. Each step creaked as I jogged down to the street.

I went straight for what Gary loved more than anything—

His shiny black F-150 parked in front of the trip where his apartment was.

A bunch of Gary's neighbors hung out on the back porches of their trips, listening to a game on the tube and shouting at each other from one balcony to another as the game blasted from their TVs. Smells of popcorn, hot dogs, and beer floated from the balconies.

Not likely anyone could hear what I was about to do over all the noise.

The butcher knife sank between the tread of the rear driver's-side tire as easily as Gary had been sliding into that blond who was starting to get the neighbors' attention with her shrieking.

I focused on the truck and tried not to picture what I'd just seen. That—that—

The pain that had taken hold in my chest now made my entire body ache. I'd trusted him. I'd cared for him.

The front driver's-side tire seemed like a good place to leave the butcher knife. *Gary cheated on me* hammered my mind, and by the time I picked up the baseball bat I was practically on fire again.

"You." My Southie accent revved up. "Fucking." I raised the bat just over my shoulder. "Sonofa—" I reached the driver's door. *"—bitch."*

Glass scattered over the back of my hands as the driver's side window shattered. My hair swung in my eyes as I gave another good swing and took the bat to the door. Metal gave way with a satisfying crunch, the impact reverberating through my arms.

Coach Pacholewski would be proud. What a way to put to use my four years as a star player on my high school baseball team.

Then Randolph's death hit me again like another blow. I'd come over for comfort and intimacy with Gary. I'd *needed* him.

More anger, hurt, and pain went into every swing of the bat. The headlights and fog lamps went next as I put every bit of pain into each swing. The windshield spider-webbed when the bat made contact, but the passenger door window shattered all over his leather seat.

Like a hammer punch to my heart, Gary's betrayal and Randolph's death hit me hard enough that my eyes began to ache.

Not now. Not now, not now, not now.

I didn't do tears. I didn't do crying.

If I couldn't cry over Randolph, I certainly wasn't going to cry because of Gary.

Damnit. Moisture gathered at the corners of my eyes and I had to fight to keep even a single tear from rolling down my cheek.

Screw Gary.

Putting everything into every swing helped me fight back the pain, and I let it all out with that bat.

This one was for Gary.

This one was for Randolph.

This one was for me.

Some of Gary's neighbors now leaned over the railings of their porches or came out and stood in the street. A few were laughing their asses off and made cracks at Gary while one guy said, "Fuck, that's gotta hurt."

In this Boston neighborhood, no one interfered—we Southies stuck together and stayed out of each other's business.

Before I could take a swing at the passenger door, large hands grabbed my shoulders from behind.

My heart hurt when I whirled around and met Gary's blue eyes.

He wore a pair of jeans but no shoes. I wanted to pound on his large bare chest. To shout, to scream.

Gary gripped me harder by the shoulders. He'd seen me bring down men twice my size in jujitsu sparring, so he was taking a big risk. Didn't matter that he was a massive bodybuilder. I'd put him in a world of hurt.

"How could you?" My voice came out hoarse as I looked into his handsome face. A face I had trusted.

"I'm sorry." He squeezed my shoulders, and he looked

like the Gary I had cared about . . . before now. "I was going to tell you, but I didn't know how."

I shook out of his hold. My throat felt like it was closing off. "You don't screw around before breaking off a relationship."

"I'm sorry—"

"Fuck you, Gary." I gestured to the door where the blond had disappeared. "Better yet, go back to screwing her."

He didn't let me go. "You've been closing me out, Lex. More and more all the time. There are parts of you that I could never reach even when we were together."

For a moment I couldn't say anything. The job. The job that meant the world to me forced me to keep secrets, even from Gary.

"You could have talked to me." My voice was hoarse with anger and pain. "You never said a word."

"Lex—"

I was trembling all over now. "Stacy Randolph is dead."

The shock on his face was real. Gary thought Randolph worked for the same language interpreting agency as I did so he knew her.

He dropped his hands away from my shoulders. I could see his desire to comfort me, to wrap me in his arms. No friggin' way. "Oh God, I'm sorry."

So much more pain wanted to explode from me that I backed away from him, turned, and took the hardest swing yet. This time at his passenger door. I don't know why the crunch of metal was so satisfying, but it was.

Pain, anger, hurt, betrayal, shock, guilt. Could anyone feel so much balled up within and not be turned inside out?

I raised my chin and whirled to face Gary—

And came face-to-face with a pair of men in blue.

Christ.

The frantic beat of my heart increased as I looked from one stern face to the other.

Not jail. Oh, God.

One of the cops looked at the damage to the truck. "Must

have pissed you off good," he said in a strong Southie accent. I swore I heard amusement in his voice.

The other officer marched me the few steps to the cruiser and forced me up against it, my back to him, my arms and legs stretched out as I braced myself against the car. I could smell the soap he must have used to shower, and the dry-cleaner scent of his pressed uniform.

My anger started to fade, and instead a sense of defeat made my body ache. Right then I wanted to curl up in a ball and hope this was all a dream. A nightmare as bad as the ones I had nearly every night.

"I'm not pressing charges," Gary started to say when the cop's words cut across his.

"What the hell—?" the cop was saying as he found the Glock at my hip, before he discovered the knife strapped to my ankle. "Do you have a license to carry concealed weapons?"

Oh, shit. I always locked my handgun in the glove compartment of my Cherokee before I saw Gary, but today I'd been too distracted.

"No," I muttered, part of my anger draining away into cold, hard reality. Lexi Steele was an interpreter. She wouldn't have a concealed weapons permit. "I don't."

"Then I guess it's a trip to the station for you," the cop said.

"I'm not pressing charges," Gary repeated.

"That's fine," the officer said. "But we're taking her in for possession of illegal weapons on her person."

I was so in for it when Oxford found out.

The people standing around or peering over their balconies only knew me by my real name of course—I'd grown up with a lot of them. To everyone I knew in "real life" I was just Lexi Steele. Pint-sized tough chick who could speak nine different languages.

The officer finished searching me, and I heard the jangle of cuffs. He jerked my arms behind my back before the cold metal bit into my skin.

The officer started reading my Miranda rights.

Icy realization hit me.

I was really going to jail.

I was going to be put behind bars.

Now I've really blown everything, haven't I?

When they shoved me into the back of their cruiser, I met Gary's eyes. His were filled with regret, not anger. And that hurt worse than if he'd been furious with me.

I looked out the cruiser's other window and swallowed so hard I coughed. Everything familiar now seemed alien as the officers drove through Southie toward the District 6 station on Broadway.

Like an egg separated from the yolk, what was real separated from what couldn't be.

Gary had been a safe place in my not-so-safe life, and now that was gone.

CHAPTER 7

Nick

March 28
Thursday morning

Nick scrubbed his hand through his hair. *Just great.* He had a partner who apparently didn't know the meaning of the words "low profile."

He clenched his jaw as he leaned back in the chair of his home surveillance room. Blue light from the several computer screens was the only illumination in the room, which suited him just fine.

Just looking at one club in particular had him clenching his hands and ready to punch holes through the walls. He hadn't been one to destroy property, but goddamn, just seeing the Diamond Castle made him want to go to the nightclub and tear the place apart. He wanted it so bad his palms itched.

Now he had a partner who could possibly have fucked things up unless RED had gotten the situation under control and kept what she'd done out of the media.

He felt a surge of frustrated anger. He didn't need this shit. Not now.

Nick got up from his chair and headed toward his bedroom to change into his sneakers and shorts. He needed to go for a run. He'd be no good to anyone if he lost control.

He was too close to achieving his goal. And yes, he'd mow down anyone who got in his way, but he'd try to make sure that Lexi Steele was safely out of the way. However, not even she would have the power to stop him.

CHAPTER 8

I've really done it this time

March 28
Late Thursday morning

I don't handle cold metal bars well so I was more than a little relieved when a short, stocky female officer strolled up to my cell and said, "You're in luck, babe," she said as the lock clanked and she rolled the door open. "You've got yourself a 'Get out of jail free' card."

I pushed myself to my feet in time to see two men enter the corridor. A combination of relief and dread went through me in a harsh rush.

It was two of my own agents, Takamoto and Smithe. This was just the beginning of Oxford's punishment.

God.

The BPD officer winked at me before she led us down a couple of corridors.

"To think," Smithe said with a grin, "we'd end up bailing our TS out of jail."

I glared up at him. "Screw you."

Takamoto laughed and I glared at him, too.

I'd tried calling Georgina last night. But she never answered her cell and I couldn't think of anyone else to call. Not my family. Not even my brother Zane, who was a RED Special Agent, too. He knew Gary and I didn't want Zane to end up in jail, too, for killing my now ex-boyfriend.

No, I'd had to face the lion's den and place my call to Oxford.

The officer escorted us through a main door and into the

police station itself. The breath I took felt like I'd just sucked in a lungful of spring air compared to how it had smelled where we just came from.

"Tsk." Smithe wasn't going to give up as he signed out the two weapons that had been taken from me. The knife and the Glock—both had saved my life one time or another, or had ended someone else's. "Beating some guy's truck in broad daylight—yeah, that's low profile."

I gritted my teeth and gave Smithe a harder look. "I have a pretty nasty assignment I'm almost ready to put someone on. I think you'd be a good candidate."

Ha. That shut him up. Takamoto looked like he was holding back a smile.

I didn't have a permit as part of the job, so those weapons weren't coming near my hands until we got into the transportation they'd brought. I might as well have been naked. While still in the BPD station, Takamoto handed me my wallet with my civilian ID and I shoved it into my back pocket.

I blinked when we walked into the sunshine. Was it already almost noon? Crap. Since I hadn't eaten for so long, I was light-headed on top of being exhausted, hurt, angry, and filled with so much pain I couldn't begin to think straight.

One black Ford Expedition with dark-tinted windows waited in the back of the police department parking lot.

A cool breeze hit me and I shivered. Spring had only made it to us a week ago.

Christ, what an inane thought. Who cared that it was spring now? I might be losing my job.

The breeze became a light wind and threw my dark hair across my face, a face that could probably use a whole bar of soap. My mouth tasted sour, and no doubt my breath would bowl over Superman. As soon as I had faced the firing squad I had a date with a toothbrush and a shower.

I walked toward the SUV with Takamoto and Smithe. "You know how to do it up good, Steele," Takamoto said with a grin as we reach the SUV

"We've all got our talents," I muttered.

Smithe opened the rear driver's-side door for me. "And

yours seems to be getting in deep whenever you get a chance."

I scowled at him as I buckled my seat belt. "Bite me."

"One of these days I'll take you up on that," he said before he shut the door.

The leather was smooth against my back as I slid down in my seat, exhaustion rolling through me. I'd faced Randolph's death and had gone over everything I could about her case. I'd had my head agents brief me before I stopped at Gary's, took a bat to his truck, ended up in jail, and had a nightmare that made me feel like I hadn't slept at all.

My eyes fluttered and Takamoto's and Smithe's conversation faded as sleep came.

March 28
Thursday afternoon

"Time to face your doom, Steele," Smithe said.

The words barely registered as my eyes blinked open and I stared at the seat in front of me.

Shit.

Oxford.

The familiar parking garage for RED's cover operation made it easy to tell where I was. I didn't want to be here right now. I'd rather have stayed on that backseat and slept for a million years than face what I had to now.

In the agency only Oxford knew I'd been an assassin. All anyone knew was that I'd been in Special Forces in the Army before joining RED as a special agent.

I owed her, and I hated the thought of disappointing her or, even worse, putting her in a position where she might have to can me.

Damn. The thought of being forced to leave RED hit me like a punch to the gut.

I rubbed my goose bump-covered arms. If I lost my job, I'd lose my identity. Everything that I'd worked for since she saved my ass.

Takamoto and Smithe headed out of the lower level of the garage with me trailing in their wake. My scalp itched and

I knew I had to look like I'd just come off of one of those survival reality TV shows, and lost. If I was a girly-girl I might have cared. Right now I didn't.

Feeling started coming back into my limbs and my body as we took the parking garage elevator up to the first floor. My feet dragged like a kid being taken to the principal's office as we reached the pseudo interpreter agency.

After my ASAC canned me from the Recovery Enforcement Division, would any other branch of the NSA take me on?

Ha. The NSA didn't know I existed. After all, RED didn't exist, right?

When the three of us passed the glass-walled reception area where the blinds were always kept shut, my reflection made it clear I looked even worse than I'd thought—which was pretty damned bad.

I glanced down the hallway that led to the exercise center and wished I could jump into the shower in the women's locker room before it was time to face Oxford.

Yeah, like she would wait for a little thing like a shower.

Takamoto touched the fingerprint scanner; then he, Smithe, and I entered the empty elevator and Takamoto punched the button for the fifth floor.

"This year the Yanks don't stand a chance against the Red Sox," Takamoto said, and I turned my attention to him.

Thinking about the baseball season that was going to start Monday was a lot better than thinking about what I was about to face.

Oxford's disappointment. And no doubt anger.

"The boys kicked ass in the Grapefruit League during spring training," I said.

"Zapato's looking particularly good," Smithe said. "He's one hell of a pitcher."

As a city we were still pissed about last year's ninth-inning loss to the Yanks on a home run by Andy Dominique in the World Series.

Every floor seemed to pass by too fast. With a soft stop, we reached my fifth-floor doom.

I looked down at the CC and wished I was working with my team. But at this moment I was destined to stay above the CC on the catwalk that went past the TSs' glass-walled offices.

"Oxford's," Smithe said.

I glared at him. "Oh, really? Thanks for informing me of that little fact."

While Takamoto and Smithe left me and headed toward the stairs to the CC I practically dragged my feet as I went to my ASAC's office.

Darlene looked down her nose at me as she immediately showed me in, almost like she was shoving me through the door before she closed it.

I swallowed as I met Karen Oxford's dark eyes. Her gaze remained steady as she pressed a button on her glass-and-chrome desk.

Vertical black blinds hummed along their track as they covered the glass walls, giving us complete privacy.

This was so not good.

Oxford leaned forward and clasped her hands in front of her on her desk, her dark gaze shrewd and calculating. At times like this she made me feel as if she could peel me like an onion, layer by layer. She didn't invite me to sit, just stared at me for a long moment.

Oh, damn. As much as I'd cared for Gary, my career meant enough that I would have chosen my job over dating any guy. And I was about to lose it.

And Randolph. God, I couldn't leave before I took out her killers.

"You destroyed property in front of a street full of witnesses," she finally said.

"I caught my boyfriend in bed with a woman." Heat and numbness alternately gripped me.

For a moment I swore her gaze and her tone lessened their intensity. "I realize you lost an agent as well as your significant other in one day." Her tone was hard, though, as she continued, and any possible softness was gone. "Regardless of the situation, Steele, you were completely out of line."

"Yes, ma'am—"

"Have you ever thought how it might compromise yourself and your family if your escapade ended up on the evening news?"

Uh . . .

She pulled a cell phone out of her desk. "You were recorded, Steele. If RED hadn't cleaned up the mess before it ended up as a little joke on the news, your face would have shown up on every television in the Boston area."

My cheeks burned. Shit. *That* was something that never occurred to me.

I fought the urge to start begging. *Don't can me, don't can me, don't can me.* "Nothing like that will ever happen again."

"It had better not." Oxford looked at me intently. "I won't have you compromise this agency."

I wanted to collapse with relief. I hadn't been released from RED. Yeah, I'd screwed up, but she wasn't going to let me go.

A buzzing sound made me jump.

"Is it Agent Donovan, Darlene?" Oxford said to the air. I wasn't really sure where the microphone was. "If it is, send him in."

Not two seconds and a pink-faced, obviously flustered Darlene showed in one of the most gorgeous men I'd ever seen. No wonder Darlene looked so flustered.

Just his vivid blue eyes were enough to make a woman's mouth water. A black overshirt over a black T-shirt couldn't disguise what was obviously a fit, muscular body. Snug blue jeans only emphasized the fact.

Well, well, well.

Look at those broad shoulders, a well-defined chest beneath his T-shirt, and sculpted, muscular biceps. Thank God for short-sleeved shirts because those biceps were made to be seen. He wasn't body-builder big, but it was obvious he had a kind of power no mortal could match. Bet he was Superman in bed. His tapered hips, and snug Levis over muscular thighs completed the picture of a woman's wet dream.

He was rough around the edges with an unapproachable look to him, but it didn't disguise the fact that he was one hot male.

Oxford gestured toward the big hunk of a man now standing next to me. "Special Agent Nick Donovan is new to RED and has been assigned to double-team your operation. He'll work the op with you as a Team Supervisor until we complete *Operation Cinderella*. He will also be your partner when you go in undercover in the BDSM clubs."

I had been standing there staring in shock, mouth hanging open when Oxford's words finally penetrated.

"What?" I shook my head, feeling like I needed to wake up. "I mean, hold on. I've put this case together from the beginning. George Perry is going into the private clubs with me."

From the corner of my eye I saw Donovan's expression darken, but he remained silent.

My ASAC stood and braced her palms on her desk. "Steele, you will work with Agent Donovan and that is my final word on the subject."

CHAPTER 9

Revelations

March 28
Thursday afternoon

I left Oxford's office, still not sure what had hit me.

What the hell just happened? Why would Oxford stick me with another agent? TSs put together their operations using their team members, but it was rare to have two RED TSs head the same op. Why now and why me? Was it because of my bat versus truck adventure?

No, this seemed like it had been arranged already.

As soon as I took care of a few things, I would get an appointment with Oxford and discuss this little Agent Tall-Dark-and-No-Way problem. Yeah, he looked like an asset to the team, but double-teaming me as a TS for my op? I don't think so.

Donovan walked by my side as I went to my Team Center. He was silent, and when I glanced up I saw him looking at me with an intense expression, like he was analyzing me.

Screw his analysis.

"Chavez." I motioned to Isabella Chavez, indicating I wanted to see her.

She set down her comm and headed toward me. She glanced at Donovan, but I wasn't in the mood for introductions. "I want you to take over Randolph's cover and be Deseronto's partner." I met her dark eyes. She was model-gorgeous and one of my best agents. "You good with that?"

"Absolutely," she said with no hesitation and pure professionalism.

"Give me a moment and I'll brief you in my office," I said.

Since it didn't look like Donovan was going away, I might as well introduce him to the team. "Listen up," I said, loud enough to catch most of the agents' attention until they were all quiet. "This is Special Agent Nick Donovan. He's been assigned to our team. Donovan is new to RED so give him as much hell as possible."

Some of the agents laughed. Donovan didn't.

Donovan and Chavez followed me as I headed out of the CC and up the stairs. "Randolph and Deseronto penetrated a couple of BDSM clubs with ties to the group we're targeting."

When we reached my office, I motioned to the chairs in front of my desk. Chavez sat. Donovan hitched his shoulder up against the door frame and studied me with those intense blue eyes, still saying nothing. If I was the type to be easily rattled, that look would have done the job.

"I haven't had a chance to review the intel reports this morning." I focused on Chavez. "As soon as I do I'll have you completely briefed before we put you out in the field. Isabella, you'll be penetrating a BDSM club that Deseronto's in. Are you up on the scene?"

She nodded. "I know what to expect."

"Excellent. I'll let you know when I have the latest intel for you."

"Got it." Chavez stood.

"I'll be assigning more agents," I said. "You and Deseronto won't be alone."

Chavez nodded again before she turned and strode through the door past Donovan.

Finally, my gaze met Donovan's.

"We need to talk," he said as he pushed away from the door frame.

"Yeah, we do." I rubbed my temples. "But it'll have to wait."

March 28
Thursday evening

My jogging shoes squeaked on the concrete floor of RED's almost empty parking garage. Smells of dirty oil and antifreeze certainly didn't make the churning in my stomach any better.

Donovan and I didn't speak as we walked from RED and neared a Ford Explorer black enough to seem to absorb most of the surrounding light. I wouldn't exactly call it a comfortable silence.

Oxford had informed me that Donovan would be the agent to drop me off at my place. Like I had a choice. I glanced at the empty parking spot between my undercover vehicles. My black Jeep Cherokee was still parked in front of Gary's triple-decker.

As much as I didn't want to, I climbed into Donovan's vehicle, which smelled of leather and the musky, spicy scent I'd noticed when I'd walked beside Donovan to the parking garage and in Oxford's office.

Every part of me was exhausted to the point where I didn't care if I dropped onto an oil slick.

The moment I relaxed against the seat, wind just whooshed right out of me as I heaved out a long breath. I had to fight my eyelids just to keep them open.

I realized Donovan wasn't heading to Southie and I looked at him. "Uh, I live in South Boston," I said as we headed toward Little Italy, in the North End.

"We're not going to your home," he said without looking at me.

"What the hell?" I came fully awake as he reached the parking garage at the corner of Congress Street and Sudbury Street, across from the Haymarket T stop. "What are you pulling, Donovan?"

"I'm hungry." He guided his Explorer into a spot and parked. "And we need to talk."

"No way." I glared at him as he started to open his door. "You don't just make decisions like that when it involves me."

He looked at me with a calm expression. "I just did," he said before he climbed out of the SUV.

Well, sonofabitch. I got out of the Explorer and shut the door harder than I should have. When we met up at the back of the SUV, I narrowed my gaze at him. "So what's the deal?"

"We're going to an Italian place I just discovered on Salem." He turned away and I jogged a little to keep up.

"So you figured out Little Italy all on your own." Okay, I know my tone was sarcastic, but I was tired and irritated at this man's arrogance. He didn't have an accent that I could identify, so I knew he wasn't from Boston. He probably came from the western side of the United States.

He looked at me. "Are you always such a pain in the ass?"

"When someone forces me to do something I don't want to, yeah, I am." I wasn't in the mood to talk anymore, so I didn't say anything else until we reached an Italian "ristorante" and bar and were seated.

The aromas of Italian food almost made me melt. It smelled so good that my stomach started to rumble despite the fact that I was ticked at Donovan.

As soon as the host handed us menus and walked away, I set my menu aside, folded my arms on the table, and focused on Donovan. "All right. So talk."

"We need to set some things straight. His eyes had gone from vivid blue to a darker shade. Cobalt. He kept his tone neutral, but by the way the muscles in his neck corded and his jaw tensed he was obviously feeling anything but neutral.

"Let's make this clear." His gaze focused on mine and I refused to blink. "We're partners, and from this point on it's *our* op. Not yours. Ours."

A busboy set glasses of ice water on the table and bread that smelled strongly of garlic, but I didn't take my gaze from Donovan's. "I built *Operation Cinderella* from the ground up." The surface of the cloth-covered table was rough beneath my arms as I faced off with him. "I don't have a problem with you as a partner. But I call the shots."

"Bullshit." Donovan let out a sound that was like a low rumble, and his jaw worked as if he was grinding his teeth. "I'm not playing second fiddle in this op."

The waiter arrived and we could barely take our glares from one another long enough for Donovan to order a bottle of Chianti and grilled bruschetta for an appetizer. Right then I didn't care that he had the audacity to order for both of us. I cared more about his attitude about *Operation Cinderella*.

I shifted my arms, rumpling the tablecloth. "Team Supervisors don't work in pairs, and I don't need your interference."

The waiter returned, presented the bottle of Chianti, and poured it into our glasses when Donovan gave his approval. Without looking at the menu or the waiter, Donovan said, "We'll have the veal marsala."

Obviously the waiter sensed the fact that his presence wasn't wanted. He bowed and hurried away.

"Well?" My tone was entirely hostile.

"Kristin. My sister." Donovan's voice was suddenly coarse, raw. "The bastards took her. She was sold as a sex slave in that auction you're tracking. To an international buyer or domestic, I don't know."

"Christ." I stared at Donovan like I'd been slammed in the face.

There's a reason why cops aren't assigned to cases that they might be too close to. Emotions run too high and smarts and a clear head take a flying leap.

My stomach clenched at the thought of what he was going through. It wasn't like I didn't understand. I personally wanted to bring these bastards down for killing one of my own. But my relationship with Randolph wasn't that of a sister or even my partner.

The fury was still hot inside of me, but my mind was clear on what needed to be done and it would stay clear. As a matter of fact the heat of my fury was rising inside of me even now, but not because of my dead agent. I wondered what the hell Oxford was thinking letting this guy even within ten feet of my operation.

I studied Donovan more sharply as my mind worked that question over.

Karen Oxford didn't do anything without a reason. She was Machiavellian in her motives and goals, so she must be after something major here and killer boy Donovan was the key to getting it.

Yeah, I was interested in knowing what her reasons were.

It still didn't change my opinion that a man on a mission with such personal stakes didn't belong on an op he was this close to.

The tablecloth felt rough beneath my forearms as I leaned forward. "All right, we'll get to your sister in a minute. First tell me why Oxford allowed you on a case involving a family member."

Donovan's blue eyes betrayed nothing when he said, "Oxford and I have an agreement."

"That's not enough." I leaned back in my chair. "I need to know why she's willing to take such a big risk."

He narrowed his gaze. "The only risk is to my sister if I don't find her."

"We're talking about a local operation where dozens of women's lives are on the line," I said. "I understand the importance of you finding your sister, but as it stands I can't accept that anyone with such a personal interest should be a part of this op."

Donovan was silent for a long moment. "I have something she wants. Experience she can't get anywhere else."

I let what he said sink in for a moment. He hadn't told me a whole lot, but it gave me something to go on, believe it or not. When she could, Oxford collected people with unique skills, so this guy was bringing something serious to the table. Which meant Oxford also wouldn't let him go easily. So Nick Donovan was going to do RED some serious good. I sighed in resignation. After all, when had we ever done things the easy way? "All right. We'll find your sister," I said. "But let me make something very clear. I'll do everything I can to protect this op and my agents. I won't let allow anything to compromise either. Do we understand each other?"

His expression was icy. He folded his arms across his chest. "That's fair."

I nodded. This was all going from shit bad to shit worse. But I couldn't only deal with what I had in front of me right now.

"Tell me about your sister. When was she taken?"

"About two weeks ago." Donovan's voice was raw as he

spoke. "Kristin was at a nightclub with some friends from college. A nightclub you've been monitoring—the Diamond Castle. Kristin's friends saw her across the club with a man they didn't know."

Donovan glanced from my face to his hands as if he was suddenly lost. "According to one of the girls, the man took Kristin out the back of the club." Donovan looked up, fire sparking in his blue eyes. "There wasn't a sign of my sister inside or out of the building." His throat worked. "She was gone."

He shoved his hand through his dark hair, the movement terse, filled with anger. "The intel your agents gathered and the monitoring you did on that specific auction recorded the"—his voice went suddenly hoarse—"the entire transaction."

My body went numb.

"When they sold her," Donovan continued, "the slave auctioneers videotaped her, naked. They gave her first name and recorded every bit of her body, right down to the birthmark at the base of her spine."

I'd seen those vids. I'd seen all the women. I remembered her.

I'd seen Donovan's sister being auctioned.

The cold in my body sent ice down my spine.

"I came across the country the moment I was contacted and told she was missing." Donovan's voice was a growl, yet pain was there, too. "I don't have much intel despite every bit of investigative work I've done beyond what you've accomplished."

"I'm sorry," was all I could think to say at the moment.

The urge to reach out to Donovan, to comfort him somehow, was almost overwhelming. And so unlike me. I didn't do huggy-huggy. Especially with a stranger. But the thought of his sister being sold in a sex slave auction sent more flurries of cold that iced all of my insides.

The waiter arrived with the bruschetta, but we both ignored it.

Donovan looked me dead in the eye and a different kind of shiver went through me. No one should have eyes like that.

"You were clear about a few things and now I want to be clear on some things myself," he said. "I won't do anything that jeopardizes the operation or our people." The look in his eyes turned diamond hard. "But I *won't* stop until I bring these bastards down and bring my sister home."

CHAPTER 10

Cinderella, fastballs, and balloon boobs

March 29
Friday morning

When I stepped off the elevator into RED's human trafficking department, Special Agent Suzanna Jones stopped in front of me and gave me a high five. "Way to go, Lexi," she said with a grin.

I wasn't sure what the high five was for—at first, but I went with it. Suzanna hadn't given me a chance to ask before she continued down the walkway.

Angela Rollins strode by, a teasing light in her hazel eyes. "Not only did you take care of that jerkwad boyfriend, but you ended up with the sexiest partner I've seen in a long time."

Oh. That's what the high five had been for.

I shrugged even though I totally agreed with her about the sexy partner. He was so damn hot that it was dangerous having him as a partner for just that reason.

But Gary . . . was he really a jerkwad? I'd never forgive him, but I couldn't just throw out the window the good memories and the fact that he was, overall, a decent guy.

Despite being a cheating sonofabitch.

Okay, so I have a split personality.

Angela grinned over her shoulder before she headed down one set of steps to the CC.

Thoughts of my conversation with Donovan last night kept churning in my mind. I had to sort this out with Oxford.

I stood at Darlene's desk at exactly the time for my

appointment and she gave a haughty sniff that so did not go with her Beatles look.

She pressed a button. "Agent Steele is here."

"Send her in," came Oxford's voice.

"Have a seat," Oxford said as soon as I had closed the door behind me, which was a good sign.

I picked the closest chair and sat in it. Oxford studied me with her assessing dark eyes. Today she wore a deep red silk blouse over another silk shirt. She might not go out in the field, but she was as armed as we were.

My own Glock pressed against the chair. When I went undercover I wouldn't have it and the sense of safeness it gave me.

Oxford folded her hands on her table. She didn't close the blinds, so the entire CC was visible—and we were visible to them. "Is this about Agent Donovan?"

Trust her to get straight to the point.

"Yes." I tried not to squirm in my chair. She made me feel like a schoolgirl being evaluated by the principal. "If he's going to be my co-TS, I need to know what he brings to the table." I leaned forward in my chair. "And why he's allowed to work a family member's case."

"You walk a fine line questioning my decisions, Steele." Oxford's eyes hardened and I wanted to shrink away from her. "However, I do understand your concern."

Phew.

"When he served, Nick Donovan was one of the best SEALs the Navy had. One of the best they'd ever had." Oxford's tone was as hard and even as ever. "As to the whys of his leaving the Navy with an honorable discharge, that is his personal business."

She leaned forward, her hands still clasped on her desktop. "I have been attempting to recruit Donovan for six years due to his skills and how valuable an asset he would be to RED."

OK, she was barely telling me more than Donovan. Were this guy's skills that big of a state secret?

"But his sister?" I knew I should shut my mouth and of course didn't.

Oxford looked at me like I had some nerve questioning her. "This time Donovan came to me. He agreed to sign the contract tying him to RED for a limited amount of time, his only provision being that he could join the operation that would help locate his sister.

"He is an *extremely* valuable resource." She maintained her hard expression and tone. "And that is more than you need to know, Steele. I expect full cooperation with Donovan throughout this operation."

Yeah, he would be an asset, even though it was hard to accept the fact that I wouldn't be the sole TS on this op. I might have done the same thing in Oxford's shoes.

"Yes, ma'am," I said. "As far as going undercover, Perry is already trained—"

"Enough," she said. I knew if I said one more word against Donovan, I was in deep shit. "Fully brief Agent Donovan in his role as your partner." She gave a slight nod to the door. "He's expecting you now."

I got to my feet. "Thank you, ma'am," I said before I headed to the door.

"Steele." Her voice sounded a little less hard as I looked back to her. "Good luck."

"Thank you," I said before I turned and walked out the door, closing it behind me.

I didn't even have time to mull over what she'd said as Nick Donovan chose that moment to round the counter, coming straight for me.

Sweaty nights, tangled sheets, and a hard muscular body between my thighs and pinning me down were the first thoughts that came to mind the moment I saw the man. He was raw power and masculinity in one satisfying, tasty package.

Today he wore a blue overshirt that brought out the brilliant blue of his eyes. His dark gray T-shirt stretched across his well-defined chest and abs. Those biceps and big, strong hands were made to hold a woman as he brought her to orgasm after orgasm.

And this was my new partner. Christ.

Get yourself under control, Steele.

"Conference room three is available." Donovan didn't have any expression on his hard features as he inclined his head toward the row of rooms along one of the catwalks above the CC. It was almost like last night hadn't happened, and we hadn't had our friendly little heart-to-heart.

I felt like a dopey puppy trying to keep up with his long strides. My shoes made no sound on the black tile catwalk as we passed over the busy CC, past conference rooms one and two, and reached three.

As I followed him, I remembered coming in Wednesday and seeing an unfamiliar backside walking into a conference room. It'd been Donovan. Definitely the kind of ass a woman wouldn't forget.

Donovan held the door open and I walked through. The leather chair hugged my body as I slipped into a seat in front of a high-tech keyboard with a touchpad instead of keys. I registered my thumbprint on the scanner before it allowed me access to the files we needed.

At one end of the table a screen materialized, and I cued up a photograph with a list of stats beside a man's face. "This is our informant, Chancy Yeager, who coughed up more info Wednesday to Takamoto."

The informant was handsome but slick. He used his good looks and charisma to his advantage, and he liked the lifestyle he led with the money we paid him for solid information. "Yeager's a very dependable informant, so we think his info is good." I leaned forward and folded my arms on the conference table as I studied Donovan.

"According to what he leaked to us, the most recent group, thirteen women, were just sold on the auction block two weeks ago," I said. "His info is going to help us reach our objective and save those women before they're shipped to the international buyers."

Donovan remained silent but his expression grew darker and darker as I continued. "We tracked down the last auction to a chat room on the Internet. As you know, the slavers included footage of the men and women as they were auctioned."

The anger overcoming me burned as I went on and thought about Donovan's sister. "We failed to find the actual location of the auction." I tried to get a grip on my emotions as I thought of Randolph. "We were certain we were close to finding them, but that's when bad info was fed to Agent Randolph."

Donovan looked at me intently and I cleared my throat. "Our current intel leads us to believe some of the women have already been delivered to their new 'owners' within the US." Even saying the word *owners* made me want to take a bat to the head of each man involved. Or woman, if that was the case.

I glanced at Donovan, and the intense fury in his gaze was so clear that I caught my breath. All those hard, rough edges made him look dangerous now, lethal. On the table he clenched one of his hands hard enough that veins stood out on the back of it. Another taut vein ran along his neck and his jaw was tense, his eyes narrowed at the screen.

Still looking at Donovan, I continued. "The women who were sold to foreign buyers we are certain haven't been shipped yet. From what Yeager gave us, within days this group will be gone. We've got to get to them first and, hopefully, stop the next auction before it happens. The clock is ticking."

Donovan said nothing but looked back at Yeager's profile.

I clicked another button on the keypad and a second photo flickered in the air. "This is our gem, Holly Endicott." The picture I brought up was an image of a beautiful socialite posing on a red carpet and wearing a beige, ankle-length sequined dress. Long, dark hair and a brilliant smile. "She's a billion-dollar baby. A player, big into kink with the club we're going to penetrate."

The word "penetrate" made me want to cough because getting into those clubs would involve a lot of that, in particular.

"Our man Yeager charmed the pants off Endicott and she managed to get us tickets into this exclusive club." I looked at Donovan. "Yeager's a bit of a bad boy and apparently Endicott has a thing for men who Very Rich Father would be appalled to see her bring home."

Donovan leaned back in his chair and studied her picture.

"So she's our 'in' to the inner circle of these three clubs." I brought up an image to replace hers, this one of an exclusive nightclub. "The Champagne Slipper." Another. "The Crystal Twilight." A third. "The Glass House.

"Our objective is to infiltrate their exclusive inner circle and 'playrooms.'" I met Donovan's eyes again. "The three are chic nightclubs, and fronts for the BDSM clubs Endicott supplied the tickets for."

Donovan's expression remained neutral as I continued.

"Back to Yeager." I returned my gaze to the screen. "According to him there are three men who are potential ringleaders of the slave auctions. He can't give us a definite, but he gave us this much."

I touched the pad to bring up head shots of three men side by side. "Benjamin Cabot, Jason Strong, and Lucca Tarantino." I clicked to a screen with Cabot's information first.

Cabot's olive-hazel eyes stared back at me from a classically handsome face. The fortysomething man looked fit beneath his Armani suit.

"Cabot is among the megarich with a home on Marlboro Street. Old money. Boston Brahmin." I glanced at Donovan. "In case you're not familiar with it, it's one of the most prestigious properties in all of Boston. You've gotta have money to live there. Lots." I went over some more statistics. Age, net worth, activities like tennis and golfing, and so on, before bringing up Lucca Tarantino's mug and stats.

Tarantino was Italian, approximately the same age, early forties, and had a debonair air to his bearing. Angular features, olive skin, stunning emerald green eyes, and black hair.

He made a pretty picture—like a young 007 who was heavily into playing and watching *pallone*, as the Italians called soccer. "Where Cabot is old money, Tarantino is new. Made his bucks in the software industry after immigrating to the States as a child in a poor family." I shook my head. "Smart man, or had some insider information, because he pulled out of the stock market before it crashed big-time. Left him pretty wealthy." I gave more of Tarantino's stats before moving on.

"Jason Strong is all over the board." I studied the man's heart-thudding profile. Strong could be mistaken for a very hot, older Vin Diesel—shaved head, muscles and all. "Strong has quite a stash of money, and even has his own private island."

His stats were pretty much the same as the other men. Close to their forties, single, divorced—Tarantino three times—and each man donated large sums of money to various charities. Diesel, I mean Strong, was heavily into weightlifting—which was oh, so obvious, and a little interesting because of his last name. He was a major football fan. Big Red Sox fan as well, so he had a single point in his favor from me.

The laugh I gave was humorless. "Ironically enough, Tarantino gives a good deal of cash to women's shelters." I leaned back in my chair. "These three apparently get together on occasion to play racquetball and gamble a bit at their establishments. In private of course."

Donovan drummed his fingers on the black granite conference table. "What makes these three men suspects?"

I touched the pad again and the screen vanished. "Women seem to disappear every so often from all three men's clubs."

Donovan frowned. "How do we know it's related to the slave auctions?"

I frowned and tilted my head. "With the ticket Endicott gave Yeager to get him in, he had the opportunity to overhear one of the 'regular Doms' talking about buying one of the other missing girls in our case. The Dom pointed to another man's sub, and said something like, 'In the auction coming up I'd pay good money to buy that submissive. I'll talk to the Man.' "

I let out a huff of breath. "That Dom who was looking to buy the girl stopped going to the club nights. The sub he'd said he wanted to buy disappeared.

"That missing girl's real Dom was apparently pretty pissed when she vanished, from what Yeager said, so it leads us to believe 'the Man' was one of our three suspects."

"I need more than that, Steele," Donovan said.

"Well, you've got it." With another touch to the pad in

front of me, I brought up the face of a young brunette woman who looked drugged out of her mind. "Yeager recognized this woman from the vids of the last auction." I cleared my throat again. "The same auction your sister was sold in." Donovan's face turned rock solid. "Yeager is sure she's the sub who disappeared."

Donovan clenched his fist on the granite table. "But he didn't overhear any names?"

I pushed my chin-length hair behind my ears in a frustrated movement and some of it swung back against my cheeks. "All we do know is that only one 'boss man' was referred to, and that Cabot, Strong, and Tarantino own these clubs." I pressed a button and the screen vanished. "The three could be in on it together, or it could be just one, maybe two of them.

"One of the things Randolph gathered in her intel," I said, trying not to choke when I said her name, "is that there's someone higher up. Very high." I rubbed my hand over my hair. "Even if the man responsible for these girls' auction is one of the three we're checking out, there is someone higher up."

"Any more intel on that?" Donovan asked.

I shook my head. "Randolph couldn't get a name."

"What's your plan, Steele?" Donovan asked with his steady blue gaze focused on me while he tapped the manila folder. "You said you've got this op under control."

Heat crept up my neck. Damnit.

"Everything's set," I said. "The group meets on Saturdays. So tomorrow night you're replacing Perry and infiltrating the inner circle of their private little BDSM club"—I wanted to groan as I added—"with me."

Donovan nodded as if he'd expected this.

"Endicott provided Yeager with our two exclusive invitations, and RED is going to cough up some bucks," I said. "The invitations for the inner circle include a twenty-five-thousand-dollar fee once we pass whatever tests there are. Twenty-five grand for each invitation."

I opened up the file folder and withdrew the two envelopes that had "The Circle" stamped in gold leaf script on the front, and a red wax seal on the back. "These two invites already cost us fifty grand to Yeager."

"I'm assuming you've found a way to read what's on the inside of those sealed envelopes," Donovan said.

"Sure did." I slid one of the thick, creamy stationery envelopes across the table to Donovan. "In gold leaf on matching stationery, all it says is 'Bearer is granted one-time entry into the Inner Circle.' "

Donovan nodded but didn't pick up the envelope.

I blew out my breath and leaned back in my chair. "Then it's our job to pass their inner-circle 'tests' to be a part of the group."

"What tests?" Donovan asked.

"Could be anything to do with kink." I looked at him. "Are you up for the challenge?"

"Whatever it takes," he said.

"So you'll be the submissive." I barely held back a laugh. "And I'll be the dominatrix who tries to get you as her sub."

Donovan stared me directly in the eyes. "You've got it backward." I bristled as he continued, "You're going to be the good little submissive and I'm going to be the Dom who's going to spank your ass."

"Fuck you."

"Maybe."

I ground my teeth. "This isn't going to work out. We'll get Perry to go in with me as we had already planned." He was going to be a good sub to my Dom.

"Live with it, Steele." Donovan tapped the invitation. "It's you and me, and nothing's changing that."

He was right, because Oxford would back him on this, not me.

I leaned forward. "Got any bondage gear?"

March 29
Friday evening

Heat flushed my cheeks and my adrenaline was still high after a good softball game in Foley Park with my super, Marty, and some of the neighborhood guys. Marty had snagged me as soon as I stepped foot out of my Cherokee and I couldn't say no. Our team didn't win, but we'd come close. Todd, Marty, and Lou had walked me home, and we'd spent the time talking about the promising upcoming season for the Red Sox.

It had helped me work off some of the frustration after my less than productive meeting with Oxford. She wasn't giving up any goods on Donovan nor was she letting me shake him loose. I was going to be up close and personal with Donovan.

I had stared down cold-blooded killers, but the thought of Donovan seeing me, touching me, possibly tasting me left me shaking with desire, which frankly was pissing me off. If my reaction was this strong just thinking about it, what would happen when he actually put those strong hands on me or placed those delicious lips anywhere on my body? He would know how to give it to me. So intense, so hard, that I would lose all sense of myself and still end up begging for more.

Time for a cold shower and a hot meal.

I was just starting to strip down when my doorbell rang.

"Lexi's gone," I called out. "Come back next week."

"Open up, Steele." Georgina's voice was loud, with a snap to it, and that meant trouble.

"What did I do now?" I grumbled as I rearranged my shirt, walked toward the door, and yanked it open.

Georgina strode through looking more gorgeous than any woman should be allowed to. Bitch.

But I loved her.

"You look like crap," she said.

"Where'd you get that?" I checked out a glittery red dress that barely covered her boobs or her backside. "From the Barbie's-going-out-and-going-down-on-a-Marine store?"

"Screw you, Steele."

"If I swung that way, you'd be the first."

She propped her hands on her hips and cocked her head so that her dark hair swung over her shoulder as her lips quirked. "Come on, baby. We'll try it on for size."

"Let's see." I looked her up and down. "You're nearly six feet and I'm five-four." I batted my eyelashes. "Do I get to be the girl?"

"Five-ten." She smirked. "You, on the other hand, are *lucky* if you're pushing five-four."

I focused on her balloon boobs, obviously given extra oomph by Victoria's Secret. "If I poke one will it pop?"

Georgina's snort of laughter didn't go along with her exotic runway-model features.

I looked over her again. "Does Cal get the honors tonight?"

"I dumped dickhead." A smug expression twisted her lips. "Met a guy at the social after Mass last Saturday." She glanced down as if she could see through my floor to her apartment before she raised her dark eyes again. "Sweetie is waiting for me now."

"Good little Italian Catholic girl has someone to take home to Mother."

She gestured her head toward the kitchen where we usually had our girl chats. "You and I need to talk."

Uh-oh. Wasn't sure I liked her tone. "I hope this is about our girl's day tomorrow."

We pulled out chairs at the kitchen table and I plopped onto mine. She was as graceful as always when she seated herself.

I shoved aside two empty Chinese food cartons as I leaned my elbow on the table. "Okay. What gives?"

"Rumors are flying around RED that you forgot the meaning of low profile. So why don't you fill me in? Now."

I sighed. "Caught Gary with another woman." Another ache stabbed my chest as her eyes widened. "Sonofabitch was screwing her Wednesday when I stopped by his place."

"I'll kill him." She went rigid, her gaze hard. "Unless you already took care of it. Is he in the back of the Jeep? I'll help you dump the body."

"He's not worth the jail time if they dragged Boston Harbor." I braced my chin in my palm, my elbow still on the table. "I got him where it counts." My throat felt scratchy and my laugh came out hoarse. "Took a bat to his truck and slit one of his tires."

"In front of other people?" Georgina reached for her throat and made a choking sound when I nodded. "Christ.

Are you out of your mind? And Oxford didn't can you?" Her face was dead serious. "You'd better not pull that kind of crap again. Do you want to stand in the unemployment line or end up serving pastries and coffee at a Dunkin' Donuts?"

I winced at the thought. "I was afraid of that when Oxford sent Takamoto and Smithe to get me out of jail."

"Jail?" Georgina braced her palms on the table. "You ended up in *jail*? So that asshole Gary is pressing charges?"

"No." Something crawled into my throat. "He told the cops he wasn't, but they were already frisking me and found my Glock. I'd forgotten to put it in the glove compartment when I went in to see Gary."

"Damn, girl." She got up and walked to the fridge, grabbed a couple of bottles of Guinness, and cracked them open with the magnetic bottle opener that had been tacked to the fridge. She handed me a Guinness and sat back down.

The cure for anything. A bottle of Guinness and some girl talk.

"What happened to Stacy Randolph—it doesn't seem real," Georgina said in a much softer tone before either of us had taken a drink.

For a moment I glanced down at the table before looking at the Italian beauty who grew up in North End, but leased a floor of the triple-decker, with me and Marty leasing the other two levels.

"I miss her already." I gripped my cold bottle. "I'm going to the funeral—it's sometime Sunday morning."

"Stacy was the kind of girl you couldn't help but like." Georgina reached out and touched my hand. "Would you like me to go to the funeral with you? Where will it be?"

"Sure." My eyes ached and I rubbed them. "Forest Hills."

She squeezed my hand. "I'll call the mortuary and find out the exact time, and we'll drive out together, okay?"

I gave a slow nod. "Thank you."

We were both silent as we drank our beer.

"So what's with this sexy new partner I hear you have? Nick Donovan, right?" she asked after a few minutes.

"Oxford said Donovan's going in with me on this next op,

not Perry." I groaned. "Donovan wouldn't go for playing a submissive with me as the dominatrix." I almost laughed at the thought of putting a studded collar around his neck. Then I grimaced. "But I'm less than crazy about playing the part of the sub to his Dom."

"You—a, a *submissive*?" Georgina snorted and started laughing so loud and so long that her eyes grew wet and mascara streaked her face.

I gripped the cold bottle as she kept giggling. "It's not like I haven't been through worse. How about when I helped you with that huge narcotics bust last week, in that warehouse that smelled like endless gallons of horse piss? That's gotta be worse than a—" Crap. "A BDSM club."

She gave another snort of laughter and smacked her bottle of Guinness on the tabletop hard enough to make a loud *thunk*.

"Hey, you're gonna damage the pricey laminate."

She rolled her eyes. "It's only as old as this trip we live in."

I sniffed. "It's an antique."

"Those dark circles under your eyes aren't from this thing with Gary." She looked me up and down. "Or Randolph."

The short strands felt scratchy against my cheeks as I shoved my hair out of my face. "Been a long couple of days. *Operation Cinderella* is coming together, but it's been a total bitch getting the inside intel we need to make a move." And the nightmares weren't helping a damned bit. It was almost like not getting sleep at all sometimes.

"Get some rest, Lexi." Georgina sounded like the concerned friend she was, one who'd been through so much with me.

I waved my hand in a dismissive gesture. "Don't you have a party or something to get to with that sweet little Catholic boy?"

"Sam's not going anywhere." She shrugged. "He's probably watching the tube while he waits."

I drained my bottle of Guinness and stood. "So go find out if he's a good lay."

"He's got big feet and hands." She put on a sultry look

and used her low, sexy voice. "I just hope he lives up to expectations."

With a grin, I shook my head. Then pictured Donovan's good-sized feet and hands and nearly groaned again.

Georgina's smile turned into a frown. "I'm not so sure I like the idea of you in a BDSM club."

I wasn't so sure either.

"It'll be fine." I rolled my empty bottle in my palms. "We'll be in and out."

"That's what I'm afraid of." She narrowed her brows. "A little in-and-out action. You know what goes on in those places, don't you?"

"I've done my research, and I've visited some of the tamer clubs, where you can watch and don't have to play." Warmth flushed up my face to the roots of my hair. "As far as this op, we'll just make sure we get what we need as fast as we can."

"If this Nick Donovan is as hot as rumor has it, this op might not be so bad if it does come along." Her mouth curved from the frown to a slight smile.

"He's just my partner." The heat in my face grew hotter as I pictured just that—him coming. "Now, for our shopping trip tomorrow."

"Oh, honey, I'll take care of you." Georgina's exotic dark eyes sparkled as she stood on her tiny red heels. "I know exactly what places we need to hit."

"I've got a hair appointment at ten." We walked to the front door. "Followed by a manicure and a pedicure." And oh, lord, a wax job I really wasn't looking forward to.

"Meet you here at nine-thirty," she said before she let herself out the door.

I rolled my eyes as I locked the door with the industrial chain. Yeah, this little shopping trip with Georgina ought to be interesting. And just wait until Oxford got a look at the expense voucher.

CHAPTER 11

Kristin

March 16
Saturday, two weeks ago

The hum of voices, and what sounded like the scratch of metal over metal, caused a shudder to run down Kristin's spine as she slowly became aware of the sounds. Whimpers and cries from other women—barely there.

Smells of new carpeting and paint tickled her nose, almost making her sneeze. An air conditioner kicked on and she shivered from cool air caressing her skin.

Naked. She was naked.

True reality seeped into Kristin and her slack body tensed. But she hung from something, her arms stretched over her head.

No strength. She had no strength.

Was she really here? Where was here? Was this her body? Even though her arms ached and her wrists stung from metal handcuffs, she felt almost separated from her own bones and muscle.

She found the strength to lift her head and look up. As heavy as her head felt, it was a wonder she could raise it.

The haziness in her mind started to clear along with her eyesight. The handcuffs' links had been secured over a big meat hook attached to a thick chain in a ceiling that could be in any office building.

Strange to see the circular area around her. Blue drapes hung from a big metal hoop, and she couldn't see past the drapes.

Hours, days, weeks, years. Who knew how long she'd been drugged? Too drugged to even move most of the time. She couldn't remember when she'd been shot up last. It must have been a while ago since things looked so much clearer as she stared at her bare toes.

It hadn't surprised her that she was naked. The only thing that surprised her was that she hadn't been raped.

Her lungs didn't want to work as her thoughts went places she tried to avoid but couldn't.

Yet. They haven't raped me yet.

The men could have. The ones who kept her locked up in a room, fed her cold pizza, and gave her bottled water when she was coherent. Ricco and Danny she thought their names were.

Whenever she was alert enough, she wondered if there was any chance in the world that she could escape.

Nick would find her. Her brother. Her only family.

He would never stop until he did find her. There was no way in the world he wouldn't be looking for her the moment he discovered she was missing.

Did he know she was gone yet?

The murmur of voices around her became more distinct as the fog started to lift from her mind. Men moved inside the drapes, ignoring her as they set up computer monitors, lights, and what looked like recording cameras.

"This auction had better go down smooth or the Man will blow a goddamned fuse," one of the men said. Danny maybe?

The men had frequently talked about an auction when they were around her. They often referred to someone called "the Man" and how he'd make sure she and other unspoiled candy went for top dollar.

Candy?

The words made no sense when she was doped up. But as she hung from the ceiling, her mind started functioning better. What kind of auction?

Her heart started throbbing so fast her chest hurt. It was pumping hard enough to push away more of the haze.

She was going to be *sold*?

Kristin swallowed as pieces of what the men often said started matching up. She was going to be somebody's sex slave.

Tears pushed their way through her closed eyelids and her cheeks were wet within an instant. She gave a sob and tried to raise her head.

Nick. Where are you?

"Shit." Ricco's voice came from her right. "The dope is wearing off of this one. We can't have her bawling during the videotaping and auction."

More sobs rolled from Kristin as she felt a familiar prick in her arm. Within moments she wondered why she was crying.

Everything was fine.

Why was she hanging from something?

It didn't matter.

The chain was lowered so that she was standing flat on her feet instead of her toes, but they kept her arms over her head. Still she felt some relief in the ache from her armpits up to her wrists. Plush carpeting beneath her bare feet. Strange.

Someone put his palm on her forehead and pushed her head up. She tried to focus. Joe, the man who'd put her into the van, right?

Maybe. Whatever.

"Grace." Joe looked over his shoulder and smiled at someone Kristin couldn't see. "Do your thing."

Her mind swirling, Kristen felt like a leaf floating on water and nonsensical singsong music made her want to hum.

Joe faced her again and he smiled. Such a handsome smile. How easily he had taken her in. Flirted with her, bought her a drink, and bam, she was gone.

So easy.

No emotion existed in Kristin. She just was. She watched as an old lady pushed a cart close to her. Looked like makeup and stuff was on it.

"Let me do her nipples." Joe grinned and opened a container with a pink substance.

He pinched first one nipple then the other, and squeezed hard. The pink stuff had the consistency of lipstick and caused her to gasp as he rubbed it around her areola and all over her nipple. The sudden sensation was powerful enough to cause her to catch her breath. Her nipples were hard, distended, and they ached like a small vise was clamped on them.

The old lady moved in close to Kristin as Joe cleaned his fingers with a wet wipe from the cart, smirked, and walked away.

Grace started fussing with Kristin's long hair, which had been washed earlier when she'd been dragged into a shower. Kristin's hair was dry now, and Grace teased it and curled the naturally blond hair so that it fell in soft swirls and waves to her shoulders.

Next Grace applied makeup to Kristin's face, and finished with lipstick and gloss. The makeup felt thicker and heavier than she normally wore, almost like a mask.

The old lady nodded with approval in her expression before rolling her cart away. Joe directed Grace to go to another place where she was needed and the old woman headed through a gap in the drapes.

Kristin's mind couldn't settle on anything, bouncing from one thing to another. Blue drapes in a circle around her. Cameras. Lights that weren't on. Computer monitors. Microphone.

Interesting, too.

She supposed.

Kristin hummed along with the odd music dancing in her head.

And then her thoughts took flight. To nowhere. Anywhere at all.

The lights around her came on so brightly she had to blink in their glare. Three or four people were with her in the circular curtained area. Joe held a recording camera up and was filming her. A mild sense of curiosity had her watching him, and then he started moving slowly around her, recording every bit of her naked body.

Joe began listing all of her attributes out loud, starting

with her being a college student, her body unspoiled, never prostituted. He gave her measurements, showed the birthmark on her lower back.

All so strange.

Disembodied voices began shouting out numbers. Dollars. The voices reminded her of the teacher in the Charlie Brown cartoons, only she could understand the words. Some. One voice said, "Five thousand," another said, "Ten." More numbers increased with bids from other computer-enhanced voices.

"Twenty thousand dollars to triumph2000." Joe gave a satisfied smile as he looked at Kristin. "A worthwhile investment."

"Smile, baby." Joe came up to her as all the lights and computer monitors were shut down. "You were just purchased by a man who wanted you real bad. He's the reason you ended up here."

Joe settled his palm on her hip as he leaned closer. "One good screw won't spoil you before we deliver."

"Back off." Grace elbowed past him and began removing the heavy makeup from Kristin's face with a damp cloth. "You don't screw the merchandise."

Joe gave a wink and a grin, and left the room while Grace continued to wipe Kristin down, from her face to her rosy, distended nipples.

Grace pushed Kristin's hair over her shoulders before signaling to two men in the room to come to them. When she looked back at Kristin, Grace said with a motherly smile, "Just enjoy your new life, pumpkin."

Kristin frowned and wondered if she cared what the old woman meant.

Grace patted Kristin's cheek. "Be thankful you'll be one man's property, and that you won't be prostituted and have too many men to count screwing you every night."

CHAPTER 12

Leather and lace will take a girl a long way

March 30
Saturday night

The sleek Mercedes convertible registered to Alexi Adams was made just for me and I looked damned good in the sinfully red sports car.

I drove up to the entrance of the Crystal Twilight, near Beacon Hill, and parked the hot little number. The young, overly eager valet opened my door, took my hand, and helped me step out in a smooth movement.

Yep.

His eyes just about popped out of his head.

Amazing what a short skirt and a leather-and-lace corset could do to a man.

Years of experience undercover had taught me to dress and act like I belonged in whatever situation I might be in. But with Donovan now in the picture, tonight would no doubt be . . . interesting.

The snug black leather skirt was smooth beneath my palm as I gave it a single tug to take it from where it had scooted up to just below crotch level. In my other hand I held the small clutch containing cash, ID, and the invitation to the Inner Circle.

A cool, clean-scented wind brushed my legs, which were bare save for the specially equipped studded-leather ankle cuff. Martinez had designed the cuff to include a gadget that hid a high-tech USB device along with a signal scrambler to use when we needed it. Martinez was kick-ass when it came to designing gadgets. From my lipstick camera to the pen that would get me out of deep shit, which I kept in my purse. I only needed to click the pen twice to call in RED agents if an undercover operation went bad.

I slipped my fingers into my Versace clutch and handed a big enough bill to the valet to make his eyes pop out almost as much as they had when he'd gotten a look at me. "Take good care of my baby, won't you?" I said, my voice soft and sultry.

His throat worked as he said, "The best," before giving me a claim ticket that I tucked into my handbag. I winked at him as I saw him look from my breasts to my face. His blush was instantaneous.

My leather corset had a wide V of lace between my breasts. The lace traveled downward and nearly reached my belly before it stopped. The half-carat diamond piercing through my belly button sparkled in the glow of the Crystal Twilight. The lace exposed the swells of either side of my breasts. I wouldn't have any trouble getting attention tonight.

As I turned from the valet, another man took my arm and escorted me to the door, where yet a third man was checking his guest list before allowing members to enter.

"Alexi Adams." I slipped my invitation from my clutch and handed it to him along with my ID. My ID showed one of the most exclusive addresses in all of Boston.

The man returned my ID and the invitation. "Mr. Tarantino himself will join you shortly for the exclusive gathering," the man said with a slight nod.

I passed him a large bill before walking through the door into the nightclub.

Hey, it was RED's money.

The music's beat pulsed through my body as I stepped through the doors of the Crystal Twilight. Smells of alcohol, perfumes, and aftershave swept over me.

Georgina had made sure my chin-length hair and makeup were perfect. My lipstick felt smooth and glossy on my lips, my makeup applied in a way that accented my features. I looked pretty hot if I said so myself.

It was hard to keep from smiling as men literally turned their heads to watch me walk into the club. By their scowls, a few women didn't seem to appreciate the attention I was getting from their dates as I gently swayed my hips. The click of my heels against the marble floor was nearly lost in the beat of the music.

Only the rich could afford the Crystal Twilight, so it wasn't as packed as some nightclubs, meaning there was breathing room. From the research I'd done, Lucca Tarantino had ensured this club built its rep as the classiest, most elitist nightclub in Boston.

A long-legged blond stepped in front of me and headed toward the bar. For just a moment something twisted in my belly as I remembered the blond with her legs wrapped around Gary's hips—

Someone grabbed my ass.

I swung around to face a cocky-looking college-aged kid.

The smile I gave him had his expression turning from cocky to "oh, crap," in a second. I moved close and murmured. "Touch me again and your balls will be in your throat."

One second flat and he was gone.

I enjoyed being a petite package that most people underestimated. I'd taken down men as big as Donovan, as well as big flabby SOBs with guts the size of Rhode Island.

Papa had put me in jujitsu classes after Rick Larson knocked out my front tooth when I was eight.

Let's just say that, after a few lessons, Rick never came near me again. At least not until we dated our senior year in high school. He grew up to be *hot*.

I never stopped my training, so under my belt was around twenty-three years of jujitsu, as well as experience with all the forms of weaponry I'd excelled with in Special Forces. Not only did I work out with weights, but my routine included boxing, sparring, and jogging when I wasn't deep undercover. I could do a hell of a job of protecting myself and kicking ass.

But tonight I would be playing the part of a submissive and I kept my expression sultry as I turned away from him.

My lips wanted to twist into a scowl at the thought of being submissive to anyone.

And that "anyone" was going to be Nick Donovan if everything went as planned.

The strange tingling in by belly caught me off guard. A flash of Donovan and me naked, with him sliding inside me almost made me falter in my three-inch heels.

A shiver strobed through me, as intense as the lights flashing over the dance floor. I responded by straightening my spine as I moved toward the bar.

I walked like a woman who knew what she wanted and how to get it. I made a discreet sweep of the room with my gaze.

With my countless years of training and instinct, I knew approximately how many people were in the bar; the number of bouncers—and had a good idea how many of them were armed; the best route to the front and back exits; common items that would make good weapons in a down-and-dirty fight; and which men were likely to come on to me before I located my prey. Lots of other little things I also filed away in my memory.

I eased onto the soft calfskin-leather bar seat and crossed my leg with the cuff clearly visible. My legs felt silky and soft from the wax job I'd had earlier today. The short skirt hiked up just enough that air cooled the skin where the movement revealed the bottom curve of one bare cheek.

"Lemon drop." I leaned forward and smiled at the bartender, exposing more cleavage. "Sugar on the rim."

"You've got it, babe." In a few moments, the bartender set the martini on a cocktail napkin. "Tab?"

The sugar around the rim was tart and sweet as I raised it to my mouth, took a sip, then smiled at him. "Please."

My manicured fingernails grazed the rich wood of the mahogany-and-granite bar as I pushed away just enough to turn slightly and survey the room beneath my lashes.

I wondered how long it would take Lucca Tarantino to find me and escort me back to the Inner Circle.

And I wondered how many men would approach me before Tarantino did.

Music pounded loud enough to vibrate the stool where I perched. The lemon scent of the martini as I sipped blocked out some of the smells that had hit me when I walked into the place.

After each tiny sip I slowly licked the sugar off my lower lip. It wasn't long before the first sucker approached me and I quickly dispatched him and the two who came after him. I knew who I was waiting for.

I sat there for another fifteen minutes before a tickle along my spine told me someone was approaching from behind.

Finally.

This one flashed a too-white movie-star grin, and no doubt that was Versace he was wearing. He carried the light scent of a French spa cologne. Hey, I knew my stuff, my training was extensive. This guy had to have loads of cash.

"Would you like to join me at my table?" He had a line that wasn't original enough for a girl like me even if I was interested.

"No, thank you," I said, and looked away, dismissing him.

Door number five casually made his way to me through the crowd.

"First time I've seen you here," the blond said. Not original but he had the look of a man's man, so I let it pass. He had the body of a runner, slim and athletic, and wore a button-up blue shirt and Levis.

"First time I've been here." The smile that touched my lips was sultry and seductive. I reached out my free hand and touched the top button of his shirt. And my, my, my. A bulge started to expand his jeans. Hmmm. Not bad.

I adjusted my legs so that the studs on the leather ankle cuff caught sparks of light.

He glanced at it and I fisted my hand in his shirt and drew him close. "Do you know what that signifies?" I said before I released him. I glanced at his jeans. That man had one nice package.

When my eyes met his he shrugged. "A leather ankle cuff."

Too bad. "If you don't know what it means, then I guess you'll never find out." I sipped my lemon drop before I added, "From me."

He shook his head and smiled before turning away.

A low, rich voice came from behind me, a voice I didn't recognize. "I know."

I almost spit out the drink I'd just taken.

He placed his warm hands on my shoulders and wouldn't let me swivel in my seat to face him. Then his mouth was next to my ear and he said in a smooth-as-melted-chocolate voice, "I know exactly why you wear that cuff."

I swallowed, my chin high, and wished I could face him. "So tell me."

"You enjoy indulging in certain, shall we say . . . proclivities? The cuff means you're currently unattached." He massaged my shoulders and I shivered. "If you were wearing a collar I'd know you had a Dom."

He slowly turned me to face him.

Lucca Tarantino.

The owner of the Crystal Twilight and target number one.

Dark, handsome, and sexy as an Italian god.

He faced the bartender and I maintained my sensual expression. "I'll have a martini straight up, and the lady's drink is on the house."

When he faced me again, I put all the desire I could into my smile that showed I was interested, *very* interested.

"And who is the gentleman buying my martini?" I said as I leaned against the bar and let my breasts jut out.

By the look in his incredible green eyes, it was clear he liked what he saw. "Lucca Tarantino. I own the Twilight." He took my hand and ran his finger over my palm in a slow stroke. He smiled. "What is your name, *cara*?"

"Alexi Adams."

"Alexi . . ." My name rolling out in that oh-so-hot Italian accent caused warmth to flush beneath my skin. "I understand you have a special invitation for tonight."

"Yes," I said, making my voice husky with desire. Lucca

Tarantino was sensual and gorgeous so it wasn't that much of a hardship to pretend. If he were a different man, I might even seriously be interested.

Tarantino didn't release my hand as he ran his gaze down my body, skimming slowly over my nearly bared breasts, on to my midriff with the diamond piercing, and the minuscule leather skirt. He paused for a moment as he looked at the studded cuff on my right ankle, above my three-inch spiked heels.

He stroked my palm a little more, still not releasing my hand. "Tell me, Alexi, why exactly do you think you might find a Dom here?"

I opened my handbag and slipped out the invitation. I leaned closer to let him feel my body heat without allowing myself to actually touch him. Or fall off my seat. "A friend told me that I might find what I'm looking for in the Crystal Twilight."

Tarantino slipped the invitation from my fingers. He was a good six inches taller than me so he had to lower his head to move his mouth to my ear. "Bondage? Domination?"

"Mmmmmm." I let my lips barely slide along his jawline and breathed in his sandalwood aftershave. "The whole package."

When Tarantino drew away, his expression was intensely sexual. He had that 007 and Italian playboy look down pat. "Then I'm sure you'll enjoy this evening."

I sipped my martini, its flavor tart in my mouth. I lowered my glass and ran my tongue along my lower lip, tasting the sugar left from the edge of the martini glass. I met Tarantino's gaze. "I'm ready when you are."

CHAPTER 13

Your tax dollars at work

March 30
Saturday night

Tarantino tucked the envelope into his suit jacket before he took my hand and helped me down from the stool. Even while I held my lemon drop martini in my other hand, I managed to move gracefully.

Damn, I'm good.

When I was on my feet, Tarantino released me to take his own martini.

Tarantino got points for making sure he measured his strides to match mine. He placed his hand on the bare skin at the base of my spine, below my corset. I gave myself credit for not moving away when he moved his finger in a slow, erotic circle. He was gorgeous, but that didn't mean every gorgeous guy got to pet me. But I was here to play a role and I'd play it good.

Then the thought flashed through my mind that he could be taking me to be auctioned like the women who'd been kidnapped. But that thought fled as we slipped through a back entrance and past a guard who nodded to Tarantino.

The lounge had definite Italian flare. Robust and beautifully decorated accessories including knickknacks on the strategically displayed tables and end tables gave the room Italian charm. Oil paintings graced the walls, and there were too many carved wood and alabaster items to count. It didn't look cluttered at all. It was fabulous and made me feel like I was in Old Italy. A full bar also ran along one side of the room.

The room smelled like what I remembered of the intoxicating scents of the Riviera dei Fiori when I did a job for RED in Italy. The River of Flowers. Beautiful.

I gradually returned to reality—

And realized I was virtually on display.

The eyes of every man and woman in the cozy lounge focused on me. Some of the men and women made it obvious they were stripping me with their gazes, while others gave appreciative smiles. None of them wore collars. This was a Dom's lounge.

Tarantino stood behind me as I swallowed back the desire to turn and run.

No, I *could* do this.

Men and women decked out in various forms of fairly revealing leather lounged around on the luxurious furniture, while many stood at the bar.

I lowered my eyes like a sub would. And realized my fingers were aching from gripping my clutch purse so tightly.

Where was Donovan? He was supposed to arrive before me.

As I adjusted myself to my surroundings, I almost didn't notice Tarantino's warm hands on my backside until he started massaging through the soft leather skirt.

He murmured close to my ear in his melting Italian accent. "I'd love to take you for one of my subs." He trailed his lips along my jawline. "If I was in the position to, I would," he added. "But you can have your choice of any unattached Dom you'd like."

Tarantino nipped my earlobe. "Not only are you one of the most beautiful women here," he continued, "we're short on females at the present." He moved one hand under my leather skirt and rubbed it over one of the cheeks that had been left bare thanks to the thong I was wearing. "I could never imagine any of the men—or women—refusing *you*."

I forced myself to stand still and, instead of letting my surprise show, I sipped my martini, then looked at Tarantino over my shoulder. "And if I refuse any of them?"

Tarantino took me by the shoulders and brought me around

to face him, but I still kept my eyes lowered like I'd be expected to. "No one is forced to do anything they choose not to at the Twilight."

I nodded and his fingers slid across mine as he took my empty martini glass from my hand. When did I finish drinking it?

"Sex is reserved for the private rooms. Some of the rooms you can watch or be watched. Other rooms you may enjoy your partner or partners in solitude."

I could deal with the private room part. Donovan and I could lock ourselves away and do nothing. Or maybe we would end up doing far too much.

Yes, please, my rowdy hormones seemed to plead.

Tarantino leaned close. "Every new Dom and sub go through a 'test' that is very public. Entirely revealing. Helps with our screening process."

Yeager had prepared us on this and, even though the thought still made me nervous as hell, I nodded. "Of course."

Tarantino gave a smile filled with sexual promise. "As they say, 'what happens in the heart of the Crystal Twilight stays in the Twilight.' "

Then he leaned in close and whispered in my ear. "The other three club owners have one more special provision in our inner circle." I couldn't help the little shiver of unease that ran down my spine. What provision? "The three of us get to enjoy all of the new subs at least once, with or without their Doms present. Our club, our rules."

I nodded. Damn. That wasn't standard protocol for a BDSM club or relationship.

"And," he added in that same voice that was making me so hot, "I think I might have to fuck you before anyone else has a chance to."

Not on your life, I thought, but managed to keep my mouth shut.

He gave me a sensual smile. "But first things first."

He gave a slight incline of his head to his right and I followed his gaze. A woman with flawless dark brown skin and long, shapely legs approached us. She was unbelievably tall in her five-inch-heeled thigh-high boots. She had lush red lips, countless long black braids, and a body as great as Georgina's. She wore a leather corset and a leather thong—

And she carried a whip. One hell of a whip. "Mistress Danica will have you prepared," Lucca Tarantino said, and this time there was a little amusement to his tone. "She has a special touch with submissives." She snapped the whip almost lightly, but still with a cracking sound.

I looked up at Tarantino. "Enjoy, little sub." He gave another sensual smile and walked away.

Donovan. Where was he? What if he didn't make it in for some reason?

"Slave." Danica's voice was harsh. She sounded like a major bitch. I met her brown eyes and she frowned and snapped the whip. She glanced at my ankle cuff. "You should know better than to look up without permission from a Dom."

Bite me, I wanted to say. But she probably would have.

I kept my eyes downcast and stared at those five-inch-heeled boots. How the hell did she wear such high—

"I just gave you an order. What do you say, slave?"

Of course, with my research, I knew what she expected. With Perry I'd planned on being on her end of the whip, not on the receiving end.

"Yes, Mistress Danica," I said, as submissively as I could.

"Keep your eyes down and come forward, slave."

Now I was staring at her rounded backside as it swayed almost hypnotically in front of me. With her height and those heels I was practically eye-to-butt level.

The hardwood floor clicked under our heels as Mistress Danica led me through the room. From the corners of my eyes I saw more appreciative glances from men and women, and even heard murmurs about my attributes. "I'd like to spank that cute—" "That one's got fire in her." "All the better to burn." "Hot little package."

Moisture didn't want to go down my throat as I tried to swallow. We passed one blond woman sitting on the arm of a couch and she pinched me under my skirt as I walked by. I made a little sound of surprise and almost stumbled. The blond laughed.

"Don't make a sound without my permission, slave," Danica said as she continued walking.

"Yes, Mistress Danica," I said to her butt.

In truth, submissives weren't doormats. They held the power over their Doms, which was something I'd learned right from the start of my research. According to everything I'd read and seen subs held the true power—the power of giving their Dom pleasure.

But as I followed Danica and held onto my clutch, I had a feeling nothing was going to be easy tonight.

Danica guided me to a room that smelled of almonds and vanilla, and reminded me of a massage parlor. It had a couple of massage tables, vials of oils, and warmers for hot towels. The clear view of a shower was to my left, and rows of tall and short lockers in front of me. To my right were a man and a woman. Each stood with their feet shoulder-width apart, their hands clasped behind their backs, and their eyes lowered. And each of them wore black leather that didn't cover a whole lot.

A slow burn rolled under my skin. Here we go.

"Slave Kathy and slave Samuel, this is our newest slave. She hasn't earned the right to be called by her name. Yet."

Oh, great. Slave no-name, that's me.

Danica swung around to face me, and now I was looking at her crotch instead of her backside. Terrific.

"Slaves Kathy and Samuel will strip you and prepare you for your first test."

Strip. Me.

This was real now. It wasn't practice, it wasn't something I was still working through in my mind to make sure I got it right. It was real.

Game on.

"Yes, Mistress Danica," I said, trying to keep my voice respectful.

Danica turned slightly toward Kathy and Samuel. "Put

her in that new little crisscross number we just got in. Leave on her heels and her ankle cuff."

The sigh of relief that they weren't going to take my ankle cuff almost came out of me in a rush. I managed to hold it in.

"Yes, Mistress Danica," the two slaves said as one.

Danica stepped close to me and cupped my chin in her hand before raising my head so that my eyes met hers. Her long braids swung over her shoulders as she leaned down and brought her face close to mine.

"I bet you're delicious," she murmured before she kissed me.

To say I was shocked was an understatement. I'd never been kissed by a woman before. I can't say it was unpleasant. Her lips were soft, and she slipped her tongue inside my mouth when I opened it in surprise. She tasted sweet and like she'd just had a glass of fine wine, and she smelled like jasmine.

Still, I was happy when she drew away. Women just didn't do it for me and I didn't really have any desire to repeat the experience, though, honestly, it looked like the night was young yet, and who knew what would be required of me while I was tested.

But then I thought about the girls I was trying to save and knew that this was nothing. I would do what I needed to do to save them.

Danica smiled at me, thinking my stunned reaction was due to her prowess and not my shock. Well, whatever did it for her.

"Here the sub chooses her Dom, if the Dom reciprocates," she said. She ran her finger down the side of my throat and rested her hand on my breast. "I'd enjoy having you for a sub."

She kissed me with her soft lips again before she nodded to the other two slaves. Then she turned and strode out the door.

The imprint of Danica's mouth seemed to remain on mine, and my lips tingled. The sound of a zipper and air caressing my spine brought me to the present in a hurry.

Kathy slipped my clutch out of my hands, which left Samuel as the one stripping me. His grip on my waist was firm and the corset was already falling away. It landed in a pile on the floor with a soft brushing sound.

Samuel unzipped my leather skirt and let it drop around my heels. "Nice." He was behind me so I couldn't see his expression. "But I prefer dick over pussy."

Oh, good. Then his pulling my thong down around my ankles wasn't arousing him.

Sometimes this job was insane. Beating my head against the wall felt like a real idea right now. *I* was insane for coming up with the infiltration idea.

But really, what choice did we have?

I stepped out of the thong and skirt, and Kathy grinned up at me as she knelt and gathered my stuff. She folded everything neatly, arranged my clutch on top, and pushed the pile into one of the shorter lockers.

The smells of almonds and vanilla grew stronger as Kathy and Samuel had me lie facedown on one of the massage tables and my preparations began. By the time they were done with me, I had been massaged, oiled, and trussed up in mere strips of leather. I hadn't been crazy about it, but at least I'd had the complete wax job done earlier, or they would have done it. I could smell the melted wax they used for that purpose.

I was so getting extra pay for this. No idea how I'd turn it in, but I'd figure something out. Hazard pay? The look on Oxford's face would almost be worth the current embarrassment. Good thing I wasn't a regular Fed. The newspapers would have too much fun with an exposé on something like this.

Agent gets Brazilian wax on the clock. Your tax dollars at work . . .

Thank God my lower part was covered with the strips of leather, even though the bottom half was just a thong so my butt was completely bare. I had a feeling I wouldn't be wearing any skirt to cover myself.

Samuel and Kathy raised more strips and crossed my

nipples with about one inch of leather, and fastened the straps over my shoulders.

"Perfect," Kathy said as she looked at me.

My entire backside and belly were bare, and only thin leather strips covered my nipples. That was it.

I absolutely did not want to go strutting through a room of people dressed in the equivalent of three leather tongue depressors.

Samuel put his hand on his chin and twirled his fingers in a way that told me he wanted me to turn around. I did as he said, sure that certain leather parts would fall away from all of my important parts, but it stayed put. Good sign.

When I met Samuel's gaze again his expression was almost serious, appraising. "Excellent. Stunning."

"And with your backside bare like that, it'll be perfect for your test," Kathy said.

"I haven't been told yet." I cleared my throat. "What's the test?"

"You're going to love it." She smiled. "A good flogging in front of the whole club."

CHAPTER 14

Ouch

March 30
Saturday night

I had broken out into a sweat and it and the oil was slick on my skin as my arms brushed my sides while I walked, with Karen and Samuel on either side of me, toward . . . toward what? The scent of almond was so strong, it blocked out any other kind of smell. Must have gotten some of the oil up my nose.

How strange my mound had felt all day, waxed and bare, and even more so now that I was oiled. The roiling sensation in my belly accompanied the pain in my chest that could have been from the pounding of my heart.

Christ, Steele. When you worked narcotics, you were in knife fights with drug-dealing gangs—and managed to escape with a few slashes before taking the assholes down with other RED agents. A lot you've taken down yourself. You've had to smoke pot, snort coke, all in the name of playing an undercover part.

And you've killed, Steele. Many times. Many, many times,

You can do this.

My tits were going to fall out of those straps, I just knew it. If I moved the wrong way I'd flash anyone who passed us while we made our way through a maze of high-ceilinged, arched hallways.

The ankle cuff was a constant reminder that I needed to find a way to download info off Tarantino's computer. Not that I needed a reminder, because thinking of saving those girls from being auctioned was what kept me going.

It was almost painful to swallow as I managed to walk with what looked like confidence down a long hallway. Whenever we passed a Dom, I lowered my gaze.

Faking illness didn't sound like too bad an idea right now. Of course that would ruin my chances of getting "in" with this BDSM crowd.

Where was Donovan?

Kathy and Samuel hadn't spoken, but Kathy took my hand and squeezed it briefly before she let go. I looked at her smile. "It's been a while, hasn't it?"

No doubt she felt the tremors in my hand. I nodded.

"Master Tarantino believes only in pleasure for the sub." She gave one more squeeze before releasing me. "You can always use your safe word." She frowned. "But then you'd fail the test and we wouldn't see you around anymore."

I blinked. Were women who didn't make the cut taken to the auctions?

I'd better make the cut. That's all there was to it.

At the end of one long hallway was my virtual doom. Through the tall, wide-open double doors, I saw what looked like a casual party. Apparently it was a very private party considering the number of uncovered breasts of women wearing collars and the men in skimpy thongs that barely covered their packages while they walked behind their Doms. Some of the subs were being tugged along with chains or leather leashes attached to their thick leather collars.

We walked closer.

And closer.

At the threshold.

Everyone stopped what they were doing and looked at me.

In the crowd of onlookers, I registered Benjamin Cabot and Jason Strong, our other two major suspects. Strong really did look like a buff Vin Diesel in a sleeveless shirt, with muscles in all the right places, including the one in his tight leather pants.

Cabot was better looking in person than he had been in the photo we had on record. I'd been right about him being classically handsome, but he was much more of a snob—or looked like one—than I'd gathered from his pic. Like Tarantino and unlike all the leather and lack thereof on the people around us, Cabot wore a suit. Armani.

Cabot had a satisfied smile and as he studied me, and I knew he was taking great pleasure in what I was about to go experience. I glanced at Strong and Tarantino, and saw the same expressions of pleasure on each of their faces.

I remembered the part about the three of them having the option to use my body, with or without my Dom, as part of the club package. Christ.

Samuel touched the base of my spine and gently propelled me forward, guiding me to the center of the room. The plush evergreen-shaded carpeting muffled the sound of my three-inch heels.

When we reached the center of the room, I knew the drill. I immediately took a sub's stance. My feet shoulder-width apart, my breasts thrust out, my hands clasped behind my back. I wouldn't raise my eyes unless I was told to.

I'd been beaten in the Cuban and Mexican jails, whipped, punched, knocked out. This was nothing.

At least that's what I told myself.

Samuel and Kathy moved away. With my eyes downcast, it was hard to make a sweep of the room with my gaze to analyze it and look for Donovan, but I did my best.

The scent of sandalwood met my senses just before Lucca Tarantino stood before me, still dressed in the suit that was obviously tailored and made just for him. Was he going to do what he'd said? Fuck me before anyone else could? I have to admit I'd take him over anyone else I'd seen.

Except Donovan.

Where'd that come from? Maybe because I'd fantasized about him too many times to count since meeting him.

"Very good, Mistress Danica," Tarantino said in his smooth Italian accent. He reached up—and pushed aside one of the straps, completely baring my breast. I barely held back a gasp. He stroked my breast, my skin still moist from the almond oil. "You had your slaves prepare her well."

He pushed aside the other strap and that breast felt the coolness of the room.

Now everyone could see my breasts and my nipples, which hardened and stood out.

I deserved a bonus for this.

Tarantino hooked his finger under my chin and tilted my head back, forcing me to look at him. With a sensual smile, he brought his lips to mine.

His kiss was slow, inviting. But it was a kiss of ownership. I felt it in every cell of my body. He'd decided he owned me, no matter what Dom I chose.

But nobody owned me.

When Tarantino drew away from the kiss he smiled, his expression filled with sex and passion. Those green eyes of his were somehow mesmerizing. "Cuffs," he said in a voice that sounded distant as he spoke to someone else, but he kept his gaze on me. "Hands in front of you, little slave."

I obeyed, and the skin around his beautiful green eyes crinkled with pleasure. It took me a moment to realize he was buckling a pair of leather handcuffs to my wrists.

"Raise your arms." He guided my arms over my head.

My gaze drifted up as he raised my arms and I saw that I was beneath a very large silver hook hanging from a long silver chain. Tarantino took me by the waist, raised me slightly so that I was on the tips of my toes, and someone else hooked the chain linking the cuffs over the hook.

I was cuffed. Hanging from a hook in the ceiling. Most of my body bared.

Tarantino turned his head to the crowd of onlookers. "Mistress Danica. Have one of your subs strip this slave. Leave the cuff."

Oh, shit.

He returned his gaze to mine. "Any time you want to stop, say the safe word you will give your Dom. It will all be over and you'll have failed the test."

Fail? Yeah, right. Bring it on.

Kathy and Samuel moved toward me and removed the bits of leather and took off my heels.

Even though I'd half expected this, when they finished everyone had to see how red my entire body must be from embarrassment. It was like I was on fire, the flames rising from my toes to my scalp and then never stopping.

"Beautiful," I heard through the buzzing in my ears. "Who gets to flog her?"

"No idea who Tarantino will pick, but if it's me, I'll give it to her good."

I prayed it wasn't that last voice.

"We have a new Dom joining us tonight." Tarantino gestured with a nod to my right. "Known elsewhere as Sire Dunning. This slave will be his test to see if he earns that title here."

My gaze followed Tarantino's and my stomach gave a lurch.

Donovan. Carrying a very long bullwhip.

I didn't know if the twisting in my belly was from relief at seeing him, from the desire to be on the other end of that whip, or from embarrassment. It was bad enough having a roomful of people seeing me naked while I was whipped, much less my new partner.

But damn did he fill out a tight pair of leather pants extraordinarily well. They molded to his muscular legs and I could imagine just how butter-soft that leather would be beneath my hands. His hips were trim, and I bet his backside was just as nice.

And dear God, his chest was bared. All those muscles that had been hidden by shirts before were now slick with oil.

Donovan was so different from Gary, and not nearly as packed with muscle.

But Donovan was so much more powerful-looking and in his presence, in every well-defined cut of his muscles, his potent sexuality radiated from him. His shoulders were broader than I realized. His arms and chest bunched with raw power. Not only did his biceps look more cut, his thick forearms and strong wrists seemed more so now that he was bare-chested. Not an ounce of spare flesh on his body.

On those thick wrists he was wearing his cuffs, one on each wrist.

But he had a dark look on his features and when his brilliant blue eyes met mine he narrowed his, like he was pissed.

"Lower your eyes, slave." The order came out in a bark and he snapped the whip. It gave a loud crack that startled me into remembering my role, and I looked at his crotch instead of his eyes. Not a bad view.

"May I?" Donovan said, and I knew he was asking Tarantino if he could start.

My arms ached from bearing my weight. This reminded me of the time I was in the Mexican prison, before I escaped. Then the Cuban prison before I was recruited by RED.

This would be a piece of cake.

Angel food cake, which I hated.

"Make sure you don't mark her below her ass, above her breasts, or on her arms," Tarantino was saying. "It wouldn't do to have signs of her test show once she's dressed again and walking out of my club."

Every word he said brought me closer and closer to the realization that this was real.

"Thank you, Master Tarantino." Donovan gave a quick bow of his head that I saw from beneath my lashes.

"Every Dom should be highly skilled with a bullwhip," Tarantino said. "You might be considered a Sire elsewhere, but we require that you show us your abilities before you earn your title here."

Donovan said, "Of course, Master Tarantino."

The beating of my heart grew harder and faster as Tarantino took his seat on a couch and observed Donovan and me as if he were watching a television show.

Donovan moved so close that his chest nearly brushed my breasts. His familiar scent was masked by the musky scent his torso was oiled with.

He put the handle of the whip under my chin and forced me to look at him as he leaned in close. Very close. "Lucky for both of us I'm damned good at this," he said, too quietly to be overheard. "It's going to hurt." He sounded genuinely sorry.

"*Now*, slave," he said louder so that anyone could hear. "I asked you what's your safe word?"

"Fastball," I said as the word popped into my mind. "That's my safe word. Uh, Sire. Fastball."

Someone snickered. "Bet he does have some pretty fast balls." A decidedly gay male voice said, "I'd sure like to take a couple of his fastballs."

This time I thought I saw some red creep into Donovan's swarthy features. "Don't make a sound, slave," he said. "If you do it means you'll be blindfolded. Do you understand?"

Maybe Donovan was a little too much into his part of the operation.

Being blinded was not my idea of fun. I nodded. "Yes, Sire."

"Eyes down."

I obeyed.

Because of the carpeting I couldn't hear his footsteps, but with a crawling sensation down my spine I knew he was behind me.

The incredible sting of the whip against one butt cheek and then the other in rapid succession caught me by surprise. They hurt so badly I shouted my pain without even thinking about it and my eyes watered.

Through the burn on my backside I heard Donovan say something, and the next thing I knew someone had blindfolded me. "I warned you, it's going to hurt like hell," Donovan said softly as he rubbed each butt cheek with his palm. "Try to hold in your screams."

The instinct to fight against my bonds and everything else was so strong that my body ached with the need to escape. But there was no escape. It wasn't cruel punishment. It was what a true sub craved.

Again Donovan whipped me, but this time I gritted my teeth and held back my scream. Moisture from my eyes dampened the blindfold. He whipped me everywhere within the zone Tarantino had specified. My backside, my mound, my belly, my breasts.

Not being able to see made it all the worse. I was more intensely aware of each strike. I tried to focus on some kind of "happy place," but every crack of the whip and sting on my body snapped me back to reality.

Every so often Donovan would pause and use his palm to rub the spots he'd struck. Rubbing them drew out the burn rather than easing it.

"Okay?" he'd ask quietly, and I wouldn't even answer with a nod or shake of my head. I was too busy plotting ways to kill him.

When I didn't think there was a place "in the zone" on my body that he hadn't whipped, he stopped.

My arms ached from hanging from my wrists, and my body burned like fire every place the whip had struck.

The damp blindfold was removed and I blinked against the brightness as my body went slack and I lowered my head. I wouldn't be able to sit for a week. At least.

Vaguely I was aware of someone helping me off the hook and then I collapsed against Donovan. He took me by the shoulders and held me up as I opened my eyes and looked up at him. His blue gaze met mine for a long moment before he glanced at Tarantino.

"You're good with the bullwhip, Sire Dunning," Tarantino said, using Donovan's undercover name. "Welcome to the Club."

Tarantino smiled at me. "Welcome, slave Alexi."

"I'll take this sub if she'll have me, Master Tarantino," Donovan said before Tarantino could continue.

Tarantino looked from Donovan to me. Donovan was still holding my shoulders. Otherwise I don't think my legs would have worked. "Do you want Sire Dunning to be your Dom?" Tarantino asked me.

I looked up at Donovan and, no matter how much pain I was in at that moment, I tried to put a sub's adoration into my expression rather than the desire to kill. "Yes, Master Tarantino. I would like to be Sire Dunning's slave."

Like the Pope giving us his blessing, Tarantino nodded. "You're a good match."

He focused his gaze on me. "But if your Dom ever crosses a line, you're to come to me immediately." Tarantino looked at Donovan again. "We don't tolerate abuse. Everything we do here at the Crystal Twilight and the other two clubs involves only pleasure."

Donovan lowered his head. "Of course, Master Tarantino."

"The next test for your sub—"

I almost dropped my jaw. Another test?

"—is the cage."

I could literally feel blood draining from my face. Bars. No, not bars.

Two subs with collars dragged in a shiny metal cage with bars like a jail cell. A very small jail cell. It was so small I wasn't sure I'd be able to sit up in it.

"Your slave is to stay in the cage until you feel she's worthy to come out." Tarantino looked at Donovan. "Order your sub to get in."

Donovan released my arms and pointed to the floor. "On your hands and knees, and crawl into the cage."

No. I couldn't do it. But I knew if I didn't, this whole setup would be blown to hell.

"Yes, Sire." I kept my eyes lowered as I slowly got on my hands and knees. I could feel a scream building in the back of my throat as I crawled to the cage, which was a good ten feet away. My body ached and burned from every slash of the whip, and I bit the inside of my lip until it almost bled.

"Too slow, slave." A snap, and the whip struck my ass again. The whip caught me by surprise and caused me to cry out.

I was so going to kick his ass for that, too.

When I reached the cage entrance I stared at all those bars and barely kept my body from trembling. How was I going to sit up in there with the top so low?

I got my answer when Donovan said, "You'll stay on your hands and knees until I think you've earned the right to come out."

This time a shudder did travel down my spine.

Snap. The whip connected with my ass again and I bit my lip to keep from crying out. "*Now*, slave."

I forced myself to crawl into the cage, and felt myself begin to hyperventilate.

Fastball. Say it.

No. *Breathe, Steele*. Breathe.

Everyone else in the room started laughing and chatting and thoroughly enjoying themselves like they were at a normal party. I couldn't really see much with my head bowed. I didn't have much of a choice since the top was practically touching my head.

That claustrophobic feeling wanted to close in on me.

Breathe. Just breathe, I chanted in my mind.

My body burned from the whip, my wrists ached from the cuffs, and my arms from hanging so long. My knees and palms hurt, the carpet not soft enough to even give me that much of a break. The cage was so small that I felt the cool metal bars on either side of me when I shifted. I refused to look at the ones in front of me because I didn't want to see the bars.

Hang in there. This can't last too long.

I was so wrong.

Someone poked me with a straw, like a kid poking an animal. Then, for what had to be hours, hands reached through the bars and stroked every part of me that could be reached. Oh, God, even my folds—which were damp despite my humiliating position—didn't escape someone's touch.

I was nothing but an animal in a cage.

This was something I knew slaves were often put through. But I'd planned on being a five-foot-four Dominatrix with Perry as the sub. I hadn't counted on being behind bars myself.

I prayed that what Tarantino said was true, that sex was for the private rooms and no one would try to take me from behind while I was in the cage.

The party started to wind down, and my arms were shaking by then from bracing myself the whole night.

Voices saying "Good-bye," "See you next Saturday," "Welcome to the club, Sire Dunning," and "Welcome to the inner circle, slave Alexi," met my ears, and more hands touched my burning skin and slapped me on the ass as they left.

I don't think I'd ever been more humiliated in my life.

Finally, God, finally, the door hinges scraped open behind me. "You can come out, slave Alexi," said Donovan, the man I was going to kill.

"Yes, Sire Dunning." My throat was hoarse, and my arms were so stiff, yet shaky, that I barely had the strength to back out of the cage. I had motivation, though. I'd finally be away from those bars.

When I'd backed out, I stopped. I wanted to collapse, but I knew that would be a really bad idea. If I received one more punishment, I wasn't responsible for the multiple homicides.

"You can stand, slave Alexi," Donovan said.

Gee, thanks. Let's see if that's remotely possible.

I pushed myself back onto my haunches and every muscle in my body started to shake. Donovan reached his hand out to me to help me up, and I let him, but remembered not to look at him. It might not be good for Tarantino to see red lasers shooting from my eyes at Donovan.

Oh, I was supposed to play the submissive part, but he had made me do some things he didn't have to.

"The next order of business is the twenty-five grand each to join our exclusive club." Tarantino nodded to a gentleman sitting on the couch. "Johnson will take care of you."

Donovan said, "I've got cash on me, Master Tarantino."

I said, "Will American Express do, Master Tarantino?"

"Of course. We meet each Saturday," Tarantino said as he acknowledged my question and Donovan's statement with a nod. "The Glass House is our next get-together." He looked toward Jason Strong, who had his arms across his massive chest. "Your names will be on the list with a special indicator that you are to be escorted to the 'party' in the rear of the club."

"Thank you, Master Tarantino," I said, my head still down.

"I appreciate your inclusion in what I understand is the best of the best, Masters Tarantino, Strong, and Cabot," Donovan said as he gave a slight bow from his shoulders.

"It's our pleasure," Tarantino said.

Donovan inclined his head toward the hallway. "I'd like a private room with my slave, if that's not an inconvenience."

Tarantino smiled. "Of course you do." He signaled to a gorgeous redhead with a red collar and she approached him with her eyes slightly lowered. "Slave Marissa, show Sire Dunning and slave Alexi to the Pleasure Suite."

Donovan brought one of his hands up to the column of my throat. "Now I'll need to find slave Alexi a collar."

He almost lost a front tooth.

We followed the shapely redhead, but Donovan gave me a Dom glare and made me keep a few steps behind him "to keep up appearances," I'm sure.

When I'd researched BDSM on the Net, I'd found people of all shapes and sizes in the lifestyle. But here it was like they picked only perfect bodies and beautiful faces. Guess I should be flattered to be among those chosen, I thought sarcastically.

Marissa guided us down a couple of hallways to a door. "This room is by order of Master Tarantino only, so it's empty unless he allows it to be used." She turned the knob and opened the door to heaven.

Heaven because it had an enormous bed with a huge, fluffy-looking satin comforter. I didn't care about anything but that bed. I didn't register anything but the bed—and the fact that there were no windows or mirrors that might be two-way glass. Couldn't rule out cameras, but the signal-jammers in one of Donovan's cuffs and my ankle cuff should take care of any of that kind of stuff. We really were alone, this really was private, and that really was a bed.

When Marissa left us, I started toward that piece of heaven, but stopped walking as the whole reason we were at the Crystal Twilight hit me. I glanced at my ankle cuff, then met Donovan's eyes.

"I never had the chance to . . ." I gestured to my ankle cuff.

He raised his forearm and showed me one of his wrist cuffs. “Already got it.”

I had strength enough to walk up to him. “Good,” I said and drove my knee into his balls. “Sire Sonofabitch.”

He doubled over with a shout and a growl before he dropped to his knees.

Without a look back, without giving a crap about the various creative things he was saying about me between his gritted teeth, I went straight to that bed and crawled under the covers.

I winced at each ache, pain, and burn that made me feel like I was on fire from every movement I made. I settled onto my left side, which seemed to hurt the least.

And passed out.

CHAPTER 15

Sins of the past

March 31
Sunday early, early morning

Donovan let me sleep for three hours before waking me up so we could leave the Crystal Twilight and head home.

The moment Donovan touched my burning shoulder I rolled over and clocked him.

I was in so much pain I couldn't even tell if my knuckles hurt from the impact after they connected with his jaw.

He glared and rubbed the area I'd hit. "Goddamnit, Steele, we'd agreed on this."

My entire body screamed as I pushed myself up in bed. Oh, God, it hurt to sit on my backside. The blanket and sheet fell from my naked chest and I looked down at the vivid red welts crossing my body in haphazard strokes.

I raised my eyes and glared at Donovan. "That cage. You did *not* have to make me crawl to that cage or stay in there for that long."

"I'm sorry," he said, and he really did sound like he was sorry. "To make sure I got it right, I read Tarantino's expressions." The bed gave a little as Donovan sat beside me. "We finally had his 'blessing' when he gave a cockshit grin."

Donovan's relief was apparent. "We're in," he added. "Our clothes were already in here, along with some salve for your—" He gestured to my body and didn't finish his sentence.

For the first time I paid attention to the room. Decadent was a good word for it. Enormous white oak four-poster bed—all the better to tie you up with—and stunning gold draperies and gold-shaded carpeting. Everything was in golds and whites, including all the furnishings. Kinda like being in a palace.

Donovan had to smooth salve on my back. "People actually get off on this stuff?" I said. "Get horny from having the crap beat out of them?"

I wasn't horny. I wanted to shoot something.

He shrugged. "Like they say, to each his own."

I winced as he touched another welt. A part of me had to admit that I had enjoyed some of it. I could barely accept that truth—the whipping had turned me on. God, how could it have?

I swallowed and thought about the reason I was going through this physical pain. It was to save other women from being sold into sexual slavery by a sicko, to find Kristin, and to blow away the sonsofbitches who'd killed Randolph.

When we left the Pleasure Suite, not a mark showed on any bared skin revealed by my short skirt and corset. Every step, every brush of my leather-and-lace clothing against my skin, made it hard to keep from wincing. I walked in my heels with a confident stride, as if I didn't want to scream with every step.

I pulled the claim ticket out of my clutch and handed it to the valet. Donovan did the same for whatever vehicle he was driving. He leaned close to me. "I'm going to follow you home and make sure you get there all right."

"Don't bother." I gave him a fake smile. "I'll be fine."

Donovan narrowed his gaze but didn't answer as my little red Mercedes was pulled up by a valet, followed by a sleek black Porsche.

Once I'd tipped the valet I was on my way home. I continued to clench my jaws, trying not to cry from the pain on my backside, made worse every time I shifted gears. I almost didn't notice the black Porsche following me, and scowled when I finally did.

I guided the Mercedes through my neighborhood, past a couple of kids smoking on the corner at three friggin' a.m. Dope probably. My street wasn't bad for Southie, but it wasn't Sunshine Acres, either.

From beneath my seat I pulled out my Glock and stuffed it in the back of my skirt since I didn't have a holster.

Ouch. Did anything *not* hurt?

My face, my arms, my lower legs didn't. Okay, there were positives.

Donovan was out of his Porsche before I even opened the door of the Mercedes. I let him help me out and I slammed the door shut. In keeping with our undercover agency policy, the lights didn't flash and the vehicle didn't "beep" when I locked it with the remote. I heard the subtle sound of the locks click.

We didn't speak as we walked up the steps of the trip and into the foyer inside. I faced him and held my hand up. "Far enough. I can make it the rest of the way myself."

"You're so damned stubborn, Steele."

"I'm tired." I rubbed my temples as a wave of dizziness hit me. "Just go."

He folded his arms across his chest and didn't move as I turned away and almost lost my balance.

Why the hell was I so dizzy?

My keys jangled in my hand as I started to walk up the stairs past Marty's apartment, then Georgina's.

My head spun.

Spots in front of my eyes blinded me.

I swayed.

Christ, I—I . . .

I dropped and tumbled down the stairs.

My head hit the floor.

Everything went black.

March 31
Sunday morning

Special Forces and I'm a sniper. I know I'm saving American lives every time I take out a target.

Just as I pull the trigger, orders come. Abort.

Too late.

Fuckup. Big-time.

Arrest.

Court-martial.

Standing before men in a white room.

Strange men. Men not in military uniform.

Two options.

Serve as an assassin.

Or kill me. Slowly.

They break me.

Now from a building's rooftop in France, I set my sites on two women coming out of a restaurant. I wonder who the women are. Why I'm killing them. Like I wonder every time I'm ordered to kill.

My employers never tell me. I don't even know who I work for. Only this, or death by mutilation.

I save myself by killing others.

I pull the trigger.

No one knows where the shots came from. I disassemble the agency-issued sniper's rifle and put it into a backpack. I'm just a tourist now.

A prison. I'm strapped to a chair and wherever I am stinks of sweat and urine.

Men ask questions I refuse to answer. I can't answer if I wanted to because I don't even know who I work for.

They slam fists into my head and body.

Then I see Randolph's dead face, her body floating in the harbor.

My own screaming woke me up. "No!"

Heavy footsteps and I heard a man's voice. "Lexi, wake up. You're having a nightmare."

I started swinging my fists but a male body pinned me down. "No! I've got to. I've got to."

"Wake up!" the man shouts.

Donovan.

With a gasp, every bit of reality hit me with the force of a Mack truck slamming into a brick wall. I rolled onto my side clutching my belly. My insides were sure to spill out from the terror of the dream.

I opened my eyes and looked into Donovan's blue ones.

"H-how?" Confusion clouded my mind as I realized this wasn't my bed. "What?"

"You knocked yourself cold when we got to your place." Donovan sat on the edge of the bed, and he looked concerned. "You fell down the stairs."

Tough Lexi Steele knocking herself out? This was definitely the highlight to one fucking hell of a night.

What could be more embarrassing than passing out for no goddamned reason in front of your new partner?

I wiped sweat from my forehead. My whole body felt sweaty again from the dream. "Where am I?"

"Kristin's." Donovan continued to study me. "I couldn't leave you alone after hitting your head like that. I've been checking in on you for the past few hours."

The fact that he'd been concerned enough to do that gave Donovan bonus points in spite of my embarrassment.

I blinked away some of the remaining fuzz and felt an ache on the side of my head. Yup. Goose egg.

He gestured to the floor where, a few feet away, one of my duffel bags was zipped shut. "I grabbed some of your clothes."

I cocked my head and looked at him. "Thank you."

Donovan picked up a container that was on the nightstand. "Hope you don't mind that I took off that skirt and corset thing and put some of this on the welts."

"That must be why I feel better." I winced as I pushed myself up in bed and discovered I was wearing a terrycloth robe. "Thanks for not letting me wake up naked."

"Do you want some more salve?" he asked.

My hair was damp with sweat when I pushed it out of my face and gave a sigh. "I really need a shower first."

He gestured to a door opposite to where the bed was. "Use anything you need."

"I'll just take a few minutes."

The mattress rose from where he'd been sitting as he stood. "I'll make breakfast once you're out of the shower."

"Okay." I winced as I scooted up in bed while Donovan let himself out of the bedroom door and closed it behind him.

Hallelujah, my legs cooperated as I swung them over the side of the bed.

Rock on.

My feet sank into luxurious off-white carpeting that went well with the lavender walls. I pushed myself up to stand, bracing my hand on a white nightstand that matched the rest of the furnishings. Jeez, my body was shaking. Last night was coming back to me in all its brilliance.

Not like I could forget as I winced and limped toward my duffel bag and scooped it up. Someone had to have slipped me something because no way would I pass out from a whipping. Right? Or I was totally in denial.

The carpeting was heavenly soft beneath my feet as I walked through a patch of sunshine and slipped into the bathroom.

Ugh. I so had morning mouth. And I wasn't going to be able to hold back the contents of my full bladder if I didn't make it to that bathroom real fast.

After I took care of business, my butt burning the entire time, I then proceeded to cause myself more pain by showering and drying myself with a towel before dressing.

I had to search through the duffel Donovan had brought, but I finally found a pair of matching socks. My damp hair irritated me, as it kept getting in my face while I tugged on green jogging shorts, a matching T-shirt, and my favorite pair of running shoes. He'd been nice enough to pack what had to be my most comfortable clothes.

The room I'd slept in was filled with sunshine and oil paintings on the lavender walls and photographs on the surfaces of the white furnishings.

One of the pewter-framed photos caught my attention. Oh, cool. Nick Donovan—had to be. But he was actually smiling. Not a big smile, but hey, from the short time I'd known him, I'd thought he didn't know how to.

A girl leaned against him, her own smile somewhat wistful. Donovan had his arm around her. A heavy sensation settled in my gut. Was she one of the two slaves already delivered to domestic buyers, or was she scheduled to be shipped to a foreign country?

I swallowed hard. This was one messed-up world.

My stomach growled like it was going to go AWOL on me if I didn't get some food in there now. I forced myself to push thoughts of what we were dealing with aside, and headed out of the room.

I walked past the only other door in the dim hall. Donovan's bedroom, no doubt.

I passed it, then walked into a beautiful living room with a brick wall to the left and the front that included a bay window and a brick fireplace between with photos arranged on the mantel. It was very cozy and feminine, with floral-patterned furniture, lots of throw pillows, houseplants, and expensive-looking treasures and artwork.

To my right was an archway and I walked through it into a kitchen as spotless as the rest of the house. A cliché of a copper tea kettle clock was over a stainless-steel stove. Seven a.m. If nothing else, I'm consistent.

"Hey there," I said.

Donovan turned from whatever he was doing on a counter. "I'm just starting the crepes." His voice was deep and rumbly. As he faced me a shivery sensation traveled the length of my body.

No man should be allowed to look that devastatingly sexy—it was nearly overwhelming. His T-shirt matched the brilliant blue of his eyes. His muscles flexed beneath his clothing, from his shoulders to his abs. Mmmm, firm thighs, too. I'd seen his chest last night and would I ever like to see the rest of him.

Get it together, Steele.

"You make it, I'll eat it," I said.

His nod was brief and he strode across the kitchen. Nothing casual about this man. Every movement he made was decisive. Muscle and sinew on his forearms tightened when he opened the refrigerator. He ducked and leaned into the fridge.

Dear God.

My palms itched and I had the urge to touch that tight ass I now had a perfect view of.

What was the matter with me? He'd just whipped the crap out of me and made me stay in a cage all night on my hands and knees. *And* saw me naked. Every inch of me.

I know, I know. All part of the op. But the cage thing still irked the hell out of me.

But it was really nice of him to do what he did for me when I knocked myself out like an idiot.

A quick flare heated my skin as I watched him and felt something stir inside me. I pushed my hand through my damp hair as I turned away. A Boston seasonal calendar hung from the wall next to a row of mahogany cabinets. In the current month's picture the city looked sparkling clean, as if the area was perfect from the underground up.

Ha.

The sounds of the fridge closing, the thump of a cabinet door, and the clang of a pan on the stove top came from behind me. Safe to face him again.

Well, maybe not.

Donovan's back was to me, his shoulder muscles flexing as he dumped what looked like flour and sugar and salt into a bowl.

Hell if I knew what he was putting together. As far as I was concerned, my mobile phone led to a perfectly balanced meal. Just hit speed dial for any number of restaurants and I was set. That or it was Pecan Sandies and Mountain Dew.

The best breakfast was cold cheese pizza with extra cheese, garlic, and green olives.

Mmmm.

Crepes, though. Never had those.

I moved a little to the side so I could watch Donovan, who threw this and that together without even looking at a recipe book.

"Need any help?" I asked, hoping he wouldn't want any.

I spotted the egg carton on the counter.

"Uh, except I'm not good with eggs," I said as he looked over his shoulder at me. "My version of cracking an egg ends with the shell exploding in my hand and a little egg and a bunch of shell making it into the bowl." I swear I saw the corner of his mouth twitch. "Unless you don't mind the yolk, whites, and eggshells being well blended, another job might be better."

"Nah," Donovan said. "It's under control,"

A loud "Meow" from behind startled me into whirling around. A calico cat casually padded into the kitchen with its head held at a regal angle. It ignored Donovan and me before going straight for a dainty dish on the floor near the stainless-steel refrigerator. The dish was empty and the cat gave Donovan a disdainful look.

"Kristin's cat?" I asked as Donovan grabbed a can of Fancy Feast from the pantry. "What's its name?"

"Dixie." Donovan took a can opener from a drawer and opened the cat food. I detected a grumble in his voice. "You might say I inherited her from an elderly lady where I lived out west, before coming to Boston to find Kristin." He glanced at Dixie and they exchanged looks of mutual toleration.

A cat. I laughed. "You're the last person in the world I'd have thought would own a cat."

Donovan crouched down and scooped some of the cat food into the bowl. "If you ask her she'll tell you that she owns me."

I laughed again, and then he stood and finished making the crepes. They smelled so good I thought I'd pass out from hunger this time.

Not much longer and we were sitting at the kitchen table and I breathed in the incredible smells. "I think I'm in love," I said before my mind caught up with my mouth.

Heat flushed over me and I didn't meet Donovan's eyes as he put a plate on a mat in front of me. Instead I focused on using a spatula—hey, I know what those things are called—to put five of the ten crepes onto my plate.

"These are heaven," I said as I closed my mind for a moment and savored a mouthful before opening my eyes again. As usual, I could have cared less about how much I was eating around a man. I proceeded to prove that by stuffing my face.

"Where did you learn to cook?" I asked him as we were eating.

He shrugged. "Picked it up when I came home to raise Kristin."

I blinked and set my fork down. "You raised your sister?"

"Our parents died when their small plane collided with another when Kristin was fifteen." Donovan met my gaze. "No way in hell was I going to let her be raised in foster care."

"So that's why you left the Navy when you were a SEAL," I said. He raised his brows. "That's pretty much all Oxford told me," I hurried to say. "Just that you were the best of the best before you had to leave. She didn't tell me anything else." Wouldn't, I added to myself.

"How long were you a SEAL?" I asked.

"Eight years."

"Then you left to take care of your sister," I said.

He took another bite, then met my eyes. "Are you okay?"

His sudden change in conversation was one hell of an indicator he wasn't crazy about talking about his past.

I could so relate.

"What do you mean?" I asked.

"The welts from the whip." Donovan's voice was hard, and his gaze even harder when I stared into his blue eyes. "And being forced into that goddamned cage."

A shiver wracked my body at his intriguing yet terrifying gaze. Perhaps terrifying was more appropriate, because he looked like he could snap a man's neck without an ounce of remorse.

"Yeah." I nodded despite the burn. Especially in my butt, since I was sitting on it. "You were right. We agreed on it and it was part of the job."

"I heard you were Special Ops in the Army," Donovan said.

So we were going to skip to my past. "For a while."

"Why did you leave?"

Talking about my past ruined my appetite and I couldn't eat anymore. I set my fork on my plate, two crepes still remaining, and I looked out the window over the kitchen sink.

"Screwed up." I rubbed my temples. "Made one big mistake."

He ate his last bite of crepe. "Want to talk about it?"

"As much as you want to talk about your past," I said.

He studied me. "Yours is eating at you enough that your nightmares have you waking up screaming."

I frowned. "How did you know?"

"The walls are thin." He folded his arms on the table. "You talk a lot in your sleep."

"Jeez." I ruffled my hair.

He studied me. "And you've got a thing about bars."

"Noticed that, too, did you?" I asked, trying to joke.

Nick didn't say anything, just continued to look at me.

I pushed my hand through my hair again. "Okay, fine. I got trapped in a storm drain when I was five." The memory of that day still threatened to make me shudder. "It had rained earlier in the day and I'd been playing street hockey with my four older brothers and my sister. My little brother wasn't born yet."

Why it was so hard to talk about something that happened when I was so young—I don't know. Maybe because bars still bothered me after all of these years.

"While we were playing, the ball had gotten away and rolled into the storm drain." I should have listened but even then I was stubborn. "My brothers and sister yelled at me not to go after it, and started running after me, but I was so sure I could get the ball and they'd be proud of me."

I closed my eyes as the horrible memories rushed over me. "And I fell in."

My throat felt dry as I swallowed and opened my eyes to meet Donovan's intent blue gaze. "I was trapped. Crying, sobbing, begging my parents to come and get me as I clung to the grate." I could almost feel the water rising to my throat as I remembered the horrible moment. "I clung to the grate and tried to keep my head above the rushing water.

"Papa had called to me, telling me it would be okay. He sounded like he was trying to keep calm for me, but I knew he wasn't." Mammy's cries still echoed in my ears. "My mother was crying and I still remember the sound echoing inside the drain."

I think the sirens of the rescue units scared me even more. "The extraction team fought to rip away the grate against the rushing water. It had passed my lips and I'd had to tilt my head back to breathe. My heart had been beating so hard my chest hurt.

Donovan held my gaze as I finished. "Then the men saved me and I was in Mammy and Daddy's arms."

For a few moments all I heard was the ticking of the kitchen clock as Donovan seemed to think about what I'd just told him. "I can't imagine what you must have gone through," he said.

I shrugged. "It happened a long, long time ago."

"You also cry out about things like assassinations, Special Ops, Cubans," he said and I straightened in my chair.

"I didn't realize I carry on like that in my dreams." I rubbed my palm on my shorts. "I wake up feeling like I've had the crap beaten out of me, but I just had no idea . . ."

"Tell me." The words came out like he was a concerned friend, not like he was demanding that I spill my guts.

Maybe I needed to talk about it because it was something I never did—share what I'd been through.

I took a deep breath. "In the Army I was a sniper in Special Ops." I gave a rueful smile. "There was still a stigma about allowing women in Special Forces, and my captain hated me."

Donovan narrowed his brows.

"We were on location and I had a target to take out." I ground my teeth. "I'd had the perfect shot. But orders came through at the last second to abort the op. Too late, because I'd already pulled the trigger without the official go-ahead."

"Wild guess." Donovan's tone was flat. "You were court-martialed.

"Good guess." I couldn't look at him anymore. "My asshole captain made sure every bit of blame was on my shoulders. Made a huge deal of it."

Donovan stayed quiet and I brushed a wrinkle out of the cornflower blue tablecloth as I avoided his gaze.

"Somehow I ended up in a cell with men I'd never met before. Men who gave me an ultimatum.

"Two choices." This time I did look at Donovan. "Either assassinate people for them, never knowing who I was killing or why."

I swallowed. "Or they would slowly kill me. They would mutilate me, keep me hidden. Then they'd cut off a couple of fingers one day. Maybe chop off a leg the next. An arm the following day. They would stop the blood flow only so that I could live for more mutilation. Until slowly I died."

The sudden look of fury on Donovan's face almost made me lean back from him in my chair. But I continued. "I was beaten, nearly drowned, electrocuted, whipped, and threatened with rape."

Shame rolled through me in waves. "They broke me."

"Jesus Christ." The fury on Nick's face was enough to send me reeling, and he hit the table hard enough with his hand that it made the plates and the silverware on the table bounce and clatter. "You give me the names and approximate location of those men who gave you that ultimatum and I'll kill every goddamned one of them."

I sighed before I said quietly, "I already did."

CHAPTER 16

Life and Death

March 31
Sunday morning

The vibration of my cell phone cut me off from saying anything else. It was my personal line, and Georgina had unblocked her number so that I could see it was her.

"Georgina," I answered before she could respond. "Randolph's funeral. Did I screw up and miss it?"

"No, honey." Georgina's voice was subdued. "The funeral's at ten and it's only eight now. Where are you?"

"I'll tell you about it on the way." I looked at Donovan. "I'm running home right now."

"Let me know when you get here."

"I will."

The urge to cry was almost overwhelming and I wished I could have. I'd just gotten through telling Donovan how I had killed for others and killed for myself.

And now I was going to a funeral for one of my own.

March 31
Sunday late morning

"I can't look." I squeezed Georgina's hand as we stood outside with a group of other mourners and I stared at the open silver casket.

"It will help give you closure." Georgina squeezed my hand in return.

"I know what will really give me closure." Yeah. Kill every one of those bastards. That would give me some closure.

"You need to see her." Georgina drew me toward the casket. "And say good-bye."

It was a sunny, beautiful day with a light breeze and birds chirping. It should have been dark, with the wind whipping the trees back and forth and thunder crashing in our ears as rain pummeled our bodies.

It was too bright. Too cheerful a day. Except for the crowds of people in black, many weeping and some openly sobbing, like Randolph's mother.

Other RED agents had come to see Randolph one last time, and to say good-bye.

If only these people knew what a hero Stacy was. Everything she had done for her country.

It was so unfair.

But so was the fact that she was dead.

I let Georgina draw me toward the casket, and I closed my eyes at first so that I couldn't see. Then I opened them and there she was.

She could have been sleeping. Her blond curls were soft around her face and they'd put makeup on her that made her look warm and real. She was in a high-necked dress. To hide the slit in her throat.

"Stacy." I could barely get any words out. There was so much I wanted to say. "I'm sorry. You don't know how sorry I am. I'm going to miss you so much." I wanted to touch her face but I didn't want to feel cold skin. I wanted her warmth and vitality back. "Good-bye." I whispered.

And don't worry, I said to her in my thoughts. *I'll get them all.*

March 31
Sunday afternoon

My brother Ryan gave a quick grin to Mammy as he spooned out big helpings from a large stewpot. "You don't know how much I've missed your wicked-good Irish stew."

Our oldest brother, Zane, reached to take the pot from Ryan. "Stop hogging it all to yourself, Marine."

"There's plenty for the bunch of you." Mammy smiled,

clearly happy to have all nine of us at the table. "Eat up," she said, and passed around a huge plate of soda bread.

Daddy took two pieces for himself before handing the plate to our younger sister, Rori. "I'm on a diet," she said as she passed it on to our next oldest brother.

"You're always on a diet and you're stick-thin." Troy practically took the rest of the plateful for himself.

"As if." Rori mostly ate the meat out of the stew. "I have to watch what I eat or—"

"Yeah, yeah," Evan interrupted as he piled Dublin Coddle on his own plate. "You're a flight attendant. Gotta watch those carbs."

"Bangers." Sean bounced up and down in his chair at the huge table. "I want some sausages, and Ryan's going to eat them all." Sean was a late-in-life surprise and was only twelve, where the other six of us ranged from twenty-nine to thirty-six years old. But as hyper as Sean was, Mammy might as well have had three kids his age.

"Calm down, Sean." Daddy made a motion with his hand indicating that our little brother needed to glue his butt to his seat.

"Heaven help us all when that kid hits puberty," Evan said.

Sean glared at Evan. "Shut up."

"We'll have none of that at the table, Sean." Mammy gave him a stern look. "Now eat your stew."

"What's up in the world of translations, Lex?" Ryan asked in between healthy bites of stew.

If they only knew. I shrugged and the movement caused the welts on my body to burn. "Not much. I might be going to Italy in a couple of weeks. It's not definite."

"Zane just returned from DC." Mammy was so proud of him, too, believing he was still in the Secret Service and having no idea he was a RED agent now. She was thrilled with all of us, including the bouncing twelve-year-old next to her.

Evan stopped eating his soda bread long enough to look at Ryan. "How long are you shored up for?"

"We're shipping out next Wednesday." Ryan glanced at Mammy and smiled. "So I'll be home a few more days."

"Damned good to have us all together again," Daddy said, and we all grinned. "Been a hell of a long time."

"At least a year." Troy jabbed his fork into his potatoes. He was a firefighter in Roxbury. "Where you flying to next, Rori?"

"I've been mostly on the Phoenix and LA route." Rori grimaced. "I am so ready for a change. I might start traveling to Paris and back."

I would have said I loved Paris if I hadn't had to assassinate someone there. My mind wandered, the thought reminding me of how I'd spilled my guts to Donovan this morning. And that thought took me to last night and being naked—

"*Lex.*" I jerked my attention to Evan, who'd said it loud enough that everyone was looking at me. "I was just trying to catch your attention. You seemed like you were in outer space or something."

"Or something." I forced a smile. "Just thinking of the creative ways I'm going to kick major butt later when we play some three on three."

Evan snorted. "This time you won't get so lucky."

March 31
Sunday late afternoon

The rain-scented wind pressed my clothes against my body while Zane and I walked down the street in our parents' neighborhood of Cedar Grove.

Now the rain was coming that should have been here this morning.

Even the feel of material against my skin made my eyes threaten to water, and I ground my teeth. I should have worn something looser than the jeans I changed into after the funeral.

As we walked, Zane's hair ruffled and looked messy from the harsh breeze. But with the black hair and green eyes he'd inherited from our father, and Zane's quarterback build, he still looked damn good.

He was the only other member of the family who knew I worked for RED, because he worked for the same agency.

Zane's cover was that he still worked for the Secret Service. He'd been Secret Service for eleven years before being recruited into RED, but he couldn't tell anyone the true story, same as me. So he just let everyone continue to think he was with the SS.

"Now that we've ditched everyone, what's up in HQ?" Zane looked down at me. "I hear you have a new partner."

A wince followed the memory of the whip, and the burning stripes all over my body that my "wonderful" new partner had been forced to inflict on me.

I clasped my hands behind my back. "How did that news get down to weapons trafficking?"

"You're my kid sister." Zane shrugged and smiled. "Everyone knows better than to keep me out of the loop when it comes to any big news that has to do with you."

"Georgina, wasn't it?" My scowl only made him give me a more amused expression. "I'll have a talk with that girl."

"His name's Donovan, right?"

I nodded.

"Think he'll make a decent partner?" Zane asked.

"Depends on what you mean by decent," I grumbled.

Zane frowned. "You know I'll tear him apart if he gets out of line."

I thought about the club, Donovan taking care of me last night and listening to my story. And I thought of his sister and what he was going through.

"Yeah, Donovan's a good guy." Despite the burn of every lash on my body the words came easily. He'd had to do it or we'd never had made it into that BDSM fold. Maybe I shouldn't have kneed him in the groin.

But it had made me feel *so* much better.

"You know I'm here for you." Zane's tone was serious. "Anytime. Anywhere."

The wind's chill bit at my face and bare arms, and I rubbed my arms with both hands as I met his gaze. "Sometimes you forget I can take care of myself, Zane."

"I never forget." He stopped me in midstride by grasping my shoulders. "But it's okay to ask for help if you need it."

The warmth in my chest from the depth of his caring made the chill back off. "Right back atcha."

He released me and it seemed like he was struggling to find words for what he wanted to say. "I've just had this bad feeling lately. Be careful, Lex."

He tugged my hair, and we turned around and started walking to our parents' home.

I didn't say anything because I'd had a bad feeling for awhile, too.

March 31
Sunday evening

"No way." I glared up at my six-two brother, Ryan, as we played three-on-three basketball. "That was a clear foul."

"Listen, shrimp," Ryan said with a cocky grin as he dribbled the basketball that he'd just knocked out of my grasp. "You're just too damned short."

"I'll show you short." I made an easy steal from him, dribbled around Sean and Evan, and made a jump shot.

Swish.

"Nothing but net." Zane slapped my sore butt and I almost punched him. Reflex, of course. "Good job, Lex."

"You should know better than to piss Lexi off." Troy grinned at Ryan. "Now we're tied."

Evan grasped the ball. "Next basket is the tiebreaker."

"Five bucks on Lexi," Rori said from her seat between Mammy and Daddy on the porch swing. "You'll never win after calling her shrimp."

"You're on," Ryan said.

"And you just lost five dollars," I said with my evilest grin.

Out of a family of nine, I drew the shortest straw. My sister and mother were both around five-eight and my twelve-year-old brother was five-six already. Not to mention our four older brothers, who were all six feet and taller.

I just didn't get it.

But Rori was right. Nobody pisses me off and gets away with it.

That last point was a good, hard battle. But sometimes being short had serious advantages, and I dodged around Ryan and made an easy layup for the win.

"Take that, badass Marine," I said and then cried out when he swung me over his shoulder and swatted my butt.

"I am so going to kill you," I said as he set me on the grass and I proceeded to knock Mr. Badass Marine flat on that badass when I swept his feet out from under him. "The bigger they are—"

Everyone started laughing.

Ryan growled and lunged to his feet, and I laughed and dodged around him and up to the "safe zone" with Mammy, Daddy, and Rori.

"Safe!" I grinned as he glared at me. If it wasn't for the fact that I was already in a world of hurt, I'd have had some fun sparring with him.

"I've got to go." I kissed Mammy's, Daddy's, and Rori's cheeks. "It's been a really long day." It had been an exhausting five days, actually, but especially last night and today, and I was ready to collapse.

I hugged and kissed my five brothers' cheeks, too, and barely avoided getting slapped on my butt by Ryan. I waved before unlocking my Cherokee, climbing in, and driving home.

My thoughts turned to *Operation Cinderella* and the next phase of the assignment. Saving those girls was never far from my mind. Especially Donovan's sister.

CHAPTER 17

War room

April 1
Monday morning

It was almost nine by the time I made it to RED. I think I could have slept until noon after the weekend I'd had.

Once I got off the elevator, I headed past my office to Donovan's. His door was open and he looked up from his monitor as soon as I stepped into the doorway.

Delicious. Why did he always have to look so good? My mind flashed to Saturday night, when he'd been naked from the waist up. How could he look just as powerful with clothes on, covering all that well-defined muscle?

After talking with Donovan a little this weekend, and knowing he had left the Navy to raise his kid sister, his edges didn't seem so rough now.

His reaction to what I went through made him seem different somehow, too.

"Ready, Steele?" he asked after we had both stared at one another for a long moment. "Now that you're here, we can go through the data we obtained Saturday night."

"Let's see what we've got." I tried not to yawn and ruffled my hair. "Which conference room?"

"Three." He reached into a duffel on his desk and drew out the pair of leather cuffs he'd worn Saturday night.

He got up and came around his desk, and I swore I felt his body heat before he even reached me.

We headed down to the conference room, and he shut the door behind him when we walked in.

I looked at the chair I so wanted to sit in. The burn on my backside said otherwise. Sleeping had been a real bitch.

Donovan took his own seat. "Aren't you going to sit?"

The look I gave him said, are you out of your mind? "Right now standing is better."

He winced. "Sorry, Steele."

I braced my hands on the back of the chair I would like to be sitting in. "All in the name of the job, right?"

"You want to do this later?" Donovan asked. "You can take a breather in the lounge."

"Nah. Let's go."

Donovan used a touchpad to bring up Tarantino's photo on the screen that materialized at the end of the table.

My cheeks and body burned at the thought of what he'd put me through. "Too bad I couldn't have kneed *him* in the balls Saturday night instead of you," I grumbled.

"Same here." He grimaced and touched the pad again to run the familiar stats we had already gathered alongside Tarantino's photo.

Donovan held one of the cuffs he'd worn Saturday night. The cuff looked thick, and the device Hector Martinez and his "gadget" staff had implemented was virtually invisible the way it fit into the leather. It was small, but could mirror an entire hard drive. An identical device had been implanted in the ankle cuff I'd had on.

When Donovan pressed one of the studs on the outside of the cuff, the device popped out. The gadget was about an inch long, with an embedded button that Donovan used to slide out the port access. He injected the device into a slot near the computer touchpad.

In an instant, the information from Tarantino's hard drive came up on the screen, information organized into document folders. Each folder had a different name.

I straightened and crossed my arms in front of my chest. "Click on the folder for 'Special Projects.' "

"Good enough place to start."

The folder was filled with files showing large donations to various charities.

"Jeez," I said as we went through file after file. "Everything's documented so well that it has to be an accountant's dream."

Donovan closed a spreadsheet. "We'll have some of the agents get on top of the charities to make sure they're legit."

I nodded. "Either they're legit, or he's damned good at hiding his money."

Folder after folder of information showed us nothing more than employee records, along with his expenses and various streams of income.

"Christ, the man makes a truckload of cash." I leaned on one elbow. "Investments and clubs, including the Crystal Twilight."

After we'd spent at least three hours working our way through the info, Donovan rubbed his eyes with his thumb and forefinger. I was ready to drop.

"Enough." I raised my arms, clasped my hands, and started in on a number of stretches. "We'll let the geek squad tear apart the copy of everything we got from the hard drive." I leaned to one side while stretching my opposite. "We've gone through everything obvious, and we might as well let the guys do their thing."

Donovan touched the pad and the screen dematerialized. He ejected the device with Tarantino's information on it and stood. "Taylor seems to know his stuff."

"He sure does."

When Donovan stood and stretched it was something to behold. All those muscles flexing and bunching.

I had to turn away, or embarrass myself by tackling him and kissing that firm mouth and tasting his male flavor.

Donovan and I took the device with Tarantino's hard drive to Seth Taylor, a self-proclaimed "geek" who headed up the team of agents who were technological analysts and hackers.

Taylor might call himself a geek, but he looked nothing like the stereotypical moniker. Sharp blue eyes; a sexy grin on a movie-star face; a build like a swimmer and the tan to go along with it.

"What's up?" Taylor stood. He'd been sitting in a chair in front of a monitor, viewing code, as we entered the room his team worked in.

Donovan handed him the device with Tarantino's hard drive information. "We need every nook and cranny explored to see if there's anything dirty on this guy. Lucca Tarantino."

Taylor took the gadget. "Anything in particular we're searching for?"

I frowned. "Mainly auction information. If you see something that looks like Tarantino's involved in auctions with any kind of 'merchandise,' or you find odd transactions, those are things we need to know about right away."

Taylor glanced over his shoulder at a guy who *did* look more like a hacker geek with his slightly larger belly, shaggy hair, and T-shirt with a *Battlestar Galactica* logo. Hmmm. Guess RED had different appearance standards for geeks than special agents. "I'll give it to Sparks. Sparky will dissect it in no time."

Donovan nodded. "Thanks, Taylor."

I glanced up at the big clock on one wall of the CC. "Just in time for our briefing with Oxford. She so does not tolerate tardiness, except for extreme circumstances. Better to be early with her."

When we reached Oxford's reception area, Darlene smiled at Donovan, her cheeks turning pink. She pretended I didn't exist, and her tone was sweet and girlish when she spoke to him. "You are a little early, but I'll let Agent Oxford know you're here."

I couldn't help it. I rolled my eyes. She caught me doing it and glared at me when Donovan wasn't looking.

"Send them in," Oxford said when Darlene buzzed her, and we went in.

"Have a seat." Oxford gestured to the chairs in front of her desk.

"I'd prefer to stand," I said. "I'm a little sore from Saturday night."

She looked at me with her keen, dark gaze. "Sit."

"Yes, ma'am." I winced and my eyes watered as I obeyed, but I sure as hell obeyed.

Donovan and I took turns filling her in on Saturday at the Crystal Twilight. I glossed over the more embarrassing parts and I was glad Donovan didn't mention the kneeling-on-all-fours all-night-cage thing.

I wanted to bring up my earlier thoughts of asking for "hazard pay," but I doubted Oxford would find it amusing. She was going to find those expense reports interesting enough as it was. Butt plugs, dildos, whips, and black latex were going to have her brows rising. Hey, we had to get to know all the equipment we could. Not that we had to actually use it to get the entire experience.

After we filled her in on everything from the club to the contents of the copied hard drive, Donovan's expression grew dark. "Agent Steele shouldn't have to go through shit like that." His voice had a hardness to it that caught me off guard. The words just came out of nowhere. "I should handle this alone. I'm in tight, so that part of our mission was accomplished."

"What?" I said, his comment setting me off balance before I regained my senses. "Oh, no way. You are not pulling this chauvinistic crap on me."

Oxford gave the slightest wave of her hand toward the door in a dismissive gesture. "Protect her ass and she'll protect yours."

I winced at the "ass" part.

"Steele shouldn't have to go through this shit," he said again. Donovan always sounded like he was holding back a low growl. "She was whipped and humiliated in front of a crowd of people. They put her in a small cage like a goddamned animal, and poked and prodded her for fun. I don't know what they might do to her next."

So much for him not mentioning that little tidbit of information.

Our ASAC gave him a steady look. "If we pull her out now, six months of investigative work will be tossed down the drain. It's up to Steele how much she can take, how much she's willing to endure. Not me, not you."

Oxford leaned forward in her chair, her forearms resting on her desk. "Tell me, Donovan. Do you think a woman is any less capable than a man when it comes to dealing with undercover work?"

Donovan scrubbed his hand over his face. "No, goddamnit."

"I'm fine, and she's right." Maybe I should punch him. If I was a man, Donovan wouldn't be talking to our ASAC about his partner being forced into these kinds of degrading acts. "Every undercover goes into an operation knowing there could be a price to pay." The armrests bit into my hands as I clenched them. "At least I didn't have to snort coke or something." This time.

Donovan looked twice as pissed. "I've just got a bad feeling."

"Is that all you have to go on, Donovan? A feeling?" Oxford got to her feet. Yeah, I'd say that was a real clear statement that she wanted us to leave. "Unless you have proof otherwise, a feeling's not good enough to take down this operation, especially not now."

April 5
Friday afternoon

Friday, Donovan and I were poring over more intel from Jensen, Takamoto, and Smithe until one-thirty in the afternoon. Tomorrow we'd be going to the next club to get Strong's hard drive contents. Great. Probably some more humiliation to look for in the meantime.

"Ready for some lunch?" Donovan asked when we reached a stopping point.

I grimaced. "RED cafeteria food just doesn't appeal to me right now. I think today the special is meatloaf."

Donovan stood and stretched. I tried to hold back a sigh as I watched him. "Come with me to Kristin's. I've got a room set up with enough equipment, and we can keep ourselves busy all afternoon working on *Cinderella*."

"Work?" I shifted in my chair. The pain had settled into a more reasonable burn. "You're trying to get me to your place with *work*?"

"Nah." Donovan gathered the file folder he'd been going through. "I know the way to you, Steele, is through your stomach. I'll fix lunch."

I scooted back my chair in a hurry. "If you can cook anything as well as you did those crepes, I am so there."

It didn't take us long to gather our things and what files we needed, and anything that would help with the case.

I followed him from RED HQ to Kristin's home in Back Bay. She lived on the lowest floor of a brownstone. It had a front yard filled with flowers and wrought-iron gates and fencing. Huge trees shadowed the line of brownstones and sunlight winked through the leaves and onto my Cherokee when I parked in front of her place.

"Dibs on the couch," I called and flopped on the pretty, comfortable piece of furniture. "Maybe I'll just nap. Forget eating. I'm going to fall asleep and then you'll never get rid of me."

"Who said I wanted to get rid of you?" Donovan's expression was intense. Then he disappeared into the kitchen.

The look on his face did funny things to my belly that shot straight between my thighs. Damn. I so had the hots for my partner.

My stomach rumbled and I wondered when was the last time I'd eaten anything? Ever since last Wednesday, when the world seemed to fall apart, I kept forgetting to eat. I was going to end up as stick-thin as my sister if I didn't start eating. She was way too thin as far as I was concerned. Mammy and Daddy thought so, too, of course.

The most delicious smell, like roasted meat, began drifting from the kitchen. I thought I'd die from hunger if I didn't get something in my stomach, like *now*. I wanted to follow the incredible smells but I was soooo comfortable on that couch. My legs wouldn't move, and I felt as if someone could stretch my arms and snap them back like rubber bands.

Yeah, it had been a long week.

Pain for Donovan and his sister gripped me as I studied Kristin's living room again. At the same time I couldn't help but wonder about Donovan's sister as a young girl, and a younger Donovan.

The pictures I'd noticed before on the fireplace mantel drew me. Despite my exhaustion I pushed myself from that comfortable couch and made my way to the fireplace.

So many photos . . . a black-and-white that must have been taken in the sixties of a newly married couple. I saw two pictures of a family of four. The father was stern-faced and the mother unsmiling. Only Kristin smiled as she leaned against Donovan. He looked like he'd earned some of his hard edges by then, and I had a feeling his father had a lot to do with that.

I moved on to photos of an older boy watching a little girl splashing in a play pool, another one of the two of them eating ice cream, and one with the little girl on top of the boy's shoulders. Even then Donovan was a solidly built young man, but he didn't have the hardness to him that he had now.

A photo caught my eye that looked like it hadn't been taken that long ago. I picked it up and something jerk-pulled my stomach as I saw the little girl grown up into a young woman and Donovan's arm around her shoulders. She had her head against his chest and he was smiling down at her. You could see the love and caring so clearly on his face that the pull in my belly was stronger.

Seeing Donovan with his sister in such happier times made it all hit me even harder. Before, Donovan's sister was a faint image in my mind. She wasn't anymore. I'd been determined to find his sister from the beginning, but somehow it now seemed more urgent and more real.

"Ready to fill that bottomless pit?" Donovan's voice from behind startled me and I almost dropped the photo.

I set the picture back on the mantel and turned to face him. "Kristin is beautiful."

He looked at me and said, "Not only is she beautiful, but she's a sweet kid. Genuine."

I moved closer to him. His presence was large and powerful

no matter what he was doing. The handles of the serving tray he was gripping seemed so small in his hands.

The serving tray even matched the rich mahogany furnishings. “Threw together some things from the fridge and pantry, and heated some roast chicken.” He set the tray on the glass-topped coffee table. “Didn’t know how hungry you’d be.” His gaze met mine. “I can tell you haven’t been eating enough.”

My mouth watered as I sat on the edge of the couch. I rubbed my palms on my jeans as I held myself back from snatching up food and stuffing it in my face like a street urchin who hadn’t seen a meal for months.

Roast chicken was on the tray, along with fresh green grapes, several cheeses, and bread that was obviously homemade.

“I have *got* to follow you home more often,” I said as he handed me a plate and I dove into the minibanquet.

He looked at me, his gaze steady. “Any time, Steele.”

The way he said it, so serious, made me want to squirm in my seat. Somehow we’d hit a mutual understanding, and maybe something more.

Did I want to think about the something more?

Onto my plate went lots of roast chicken, thick bread, one of every kind of cheese he had on the tray. And grapes. I so loved firm, sweet grapes.

This time we ate in silence, not having a share-fest like we did the last time he’d cooked for us. It was not an entirely comfortable silence, I think because we’d told each other so much, yet hadn’t shared everything. We were keeping our cards close to our chests and neither of us wanted to call.

“So, you have equipment set up to do some work on *Operation Cinderella*? I asked as we took the tray—just about every crumb gone off the plates—into the kitchen.

“Yeah.” Nick started washing off the plates and I was surprised that a guy would automatically clean up. I used paper plates—tossing them in the garbage was my version of cleaning up after supper. “I’ve got a little equipment set up in the spare bedroom,” he said.

"The whole kitchen is clean," I said with amazement. "I can't even tell you fixed anything for dinner."

Nick shrugged. "I like a clean house."

"You wouldn't like my apartment then." I pictured bottles of Mountain Dew and Guinness on my end tables and clothes on the floor. "Just call first if you're ever going to stop by."

He looked at me and raised one of his eyebrows. "I'll try and remember that."

When we finished cleaning up—or rather Donovan did, wasn't much I could do—he directed me to the spare room.

The door to the room was slightly open and a blue glow spilled out through the opening. The glow was accompanied by the familiar smell of hardware and plastic that all high-tech equipment seemed to have.

I stopped in the doorway while he continued on in. "Looks like your equipment is as high-tech as RED's." My gaze traveled over the surveillance cameras, holographic maps, and gadgets, along with several camera monitors, each focused on a different place. I had no doubt he'd installed it all to help him in his search for Kristin.

Donovan sat in one of the office chairs and immediately began analyzing a screen in the middle of a bank of computers and monitors. "Come on in," he said without looking at me.

I walked all the way in. "You have your own 'war room.' "

He glanced at me over his shoulder. "Guess you could call it that."

The room was clear of any furniture save for a cot along one wall. Every other bit of available space in what was a former bedroom was taken up by Donovan's equipment. When I moved closer to him, the clean smell of his spice-and-leather scent met me.

The leather was soft and comforting when I pulled up one of the six office chairs in the room. "Expecting company?" I said as I gestured to the other four chairs.

"Have a team coming in." Donovan moved his gaze to the camera monitors that showed parking lots and various other locations. "Recovery specialists."

I frowned. "That's what RED agents are."

Donovan still didn't look away from the monitors he was scanning. "These guys are what you'd call 'special.' "

"Okay. Special Special Agents." I rolled my eyes to the off-white ceiling before looking at Donovan again. "I can go with that." Sure.

And then we buckled in and worked our butts off trying to find more leads on *Operation Cinderella*, and evaluating those we already had.

"My head's spinning." When it hit eight p.m. I must have given the world's biggest yawn. "I've got to get home and get some sleep."

"I'll walk you out." He pushed his chair away from the bank of equipment and got to his feet.

I could have said I knew the way, but I found myself wanting to stay near Donovan a little longer. Thoughts of him touching me, kissing me, kept slipping through my mind. God, I'd bet he tasted so good.

When I rose from my chair I almost froze when I saw the intensely sexual look in his blue eyes.

I swallowed. Partner, Steele. This is your partner.

A shivery feeling sensitized my skin as we walked side by side down the hall and out the front door.

I used the remote to unlock the Cherokee's door and turned to say good-bye. I caught my breath. Donovan had one hand braced on the open door, and one on the roof of my SUV. I was caged in.

But this wasn't like that night when I was in a real metal cage. This was the kind of cage that gave me the sensation of being wrapped in his arms.

The glow that came from the light post barely made it through the tree leaves and Donovan's face was shadowed. I could still see his expression which was intent as he studied me.

"Why don't you meet me here tomorrow night," he said, "and we'll go to the Glass House together?"

"Sure," I said in a soft tone. "I'll be here around eight thirty."

He was close enough to kiss and I almost did just that. I almost flung my arms around his neck to draw him to me to share what I knew would be an incredible kiss.

But he stepped back so that he was a couple of feet away. "Good night, Steele," he said, one of his hands still braced on the SUV's door. Donovan had been so close to kissing me, I knew he had. So why had he backed off?

I clenched my fingers to control myself. He was so sexy in the near darkness. All those hard muscles, his broad shoulders, his long fingers and his intent expression—I wanted him. And I wanted him now.

"Be careful," he said and I could swear his voice was tight, restrained.

"See you tomorrow," I said as I climbed into the Cherokee, dug my keys out of my pocket, and put them into the ignition.

He didn't say anything else and shut the door. But when I pulled out onto the quiet street, I looked in my rearview mirror and saw him still standing there, watching me drive away.

CHAPTER 18

Can we skip the flogger?

April 6
Saturday night

"You going to be okay tonight?" Donovan looked so serious as he put his hands on my bare arms. We were in Kristin's home, about to walk out and head to the Glass House for our second night of bondage fun. "Goddamnit, but I hate the idea of you going through any more of that."

The way he studied me—it was more like he cared what happened to *me*. Not because of me being a woman, but because he really cared.

"I'll be fine." I tilted my face up and smiled, trying to reassure him.

My smile faded when I saw the change in the way he was looking at me. His gaze fixed on my lips as he raised his hand and cupped my cheek in his warm palm. He moved his thumb from my mouth and across my cheek in a slow caress.

The sudden thudding of my heart and the catch in my breath caught me off guard. All I could do was feel his hand on my face, his thumb stroking my cheek. His scent of spice and leather and man intoxicated me.

Did I move? Somehow I had melted into the warmth of his body, and the hard muscles of his chest pressed against my much softer breasts.

He slipped his hand from my face into my hair and I gave a small cry of surprise when he clenched his fingers tight. At the same time he grasped my hip in his hand and pulled me to him so that I felt his erection digging into my belly.

Oh, my.

Because of the way Donovan had first touched me, I'd expected a gentle kiss, but there was nothing gentle about this man. His lips came down hard on mine, and he thrust his tongue into my mouth while kissing me with fierce intensity.

The whole house felt like it spun around us as I groaned my need for him.

I loved it. I wanted more of it. I wanted every damned thing he could give me, and I kissed him with just as much intensity. I would have climbed him if the little dress I was wearing would have let me.

Instead, I ran my palms over his chest, his biceps, his shoulders. I needed to feel every part of him.

His hands pushed up the back of my dress and he palmed my bare butt cheeks as he dragged me closer to him. Harder. Tighter.

My body was on fire and my thong was damp with the need to make my fantasies come true and have Donovan inside me. How many times had I thought about that since I met the man?

Countless times.

Every day.

Every time I looked at him, was near him.

We'd barely known each other for, what, a week and a half? But it felt like I'd wanted him forever.

God, he tasted good. So masculine. So Donovan.

How long did we kiss? It didn't seem long enough when we drew apart. I couldn't take my gaze from his, my lips still parted in wonderment, astonishment, and need.

He stroked my cheek again. "I love your green eyes, the way they're looking now, when you're aroused."

I turned my head and slipped his thumb into my mouth and sucked. He groaned. When I drew away I looked back at him. "Who says I'm aroused?"

Donovan's mouth quirked in a way that sent more desire through me. "We'd better get to the Glass House." He gave me a critical, but teasing look. "You might need more lipstick."

I grinned. "That's because you're wearing it."

April 6
Saturday night

My head still reeled from the kiss thirty minutes later, when Donovan—now Sire Dunning—and I arrived at the Glass House. The House was owned by Jason Strong, our next suspect.

During the week since our adventures at the Crystal Twilight, we hadn't found a thing on Tarantino. We'd pulled as much intel as we could on Strong and Cabot, too, but were coming up with big fat zeros. Except for the fact they were all heavily into BDSM according to our sources—and our own observations.

The interior of the nightclub lived up to its name—everything was clear and frosted glass, with green, blue, orange, and yellow lights reflecting from strategically placed colored bulbs. The place was a little rowdier than Tarantino's, but still extremely classy.

Once our names were checked on the guest list, we were escorted directly to the very back of the nightclub, to a set of heavy, thick, frosted-glass doors.

The white granite stairs we were taken to wound to a floor above the nightclub. As my stiletto heels clicked on the stone, I held my hand to my belly, the silky midnight blue wraparound dress a reminder that my clothes probably wouldn't be on for too long.

This time I'd come prepared, though, after visiting an adult store with Georgina earlier today. We'd found a mega-sexy, very revealing outfit that I had on beneath the dress. The beauty of the getup was that it completely covered my breasts and all the important parts of my bottom half. It was as if I was wearing a bikini connected with strips of black Spandex down each side. No slip, lots of grip, worked for me.

I stayed one step behind "Sire Dunning," as I'd reluctantly agreed to earlier, and brought my fingers to the black leather collar now chafing my neck. Because I was supposedly a slave with a Dom, I had taken off the ankle cuff. Martinez had provided this collar, designed with a signal-jammer and a download device similar to the ones in Donovan's wrist cuffs.

Thank God, Martinez hadn't put a D ring on the damned thing. I'd probably seriously hurt anyone who tried to put a leash on *me*.

My mind wandered to Donovan's incredible kiss. I still felt the imprint of his lips, and his taste was on my tongue. I could practically feel his cock hard against my belly.

Since I had to walk behind him anyway, I admired Donovan's backside as he took each step. He had such a tight ass, which flexed beneath his black leather pants. His shoulders and back muscles made my mouth water as I watched him move.

When we got back to Kristin's I was so going to jump him.

Rock music floated from above us. When we finally reached the upper floor of Strong's establishment, I couldn't keep my gaze lowered. My eyes were too wide with astonishment.

Downstairs was nothing compared to this. It virtually *was* a glass house. Walls of patterned, mostly frosted, glass made up the individual rooms that were on the other side from the frosted walls in the greeting area. Carefully arranged colored lights made the frosted walls glow green, blue, yellow, gold, much prettier than downstairs. In random areas clear glass swirls broke up the frosted glass.

It was nothing short of stunning, and I had to force myself to close my mouth, which had been hanging open at the sight.

Glass art was positioned everywhere. Crystal statues as tall as the ceiling watched over everything, and statuettes were positioned on glass pillars of all sizes and heights. The furniture and carpeting were pure white and, of course, all of the end tables and coffee tables were glass-topped, but each glass surface was held up by a naked crystal woman.

An open bar took up one wall alongside the main room. It, too, was made of frosted glass, in keeping with the rest of the area. The scent of alcohol was mild, but I could swear I smelled marijuana. Tarantino's place had been clean as far as I knew, but here it seemed they were into a little more.

A Dom with two slaves sitting on a white couch in the corner confirmed that suspicion. The Dom cut three lines of coke on a mirror with a razor blade, then he and his two subs each took a turn snorting a line.

Crap.

When I'd been undercover in RED's narcotics division I'd had to do some dope to get in with the gangs, just like I'd had to allow myself to be stripped and flogged publicly to gain entrance to this BDSM world. I really hoped drugs weren't on the menu for tonight.

I was so busy staring at all the amazing glass decor and wrapping my thoughts around the drugs that it took me a moment to notice the silhouettes of people behind those mostly frosted walls.

If my eyes got any wider my eyeballs would pop out. Silhouettes of people being flogged, spanked, and other things that I had no clue about. But the sex wasn't too hard to miss as the shadows went at it.

How had I not heard the moans, the cries of ecstasy, the shouts of pain, along with the commanding voices of Doms, over the rock music? The music was at a decent level, not earsplitting loud.

Even though I could only see their dark silhouettes, I still felt like a voyeur, and the tingling between my thighs wasn't from the need to find a ladies' room.

I glanced at one of the glass walls, where a powerfully built moving shadow made it clear a man was flogging a woman as he raised his arm and the silhouette of the whip came down.

High-pitched screams came from the other side of that glass wall and I hoped the sub was enjoying whatever whoever was doing to her. It sure didn't sound to me like she was having a good time.

But from what Danica told me yesterday, and Tarantino's statement, everything this exclusive group participated in was "safe, sane, and consensual" sex. Everyone had a safe word. But if they used it, they were out of the club. Permanently.

"Does your slave like women?" Jason Strong's voice startled me into looking up. Other than the deep chocolate color of his eyes, he really was a Vin Diesel lookalike. He frowned at me and I lowered my gaze. "Does she like to watch you get sucked off by other slaves?"

The thought of Donovan being with another woman in any way made something squeeze tight inside my belly.

Donovan paused and looked at me. I could see him through my lashes.

"That's right." Strong hooked his thumbs in the loops of his leather pants, the loops holding up a thick leather belt. "You only met a week ago, so you probably haven't had a chance to explore."

More and more the thought of being with another woman or watching someone giving Donovan a blow job churned my stomach and made my body heat.

"Neither appeals to me, Master Strong." I tried to keep my words low and contrite. "I prefer to be with Sire Dunning."

"You weren't given permission to join this discussion." Strong brought his hands to the skull-shaped belt buckle. "My belt will be all over your ass if you say anything else."

No more whippings. No more whippings.

Usually protocol called for a sub's Master to approve of another Master touching his slave. But from what Tarantino had said, and Strong's actions, they and Cabot believed they were above that little bit of protocol because they owned these BDSM clubs.

I acted as contrite as possible. "Yes, Master Strong."

"I've got two slaves waiting right now. It's your first time here, though, so let me show you around the Glass House's 'special' addition."

Strong led us from the main room, around a glass wall, and through a maze of glass rooms. Some without doors, but with wide doorways and crowds of onlookers. Some rooms had frosted doors and silhouettes of BDSM activities on the other sides.

Strong gestured toward various themed rooms as we passed them. "Naughty schoolgirl room includes a blackboard and school desks. Cops and criminal play in this room, which even includes a black-and-white cruiser in it." I could actually see the outline of a car through the glass blocks.

We moved toward another, much larger, room with fainter shadows that seemed to be moving in circles. "Inside here is the ponygirl arena and puppygirl play area."

I'd read about and had visited BDSM playhouses that catered toward Masters and their ponygirls or puppygirls, and I really hoped that wasn't on the menu.

Ponygirls were outfitted—bit and all—just like ponies and completely treated as such. Puppygirls were treated like dogs, put on a leash to go for a walk, eating out of a dog food dish, and so on. Some people in the lifestyle really got off on it, but I wasn't one of them.

"Hardcore bondage here, where the sub is tied up thoroughly, with absolutely no way to untie herself. And there's the ménage room." Strong gestured to another wall. "And this room"—he pointed toward yet another—"is dedicated to traditional dungeon fare."

I could see the image of a crystal St. Andrew's cross through the frosted glass and the swirls of clear glass.

"The restrooms are down that hallway, just past my office." Strong pointed in the direction of a brightly lit glass corridor, and my ears most definitely perked up at the words, "my office."

"This is the spanking room," Strong said as we followed, and I winced. "And this is one of my playrooms." He grinned as we reached a closed door that was only frosted glass from my eye level up. Which meant it wasn't very high.

"Slave Kathy is waiting for a good flogging." Strong pushed the door open. "Slave Janice can suck you off, Dunning, while your slave watches."

At the thought of watching Janice sucking Donovan's cock, my whole body burned more. The thought of *any* woman going down on him made me want to clench my fists tight around Strong's neck.

The door swung shut behind us as we walked into a room where two naked, collared women lounged on the white furniture that wasn't exactly traditional furniture. By the restraints and odd positions of the pieces, and from my research on the Net, I knew this furniture was made for more creative activities than sitting down and relaxing with a glass of chardonnay.

Through the walls on either side were silhouettes of people whipping, spanking, and going at it. Their voices, cries, and moans carried over the glass walls.

On one couch perched the beautiful redheaded slave Kathy, the one who'd oiled me up and prepared me for the show last week. I swallowed and my heart beat faster as my three-inch heels sank in the plush white carpeting. Oh, hell. There was no way out, was there? I was going to have to watch that gorgeous black-haired woman on the settee give Donovan head.

I swallowed. Damnit.

Not after that kiss. Not when he'd been making me feel the way I now felt around him. Maybe it was irrational after knowing him for such a short time, but right now I wanted to claim him and say, *"Mine!"*

Wasn't that normally a he-man type of reaction?

Well, nobody said I was a lady. Often.

Donovan didn't look at me when we came to a stop and he spoke. "It's been a while since I've had one of my slaves watch another slave giving me a blow job."

I tried not to let my jaw drop as Donovan continued, "But slave Alexi hasn't had a chance to go down on me." He looked directly at me, and this time my eyes widened beneath my lashes. "I'd like my slave sucking me off while slave Janice watches and masturbates."

The room seemed to tip and I almost stumbled.

Me, giving Donovan a blow job in front of other people? That kiss had made me want to taste him *everywhere*. But with an audience?

Strong winked at Donovan. "Kinda partial to that little sub, aren't you?" he stated.

Donovan looked at me, his eyes intense. "Yeah." He moved closer, and my heart beat faster and faster. "I've been waiting for this all week."

He looked like he meant it, the way he was studying me, and I shivered as he brought his hands to the ties of my wrap-around dress. It fell to the floor, a deep, dark blue against the creamy white carpet.

"She's so friggin' hot." Strong had crossed his arms over his chest and was watching me and Donovan. "Let's get a good look at that great set of breasts we got an eyeful of last week."

Flames licked my body at the memory, and every place I'd been struck seemed to burn blazing hot again.

"Look at me, slave Alexi," Donovan commanded, and I raised my eyes to meet his. My lips parted and I wanted him to kiss me. To taste him, to feel him.

As our gazes held, Donovan put his hands on my shoulders and pushed the straps of my outfit down low enough that it fell away from my breasts to my hips. My nipples grew tight as air touched them, then they grew tighter yet when he brushed the back of his hand over my nipples.

"Kneel," he commanded. "Unfasten my pants."

I barely had the presence of mind to say, "Yes, Sire Dunning," before I was on the floor and his crotch was close to my face.

My mouth watered. Right then I wanted his cock in my mouth in the worst way. And then I wanted him inside me. I couldn't shake the thoughts out—and then I didn't want to.

It surprised me how steady my hands were as I unfastened the button on Donovan's leather pants and unzipped them. And then his cock and balls were in my hands.

Nothing seemed to exist but sliding my tongue down Donovan's long, thick erection, and him sucking in a harsh breath. I closed my eyes as I smelled and tasted his salty flesh, and felt the weight of his balls in my hands. I ran my tongue up and down his length before he grabbed my hair in his fists and guided me so that my mouth was directly over the head of his cock.

Mmmm. The little drop of semen at the tip of his erection rolled over my tongue as I slid him into my mouth as far as possible. The sting of his hold on my hair excited and turned me on as he thrust in and out, fucking my mouth.

Everything grew more intense as I worked his cock with one hand at the same time that he thrust. The soft curls around his groin tickled my nose as I breathed in deeply. I could feel the tension in him. Could feel his orgasm building and building. I squeezed his balls.

He gave a loud sound of pleasure as his cock pulsed in my mouth. He gripped my hair even tighter, and his semen pumped into my mouth and down my throat. I swallowed as I sucked, but he could only take a few more thrusts before he pulled his cock out of my mouth.

My gaze met his, and I smiled at the shock and amazement on his face. Bet he hadn't known I could give such a good blow job.

"Damn, that was hot." Jason Strong's voice jerked me to the present. I'd been lost in the moment I'd just shared with Donovan and had forgotten anyone else was in there with us.

Would my body ever stop burning?

"Your slave gives the best head I've seen in a while." Strong came up close enough that his crotch was nearly in my face, too. From the corner of my eye I saw Janice scowl, but then Strong's next words had me ready to bolt from the room. "I'd like slave Alexi to go down on me."

"No." Donovan's voice was hoarse, the word immediate. "Slave Alexi needs punishment for making me come too fast." He grasped my upper arms and his fingers dug into my flesh as he jerked me to my feet. "Then I'm going to fuck the hell out of her."

"This time." Strong's voice was disappointed, but serious. "Around here we share with the host."

I stared at my toes, not daring to look at Strong and give him an excuse to carry through with his desire to have me give him a blow job.

"I'll show you to a private room," Strong said, and I let out a silent breath of relief as he opened the door. Donovan tucked himself back into his pants, and I scooped up my dress before following them both out.

Air cooled my bare nipples as we walked, but fortunately my bottom half was still covered. I clutched my dress to me, wanting to raise it to hide my naked breasts, but I knew that would get me into trouble, and in this place I so didn't want to invite any.

Once we had walked a little way down the glass-walled hallway, Strong nodded to an empty room that actually had a door Donovan and I could close. Thank you, thank you, thank you.

Although our silhouettes would show everything we did. And "they" might be watching through the glass, so we had to make it look good. Our signal-jammers, whenever we chose to turn them on, would screw with cameras and microphones, but they couldn't hide us through frosted glass.

Strong closed the door.

Donovan and I were alone.

The brilliant blue of his eyes had turned a darker shade of cobalt. He stared down at me like he'd never seen me before. Like he hadn't just given me the most incredible kiss of my life only an hour ago. Like I hadn't just given him a really good blow job. I licked my lips, the taste of him still in my mouth.

He gripped my shoulders and jerked me to him so fast it startled me into crying out, and I lost my balance on my heels and fell against him. Then his lips were on mine, muffling the sound.

His tongue invaded my mouth, this time in a way that could really be called harsh. Formidable. Conquering. Demanding. Like he was staking a claim and telling everyone, including me, that I belonged to him.

Like hell.

CHAPTER 19

Side benefits

April 6
Saturday night

Okay, let Donovan have his illusions.

Mmmm.

Where'd the man learn to kiss? He was doing a great job of showing me just how good he was at it.

Donovan's tongue and mouth were so rough and demanding that I almost felt like a romance heroine being taken by a villainous pirate or a barbarian. He sank his teeth into my lower lip, and when I groaned he thrust his tongue back into my mouth.

No mercy. The man showed no mercy.

He palmed my bare breasts, then pinched my nipples hard enough to make me cry out. The stubble along his jaws was rough against my skin as he nipped and licked his way down the column of my neck to my breasts.

As roughly as he was handling me, the silkiness of his dark hair was a surprise when I slipped my fingers into it. He bit one of my nipples hard enough that the sound that came out of my mouth was almost a scream, and I clenched my hands tighter in his hair.

I couldn't think. What Donovan was doing to me was scrambling my brain waves. Who needed signal-jammers?

Then he was on his knees, purposely rubbing his stubbled jaws over my soft skin before his tongue found the diamond piercing. He licked all around it and even sucked it into his mouth.

Somewhere I knew there was something we should be doing that we weren't. Oh, yeah.

Donovan stuck his tongue in my belly button, then circled my belly piercing again, sending crazy sensations straight to every part of my anatomy.

"Wait." I whimpered as he nuzzled my mound through the material of my bondage outfit.

"Shut up for once," he growled before nipping my folds through the cloth, right before he bunched his hands in the material and jerked it all the way down.

His mouth was headed directly where I wanted it, but I kept my voice low as I said to him in a hurried tone. "You're supposed to be punishing me."

"What?" He had an almost dazed expression as he looked up at me. "Punish. Yeah. Give me a minute."

He yanked off my outfit completely, with my help, and removed my shoes. When I was naked he said in a loud voice, "Hands and knees, slave. I'm going to punish you good."

"Yes, Sire," I said, equally as loud. "I only wanted to please you."

"You didn't, and you're getting what's coming to you." He pushed the back of my neck so that my cheek was against the carpet. "Spread your knees, slave."

"Yes, Sire," I said, just before he slapped my backside freaking hard enough to make me shout out in pain.

Okay, don't take this so seriously, Donovan.

He spanked me even harder.

I shouted louder.

The fact that we were putting on a show made it easier to belt out how much it hurt. I was good at holding back cries of pain no matter how badly I was tortured, but now I had an excuse to let it all out.

Then his free hand was rubbing my clit, and I was gasping and crying out at the same time whenever he spanked me. I could feel an all-time record of an orgasm on its way.

Oh, my God. I suddenly understood the meaning of pleasure and pain, and how the two could intensify a climax. My whole body was trembling and I could barely keep from collapsing completely to the floor.

"You're not allowed to come, slave." Donovan fingered me even more, his voice so harsh I almost didn't recognize it. "I have to give you permission."

"Wha—"

He spanked me again and I screamed again. Screw him. This was going to be an orgasm to end all orgasms.

Donovan stopped. He dragged his hand from my slit, drawing the moisture from between my thighs over my belly. And he stopped spanking me.

"D—Sire." I looked up at him. "I've got to come."

He gave me a dark look before he unfastened his pants and released his erection. He jerked something out of his pocket, and I didn't even have the presence of mind to realize it was a condom until he had slid it down his erection.

Donovan dug his fingers into my stinging ass cheeks and slammed his cock inside me. No more foreplay.

I cried out at the sudden thrust.

Now he was fucking me.

Dear lord, he was big and thick, and I felt him clear to my G-spot. I thought I was going to die from the exquisite pleasure. He drove in and out so hard it was almost painful.

"I can't wait anymore." I slammed back every time he rammed into me so that I was taking him deeper. "I've got to come. Sire."

"Not yet, slave." He sounded like he was talking through gritted teeth, and I had a feeling he was having a hard time remembering the Master/slave thing, too.

Not that I cared. My whole body was nothing but nerve endings that were on fire. Hold back the climax. Hold back the climax. Do it for the show.

Do it for Donovan.

"Now, slave," he shouted. "Come now!"

I came.

Oh, God, did I come.

I came so hard that my mind went entirely blank and all I could do was feel the most extraordinary orgasm of my life.

And I'd had a lot of orgasms. This one was unbelievable. Never-ending.

When I started returning to full consciousness, Donovan was still pounding in and out of me, making my spasms go on and on. They wouldn't stop. He wouldn't stop. It was almost painful, the way my contractions continued around his thick cock.

I hadn't even remembered he had his hands on my ass cheeks until he gripped them harder and shouted as he climaxed. I'd never felt a cock pulse inside me the way Donovan's did. It throbbed, and I swear I had a contraction with every pulse.

Was it forever? Or was it not long enough?

I didn't care.

Donovan rolled us over onto the carpet so that we were spooned together and he was still inside me. His skin was slick, like mine, and sweat dampened my hair. The rise and fall of his chest matched my breathing and was just as harsh.

He moved his lips close to my ear after he pushed one of the silver studs on my collar that activated the scrambler. "I didn't know there were such great side benefits."

I elbowed him in his gut, but I smiled.

Neither one of us seemed to be able to move. At least I knew *I* couldn't. I started to slip into a sort of haze, listening to the sounds of pleasure throughout the Glass House.

Then I heard words that captured my attention and I caught my breath.

"The shipment of auctioned merchandise goes out Thursday night," a man's voice said, and Donovan went still behind me.

I started to tip my head to look in the direction the voice was coming from, but Donovan held me tighter. He nuzzled my hair. "Just pretend you don't hear them, in case we're being watched through the glass."

"The merchandise will be transferred from a secret location to a yacht, the *Sweet Cherry*, that will arrive at the yacht club in Charlestown Thursday night," the same man continued. "The cover will be a rather exclusive party that will start on the upper deck when the merchandise is loaded onto the yacht."

A woman gave a soft laugh.

"You can inform the investors they'll have their merchandise," a different unrecognizable voice said, "once each piece arrives at the individual destination."

Auctioned merchandise. Each piece.

The girls.

It was as clear to me as if the men were informing me themselves.

"When is the next auction, Master Schilling?" This time it was a female. Maybe the woman who'd laughed.

"In . . ."—the first voice was fading—"weeks . . . the usual . . . online . . ."

A few faint murmurs more.

They were gone.

Schilling. Schilling. Who was he?

"Say nothing," Donovan murmured against my hair. "Just act like you want more sex or something."

"That wouldn't be a hardship," I said as I rolled in his arms to face him. I brushed my lips over his, then kissed my way to his ear. "I think I'll go to the 'ladies' room' if you can find Strong and keep him occupied."

"Yeah," Donovan said, his tone hard. "I'd probably end up cutting Strong's balls off because of what he'd make you do if I left you alone with him and I went to find the john to 'take care of business.' "

April 6
Saturday late night

Adrenaline always made it easier to get the job done. I liked the charge it gave me. The feeling of invincibility.

Sure, I was nervous. But the challenge was what excited me and made my blood tingle.

Of course tonight my blood and other parts of me were tingling a lot more than usual, thanks to Donovan.

After he left to find Strong, I'd shimmied into the outfit that I'd worn under my clothing and left the dress behind.

I couldn't afford anyone that I might pass being suspicious if they saw me fully clothed. I left my stilettos off, and the off-white carpet was soft and rich as I walked.

The blue, green, and yellow lighting made the trip through the glass-walled hallways almost surreal. So much pleasure was going on behind those walls that it was enough to make my head spin. My heart jerked as I passed a couple of Doms, and I kept my head lowered, not just my eyes. They made comments about my "assets" but didn't stop me. At least they knew how to follow protocol.

Just around the corner from Strong's office was the ladies' room. I made a visit there first to check it out. Oh, just perfect. A frosted glass door with a gold-plated sign led to the bathroom. Inside were glass stalls, along with white marble floors and countertops. Lovely. Not a place where one could easily hide if necessary.

Still, I went into one of the stalls and, after closing the door, removed the collar. It took me only a moment to press the right stud on the collar to activate the signal scrambler that would block sound and make cameras fuzzy or dead.

On the inside of the collar was a port device identical to the one in Donovan's wrist cuffs. The leather was hard and thick enough to snap the gadget back into it without a problem once I downloaded all the contents of a hard drive.

I rubbed my neck where the leather had chafed me. The roughness of the leather was something Martinez and I would have a little chat about.

Next I activated a camera with a press of another button. The camera was embedded in the outside of the leather, and for it, I didn't need to do anything. It would stay on as long as I left it on. Martinez was fast and good when it came to designing just about any kind of recon device.

Once everything was activated, I slipped one more thing from the collar—a small lock-picking kit. The kit was flat enough to stuff below the material of the bikini bottom, slightly over my mound.

The port device was thin enough, too, that I could slide it on the other side of my mound. Felt a little weird, but hey, whatever worked. I didn't think the top part of my outfit would hold either device well enough to keep them from slipping down or out.

I fastened the collar around my neck, took a deep breath, and walked out of the restroom. My bare feet traveled from the cool marble of the bathroom to the plush carpeting. Strong's office was just around the corner.

A puffy-cheeked, not-so-good-looking Dom carrying a whip came down the hallway just as I neared Strong's office and was eyeing the glass doorknob. I met the brown gaze of the puffy-cheeked man.

He was not one of the "beautiful people" that I'd seen so far at the clubs. When he reached me, he grabbed my arm with a bruising grip that caused me to gasp in surprise as he brought me to an abrupt stop in the hallway.

Damn. I'd forgotten to lower my eyes. I looked down at once. Still, he shouldn't have touched me.

"Your name, slave," the Dom demanded in a familiar voice that almost had me jerking my head up.

Schilling! The voice from the other side of the glass.

The dryness of my throat almost kept me from answering, but I managed. "Alexi."

"I do very special things to bad girls, slave Alexi." He pressed his big body close to mine and I had to struggle to keep from shuddering. "Are you a bad girl?"

My hair swung in my eyes when I shook my head while I stared at the carpet beneath Puff Cheeks Schilling's steel-toed boots. "No, Master," I said in as strong a voice as I could manage.

"Do you have a Master?" He brought his face nearer.

"Yes, Master." I nodded so fast it was a wonder my head didn't hit his chin. "Sire Dunning."

"Too bad you're taken." Puff Cheeks brushed his lips along my ear, and it wasn't a shiver that traveled through my body but a shudder from wanting to puke. "You still deserve a little punishment, slave."

I expected him to drag me to Donovan but he shoved me against a glass block wall and stars sparked in my eyes as my head hit the blocks hard. Before I connected the dots, Puff Cheeks Schilling jerked down the front of my outfit, baring my breasts, and pinched one of my nipples with his free hand.

Thank God I didn't have my tools or the port device in the top half.

Even as that thought came to me, my muscles tensed as I almost gave in to automatic reflexes, grabbed him, and twisted his arm behind his back.

He took two steps away from me, cracked his whip, and snapped the end across my breasts.

My eyes watered. The strike felt as if someone had branded me with a hot poker.

The cry rising in my throat was hard to choke down, and I shook with the need to retaliate. He had no right to be doing this. He wasn't my Master. An ache traveled through my hands as I struggled against balling my fists. I forced myself to keep my gaze down, praying he wouldn't do that again.

Puff Cheeks Schilling laughed and came back to me, obviously to admire his handiwork. He rubbed his big fleshy palm over the stinging flesh and growing red welts. What he was doing had me biting the inside of my cheek to keep from shrinking from the creep's touch.

My knee. His balls.

Can't blow my cover. Can't blow it.

Remember the girls.

"Next time," he said as he rubbed his thick erection against me, "I'll have to punish you in a very special way."

Rage had my voice trembling. "Yes, Master."

Schilling laughed again. "Go to your Sire and tell him you were punished for being disobedient and not obeying a Master when he told you to fetch a glass of water." He leaned in close. "Say anything else and I'll make sure you have a *real* punishment."

"Yes, Master." Sick SOB.

He slapped one of my breasts before he turned and headed for the men's room. His chuckle had me wanting to run up behind him, wrap his own whip around his throat, and strangle him with it.

When he disappeared behind the swinging door of the men's room, I pulled my top up for yet another time that night and winced at the feel of the material sliding over the welts.

Now I really had to hurry. I looked both ways and went for Strong's doorknob.

The lock was standard fare. I was confident that, if Strong had an alarm, another device Martinez had built into the collar would keep the alarm from activating.

Picking the lock was, thankfully, a breeze. I eased the glass door open before closing it behind me and stuffing the tools into my bikini panties again. I was so damned glad I hadn't put them in the top half of my suit. I locked the door.

Desk, shelves, art—everything was some form of glass or crystal, with the exception of the white chairs and carpet. If anyone came in here, there would be *no* place to hide. Except maybe in the shower in the bathroom that led off from the office. As long as no one looked in there. Even then, the shower was made of glass block.

I hurried around the desk to his pristine white computer, with a screensaver of a bound girl being whipped. It was the first picture in a slideshow screensaver with lots of women in different positions—

And then I saw myself, hanging from that hook, blindfolded, with Donovan whipping me.

I wanted to pick up the crystal paperweight next to the computer so badly that I shook with the need to smash the screen.

Asshole, asshole, asshole!

The picture changed to another woman and man, and relief at not seeing myself anymore helped me focus on my job.

It took me only a few minutes to download the entire hard drive's contents. Now I could let the geeks worry about cracking any codes.

My cheeks burned at the thought of anyone at RED seeing that screensaver. I'd have to convince Taylor to handle this one himself, and to discreetly remove that particular photograph before his geek squad got a hold of it. Still, it was going to be embarrassing as hell having him see me like that. Donovan and I could remove it, but it might show up on a more intensive search.

I slipped the port with the hard drive back into the lower part of my outfit and started to the door. I looked over my shoulder and saw my footprints in the once perfectly smooth carpet that must have been vacuumed by one of Strong's maids.

What could I do to cover my tracks? And do it in a hurry. My blood raced and my face felt flushed.

There. The book closest to me on one of the nearby shelves might do the job. I grabbed it and ran to the desk, maintaining the same footpath. I leaned over and started dragging the book behind me, through the carpet, removing my tracks. Unfortunately, if someone was paying attention, it looked like something had been dragged on the floor.

Never mind. Maybe he wouldn't notice. But I didn't have time to set the book upright on the shelf, and I needed to back out of the office, erasing the rest of my tracks. Strong would just have to lose a book, and I had to hope he didn't miss it.

After listening to the door to make sure everything was quiet, I unlocked the door as quietly as I could, then relocked it after I covered the rest of my footprints.

After a quick glance around, I hurried to the ladies' room. I was just about to lay the book on the counter when I caught a glimpse of the title. *Screw the Roses, Send Me the Thorns* by Philip Miller and Molly Devon. I almost laughed. From everything I'd read, this was a classic BDSM book.

Female voices came toward the ladies' room and my heart pounded as I looked for someplace to hide the book. I dashed into one of the stalls, set the book on the toilet tank and plopped down on the seat.

The girls were giggling and talking about Master Strong and Mistress Danica, and how they couldn't wait to get back to them. After two toilet flushes and water running in the sink with more giggling, the girls left.

I held my hand to my chest. Close, close, close. I got up

and looked at the book lying on top of the toilet tank and I smiled. The tank lid was a little heavy and scraped when I moved it, but I opened it wide enough to drop the book in before it grated shut.

Oh. The collar scraped my skin as I took it off before slipping the hard drive port and lock pick set from my bikini panties into it. I smiled at the thought of what Taylor or Martinez would think about where those things had been. I'd never tell.

I shut off the camera and the signal scrambler before fastening the collar around my neck. With satisfaction I realized the camera would have recorded Schilling's face and body. It would make it that much easier to take the slaver down.

Was he the man we were looking for? Or was there someone above him? I had a good feeling Schilling was a pawn.

Once I was out of the restroom, down the hall, and back in the room I'd been in with Donovan, I could finally breathe easier. I stripped and took the position we'd agreed on before I left, so that I looked like he was punishing me.

My belly rested on the carpeted surface of a piece of BDSM furniture so that my head hung on one side and I was kneeling on the other. I was in a position where my butt was up high and blood was rushing to my head. Forever and a day Donovan left me there, and stars started popping in front of my eyes.

"We'll see you at the Champagne Slipper next week," came Donovan's voice from the doorway.

"Looks like your slave was obedient while you were gone," Strong said. "Maybe she'll need a reward."

"I plan to give her one," Donovan said in a deep, vibrant tone that sent lust spiraling from my belly to that needy place between my thighs.

After he closed the door, Donovan rubbed my backside when he reached me. "Everything okay?"

When I rose, my head spun a little from all that hanging down. I worked to bring my mind back into focus and fully turned so that he could see the new beauty mark on my naked breasts. "It would be absolutely perfect if not for this."

The flash of anger on Donovan's face was intense. "Who?"

It didn't take me long to tell him in a low voice about the rendezvous with Schilling. The fury on Donovan's features grew.

"But the important thing," I whispered, despite the burn on my chest, "is that I have recorded ID on the sicko." I pointed to the place where the camera was hidden. "It will make it so much easier to take him down."

"Are you all right?" Donovan still looked angry and I felt his rough edges again. "Let's get out of here."

A moment of silence hung between us, thick and heavy.

"You're doing all you can do." I slipped my arms around Donovan's neck and brought my mouth close to his. "And you do it *very* well."

Donovan cupped my butt and pressed his erection against me. "Or we could stay a while longer," he said, all deep and rumbly.

I smiled.

CHAPTER 20

Score one for the home team

April 11
Thursday night

Helmets weren't my style, but Donovan and I couldn't afford to be recognized when we made the bust. We were camped out in the yacht club in Charlestown, in the old Navy Shipyard. The next wharf over was the USS Constitution.

The irony. A symbol of freedom parked next to the place where women were being taken out of the country to be used as sex slaves.

Hidden throughout the area were the rest of the RED raid teams, waiting for that private yacht named *Sweet Cherry*.

Ha ha. Funny.

Not.

We'd done our research on the *Cherry*. It was enormous, and could easily hide women in cargo holds that were probably laced with chemicals that made it difficult for even K-9s to locate them.

We'd also done recon on the area, but couldn't locate the women, wherever they were being held, before the transfer was even made. Of course it couldn't be that simple, now could it.

No way was I going to miss this bust, no matter what my ASAC said. I needed to feel like I was doing something productive other than getting my butt whipped. Otherwise, all I had was the sick feeling in my belly at the thought of those girls being auctioned off. *Auctioned off*.

The welt across my breasts burned as sweat dampened

my skin beneath my T-shirt. Maybe Schilling would be here and I could shoot him.

What a gold mine the information on and pictures of Schilling had been. Over the past few days our agents had been able to dissect his life down to his penchant for visiting porno sites. How's that for in-depth research? Plenty of money being funneled to Swiss accounts. Ah, the trails one does leave when one isn't careful enough.

And he owned the *Sweet Cherry*.

The now constant burning of the welt, but more importantly the fact that he was the scum of the earth for auctioning those girls, made me want to pop his head between my hands like a giant zit.

Jason Strong—still clean. Like Tarantino, nothing was on his hard drive to implicate him in anything illegal. Strong's records weren't as well kept as Tarantino's—it looked like Strong needed a better assistant or accountant. That was if he didn't already have an assistant whom he kept tied up. Literally.

I pushed aside thoughts of Strong and narrowed my gaze, hoping to see some sign of the *Sweet Cherry*.

My skin crawled as I tried to shake off last night's dream. It always changed, morphed. It was never the same. But it left me feeling exhausted, battered, almost hopeless.

Hopelessness was something I would never accept into my life.

If I'd ever allowed hopelessness to enter my mind, how would I have made it through those years as an assassin? Watching people die? *Killing* them.

The thought of not even knowing who I was killing, or why, made my stomach churn. At least as a sniper in the Army I knew why we were taking out certain targets that were a danger to the US.

Even as a RED agent I'd been forced to take a life to defend my own, or that of another agent.

I could live with that.

It was so much harder to accept the fact that I'd killed in order to save myself from mutilation and death.

That was something I'd had to live with the rest of my life, and sometimes I understood why people turned to drugs or alcohol to forget their pain and mistakes.

But I refused to feel helpless. Refused to waste my life, because now I could save others.

By taking down the sonsofbitches auctioning off these women.

I swallowed. Like that made my past sins any better.

Flashes of moonlight and ripples of water in the harbor reminded me of shards of broken glass. Like the pieces that had scattered over my hand when I took the bat to Gary's truck. My stomach tightened as I thought of what he'd done. But then I thought of Donovan, and suddenly Gary seemed like a part of my distant past.

Cool, salty air reached me under my helmet's shield. My M40 sniper's rifle felt good and solid in my hands as I crouched next to Donovan, one of my many evil twins decked out in black raid gear, as we held our places. I had the added comfort of my Glock in my utility belt, along with my dagger.

I kept my head perfectly still as I glanced at Donovan from the corner of my eye. Even in shadow and wearing a helmet, so much power emanated from him straight to me.

My belly tingled and the feeling shot straight between my thighs. Saturday's sexual adventure had turned into something hot and ravenous that we hadn't begun to be able to satisfy over the past five days. Just one look and the next thing we knew clothes were flying everywhere, and then we were at it hard and fast.

Never slow. No, our need for each other was so extreme that he took me up against the wall, on the kitchen table, the kitchen counter, in the shower, on the floor, on a chair in his war room. Come to think of it, we never actually made it to a bed.

Push away thoughts of animal sex, Lexi Steele. Save that for after the party.

How could I want him so much, even now?

Somehow he made me feel safe, untouchable.

Feelings like that were dangerous. No one was untouchable, and if anyone was going to protect my ass it would be me.

I glanced at Donovan again in the darkness, sensing even more darkness around him from his anger and fear for his sister.

My chest ached as I swallowed and gripped my rifle tighter.

I wanted to take off the helmet and swipe my hand over my damp scalp. Instead I settled for wiping away a bead of sweat rolling down my cheek.

Two times large yachts glided into the harbor and the thrumming of my heart vibrated through me. Neither had been the *Sweet Cherry*. They hadn't even come close to matching the description, in case the name had been painted over.

Every now and then Donovan or I would break the silence, keeping our voices low as we spoke into the comms and gave status reports to the other teams—the status reports were basically nothing. It wasn't necessary to tell anyone to maintain position because not a RED agent would move until the order was given. Even the K-9s wouldn't twitch a muscle.

Tonight we'd taken out most of the lights when we arrived, so our teams were even more difficult to see in the darkness.

Three friggin' hours and the yacht still wasn't here. Donovan and I knew our information was good. What we'd overheard at the Glass House—we had no doubt that tonight Schilling and his cohorts were shipping the women out.

Right?

Using the yacht—an interesting way to move the merchandise. And a swinging, exclusive party above deck. High-class human trafficking. Whaddya know?

One of the RED agents constantly monitored the Coast Guard's communications to make sure they hadn't gotten to the yacht before us. Hadn't heard a thing, though, and we would have.

The ache in my legs and lower back begged me to move so I could stretch. Hell if I'd break position.

A brilliant spot in the distance, diamond-bright on the

water. Adrenaline made my muscles sing, chasing away aches and fatigue.

"Target in range," came Special Agent Fowler's voice. The high-powered scope Fowler used was designed by RED's technology department.

"Target name confirmed," Fowler said. "*Sweet Cherry.*"

About damned time.

We still didn't move. Donovan and I didn't even look at each other.

My blood pumped double-time as the yacht sliced through the water. Closer. Closer. White lights looped in long strands above the deck, so bright it seemed like stars had converged in that one place.

The closer the yacht came toward us, the tighter my grip on my sniper's rifle, and the more adrenaline flowed through me. I was so ready to hurt these pricks.

Soon the decorations, smorgasbords of food, and even a five-piece band were easy to spot. Yeah, a party. Smart. Wonder if the partyers would have a clue what the bad guys intended to store belowdecks?

Where were those partyers? Where were the girls?

I flicked my gaze around the dock and didn't see the silhouette of a single agent. We were a part of the night. Every one of our agents came from branches of the military or government or clandestine agencies, and every agent was trained to be invisible.

RED had men and women who were former Special Ops, Navy SEALS, Secret Service, government spies, or trained assassins like me. RED recruited only the best.

The yacht slid through the water like a cutter through glass. Almost ready to dock.

Hurry. I was going to start blowing shit up with my M40 if my body got any hotter. No one could accuse me of patience being one of my virtues. I only practiced it out of necessity.

I thought the yacht would never come to a stop, and my chest ached when I finally let air out in a rush. The scraping sounds of the *Sweet Cherry* docking made my spine crawl, but better that than all the waiting.

A man aboard the *Sweet Cherry* shouted orders in Swedish. I squinted and got a good look at him. Other men scurried to follow his orders as they secured the yacht.

"Limos arriving and parking near the yacht club," Fowler said through the comm. "Looks like the party's about to start."

Were the girls in those limos with the partyers? Maybe hidden in the trunks, drugged and kept in enclosed crates with only airholes to breathe through?

The burn in my gut nearly sent acid washing up my throat.

"Civilians out of the limos and approaching target," Fowler said. "No sign of any cargo."

Donovan growled loud enough for me to hear. I knew he was thinking about his sister being among the "cargo."

Male laughter and female giggles broke the silence. It wasn't long before eleven couples approached the yacht. Most of the women leaned against the men they were with as if for support. A few of the women stumbled like they were already drunk. But the giggling didn't stop. It was as if laughing gas had been given to every woman.

Then I saw the guns in the bright lighting cast from the strings of lights. The men on deck were armed with weapons in holsters—which didn't really surprise me.

But the male partygoers—they wore holsters, too. Why would the men need to be armed?

Something crawled down my spine.

I frowned. Not right. The whole party setup wasn't right.

The women kept giggling and it was obvious the men were keeping them on their feet.

More armed men appeared on deck, and started gesturing and talking.

The women's slightly dazed expressions as they giggled made everything snap perfectly into place.

The female partyers were the auctioned women.

When I looked at Donovan, I saw he'd pushed his helmet back. By his expression when he looked at me, it was obvious he was on the same mental path as me. His gaze snapped back to the couples on board, and for a moment I saw hope and fear mixed with fury on his features.

He was searching for Kristin.

I murmured into the comm, "Yellow Team. When you take everyone on deck into custody, separate the men from the women. Don't allow any couples to stay together."

Without pause, Fowler said, "Acknowledged. Yellow Team out."

"Orange Team," I said. "Hold back the K-9s until Yellow Team has secured the deck."

"Ready on your order," Quincy said. "Orange Team out."

"All teams, most of the men are armed." Donovan said into his comm.

The five team leaders came back with their cool acknowledgments. These agents never made apologies for what they had to do, no matter what it might mean.

"All teams, green light," Donovan commanded. "Go!"

"Police!" Smithe shouted the universal word for law enforcement as RED agents poured from every hiding place they'd been stationed in.

On the deck of the *Sweet Cherry*, everything became complete chaos. Screams. Shouts. Cries.

The RED special agents on the other hand performed their jobs with cool efficiency.

Using the high-powered telescope on my M40, I sighted my first target. The asshole was shooting into the darkness with a fierce expression. Not for long. He crumpled the moment my bullet pierced his forehead.

Sharp retorts from weaponry tore through the night as men on board shot at agents converging on the yacht. The bad guys dropped so fast they didn't get off many rounds.

Screams and shouts came from the former partyers. Why did people run around in random directions when shooting started instead of literally hitting the deck to stay out of the line of fire? How stupid could you get?

My hands remained steady as I took down two more targets. I never missed. I never made mistakes—at least in marksmanship—when it came to my former profession as an assassin. That was one part of my life where I'd had no problem keeping calm and not losing my temper. I'd had to in order to make it through every assignment.

Would the gunfire never end? Would assholes with weapons ever stop appearing from the lower decks?

No sirens pierced a night that was also empty of flashing emergency lights. RED had ways of warning off other law enforcement agencies when we made a bust.

RED agents systematically took care of business. All of the men who'd been guarding the dock were down.

Ah, there. On the deck. One shot of my M40. Former last man standing was history. The rest of the men were cowering on the deck. Believe me, our agents still had weapons trained on every person on board.

I swung my rifle over my shoulder. Time to take care of business.

I kept my Glock in a two-handed grip as I skirted dead men and walked through splatters of blood while I hurried onto the yacht. I had to put bullets into two men who were down but not totally out and who were trying to go for their guns.

Yellow Team was already on deck and they'd had the situation under control, the men and women separated, in moments. Green Team remained in place on the dock, prepared to take out any more armed opponents.

When I gave the signal, Orange Team converged on the deck with the K-9s to start searching for humans in places they didn't belong—like hidden compartments—just in case.

Red Team started at the top while Blue Team headed below with Orange Team. All team leaders checked in on the comms as they searched the yacht from top to bottom in a predetermined plan, even though we were certain the "merchandise" was right on deck.

Occasionally gunfire would break the silence as our agents covered the yacht. As always, I hoped none of our agents were down, but as professionals we went on. We did our job.

Donovan threw his helmet aside and rushed straight for

the women. I'd never seen him look frantic, as he did as he checked every one of the women.

And then I'd never seen him look so vulnerable, so full of anguish, as when he finished.

"She's not here." Donovan cleared his throat after he returned to me, and he looked into the distance. "Kristin must have been one of the two domestic—'sales.'" I was sure I heard a crack in his voice.

I rubbed my chest, over the Kevlar that covered the ache in my heart. That meant Kristin's nightmare had already begun. These others—their buyers were waiting for delivery, and the girls probably hadn't been touched. I hoped.

But if Kristin had been delivered . . .

Dear God.

Donovan and I stood side by side on the deck, watching Yellow Team finish separating, disarming, and cuffing all of the men who'd been escorting the women. The men who'd survived, that was.

The eleven women looked dazed, yet were still giggling on one end of the yacht.

Donovan and I moved closer to the restrained men. The kidnappers. I could feel Donovan's rage and desire to kill them all for what they were doing to countless young women—including his sister.

My gaze slid over one of the cuffed men who was staring at Donovan, who'd taken his helmet off. The catch in my breath hurt my throat when I realized it was Schilling.

Did he recognize Donovan? Did he recognize me?

No way he'd ID me. Puff Cheeks wouldn't know. I was unrecognizable in my gear.

Wasn't I?

Schilling stared at Donovan.

"So, it's 'Sire Dunning.'" Then he looked from Donovan to me. "And I'd bet behind that helmet and under those clothes is the supposed 'slave Alexi.'"

Oh, crap.

Donovan made a low growl as he gripped his Beretta in

one hand and stepped across the bloody deck. He headed straight for Puff Cheeks, who recoiled.

Donovan clipped Schilling in the head with the grip of the Beretta.

I should have thought of that.

Schilling slumped onto his side.

When Donovan returned to me, I looked at him through my helmet's shield. "I understand him recognizing you. But me?"

Donovan scowled as he stared at the man he had just knocked the crap out of. "Hate to break it to you, Steele, but you have the kind of body a man doesn't forget easily."

My jaw dropped as I looked up at him. Say what?

He folded his arms over his chest. "I think it was a natural guess, judging by your height and the fact that you're with me."

I gestured toward the out-cold Puff Cheeks. "We're in deep, aren't we?"

"Nah." Donovan stared at the man. "We can keep him restrained."

"How about dead?" I tested the weight of my Glock in my hand. "Can't identify me if he's in the big porn house on the other side."

"Bloodthirsty little thing, aren't you, Steele?" Donovan shook his head. "He might just be the break we need to get to the top."

"Yeah." I holstered my Glock and immediately missed the feel of it in my palm. "I can put a bullet in his balls, followed by one in his brain, *after* we get the man we're really going for."

I glanced at the women. "Time to do a little interviewing." I sighed. It was going to be a friggin' long night. "I'll take the girls, you go after the dickheads."

Donovan stared at the women for a moment and I could sense how badly he wished his sister was one of those girls we'd saved.

Then he seemed relieved to not have to talk with the women. Like it would be too painful. He started toward the men. "You got it, Steele."

The women looked pitiful as they slumped on the deck. I'd bet a box of Dixie's treats and face the calico cat's wrath if I was wrong. It wasn't going to be easy interviewing them when they were so obviously high and dazed. More than likely we'd do our interviewing after they'd been in RED's infirmary for a while.

I went to a woman who looked like she was coming down from the drug. Her chest rose and fell as she took harsh breaths. Fear sparked in her gaze and she tried to scrabble away until I took off my helmet and she saw I was female.

"You okay?" I asked, keeping my voice low and trying to sound comforting.

The terror in her brown eyes made me feel like someone had jerked my guts straight through my belly button.

"We'll get you all someplace safe," I said, "and then we'll talk, okay?"

She didn't say anything. I didn't expect her to. It wasn't the drug that had her scared out of her mind. I was positive she'd been threatened with any number of punishments if she talked.

Yeah, we'd have to work on her and the other women later, once they'd had a chance to realize they were okay.

This job really sucked sometimes. Most of the time. Even when we saved the women from captivity, we couldn't save them from their fear.

One thing that kept me going on this assignment was the fact that I would help countless women once I got to the top of that awful ladder and found out who was the scumbag running the entire show. The major player calling the shots.

The other things that kept the fire burning inside me were finding Kristin Donovan, and killing every asshole involved in murdering Randolph.

CHAPTER 21

Kristin

March 17
Sunday, two weeks ago

The hangover from hell. Usually she was too doped up to feel anything, but right now her head felt like an ice pick was piercing her skull again and again. Hopefully it wasn't a migraine coming on.

Kristin opened her eyes to dimness, flat on her back, and started to rub her temples. Her heart jerked. She couldn't move. She went from sleepy to alert as she tried to wiggle her wrists and her ankles. She was spread-eagled on a soft mattress, completely naked. Warm air brushed every part of her exposed body.

These days fear only came to her when she hadn't been shot up, and right now every organ inside her was twisting so tight it felt like she might die.

She wasn't in a roach-infested room. She wasn't shot up. She was in some kind of bedroom, with rose-colored walls and furniture that looked like it might be made of cherrywood. A feminine-looking room. She was lying on a four-poster bed—which was convenient for her to be chained up. Everything in the room looked rich and luxurious, from what she could see in her spread-eagled position.

Kristin swallowed as goose bumps chilled her skin.

The transaction must have been completed. She'd been delivered to the buyer.

And she was now someone's slave. Sex slave.

Tears burned her eyes. How long ago had she'd been working on her graduate paper in abnormal psych at Harvard?

Then one mistake. Taking a drink from a stranger. And now she was someone's property.

Someone owns me.

Kristin startled when the door opened, and her heart raced as a dark figure stood at the threshold. Her owner?

Or maybe a savior? Could she be so lucky?

The figure approached her. A man. Large frame. She couldn't see his features because the room was too dim.

She wanted to scream as the bed dipped from his weight when he sat on the edge of the bed. Too much shadow on his face to make out who it was.

Kristin flinched as he raised his hand, but he reached for the stained-glass bedside lamp. The moment she saw his face a mass of confusion and hope replaced her headache and fear.

A savior.

"Professor Michaels?" Kristin let out her breath. She didn't care that she was naked in front of her Harvard professor, she was just so glad to see a familiar face. "How did you find me?"

He smiled and moved his hand to one of her breasts. A chill shot through her as he lightly squeezed her nipple. "I bought you."

CHAPTER 22

I love little red dresses

April 13
Saturday evening

My sparkly red two-piece outfit didn't cover a whole lot, which of course was the idea. It had a halter top that revealed my diamond belly piercing, and a little red skirt that barely met the tops of my thighs.

When Georgina and I had gone shopping last weekend, we'd picked up a fragrance that was citrusy yet sexy and enticing. I'd always preferred orange blossom perfumes, but this was on the exotic side and I definitely needed exotic.

I did manage to keep my hands at my sides and resist tugging down on the skirt as I walked to Donovan's bedroom. I could swear the skirt was climbing up the naked butt cheeks that my thong failed to cover.

"Christ!" The calico cat appeared out of nowhere. I almost tripped over Dixie in my four-inch heels, and would have landed on my backside if I hadn't caught myself by bracing my hand on the wall.

She gave me a look that told me that as far as she was concerned she couldn't wait to see the back of me when I wasn't staying here anymore. "Stupid cat," I shouted at her as she strutted down the hall, tail twitching high in the air.

After glaring at the calico, I reached Donovan's room and walked into the room where the door was partially open.

He looked over his shoulder. "You okay?"

"Your cat almost killed me," I grumbled. But then I brightened. "Hey, how about some washing-machine sex again, before we leave? There's a load of clothes that need to be washed."

The corner of Donovan's mouth quirked. "Steele, you are insatiable."

God, it turned me on big-time when he did that almost-smile.

Then his eyes roved over me in my little "fuck me" dress and shoes, and his Adam's apple bobbed as he swallowed.

Because of our uncontrollable need for each other, I'd started sleeping here. Which meant we now did have sex in bed, as well as every other place we could think of. Once we even did it with the top half of me on the washing machine while it was going. God, the vibrations as Donovan took me from behind—nothing like washing-machine sex.

"How about some war-room sex instead," he said in a rumbly growl.

The leather was smooth beneath my thighs as I sat in a chair next to him and let my dress hike all the way up my thighs as I crossed my legs at the knees. Even from here his masculine scent called to me and I wanted him for the twentieth time this week.

"Insatiable, huh?" I scooted my chair close to him and rubbed my palm over his cock, which hardened immediately. "And that's a bad thing?"

He made that low growling sound as he faced me completely, grabbed me by the waist, and jerked me onto his lap.

My dress had gone up around my waist when he grabbed me, and my bottom half was only covered by a leather thong. I unfastened his leather pants, released his erection, and started stroking it. At the same time he drew a condom package out of his back pocket. I took the packet and opened it in slow motion before moving even slower as I rolled the condom down his erection.

"You little tease." He reached between my thighs and pulled aside the material of my leather thong. I gasped as he rubbed my clit, which got the exact reaction he wanted from me when he raised me and slammed me down on his cock.

"Donovan!" I held onto his shoulders as he grasped my ass cheeks and fucked me while moving me up and down his erection. "You feel so good inside me." I gasped between words. "So big and full."

"You're scrambling my brains, Steele." He took me harder, slamming us together.

"Good." I tipped my head back and my breasts jutted out.

"I'm going to rip this goddamned dress off of you." His breathing was labored. "I want to suck your nipples."

"Easy." I reached up, unfastened the neckline of the halter top, and let it drop, baring my breasts.

"You just saved yourself a dress," he said before he bit one of my nipples.

I cried out as he sucked and bit my nipples, and took me so hard he was scrambling *my* brains.

My orgasm was a wonderful storm of sensations that shook my whole body. He sucked and bit me harder as my core squeezed his erection.

He came with a combination of a shout and a groan, and his cock throbbed inside me. A couple more strokes, and he brought me close to him and rested his head between my breasts.

"What the hell are you doing to me, Steele?" he mumbled against my skin as he continued to throb inside me and I shivered with each remaining contraction. "I can barely think around you."

"Apparently my dastardly plan is working." I grinned as he looked up at me. "Heh, heh, heh."

After we got off the chair, Donovan said, "I need my brains back, Steele." He tossed the condom into a wastebasket, then arranged himself in his pants and fastened them again. I'd already arranged my dress and fastened my halter top so that it covered my breasts again. "You're going to have to slow down," he said.

"Not on your life." I reached for him. "Besides, I know where your brains are." And I rubbed his cock.

"No thanks to you." He kissed me hard, then said, "Hold on while I check something out."

Donovan went back to looking at the monitors while I watched him, my whole body still tingling.

I turned my attention to the monitors and screens, too. Somehow, some way, we'd find something that would connect the dots.

If only Kristin had been one of the girls on the ship, she would be safe now. Instead she had been a "domestic sale," and was probably already going through a living hell. We'd confirmed with Schilling the fact that Kristin had already been delivered to her buyer.

Fucker.

I clenched my hands and clenched my teeth harder as Donovan's fingers flew over the touchpad.

Every time I thought of Kristin being a sex slave to some pervert I wanted to hurt something, someone. Who knew what the sonofabitch was doing to her?

The one, the tiniest of bright spots, was that we knew she was somewhere in the greater Boston area and not somewhere across the country.

Puff Cheeks, whose real name was Frederick Schilling, let us know that much after some heavy "persuading."

"Oh, *that* little piece." He'd laughed when I described her and her birthmark. He'd continued with a snort. "She's right under your noses in the Boston area. Don't know who owns her, but you can bet you'll never find the slut."

One punch and Donovan had knocked the crap out of Schilling. The man was out for a good two hours.

I shifted in my seat as I looked at the monitors that covered various rear doors of nightclubs girls had been taken from. Damn. If only we could get a big break on the whole operation.

"Maybe tonight will be the night," I said to myself. Donovan glanced at me and I met his gaze. "Our big break. A bunch of pieces of the puzzle. It's got to be Cabot, since Tarantino and Strong came up clean."

"I hope you're right." Donovan suddenly didn't look like the same man I'd just had sex with. "That bastard Schilling—fine time for RED's truth serum to cause a reaction."

"No kidding."

Without the red tape other agencies faced, our med-techs administered RED's version of a "truth serum" that had been concocted in the agency's medical lab. Instead of dragging answers from Schilling, he'd had some kind of reaction. That was a first for RED.

Schilling was now in our underground medical center covered with a full-body rash, head the size of a prize pumpkin, on a ventilator, and oh, yeah, currently in a coma.

"Friggin' great," I said. "We should have let our 'persuasion artists' have a couple more rounds with him." As far as who ran the sex slave auction ring, and how it worked, Schilling wouldn't say a word. Not even to save himself.

I gripped the lower part of the seat and dug my fingers into the leather.

Feel sorry for a man who auctioned off women, a man whose brain was close to exploding? No way. Pissed because that potential source was out of the running to interrogate? Hell yeah.

But Kristin was in our area. We didn't have to try to track her down in every city of every state. She was right here.

Somewhere.

I adjusted the leather collar I'd had to put back on for tonight. Martinez had added a trigger that would have RED agents all over the nightclub if we needed them. All I had to do was peel off one of the silver studs on the collar. Which stud was it again? The one to the left of the stud that hid the camera. Right?

Damn. When we went to Martinez, my brains had been scrambled after just having had very, very against-the-rules sex in Donovan's office. With the blinds closed, of course.

Stop thinking about earth-shattering sex, Steele.

Whenever we weren't working on *Operation Cinderella*, trying to track down more info on Cabot, Tarantino, and Strong, Donovan and I were searching for his sister in his war room.

My contacts had gotten us nowhere, Yeager hadn't come up with anything else, and as much as I wanted to help Donovan find Kristin, most of the time I felt as useful as a wind gauge in a hurricane.

Right now his attention was directed at multiple surveillance monitors—which included the front and back entrances of the Champagne Slipper, the Glass House, and the Crystal Twilight.

If they were trafficking girls from those nightclubs it wasn't showing up on any of our monitors. Of course, Donovan had been monitoring the Diamond Castle, too, the place Kristin had been kidnapped the night she was out with her friends.

"Anything new?" I asked as I watched.

More and more fury started to grow in his expression. He didn't look at me. Oh, crap, by the look on his face something had happened. And it was bad.

"Watch the monitor stationed at the back of the Diamond Castle," he said in a voice full of anger. "Last night's footage."

A tipsy young woman with long dark hair stumbled out of the back entrance of the nightclub. She was hanging onto a guy who might have been her boyfriend.

My scalp tingled as the couple moved toward a maroon van—and the guy shoved the girl through the open side door before slamming the door shut behind her. The guy climbed into the passenger seat and the van took off. Couldn't catch a visual of the driver or the man who'd thrown the girl in the van.

When I looked at Donovan, murderous rage darkened his features and the currents in the air told me just how difficult it was for him to contain his fury.

"The sonsofbitches probably kidnapped Kristin the same way," he growled.

"They must have been lying low since then." I pushed the words out. It was almost hard to talk with the heaviness of his rage filling the room.

When the van started to drive away, Donovan paused the vid and zeroed in on the license plate.

"A Massachusetts plate." My cell wasn't small enough to

fit in my bra or panties, and I'd left my purse in the bedroom, so I grabbed the cordless off the desk for its secure landline. "I'll phone it in to RED and let them know they'll have the footage in a few moments. They'll be on it in rocket time."

Donovan slammed his fist on the desk beside the monitor. "A RED agent should have been monitoring this girl's kid-napping. We'd have had the assholes last night."

I gave the info to an agent before pressing the phone's *off* button and setting the receiver back on the desk. "Must have been that new agent, but that's no excuse." RED hired the best, and this was a major screwup. I looked back at the monitor, and the license plate that was still zoomed in. "No one else in that department would miss something like this."

Donovan's scowl made me feel like thunder was about to shake the building. "It'll be the last mistake he makes."

I stood and watched him weigh his Beretta in his palm as if deciding whether or not he should take it or an AK-47 to-night.

"Uh-uh," I said. "That thing stays in the glove compart-ment while we're in the club." He turned to me, his scowl still firmly in place, and I raised my hand. "Don't go rabid on me, Donovan. We've got work to do."

After he pulled on a pair of shitkickers, he turned off the dim lighting and shut the door behind us.

CHAPTER 23

At least bamboo wasn't shoved under my fingernails

April 13
Saturday night

I don't know why, but Donovan and I just sat in the little red Mercedes at the curb in front of the Champagne Slipper instead of driving up to the valet. We just stared at the Slipper, neither of us making a move. Not sure what was going through his mind. In mine, I was wishing this was over.

Donovan remained silent, and my fingers ached as I fisted my hands in my lap. I felt like I was standing on a fine edge. Any moment I could slide down one side or topple over the other.

Why I had this feeling, I didn't know. I'd worked more dangerous undercover operations.

But something didn't feel right.

Donovan finally drove in front of the Slipper and let one of the valets take the car. Again we were checked against a list of exclusive clientele. We were escorted through the nightclub, which was thickly perfumed from the patrons, but still smelled of beer and wine, too.

We were taken to a pair of tall wooden doors halfway through the nightclub. A bouncer stood to one side. The doors were near the bar.

My heels click-click-clicked on the marble flooring of the circular foyer as we were ushered into it. The solid mahogany doors shut behind us and cut off every sound from the nightclub.

I had a major "wow" moment. My gaze roamed a beautiful

round chamber that included frescoes on the ceiling. The tall mahogany doors were the only things that broke the complete smoothness of the place. The room smelled like cherry-scented cigars.

The circular foyer was empty save for a bouncer, or guard, who could give those Special Ops guys a run for their money. He stood beside a flight of marble stairs leading below.

My stomach tightened when the single door opened. Cabot walked through it. Behind him I caught a glimpse of a mahogany desk with a flat-screen computer monitor on it, a pair of chairs in front of the desk, and shelves lined with treasures and books. Cabot closed the tall mahogany door, withdrew a key from his pocket, and the locks tumbled into place as he turned the key.

Excellent. That had to be Cabot's office.

Now what kind of lock did he use?

My stomach squeezed harder as I lowered my eyes to avoid Cabot's. I had the feeling he was a mean SOB when it came to punishments.

The dimly lit Austrian crystal chandelier threw rainbow glitters onto the marble floors as well as the walls, which were thick enough to block out the pounding beat in the main nightclub. Rachmaninov flowed at an elegant level from speakers that must have been carefully recessed so they couldn't be seen. There were three cameras, though, meant to be obvious, no doubt.

Beneath my eyelashes, I glanced to my left, where the bodyguard stood to the side of the sweeping staircase. Must lead to the BDSM part of the club.

Donovan left me behind as he strode forward and shook Cabot's hand. "Great to see you, Master Cabot."

"What a pleasure it is that you could make it to the Champagne Slipper," Cabot said in his snotty Boston Brahmin accent and too-formal manner of speech. "I'll be delighted to show you and your slave my dungeon."

Dungeon, huh.

I kept a "respectful" distance behind Donovan and Cabot. We walked down the marble staircase, crossing the boundary from the elegance of the foyer into what I could only call a raunchy underworld. This place definitely had no class, especially compared to Strong's and Tarantino's clubs. But, after taking a look around, maybe that was the intention.

It was certainly not what I'd expected of the "sophisticated" Cabot.

Hard-pounding rock music blared loudly enough to cover some of the screams of slaves being "punished." Donovan and I walked with Cabot through fog from smoke machines that gave the huge floor a misty look and lent a bitter smell to the air. Colored lights added to the sense of the surreal.

The rock music pulsed and throbbed, even more than it had in the nightclub. The nightclub had been elegant—this was so not. This room had the thick smell of too much beer and testosterone, not to mention marijuana.

We paused long enough for Cabot to let Donovan and me have a chance to take in the layout. Several slaves wearing only their collars, along with bikini underwear, thongs, or miniskirts, were humping poles.

They moved like exotic dancers in the very center of the room, over squares lit with blinking lights of blue, orange, and purple. At least twenty Doms crowded around the raised floor and crammed bills into whatever bottom parts the slaves were wearing.

"You'll certainly enjoy watching your slave turn on other Doms," Cabot said with a smile. "After you get a chance to visit the other parts of the club she can start there."

Oh no. Absolutely not.

Donovan didn't glance at me, didn't say a word as he walked beside Cabot.

We learned there were twenty rooms in the Champagne Slipper's lower level as we passed a full bar at one end of the room.

Donovan and I stopped with Cabot and looked into one of the rooms, where a man was screwing a bound and hooded woman in front of a large picture window. "As you can see, two of our twenty rooms are for voyeurs."

"The rooms each have a theme and plenty of 'toys,'" Cabot said with a satisfied smile. "Of course spanking and whipping, multiple partners, shock treatments, wax play, caging, pony- and puppygirls, and any other number of fetishes."

A wicked gleam was in his eyes that scared me more than anything. Especially when he said, "I even have two Irish wolfhounds, the tallest breed of dog, in one room. Moose and Duke have a taste for pussy." Intense fear pounded my heart against my rib cage. I know my expression was beyond stunned at Cabot's last sick statement, and I raised my head and stared at Cabot.

"You allow your slave free rein, Sire Dunning?" Cabot's eyes met mine, and for a second I forgot my role and locked gazes with him. "Your slave has failed to lower her eyes, and she has moved herself in front of you," Cabot said with a scowl and a bite to his tone.

Damn, damn, damn!

Immediately I looked down. No fucking dogs. No fucking way.

His Gucci loafers, which coordinated perfectly with his beige Armani suit, would be great for stuffing up his—

Donovan grabbed me by my hair, and I cried out in surprise as he jerked my head back. He said in a rough tone, "Looks like I'll need one of those spanking rooms to punish slave Alexi."

My heart jumped and my scalp stung where Donovan had grabbed it. Oh, jeez. Better than Moose and Duke. Yeah, bring on the whip.

"I'll be glad to show you a room with plenty of implements for punishment, Dunning." Cabot's words grew harder. "And since it affects her so much, she most definitely needs to meet my Irish wolfhounds."

I started shaking.

Oh. My. God.

No. Fucking. Way.

Anger rushed through me and I wanted to drive my heel into his balls. And fear that we'd blow this whole operation burned through me because I would be saying "fastball" in a hurry. My safe word was all that stood between me and those wolfhounds.

Donovan damned well better come up with something.

Cabot walked on like he had a stick up his ass.

Sick sonofabitch.

Cabot led us by the two voyeur rooms, and I prayed he wasn't going to insist that Donovan use one of those rooms to punish me while crowds enjoyed the show.

When we reached the back end and got to the last of the rooms along one side of the club, Cabot entered a large room that had a St. Andrew's cross.

"Over here in these cabinets we have almost every toy imaginable." He gestured toward one of the cabinets. "Nipple clamps, candles for 'wax play,' strap-on penises, violet wands, butt plugs . . ."

I swallowed. Those were really, really big butt plugs. *Huge* butt plugs.

Cabot seemed particularly attracted to a wall with every kind of whip, flogger, paddle, or cane one could imagine. Cane. They caned people here. I'd come across it in my research. It was one of the things I hadn't seen in action. I just couldn't picture people really inflicting that amount of pain on someone else, or the sub enjoying it.

When Cabot selected a natural rattan cane that was about four feet long, I kept my head down and gritted my teeth. Rattan, the most painful, of course. Donovan better get me out of this, or I'd be partnerless because I'd kill him.

Trying not to ball my hands into fists and keeping my expression stone solid was so hard as I waited to see what would happen next.

"Remove your clothing," Cabot said, slapping the cane against his palm. "I would like to see what you're wearing beneath it for your Sire."

I didn't hesitate because I wanted to make sure Cabot didn't have any additional excuses to punish me. "Yes, Master Cabot," I said.

The pounding of my heart increased and I found I had a hard time breathing. Caned? *Caned?*

My fingers shook and I fumbled with the fasteners. It seemed to take so long before the sparkly red dress and its halter top fell away, and I was left in my red stilettos and nothing else but my leather thong and minuscule leather bra.

Cabot took the handle of the cane and hooked the opposite end along the edge of the material barely covering my breasts. He scraped my skin with the hard edge of the rattan, and I almost winced as he gave a fierce tug and dragged the material down so that both of my breasts spilled out.

Donovan! I shouted in my mind.

From the corner of my eye I saw Donovan's jaw tighten as Cabot palmed each of my breasts. "Nice size. Good shape. Perky." Cabot pinched one of my nipples, then the other, forcing them to harden. "Responds well."

Cabot extended the cane to Donovan. "You have an appealing slave."

Donovan took the cane and dragged it across my nipples, making them harder, no matter that I wanted to take the cane and shove it up Cabot's ass.

"It would be my pleasure to watch," Cabot said with lust in his tone. "And then a little play with Moose and Duke."

I couldn't help it. My head shot up and I met Cabot's olive green eyes. "No!"

He met my gaze for a long moment, his eyes narrowed. "I believe *I* should teach your slave a lesson," Cabot said, his voice now hard as a two by four. "Her rudeness is unacceptable, especially to an owner of this establishment."

Oh, shit.

"Good idea." Jason Strong, the Vin Diesel lookalike, walked in, smelling like testosterone and sex, his smooth, bare chest covered with a sheen of sweat. He grinned and punched Donovan's shoulder. "All the better to watch."

Donovan better get me out of this. He'd better get me out of—

"Tarantino, Cabot and I—like I said, we get a private show from everyone now and then." Strong slapped Donovan on the back. "A little extra payment for being allowed to join the club."

Blood drained from my face. I could feel the blood drop straight to my toes. Tarantino had walked into the room just as Strong said his name. Great.

Instead of wearing a suit, this time Tarantino was bare-chested, his muscular body tanned. He wore black leather pants with what looked like a "hatch" he could pop open so his cock would be free to do whatever he wanted with it.

Not with me. Not with me.

Right now there was a really big bulge behind that hatch. Cabot and Strong had obvious hard-ons, too, as Cabot said, "I'll do the honors, Sire Dunning, as she insulted me."

If there was ever a time for crying and begging, this was it.

Donovan's chest rose as he sucked in his breath. From beneath my eyelashes, I saw him looking at me, his eyes asking me if I wanted to go through with this or say my safe word.

Fastball. That's all I'd have to say.

But the women. The auctions. Kristin. Randolph. I had to remember why I was here. I couldn't blow it now.

I bowed my head.

"Strip, slave," Cabot said, his tone harsh. "Including your shoes."

"Yes, Master Cabot." Oh, God.

Again I found myself naked in front of virtual strangers.

"This'll be good," Strong was saying. "Just fucked two slaves and I could take on another right now."

Tarantino gave a low laugh. "Slave Alexi has nice assets."

"We should take her before Cabot gets through with her," Strong said. "She won't be much good afterward."

I said a little prayer of thanks that Cabot at least wasn't stopping to let those two men have me. But I also came up with a lot of creative curse words in my mind, especially after what Strong said about me not being much good afterward.

"Stand in the middle of the room." Cabot's voice was harsh, not amused or filled with lust anymore, like the other two.

My eyes didn't want to focus, and I barely made it to the center of the room without tripping over the stilettos I'd left on the floor. A part of me recognized there was black furniture—if it could be called real furniture, since there were, as always, straps and chains and more than I wanted to know about. The carpeting was black, too.

"You continue to earn more punishments," Cabot said with a bite to his words. "How do you respond to me, slave?"

Screw you, Cabot. "Yes, Master Cabot."

"Bend over and grab your ankles so that your ass and pussy are perfectly displayed," Cabot said.

"Y-yes, Master Cabot." I couldn't see them when I obeyed, but I was sure Cabot was talking to Donovan as he continued. "I am a renowned expert in the art of caning."

Already my eyes were watering as I held my toes, and my back started to ache as my trembling increased.

"Hmmm . . . It's important that each stroke is delivered so that they are in a narrow band." I felt a smooth palm rubbing my backside and knew it wasn't Donovan. From the thick, overwhelming cologne and the smooth hand it had to be Cabot. His hands weren't roughened in any way, proving he was a man who did nothing. "This slave is not very fleshy, so this may hurt her more than someone with a fuller figure."

I squeezed my eyes shut. Great time to have a small butt.

He lightly rubbed the cane over my skin. "Now to locate exactly the right angle to administer the blows to her posterior."

I gritted my teeth and concentrated on *my* happy thoughts.

Ripping off Cabot's balls. Snapping his neck. Chopping him into tiny pieces and shoving them down the garbage disposal. Or putting them in a blender first.

A reedlike whistle.

Contact.

The first stroke was brutal, and I almost broke my promise to myself that I wouldn't scream. It stung so much more than the whip had.

I waited for the next stroke, my body shaking. Two seconds. Six seconds. Ten secon—

Another whistle of the cane right before a blow to the same spot.

I never thought anything could match what I went through in Mexico and Cuba, but this came damned close.

And this was humiliating.

Cabot's strokes were slow but intense, powerful, and cruel. I counted every second in my mind and tensed when I reached ten. Again I'd hear the whistle of the cane before he struck me, and I'd choke back a cry.

Six times. Six excruciating times.

"I normally administer twelve, but in this case six should be enough," he said with apparent satisfaction. "Enough to teach your slave a lesson, Sire Dunning, yet not so much that you can't have at her."

Strong snorted before he said, "All four of us could have screwed her if she wasn't bleeding. I think you got a little carried away, Cabot."

I was bleeding? Cabot hadn't given me permission to straighten yet, so I was still bent at the waist, grasping my ankles.

"Yes, well." A hard slap over the cane marks. I choked back another cry and almost tipped over because of the bent position I was in. "Disobedience comes with a price," Cabot said. "She was fortunate I didn't give her all twelve strokes."

"You might as well let Dunning have at her," Tarantino said. "She needs a good fucking after that, but one will be enough."

"Leave your pants on," Cabot said, apparently to Donovan. "It will cause the slave more pain and make for increased punishment as the roughness of your clothing rubs against her wounds."

"She definitely deserves that after being so disobedient," Donovan said, with what sounded to me like a forced chuckle.

"When you are finished, bring her to Moose and Duke," Cabot said.

I was going to throw up.

Strong laughed or made some kind of asinine comment before the door slammed shut.

Silence.

Donovan's big arms were suddenly around me, and then I

was standing, holding onto him. “Signal-jammers on,” he whispered.

“I hate this job sometimes.” My voice came out cracked as I spoke against his shirt.

He kissed the top of my head. “I’m so goddamned sorry, Lexi. I wanted to beat the shit out of every one of them. You don’t know how hard it was not to.”

“Tell me about it.” I gave a harsh laugh. “I was fantasizing about feeding chunks of Cabot to the sharks. Well, the blender, actually.”

Instead of laughing, Donovan sighed and held me tighter. “What do we do now?”

I leaned fully into him. I really needed the warmth and comfort of him right then. Not only was the pain worse than when I’d been whipped, but my legs wobbled so much I could barely stand.

“We do what we have to.” I sighed. “We pretend you’re taking me like he told you to, and I scream.”

Donovan sighed.

Then I scowled. “I know where his office is, and I’m going to get what we came here for.”

CHAPTER 24

High heels, thongs, and jujitsu

April 13
Saturday late night

I'd thought the whipping was painful, but the caning made the whipping seem like a few light caresses in comparison.

Same plan as last week. After the pretend sex, with me screaming my head off, Donovan went to find Cabot to keep him occupied. I'd hurry upstairs, pick the office lock, and download every bit of information on Cabot's hard drive.

The outfit I had on now—I couldn't believe I was actually leaving the room with this on. The dungeon room's closet was filled with the raunchiest clothing—if you could call it clothing—that I'd ever seen. What I'd picked out was the best—and it sure wasn't much.

Several thin strips of leather made up the "bra." The strips spread in an array from round pieces of leather that barely covered my nipples. More strips crisscrossed above the array. Pasties would probably have covered more than the spots of leather over my nipples.

The matching thong had the same kind of strips of leather at the top, then crisscrossed so low it barely, barely covered the important parts below.

And this was the best I could do?

Better than the bras that circled the breasts and let them all hang out. I put my stilettos on to add to the look. I hadn't seen anyone barefoot in this place.

If I walked out dressed in my evening clothes, someone was bound to notice. Blending in was on the menu.

I just hoped some Dom wouldn't ignore protocol and try to put me on *his* menu like these other men had.

Before I left the room, I removed my collar and hurried to take out a pinpoint of an injection needle to knock out the guard at the top of the stairs.

Martinez was damned useful when it came to coming up with the coolest stuff.

Hiding the thing was *almost* impossible. There was barely enough material to my thong, just below my mound, to arrange it along the edge. Jeez, I hoped it didn't slip so that I ended up knocking myself out.

Every movement I made while dressing, then walking, was so painful my eyes stung. Once I put it back on, my collar seemed to choke me as I walked out of the room. Suddenly my stilettos weren't as easy to walk in, as I winced with every step.

I'd thought it before and I could imagine myself doing it repeatedly—if I had the chance to shove that cane up Cabot's ass, I'd ram it through his guts and into his throat.

When I got close to the dance floor with all the slaves humping poles, two men urged me to get on stage. But I showed them my cane marks, and told them my Sire was waiting and would cane me again if I didn't hurry to the ladies' room and get back to him as soon as I could.

The Doms checked out my backside, where the huge blood-streaked welts were, and shook their heads when they saw what Cabot had done to me.

"You're ruined for tonight, babe," one of the guys said.

I ground my teeth and kept my gaze lowered.

The way air touched my breasts, waist, pelvis, and backside, I felt like I was wearing nothing but the stilettos and collar. Might as well have been naked, but at least it was something. I suppose.

It seemed like a journey and a half before I reached the sweeping marble staircase that so did not go with this sex pit.

With a casual look beneath my lashes it didn't seem like anyone noticed me by the stairs. I started up, hoping with each step no one would stop me. I was mostly silent, but the pounding music covered up any noise until I reached the halfway point that was the crossover area from one version of hell to another. On my way up I pressed the stud for the signal-jammers.

Relief caused the tenseness in my chest to relax for a moment when I reached the top and I smiled when the bald bouncer/guard came up to me, arms crossed and a mean look on his badass face.

My smile was sweet and oh-so-innocent as I moved close to him. "I'm trying to find the ladies' room." I brushed my fingers over my breasts and down to my thong. "This outfit is chafing me. I think I have it on wrong."

His gaze followed my movements, and even though his expression didn't change, the bulge in his pants sure did.

"Maybe you can help me," I said as I got him to look at my face while I slipped the minuscule injection needle from my thong. I leaned close to him. "I mean, with this outfit."

His scowl turned into a grin as I took one of his hands and placed it on my breast. "Right here is where I need help." At the same time I jabbed the tiny syringe into his thigh.

He blinked. Confusion clouded his features and his hand dropped away from my breast. I ran my finger down the middle of his chest straight to his cock, which I cupped and squeezed. "You're going to stay right here and do your job. You never saw me and never will. I'm invisible to you," I whispered near his ear.

He looked around and frowned, like he didn't know where my voice had come from.

I allowed myself a little smile of victory as I stuffed the syringe into his pocket. He could wonder where it came from later, and no one would be able to break down the elements that made up the potion. In fifteen minutes it would turn to water.

Our medical lab, and Martinez, were brilliant.

Chopin flowed from the invisible speakers as I glanced at my surroundings. The three cameras had to be scrambled by the signal-jammers. Now to get into Cabot's office.

Damn, his lock was tough. I kept feeling like something was crawling up my spine as I struggled with unlocking it.

The tumblers finally clicked. There. Not so bad.

The signal-jammers had taken care of any kind of alarm RED had encountered in the past. I was safe.

After I locked the door behind me I took a quick look around like I had in Strong's office. At least there were a couple of doors in here, probably leading to a closet and a storage area, where I could hide if I heard a key in the lock.

No time to worry about that now.

I unhooked my collar and pulled out the copying device, and hurried to slip the connection into the computer's port. The end of the device blinked. It was downloading.

Hurry, hurry, hurry.

A feeling like centipedes crawling over my skin had me straightening.

Not good.

Something wasn't right.

It felt like the centipedes now tickled the back of my neck and crawled into my hair and over my scalp.

Call it cop-sense or whatever, but I had no doubts at all.

I was being watched.

No. Oh, no.

The cameras in the room looked functional and were aimed at me. What about the signal-jammers?

One of the two doors burst open, and three men armed with AK-47s rushed through.

AK-47s? What the—

And they had their weapons trained on me.

Three on one.

My heart raced and adrenaline made my skin vibrate.

"Uh, hi?" I said as I fumbled with the collar that I was still holding. "I'm just looking for Master Cabot."

Like reading Braille, my fingers were moving over the collar as I spoke. I had to find and press the button to call in RED, because in that moment I knew there would be no way to get my butt out of this mess. Was it this stud? No, that was the camera. Damnit, why didn't I pay better attention? Talk about sex with Donovan scrambling my brains. How about—

"Don't move, lady," one of the men growled.

I caught my breath and stilled as three more men burst into Cabot's office from the foyer.

I was so screwed.

There were half a dozen men pointing their handguns and rifles at me.

Then Cabot walked past the men who had come through the door of his office.

Deadly. The only thing that could be said about his expression.

The centipedes I'd felt earlier now scrambled up my throat.

From behind Cabot, Donovan was shoved into the room, three weapons aimed at his head. Donovan's expression was total fury. His hands were cuffed behind his back.

Oh, yeah. We were good and screwed.

Ice in Cabot's eyes sent a chill straight through me. His cold voice stabbed my chest like icicles.

"Come here, *slave* Alexi." Cabot's stare was so intense, and the cold that encased me so frigid, that I wanted to rub my arms. "Come to me. Now."

I stayed behind the desk, pushing every damned stud on the collar while I stared at him. I could swear it was the one to the right—

"I tire of waiting." Cabot glanced at one of the men, who had a vicious smile on his face. A smile that made me shudder. "Get her, Danny," Cabot said to the man.

Two steps and the man had the barrel of his Beretta pressed against my temple.

Steady, Steele. Steady. I swallowed. Nothing was ever hopeless. Breathe.

"You know I don't actually plan to kill you, *slave* Alexi." Cabot gave a smile reserved for his clients. "I have a much better use for you in mind."

Funny how my hands remained steady as I clenched the collar, despite the fact that six guns pinned me down. *Peel the stud off, idiot.* I popped off the stud.

Donovan looked like he was going to come unglued, even though he had three handguns pressed to the back of his head and he was cuffed.

"Do *not* screw with me." Cabot held his hands loosely at his sides. He made a quick scan of the room, meeting the eyes of every man pointing a gun at me. "Don't shoot her. I'll deal with this bitch."

The man with the vicious smile grabbed my arm and jerked me from behind the desk. I stumbled sideways in my heels and dropped the collar.

When I wasn't behind the desk any more, Cabot studied me as I took step after step toward him in my stiletto heels. I didn't wobble. I didn't tremble as I reached Cabot, maybe a foot in front of him.

"The moment you picked that lock, I was notified." He smirked. "Your scramblers didn't work on all of my equipment. Oh, yes, we have the technology to recognize signal scramblers. We have technology you'd never dream of."

Yeah, whatever.

One of his hands flexed. He was getting ready to punch me and I could tell he was looking forward to it. But he kept his voice steady. "No doubt you managed to obtain the information about the merchandise shipment on Thursday. You cost me tens of thousands of dollars."

"A little slow on the uptake, Cabot?" I was inches from him now and gave him a smirk.

Cabot's face flushed red as he drove his fist toward me. My moves were smooth and automatic from my twenty-three years of jujitsu training.

One twist of his arm, one sweep of my foot, and he was on his back. His head hit the carpeted floor with a loud thump.

He shouted and started to get up. I jabbed my high heel straight at his throat.

The SOB was faster than I expected, and my heel hit his collarbone instead.

Cabot grabbed my opposite ankle. I lost my footing and he jerked me off my feet.

My teeth clinked as I hit the floor. I automatically rolled

to the side. Where he had caned me stung like crazy, and it only pissed me off more.

Cabot lunged for me and grasped my neck.

He gave a shout that was almost a scream as I shot my knee up, barely missing his groin but hitting the inside of his thigh. I twisted and flipped him over my head.

I was on my back and started to roll to my feet when I heard several sharp clicks close enough that my skin crawled. I went still and raised my eyes. Six guns were trained on me. Again.

My heart raced as I looked up into the calm faces of men who had no compunctions about killing.

Like me.

The sudden burn and flash of pain caught me off guard as I was yanked to my feet by my hair. Cabot swung me around to face him.

Pain burst in my head as he slammed his fist into the side of my skull. Skin split and blood started dripping down my face.

I tried to defend myself, to fight back, but two men grabbed my arms and kept me in place as Cabot attacked me.

A kick to my belly.

Another powerful kick. This one into my solar plexus.

Black spots moved in and out as I choked and went limp while the men held me from behind.

The ringing in my ears made it hard to hear, but I caught the words, "Release her," from Cabot.

As soon as the men let go, my knees gave out and I dropped to the floor.

My sight blurred and my muscles fought me as I tried to get up.

You've been through worse, Lexi. *Get up.*

I started to push myself up just enough to lunge for his ankles.

Cabot's face was bloody, bruised from what I'd done to him. Red stains streaked his beige Armani suit. He knelt, grasped me by my throat, and dug his fingers in. "Who. Do. You. Work. For?"

I struggled to take a breath. "Fuck. You."

Vaguely I was aware of Donovan fighting, even with his hands cuffed. Blood was in my eyes from the cut at the side of my head, and I could barely see. My muscles wouldn't cooperate enough for me to struggle against the two men pressing my shoulders to the floor.

Despite those cuffs, Donovan was doing a damned good job fighting every man who came near him as he tried to get to me. He used his elbows, his head, his shoulders, his steel-toed shitkickers.

Cabot probably hadn't killed Donovan—yet—because he wanted information.

But then a shot rang out and Donovan shouted. Through the blood dripping down my face into my eyes, I could make out the growing wet spot on Donovan's thigh, and knew he'd been shot.

Cabot jerked me by my hair again, so that I was looking up at him, my backside still on the floor. "If you tell me who you work for," he said, "I won't kill your partner."

"Don't tell him a goddamned thing," Donovan shouted in a furious, if pained, growl.

Before I had a chance to catch another breath or register the pain, Cabot jammed his foot into my chest with incredible force.

A rib cracked.

A long groan escaped from me as I rolled onto my side and felt the sick grinding sensation of bone against bone in my chest.

If I lived through this, Cabot would die.

By my hands.

Despite everything, I tried to fight against the men holding me down.

"Whoever you work for—right now I don't give a damn. They'll never find you." Cabot crouched in front of me, wearing a furious, hideous smile. "You're going to be auctioned once you're fit. I'll make a nice deal on that pretty ass of yours. Won't be enough to cover what you cost me, but I think you'll bring a decent amount."

He looked up at one of his men. "Remove the bitch. Use the tunnel." Cabot glared at me with such fury I thought he might kill me now. "Unfortunately she's damaged, so we'll have to let her heal before she's put on the block."

Donovan still fought against the men who held him down, and I might have smiled if my face wasn't frozen with pain. You had to admire a man who'd try to go up against nearly a dozen men to help his partner, even wounded and cuffed.

"Oh, and one more thing to remember today by, bitch." Cabot slammed his shoe against my forearm. Bone snapped. I screamed and threw up all over the carpet. The acidic stench of vomit mixed with the coppery scent of my blood and the smell of carpet freshener.

"Do it!" Cabot shouted. "Get her out of here."

One of the men grabbed me by my other arm and yanked so hard he dislocated my shoulder. Impossibly more pain screamed through my shoulder, and then he jerked me by my hair.

It seemed like forever since I'd started fighting Cabot, before his men held me. Probably all of ten minutes and I was done in. Broken. Beaten.

In the background I heard the sounds of the remaining men taking Donovan down.

I cradled my broken arm to my chest and clenched my teeth against the pain in my shoulder and my ribs. Pure agony tore through me as the man Cabot had called Danny dragged me by my hair through a door and into a dark tunnel.

Vaguely I heard Cabot's voice behind as he followed us while giving one of his men instructions.

In the growing distance I was sure I heard shouts of "Police!"

My thoughts swam. Thank God. RED had made it. I'd used the collar right.

But the door slammed shut, followed by the grating sound of metal doors and more metal, and the clunks and scraping of giant locks.

RED wouldn't be able to get to me through that door in time. They wouldn't be able to save me.

Now the only sounds were footsteps and whimpering as I was dragged by my hair.

Then I heard and saw nothing as I started to fade.

The whimpers echoing in the darkness were my own.

—black it stood as night,
Fierce as ten furies, terrible as hell,
And shook a dreadful dart; what seem'd his head
The likeness of a kingly crown had on.
Satan was now at hand.

John Milton (1608–74)
Paradise Lost, Book ii

CHAPTER 25

Nick

April 13
Saturday late night

So much rage filled Nick that he barely felt the bullet in his thigh or the fists of the men slamming into him as he fought to get across the room to the door Lexi had been taken through.

Nick's head connected with one man's jaw. He rammed his boot into a third man's gut. Blood throbbed in Nick's head so hard he barely heard Cabot's men's shouts or screams when he managed to land a blow.

One of Cabot's men punched Nick in the kidneys and stars sparked behind his eyes. He nearly doubled over from the pain.

Another jammed his foot against the bullet wound in Nick's thigh. The fucking pain was so great he dropped to one knee.

All he had to do was remind himself that Lexi had already gone through far worse than he was going through right now.

The images racing through his mind gave him the strength to fight harder even with his hands cuffed.

Cabot. Beating Lexi while two men held her.

Her crumpled, broken body.

Men dragging her through a door and out of his sight.

Nick let out a bellow of fury and lunged to his feet despite the men trying to hold him down.

RED agents had better get here soon because he had to

get to Lexi. The moment he'd come into the room, he'd pressed the special catch on one leather cuff to notify RED that the operation had gone FUBAR. Lexi might not have had the chance to trip her own call and they wouldn't be able to find her.

Over ten minutes and counting. Any second.

Pain exploded in Nick's head like a spray of white liquid as one of the bastards hit him upside the head with the butt of his gun.

Nick collapsed to his knees. Tried to get back up. But the men full-body tackled him. Smells of blood and male sweat filled his nostrils.

"Police!"

New shouts erupted in the room and Nick went slack with momentary relief before coming up swinging. He shoved his way out of the pile of men who had him down but were now scrambling to face the RED agents.

Shots echoed in the foyer. Nick knocked himself into one of the men before he could move and rolled them both behind the desk out of the line of fire.

The man growled and tried to get to his feet. Nick balanced on the knee of his leg that wasn't shot up and elbowed the Glock away from the man. Then he slammed his forehead against the other man's, knocking the guy out cold.

Nick remained on his knees, keeping out of sight behind the desk. He leaned around the desk and saw RED agents taking down every man.

Now only a couple of men remained between Nick and RED's agents. Looked like the agents now had everything under control. Pain forced Nick to rest on his ass a few seconds, his hands on his bent knees, but he still held onto the Glock.

When the shooting stopped, Nick shouted, "On the job," for the benefit of any agent who might not recognize him. Damned if he wanted to get shot again. "Special Agent Donovan."

"Weapons down," came the familiar voice of Takamoto. "Donovan's our inside man."

Takamoto appeared around the corner of the desk and

looked at Nick before shouting over his shoulder. "Clear." He looked back at Nick. "Where's Agent Steele?"

"Took you fucking long enough to get here." Nick pushed himself up, vaguely aware of the pain in his thigh, his body, and the blood dripping from his face "Uncuff me," he yelled at Takamonto. The moment he was uncuffed, Nick was already hurrying toward the door Lexi had disappeared through.

Nick called over his shoulder as he tried not to limp. "Cabot's men took her and we need to go after the sonsofbitches."

In the background he heard agents raiding the place as they rushed down the stairs outside Cabot's office. But Nick was sure Cabot had been expecting them and no doubt everyone had cleared out the moment they caught Lexi downloading the info.

Nick reached the door and grasped the handle. Locked. He stepped back and had put six bullets into the doorjamb before he could get it to open.

He rushed into the tunnel but came to a complete halt when a sound like thunder rolled over him and dust started falling from the ceiling. The entire entrance to the tunnel started to shake and rock, tossing Nick against one wall.

The whole tunnel seemed to shudder and shake as if Boston was having an earthquake. Rocks and pieces of concrete showered from the ceiling. A good-sized chunk slammed into Nick's shoulder and he stumbled to the side again.

Someone grabbed his shirt from behind and jerked him backward and out of the tunnel just in time to avoid being pounded by a bowling ball-sized hunk of cement.

Nick stared at the tunnel as more and more debris crashed down. "What the hell?"

"Booby-trapped, best guess," Takamoto said over the crashing of rock as the tunnel ceiling came down. Dust billowed through the doorway. Takamoto released the back of Nick's shirt. "Bet it'll take a while to clear the tunnel and get to wherever it leads to. Cabot and most of the other pricks are probably already on their way out of Boston."

"They've got Steele." Nick raised his fist and damn near slammed it into the marble wall of the foyer. Wouldn't do any good to try to find Lexi or Kristin with a broken hand, so instead he wiped some of the blood from his face onto his jeans. "Steele was kicking Cabot's ass before he had two men hold her down. He hurt her bad." Nick rubbed his temples as his gut clenched at the thought. "I think Cabot broke her arm and did a hell of a lot more damage than that."

"Holy shit." Smithe wiped his hand over his mouth. "Steele would have killed the bastard if he'd had the balls to fight her himself."

It was getting harder and harder for Nick to keep himself from hitting something. "She was doing a damned good job of it until Cabot's men got a hold of her."

"We need a medic to take a look at you, Donovan." Takamoto looked Nick over like he was assessing the damage.

"Screw the medics," Nick growled as he used the back of his hand to wipe more blood off his face.

"You'll have to wait for that until your leg is taken care of," Smithe said. "Then you can do whatever you want. I think the blond in narcotics and weapons trafficking has a thing for you."

Nick clenched his fists. "Fuck you."

"I'm taken," Smithe said with a grin this time.

Nick glared at the shithead. Smithe would make a good punching bag and he could use one right now.

He winced when Smithe slapped him on the shoulder where the chunk of concrete had hit him. But Smithe's expression was serious. "We'll find Steele. We'll get her back."

Memories of how badly Lexi had been injured slammed into Nick. He leaned back against a wall and repeated, "He hurt her bad. Real bad."

"Hey." Smithe stood in front of Nick and met his gaze. "If Cabot wanted to kill her she'd be dead and he never would have taken her down that tunnel. We'll find her."

The physical rush from the fight was leaving Nick's body. "I hope to God we find her in one piece."

Paramedics were already being guided into the room. Nick barely saw their faces—his mind continued to roll through what had happened and to consider the possibilities of where she could be now.

He had no goddamned idea where to start.

A pair of paramedics forced him to sit, took his vitals and wrapped his wounded leg and the blood-drenched pants around the hole where he'd been shot. He grew a little light-headed and had the sense to realize he'd lost some blood. As much as he wanted to go on a rampage the loss of blood was getting to him.

Nick refused to go out on a stretcher, instead limping his way out through the now empty club. The soundproof round foyer had cut off any possible noises from sirens or patrons being "escorted" from the club. But as he hobbled out the glare of lights and sound just reminded him of how badly he and Lexi had fucked up.

Nick

April 14

Sunday early morning

After a debriefing with a senior RED agent, Nick found himself alone sitting upright on the couch in Kristin's home. No Kristin. No Lexi.

Dixie stalked past, her tail in the air.

Nick glared at the calico.

Then Dixie did something she'd never done before. She padded up to him and rubbed herself against his legs—like she was comforting him. She didn't purr, just rubbed past one way, turned around and rubbed his legs coming from the other side. Then she left the room, her tail still high.

Nick shook his head and dragged his hand down his face. He'd had a pair of jogging shorts in his SUV that he had in a suitcase he kept under the seat in case he needed the clothing for one reason or another. Not wearing jeans kept the pressure off his thigh for now.

Screw painkillers. Nick needed to keep his mind sharp to

figure out where Lexi and Kristin were. Now not only was the image of his younger sister in his mind, but the vivid memory of Lexi being dragged away. What Cabot had done to her—

Nick pushed himself up from Kristin's couch and looked for something to hit. If he was at his own home in Arizona, he could go out in the desert and shoot something.

Here—he couldn't trash his sister's house.

But a fucking pillow—that he could replace.

He took one of her couch pillows, braced his knee on her couch, ignoring the pain in his thigh. He proceeded to beat the holy living shit out of the pillow, picturing Cabot's face. With each punch Nick shouted every curse that came to him.

Stuffing shot out of a ripped seam and the pillow grew flatter and flatter. When nothing was left but fuzz on the couch and the floor, Nick snatched another pillow. This time he saw the wavy, gray image of a man—whatever man had "purchased" Kristin. Nick shouted and punched the second pillow over and over and over again until it died, too.

The rage burning inside him blinded him to everything but the burn in his muscles as punched. And punched. And punched.

When there were no more pillows left in Kristin's living room to kill, Nick stood in the middle of all of the stuffing and wiped sweat from his face with his palm.

Dixie was at the end of the couch batting at a piece of stuffing and pouncing on it.

Nick rolled his eyes to the ceiling.

If he wouldn't lose so much blood that he'd probably pass out, he'd go for a jog right now and wouldn't stop until he'd calmed down enough to figure out where to start looking for Kristin and Lexi. That would have been a good fifteen miles at the least, thirty round-trip.

Nick avoided kicking Kristin's furniture and kicked a pile of fluff instead which sure as hell wasn't satisfying. He glanced down at his thigh and the bandage was soaked through, pretty much solid red.

Goddamnit.

He'd be fucking worthless if he didn't calm down and take care of business. Including himself.

Sonofabitch. He didn't have time for this shit.

Nick
April 15
Monday morning

"The team should have been there a hell of a lot faster than they made it Saturday night." Nick barely kept his voice under control as he tried not to limp while he paced in front of Karen Oxford's desk. "Steele wouldn't be missing if RED's response time hadn't been crap."

"Thirteen minutes and RED was inside." Oxford folded her arms across her chest as she leaned back in her chair. "An acceptable response time."

"Five minutes too long." Nick smacked one fist into his palm. "All I know is Steele is hurt real bad, that Cabot's got her, and we could have saved her ass by minutes."

"Agent Donovan." Oxford's cool voice brought Nick to a stop in his pacing. "All RED agents know the risks involved in working any kind of undercover op. What we must concern ourselves with now is retrieving Steele and bringing down the rest of Cabot's operation."

"Got him in the balls with the Glass Slipper," Nick said with only a little satisfaction. "He owns a couple more around the city and just maybe Steele is at one of those. Unless there's something I don't know, we weren't able to gather the intel on exactly which clubs he owns." Nick rubbed his hand over his face. "Shit, we don't even know if he's still in the area."

Karen Oxford picked up a pen and started tapping it on her desk. "Find Cabot and we will find Agent Steele."

Nick let out a rush of air in a heavy exhale. "I need access to all the intel from *Operation Cinderella* from the past three months."

Oxford gave a clipped nod. "You have free rein."

"One more thing." Nick turned his head just enough that

his glare might as well have pierced the wall to see the agents monitoring locations linked to specific illegal activities. "I want to kick some junior agent ass."

Nick scowled as he looked back at Oxford and her eyebrows were raised in a questioning look. He gave her the rundown on his own surveillance vid and how the incident had to match what happened to his sister when she was abducted.

"RED agents should have been all over that." Nick was tempted to draw his Beretta and scare the shit out of that junior agent. "I want Wallings's ass. Now."

"There was absolutely no excuse for his error." Oxford narrowed her brows. "I will deal with him. We do not accept nor tolerate subpar agents in RED. We hire and keep only the best."

"Not only do I want those operational records," Nick said. "I want a team of eight agents that I handpick for these two assignments. I want four on Kristin Donovan's case and four on Agent Steele's."

"You've got your teams and your records." Oxford gestured to the door. "And you have your work cut out for you."

CHAPTER 26

Is my salary enough for this?

April 14

Sunday. I only know because someone told me.

Pain shot through my head as light blinded me. Light through fog. Couldn't be heaven because after being an assassin I was destined for hell.

Brilliant white light. A white room. I thought. In the haze I wasn't sure.

It couldn't be the room where the men forced me to be an assassin. No. God, no.

All I was positive about was that my entire body hurt in every place imaginable. I was nothing but pain.

As it brushed my skin, warm air carried familiar smells.

Antiseptic. A medicinal odor.

Cologne.

The cologne was the smell I hated the most, because it belonged to the man I hated the most.

A face wavered in and out over me. Concentrating was so hard it hurt. Cold, then heat, washed over me as I recognized Satan.

Benjamin Cabot.

Vaguely I was aware my right arm felt almost too heavy to move. A cast.

The pain in my left shoulder was so great I wanted to scream. Dislocated. The guy named Danny who'd dragged me had jerked it out of its socket.

"I wanted to make sure you're awake for this part, Alexi."

Cabot smiled, then looked up at a man with a surgical mask on. "Dr. Rogers, your patient," Cabot said to the man.

"I'll take care of her, Mr. Cabot." The doctor reached for me and I became more aware of the focused pain in my dislocated shoulder.

"No." I knew what he was going to do. While I was awake. I shook my head so hard that I almost threw up from the pain just moving my head caused me. "Please. No."

Dr. Rogers grasped my shoulder and I cried out. He examined it with his fingers and hands, and I wanted to scream from every touch.

The man wrenched and twisted my shoulder into place.

I screamed so loud my throat and chest hurt. Agony. Sheer agony.

Oh, my God. Take me.

And blackness did.

April 15
Monday

I was sitting on something cold.

My arm was cradled against my belly. A cast. My right arm was in a cast and pain shot through my forearm. I almost cried at the memory of a man jerking my shoulder back into place, but I had to admit that at least my shoulder felt better now.

My arm itched beneath the cast and I wanted to scratch it. Wouldn't have had the strength to even if I could.

The wobbling in my head made it hard to focus as I tried to figure out where I was and what I was sitting on. I tried to pry my eyes open. All they would part was a slit. I was in someplace dark.

"You need to relieve yourself." A sweet voice. Not Cabot's devil's voice.

Relieve myself? Relieve myself. Oh.

I let go and emptied. A tissue was put into my left hand. Left . . . Oh, right one was in a cast. My left hand shook but managed to wipe.

Then I toppled off the cold seat and welcomed the dark again.

April 16
Tuesday

Water. Lapping at my waist, covering my legs. Warm, welcome. Lightening some of the pain.

Hands scrubbed my body with—a washcloth? Gentle hands. But still my body ached.

The swaying of the water made my head feel like it was swaying, too. My eyes—stuck. Glued together.

"What is your name?" came the sweet voice. "You never answer me."

My lips seem glued, too. Maybe it would be too much of an effort to speak. Maybe that was why I couldn't open my mouth.

"I am Alyona," the girl said. A Russian accent. "I have been caring for you. Sometimes you wake, sometimes you are in a place between wake and sleep and don't know what it is you do. Bathe. Drink water and broth. Relieve yourself. And sleep. They always drug you."

It hurt to focus on what she was saying as I tried to make sense of her words.

Then warm water spilled down my scalp, hurting but healing, too. "As always we must take care not to wet your cast or the bandages around your chest."

Yes, my heavy arm was propped on something. The warm water only went as far as my waist and my chest felt tight, constricted.

"I am sorry, but I must wash your hair." She squirted something cool on my scalp and began soaping it. "The cuts and bruises—they must hurt so."

Alyona was so gentle, yet the pain was incredible as she lathered my hair.

Sleep would be better.

April 17
Wednesday

The broth was plain and it didn't want to go down. I didn't want it. I just knew I was sick of it. But Alyona insisted. And she gave me water. Helped me up to relieve myself.

Helped me climb into bed and pass back into oblivion.

April 18
Thursday

Did I wake today? I must have.

I think, therefore I am.

Am I?

April 19
Friday

Did I really exist? The world tilted and wouldn't right itself. A snow globe with swirling white flakes tipping to the side.

Floating . . . floating . . . floating . . .

What was right or normal? Was anything real? Or was it all just . . . nothing.

Pain was real. Constant pain.

I was there. I wasn't. I was nothing at all. Nothing but pain.

Yet beyond the haze and agony there was a life that was mine. I did have a place in the world. The world that wouldn't stop tilting.

Pain. So intense.

Must be alive. To feel such pain, I must be alive.

No lying to myself anymore.

"What's your name?" came a small voice. Alyona. "One day you will tell me."

Sweet, singsong, her voice should have made me smile. Instead it echoed in my head and I wanted to scream.

I was gone again.

April 20
Saturday

"Are you awake?" the delicate voice asked through the darkness of my mind. "We must get you up to attend to your bath."

No pain. I didn't wince at the sound of the voice.

Progress.

What progress was that? Nothing made sense. Here. There. What was what?

"They make you sleep, sleep, sleep." Yes, a Russian accent. Her name—Alyona, right?

"They have kept you drugged long." Alyona sounded concerned, confused, even as she continued. "Maybe it is because you suffered much. They wait for you to heal."

The dryness of my throat made it ache when I tried to swallow. It hurt almost as badly as the rest of my body. Yes, I ached. I felt it now. So much so that I whimpered behind my closed lips.

A small hand gently touched my arm. "Your color is much better and you breathe without so much labor."

Yeah. She was right. My ribs still hurt with every inhale and exhale, but it was better.

I sucked in another breath. Jeez, that hurt.

Alyona moved close. She smelled sweet and delicate.

I had a life outside this pain, right? Beyond the fuzz fogging my mind.

My lips parted as my throat worked. I sucked in air, gasped, and coughed.

Christ. Wasn't there a single part of me that didn't feel like I'd been hit by a train?

"You need water." Alyona put something cool against my lips, and thirst hit me hard and sudden. I might crumble to dust if I didn't have a drink. Now.

Give me. Now. Now. Now.

Cool water flowed through my parched lips. Alyona was pouring it into my mouth. Only a little, like she was holding back.

More. Goddamnit, *more*!

When did I raise my head?

More.

Something anchored my right arm. Couldn't raise it.

My left hand moved, though. It shook as it reached the paper cup.

Water down the sides of my mouth. Down my neck. Wetting my chest.

More, more.

Water droplets rolled over my breasts. No clothes. I was naked beneath a light blanket.

"Slow." Alyona drew the glass away and a scream of frustration nearly tore through me. "You have never tried to force it so fast before. Perhaps it is because you are getting better."

"Now, slowly." Alyona brought the cup to my lips again and I gulped what water she gave me. "You will vomit if you don't. A little at a time."

She took the glass away from my lips.

My whole body was collapsing in on itself. Too much. It had taken too much out of me. To drink the water, raise my head, lift my hand.

"Thank you," I whispered.

I heard the smile in her voice as she said, "Finally, you speak."

The sound of a lock clicking was followed by the screech of unoiled door hinges. I winced. Alyona moved away from me.

"The bitch is awake." Who was it? I knew that voice. In my daily nightmares that voice always came. I hated whoever it was.

"Not for long," said another male. "Just get her into the shower and that needle back into her arm."

Get your eyes open. My jaws hurt when I ground my teeth while fighting to raise my eyelids.

Someone lifted my left arm. The one that didn't feel like a gorilla was sitting on it.

Everything was a blur when I finally pried my eyes open. I saw a plain room with a door to a bathroom. The men holding me got me into the tub.

Alyona bathed me. This time I realized the men were standing there, watching.

I still couldn't tell Alyona my name when she asked.

April 21

Sunday. I haven't a clue what time and don't care.

What a godawful nightmare.

"Jesus Christ." My words came out in a low croak through my aching throat. It was damned near impossible to swallow.

Open your eyes. What was that crust crap gluing them

together? Someone might as well have jerked them open with a crowbar, as bad as it hurt when I managed to get them open.

Nothing but a blur. The gunk in my eyes was like looking through a thick fog.

One breath. Another. It so hurt to breathe. Did one part of me not ache?

Blink. Blink away the gunk. There, everything came into focus.

I frowned. It looked like I was in some kind of hotel room with boarded-up windows.

Before, I couldn't open my eyes. Now I couldn't get myself to close them.

Every lump in the mattress beneath my back bruised my skin, and I felt pain at the bottom of my backside. The caning on top of everything else. A dizzying sensation wanted to take me away to some kind of black hole.

Maybe I wanted that. Maybe I wanted the black hole to swallow me. Maybe I didn't want to face reality.

Because I knew there was a reality beyond this threadbare room. A new reality. A reality I didn't want.

A reality I would find a way to overcome.

But . . . what—when—how did I get here? The how and why touched the fringes of my mind like cold fungus.

And days . . . days of broth and water and the toilet and baths . . . it all seemed surreal.

I'd been here awhile, but I'd never been so aware since I came to this place. What place?

Deep breath. Face more reality, Steele.

For some reason it hadn't occurred to me that I had a name.

Lexi Steele.

Lexi.

My chest hurt when I held my breath before turning my head to my right. A worn-out chair next to a nightstand with a reading lamp.

A flash of memories hit me from nowhere. A flood of memories. I had a partner. Donovan. Nick Donovan. I worked for—for an organization called RED. I was a special agent and was an assassin. Yes, that was me.

I was a killer.

More memories bombarded me and I wanted to hold my stomach with both hands.

Cabot.

Every blow to my body came as clear to me as if he was beating me now.

Being auctioned to the highest bidder.

He was going to auction me like he had sold Donovan's sister.

Your new reality, Steele.

Bullshit.

Pull yourself together. Analyze the situation.

Escape.

Not a single person could control my future. No one controlled Lexi Steele.

I'd been through worse.

Yet the pounding of my heart made my chest ache. How could I feel more pain?

But the pain was less than it had been when Cabot had beaten me. SOB hadn't been able to fight me without having two men hold me. Coward.

Time to assess. A cry and a gasp almost tore through me as I tried to push myself up to a sitting position and pain shot through my right arm. Something heavy encased it from my wrist to my upper arm.

A cast. Cabot had broken my arm. The pain in my lower chest and sides was thanks to the ribs he'd cracked when he kicked me. The tightness that made it even harder to breathe came from bandages wrapped around my chest.

My left shoulder hurt like hell, and I winced at the memory of it being dislocated and put back into place.

One thing after another flashed through my mind, and my heart felt like someone was twisting a stake in it. I wanted to scream as my chest rose and fell, harsh and fast, with my breathing. I was hyperventilating.

"Calm down, Steele," I growled at myself, and concentrated on slowing my breathing. Deep inhale. Slow exhale.

I swore in six different languages.

My breathing quickened again.

Okay, the freaking out and releasing every swearword I could think of didn't help.

It took all the strength I had in my left arm to push myself up, my right arm cradled against me. My left arm shook so bad from the pain in my shoulder.

Hallelujah. I managed to sit.

The light blanket fell to my waist and my stomach curdled. I was naked. It seemed like every bit of my fair skin had pale, yellowing bruises. Shadows of them, really.

How long had I been here? Wherever here was.

With the sick feeling my constant friend, I looked at the cast.

The curdling from my stomach jumped into my throat.

Cabot had signed it.

To the newest treasure of my collection.

Benjamin.

Sick bastard.

Sick, sick, sick bastard.

I'd put away a serial killer, the Harvester, who liked to eat his victims in small pieces. I'd be happy to do the honors as I indulged in my fantasy of chopping Cabot into tiny chunks myself. I'd be pleased to feed them to the man waiting on death row. Harvey might want a farewell snack.

No way was Cabot getting away with this. There would be a way to escape. I'd find it. Then I'd bring him down.

RED allowed us to use any force necessary.

Any force.

This would be necessary.

I'd do it even if it wasn't necessary.

Voices. Creaking door hinges followed. I had to figure things out. Couldn't let them know I'd woken. The lumpy mattress became my friend, along with the threadbare blanket, as I pretended to sleep.

"Bitch is still out of it," a now-familiar voice said as the door to the room squeaked open. Danny. I'd kill him after Cabot.

A girl cried out and her body hit mine as she was flung

into the room. Oh crap. My left arm. I gritted my teeth, clenching them hard enough to send a shooting pain through my head. I couldn't move, couldn't make a sound, or they'd know I was awake.

I wasn't ready for that, yet.

The doors slammed shut.

The girl crawled onto the mattress beside me and sobbed, her whole body shaking.

Flashes of memories came to me—a girl had taken care of me. Fed me. Bathed me. Helped me on the toilet.

"Alyona?" I kept my voice low as I opened my eyes and looked at the girl who had her back to me.

A loud sniffle. Her shoulders shook. "You are awake." Another sob. A moment passed before she spoke again in her strong Russian accent, and rolled to face me. "I—I worried for you."

She looked . . . familiar.

I caught my breath. She was the same dark-haired girl I'd seen abducted and thrown into a van on one of Donovan's monitors.

"Thank you for taking care of me." I reached up and brushed her cheek with my fingertips. She was model-beautiful. "How long have I been here?"

Alyona scrunched her eyebrows. "It is Sunday, yes?" she seemed to ask herself, then nodded. "Yes. A week yesterday it has been since you were brought to this"—her voice caught—"this prison."

"A week?" My voice rose before I could keep it down. I let my hand fall away from her face and forced my voice to go lower. "Are you sure?"

She nodded. "They put a needle in your arm every day after I cared for you, to make you sleep. They said"—her voice shook—"they said you needed to heal before . . . before they turned you into . . ." Her voice quavered again and I heard the tears. "Merchandise. Like me."

She continued. "I am not supposed to be touched until I—I am delivered to my new owner. But—it just now was not so."

"I'm sorry. I'm so, so sorry." The kind of feeling that rushed through me now was hot and fluid. I'd never felt anything like this. Not even when I faced pain beyond pain. Not even when the crap was beaten out of me the two times I'd screwed up after assassinations.

One man in Mexico.

Another man in Cuba.

My "employers" never telling me why I had to kill these men.

Both men were history, but I'd been tortured to hell and back by their men.

Still, I escaped.

Now, here in the good ol' US of A, Cabot considered me merchandise to auction off.

No fucking way.

What I'd said about hopelessness? No such thing. Unless you're dead, there's hope.

The pain in my ribs wasn't easy to ignore when I sucked in my breath. "They didn't drug me today?"

Alyona looked cute and young despite the tears and weariness on her features, and the fact that she'd just been raped. She looked eighteen at most.

We would have time for questions later, when I could do something about the mess I was in. The mess all of the girls were in.

I would make sure any women who might be here with us got out of here soon. That they were taken away from this place. And that the men who had done this to them paid. Paid big-time. There were so many ways to kill a man so that he felt excruciating pain in the moments before his death.

She hesitated. "I do not remember the men coming to the room before I was taken to—to the man named Cabot. For—for assessment. From the time you have been here they have always drugged you."

"*Cabot* raped you?" I was even more furious than before, if that was possible. No matter who had raped her, it was a horrible violation. Cabot doing it seemed even worse. "That man is so dead."

"I have never wished death upon anyone," Alyona said. "Until now."

The fact that they hadn't shot me up meant they knew I'd be awake anytime now. That didn't give me much time to get the lay of things.

"Sometimes I think there is no hope," she said, a sob in her voice. "No way to go back home and see my family. No hope at all."

My own thought came back to me.

Hopelessness was something I would never accept into my life.

I wouldn't. *I would not accept it.*

"Trust me." I stroked her hair away from her face. "Don't ever give up hope, Alyona. Ever. Things will get better. Everything will turn out all right. I promise you," I said just as the door hinges squeaked.

A familiar chuckle crawled down my spine and I went completely still.

Benjamin Cabot stood in the doorway.

CHAPTER 27

Kristin

April 21
Sunday, present day

Tears burned the back of Kristin's eyes and she bit her lip to keep from crying. The drug was wearing off again. God, how she didn't want it to. Staying drugged was the only way she could mentally survive, because it kept her from thinking. Feeling.

The professor liked it when the drug wasn't in her system anymore. He liked to hear her scream. Watch her cry. Hurt her. Listen to her beg for him to stop and to let her go.

If she tried to hold it in, he just hurt her more.

She tested the cuffs and the heavy chains—just in case—like she did every time the drug wore off. She wasn't a quitter; she never had been. But this . . .

Kristin swallowed hard and barely kept from letting a sob out. After all this time, what good were tears?

The only time the professor let her off the bed was to use the adjoining bathroom. She had stopped being embarrassed when he watched her relieve herself on the toilet. What did it matter?

He chained her to the showerhead and washed her body himself. Usually he would get so turned on he'd take her in the shower while the water washed away her tears. He'd slap her backside especially hard because he liked the sound of his hand hitting her wet flesh.

The professor made her take the pill every day. He told her that by skipping the pseudo tablets for the week she was supposed to have her period, he would make her jump straight to next month's pill. Then she would never have her period. She would never get pregnant.

And he could do whatever he wanted to with her. Anytime he wanted to. Day or night.

He didn't even use a condom.

She suspected he took something like Viagra. An older man like him wasn't likely to last several times a day, every day, was he?

Other than letting her use the bathroom and giving her a shower, he never let her far from the bed, much less out of the room. He kept her naked and cuffed. Always. Both wrists.

The links between the cuffs were so short that she couldn't reach for anything. All she could do was ease off the bed sometimes and kneel on the soft carpet to change positions, or curl up in a ball on the mattress and hug a thick wooden bedpost. Unless her ankles were cuffed, too.

He wouldn't even let her feed herself. He insisted on making her eat from his hands like a dog. If she refused, he slapped her so hard her ears would ring and she would cry out for him to stop.

The two-inch-wide cuffs were lined with sheepskin, which kept the metal from biting into her wrists. Still, they made her skin sore and red. In his more "kindly" moments the professor put balm on her irritated skin. That was the only time she would have a free wrist. But he always made sure her ankles were cuffed along with her other wrist before switching.

Kristin sighed. It wasn't like she had a black belt or something. Although she could scratch the professor's eyeballs out and kick him in his groin.

If only she'd taken those self-defense classes like her brother, Nick, had tried to get her to go to. Or listened to him when he wanted to teach her moves that would help her if she was ever in a dangerous situation. She pictured the last time he'd talked about her learning how to defend herself.

"Damnit, Kristin," Nick had said, his blue eyes serious

and concerned. "You're on a college campus. Some guy could rape you."

She'd flinched at the word "rape," but still she said, "I always stay in public places with someone with me." She'd kissed him on his cheek. "I'll be okay, Nick. Don't worry so much."

Her brother hugged her tight. "I love you, kiddo. I couldn't bear anything happening to you."

She'd hugged him back. "I love you, too."

She was such an idiot.

Oh, yeah, she'd been in a public place with friends. Didn't end up mattering, did it?

Her heart ached when she thought of Nick. Would she ever see him again? She squeezed her eyes tight.

Mother. Father.

If they were still alive they would have paid for not just one PI but a hundred to search for her. They could have afforded it.

But Nick would still have been the one to find her. He would find her. She knew it with all her heart, and that was what kept her going. Day to day.

Nick would find her.

Had it already been four weeks since she'd found herself strapped to Professor Michaels's bed?

The days ticked off in Kristin's head automatically. Having a photographic memory and a calculator in her head made forgetting so difficult. Even after being drugged her mind would come fully awake once the drug wore completely off.

Tick. Another day. Tick. Another day.

But she wanted to forget. Everything.

The doorknob squeaked and Kristin's body went rigid.

Professor Michaels smiled as he let the door swing open. This time he didn't close it behind him.

She couldn't stop the trembling in her body as he came toward the bed. His bald head gleamed in the low lighting from the stained-glass lamp on the nightstand. It was too far to reach or she would have kicked it over just so she didn't have to look at his pale, round face or his excited blue eyes. Eyes that showed his eagerness to take her and abuse her.

"Did you rest well, slut?" he asked when he reached the side of her bed.

Referring to her only as slut was just one more degrading thing on a list of things that he did to her that her mind continued to check off.

The tears were already starting to come as she forced herself to nod and say, "Y-yes, Professor."

She barely kept from crying out as he pinched, then twisted her nipple with his thick fingers. "I have something very special for you, slut."

Again she had to speak or he would slap her. "W—what do you have for me, Professor?"

"I'm going to have extremely important company shortly." He leaned close and she shuddered as he licked the inside of her ear. "Company that enjoys certain kinds of entertainment. Company that likes to share."

Kristin's heart pounded as horror rushed through her like needles pricking her entire body. "No." She shook her head. "Please, no."

He rose and held his hand high, his palm facing her. "You keep forgetting your place, slut."

"Professor Michaels." She found herself already wincing as she called him by the only thing he would accept. Fear continued to stab at every organ in her body. He was serious. Oh, God. It was in his eyes. The way he looked at her. The sound of his voice. "Please, Professor. No."

Images rushed through her mind of one man after another taking her, using her.

Kristin had always believed violence didn't solve problems. But now, more than anything, she wanted this man to die. She wanted Nick to come and blow the professor away like he'd probably had to do to men when he was a SEAL.

Her whole body trembled so hard the mattress shook.

She'd never even believed in the death penalty.

Until now.

"Please, no," she said again as tears rolled down the sides

of her temples and nameless, blank faces started appearing in her mind. Faces of men ready to sexually abuse her. "Please, please, Professor. I'll do anything. Anything for you. Anything you want me to."

"Don't worry, my darling Kristin." The professor smiled and lowered his hand. "You'll enjoy it." He reached into the pocket of his tan slacks. Steel blade after steel blade of terror jabbed Kristin's belly as he drew out a syringe of green liquid. "You'll want it, slut. And you'll beg for it."

CHAPTER 28

The devil wears Armani

April 21
Sunday evening, I think, but I'm not sure I care.

Cabot's smile was cold enough to ice my veins. "I would have to say you are in no position to promise anything to anyone, Alexi Adams. If that is your real name."

I narrowed my eyes and scowled at him.

The small wave of fear that sent a shiver through me made me want to hit something. I did feel some satisfaction that he had fading bruises on his face, too.

Alyona flinched as Cabot opened the door wider. "Why don't you join me, Alexi?"

My dark thoughts turned like crows circling in my mind as I shut my eyes and search for options. Any option.

"You don't have a choice." Cabot echoed what the crows cawed in my head. I opened my eyes and stared at him again. How could anyone think Cabot was handsome? All it took was one searching look into his eyes and the truth was there. "Would you prefer to have Danny drag you by your hair again?"

My scalp twinged at the thought and I held back a wince. No, thank you. That left me with getting out of the room in a hurry before he called the big dick, Danny.

Cabot stared at my breasts as I held the threadbare blanket tight against me with the hand that wasn't in a cast. Sleazebag.

Last thing I wanted to do right now was leave this room commando-style. The only things covering any part of my body were the bandages around my ribs and the cast on my arm. I gathered the blanket around me. The old, rough carpeting scraped my bare feet.

Cabot shook his head. "You can't have clothing or the blanket to cover yourself."

Heat rushed to my face. He wanted me to feel as vulnerable as possible. I bet he wanted me to beg, too.

I'd faced far worse things than walking around naked in front of an enemy, and I could deal with this. I let go of the blanket and stood.

When I got to the door, I saw the back of Cabot's hand flying toward my face just before he backhanded me.

Ah, Christ.

Pain sent stars shooting through my head when it hit the wall. The crows that had fled my mind returned and spun like I was whirling in a cloud of the wicked birds. My skull throbbed.

Cabot's hands eased up from my elbows to my upper arms, his palms and fingers cold, smooth, with no calluses. His muscles strained along his jaw as he dug his fingers into my skin. My neck whiplashed as he jerked me hard and shook me. Once, twice. Three times.

"You're going to enjoy this." His too-white teeth flashed as he smiled. "And I'll have every answer I need."

My hazy thoughts focused on what he'd said and my feet didn't want to move when he pulled me beside him and forced me out of the room and into a dim hallway. Enjoy . . . ?

Oh, shit.

Oh, shit.

Every answer he needed . . . Cabot was going to interrogate me, and no doubt torture me if I didn't give him any answers. There wasn't a question in my mind.

Did he have drugs, too? Truth-inducing drugs as good as the ones RED used?

I had been trained to withstand torture and I had a high tolerance against these kinds of drugs—but what if he had something I couldn't fight?

The plaster cast felt rough against my belly as I held my

broken arm close. A wave of dizziness made me stumble again.

Cabot's voice was cold, hard. "I kept you unconscious most of the time and only allowed you to wake long enough to take care of necessities."

Aren't you the prince.

"I let you heal just enough," he added close to my ear. "You'd already blacked out, and I couldn't have you not enjoying the pain." Chills rolled over my skin and the memory of the pain made my existing pain worse. "When I get what I need from you, I'll let you heal completely and put you up for a private auction."

I tried to jerk away but he held my left upper arm tight. And jeez did it hurt when I tried that little maneuver.

He shook his head and laughed. "If you don't talk or I don't think you've told me the truth, I'll shoot you up with the designer drug Lascivious, and you'll be begging to screw every man within five feet of you. I'll give you to a whorehouse. You'll just become another slut with all those johns who'd love to fuck a cop."

"I—I'm not a cop." Well, I wasn't.

He squeezed my arm tighter and his tone became more vicious as we walked. "You work for someone. And you, little bitch, are going to tell me everything."

Flashes of Donovan came to me and my heart squeezed. That night they'd wounded him, but hadn't killed him. Because they wanted information.

But I was sure I'd heard the word "Police!" before the slamming and locking of metal doors. He was okay. He had to be okay. He'd probably managed to notify RED with his leather wrist cuffs before having real cuffs put on him.

Images came in waves. Time I'd spent with Donovan over the two weeks we worked together. His determination to find his sister. His fierce anger at whoever was auctioning the women and the men who had killed Randolph.

The way Donovan cooked; the way he cleaned everything until it was spotless, nothing ever out of place. And how I think he secretly liked that prima donna cat.

How he'd tried to fight off a roomful of men to get to me.

The great sex—that had only been a piece of the package that was Nick Donovan.

The last image my mind settled on was when he held me in bed, cuddling me close after the second club. Telling me how he didn't want me to go through more humiliation. And that he had a bad feeling about this op.

He'd been so right.

As Cabot and I reached a door, whistles, catcalls, shouts of laughter, and vulgar suggestions came from the four men in the room. My body flamed and I wanted the chance to take them on one at a time when I was well again.

No matter how big the men were, I bet none of them could hurt me when I was at my best, unless they had two men holding me still. Like Cabot had the night he kidnapped me.

"You may get your chance with her," Cabot said to them. "Depends on whether or not she cooperates."

It was in Cabot's eyes. His expression. If I didn't talk, he planned to let these men rape me as many times as they wanted.

Cabot jerked my arm and I barely held back a cry as we headed to a door. "We have business to attend to. And I don't plan to wait any longer."

Why didn't I snap his neck when I first went after him? So what if the guys had killed me? I would have taken Benjamin Cabot along for the ride.

But now, with my ribs broken and my arm in a cast, it was going to be a lot harder to defend myself or do anything to hurt him. The bruises, the wounds, the sore shoulder, the probability of a concussion—none of that mattered. I couldn't let Cabot do it. And at the same time I couldn't tell him anything about RED.

Had to hold on. Had to figure out how to get out of this.

He pushed me through another door and down a long, black hallway that smelled of fresh paint. If he wanted to depress everyone he brought to this place, he was doing a good job of it.

All hopes faded of seeing anything I might recognize. No

windows to show me familiar landscape—if there was anything familiar here. What if he'd sent me to a foreign country? The Ukraine. Korea even. But he'd held the other auction in Boston, so likely we were still in the US. Alyona had been taken in Boston, too—I'd seen the vid.

Only fluorescent bulbs lit the hallway, and they were too high to reach. If I was lucky, he'd take me to an office in this building. I'd been fully trained in the use of common, everyday items as weapons. There were any number of things I could think of that would maim or kill.

Cabot pushed open a door at the end of the hallway and immediately the smells of leather, fresh paint, and antiseptic washed over me. He shoved me into a black room, also with a fluorescent light. I blinked and stared at everything in that room. It was a sadomasochist's dream.

Traditional BDSM equipment like a St. Andrew's cross, stretching bars, a cage, a hook dangling from the ceiling, and much more lined the walls of the enormous room—more BDSM equipment put together than everything I'd seen at the nightclubs. There was even a full-body metal cage like one I'd seen on the Internet. It was in the shape of a man and had a panel in the back where the man or woman could be taken in the ass while being kept entirely immobile.

Please not a body cage. Dear God.

Was there nothing out in the open that I could use to defend myself or hurt Cabot?

A row of metal cabinets lined one wall, and each cabinet had been secured with large padlocks.

But all of that—that wasn't really what held my attention. No, my attention was riveted on where the pain would really come from.

"I'm certain much of this is familiar to you." Cabot was leaving bruises on my arm as he dug his fingers in, but I really didn't care. He brought me to a stop in front of a heavy wooden chair that an elephant could sit on and not break. Thick leather cuffs made to secure a gorilla were attached to the armrests, chair legs, and even the back of the seat. An equally heavy-looking table was up against the chair.

"You wanted to be in the BDSM clubs, so now's your chance to get the most of it." He smiled. "Yes, this is where I have the most fun."

Black stained the chair all over. Dried blood.

This was so not BDSM. BDSM was sexual play, enjoyable to everyone involved. It was an equal exchange of power.

This—

What this sick fuck had in mind was sadistic torture.

God, just get me out of here before he can hurt me more and I promise to start going to church again with Mammy and Daddy. Really. Promise.

No divine intervention was going to swoop down and steal me away. Not unless it was for my soul once I died.

To heaven or hell.

But I was in hell right now.

Cabot continued and gestured toward the cabinets. "Of course that is where we keep special instruments that will encourage you to share all of your wonderful secrets."

He looked down and smiled at me, and I swear I saw horns. The devil didn't wear Prada. The devil wore custom-designed-and-tailored silk Armani suits.

"And here," he continued as he took me to a long metal tank of water that was at least seven feet long, five feet wide, and four feet off the floor. Restraints were at every corner of the tank, as well as a strap for the middle. "You might enjoy a little shock therapy." He smiled, and bile rose in my throat.

I didn't need a bath and electricity to make me vibrate like my whole body was electrified. I was already there.

"That's all the tour you need for now." He shoved me sideways onto the big wooden chair and I hit my shoulder on an armrest, causing pain to shoot down my broken arm. "I think you need to have a seat."

"Screw you." I pushed myself up on the seat of the chair with my good arm, but my muscles had gone on vacation and the rest of my body was crumbling. I gritted my teeth and focused on anger instead. Burning hot anger that roared through me like wildfire.

I kicked at Cabot, aiming for his groin, but he sidestepped and I missed. He backhanded me hard. Goddamn, but I was getting sick of that. The ringing in my ears, the black spots in front of my eyes, the blood in my mouth.

This time my foot connected with his leg as I rammed the sole hard against his thigh.

It caught him off guard and he dropped to one knee. I jammed my foot at his nose, but he turned and I hit the side of his face.

Devil's eyes. Loathing, hatred, fury. That's what I saw in the moment he reacted by slapping me hard enough to snap my head to the side.

"You are going to feel pain like you have never felt before." He took advantage of my momentary loss of focus and direction, and strapped down my left wrist. "The more you fight me, the worse it's going to be for you."

This time I drove the ball of my foot close to his groin. Missed my target and hit the top of his thigh.

Cabot cursed like I'd never expected from the snobby sonofabitch. This time when he backhanded the side of my head, the now very familiar black dots gathered and I felt darkness coming on.

But it didn't and he had strapped down my right arm over my cast before my sight cleared again. He jerked my arm so hard when he strapped it that I cried out as pain shot through my broken bones and my eyes watered.

Cabot had to kneel to grasp one of my ankles. He made the mistake of grabbing my left ankle first. A good soccer kick with my right foot, which connected beneath his chin. Then the satisfying clink of teeth and his shout of pain.

His head snapped back. I started to jam my foot against his head but Cabot backhanded me again, more powerfully this time. More stars. Many, many more stars. More black spots. More blood in my mouth.

Couldn't move my legs. He must have strapped them to the chair legs after the last and hardest slap. A leather strap dug into my waist, too. I must have lost it for a lot longer than I'd thought.

He had me where he wanted me.

I couldn't see a way out.

My eyes burned from the sweat dripping into them. I spit blood, aiming for Cabot, but it landed on the concrete floor.

Yeah, stupid considering it would just piss him off more. But maybe if he'd hit me again I'd pass out.

Every single breath I took seemed to make more sweat roll from my scalp. Perspiration coated my skin. In all the fun I'd actually forgotten I was naked. Now I was sitting in a chair with my legs spread completely wide, every single part of my body exposed.

Cabot wiped blood from the corner of his mouth, shook his head, and laughed.

He was laughing?

He pushed himself away while staring at my naked body. "Despite the fact that you look like hell right now, I'm going to do everything I want to do to you." He gave his devil's smile. "Unless you decide to answer each and every question I have."

"Eat shit and die, Cabot."

"Interesting choice of words." He walked away from me, his Gucci loafers echoing on the concrete floor. "I may just have you do that." Keys rattled as he pulled them from his pocket. "I might feed you shit. Moose and Duke have to be let out on occasion, and we can collect their fecal matter."

My heart was all raced out and my adrenaline shot. I completely collapsed against the wooden chair, which was so hard that I think it bruised my flesh, too.

All I knew was that the pain had only just begun.

I closed my eyes. If I kept from looking at him maybe this wasn't real.

"Open your eyes," he said several moments later, his voice almost gentle.

My jaw ached from grinding my teeth as I opened my eyes. The leather bindings constricted me like rough hands as I strained against them. I strung together every swear word in every language I could think of and shot them like poisoned arrows at Cabot.

"Finished?" He smiled and my gaze followed his movements as he reached for the tray on the table attached to the chair. "I think perhaps you may have missed Arabic."

The look I gave him had to be as poisonous as my words had been. I turned my gaze to the tray. "A little cliché, don't you think?" The glimmer of silver tools laid out on white cloth looked like standard torture fare. But there were a few things I wasn't sure about, one of them a bottle filled with some kind of black liquid. Cabot's version of truth serum? A round box of salt was next to the bottle. Rubbing salt in the wound, I'd lay a bet on that any day.

"Let's start with your name." Cabot's cologne was going to make me sick, as close as he was. "Your complete real name."

I glared at him.

"All right." Cabot picked up a pair of small metal clamps. "These always add a little bit of fun."

I swallowed. Nipple clamps. But these had sharp, jagged, jaws.

He brought the clamps to my breasts and snapped the jaws onto my nipples.

I almost screamed.

For a moment all I could think about was those clamps on my nipples and the constant, burning, piercing sensation of them as they dug their metal teeth into one of the most sensitive parts of my body. A bit of blood spotted my areolae where the teeth dug in.

He picked up another clamp as I squirmed against my bonds. With what looked like total focused pleasure, he brought that third clamp between my thighs.

Oh, no. My body vibrated. *Don't, please,* just kept going through my mind, but I didn't speak the words out loud.

He looked up at me with that same hateful smile and snapped the clamp's jaws on my clitoris.

The scream that tore from me was something I couldn't hold back. It came from deep inside my chest, the pain of my broken ribs nothing like the pain now between my thighs.

OhGodohGodohGod.

"Now tell me," he said.

I couldn't have gotten a word out even if I would break and tell him.

He chose one of the silver tools. "I'll enjoy this part more than you can imagine."

Block the pain. Block the pain. Concentrate on something else. Concentrate on the room, anything, anything else.

The stuffy room made the perspiration that had broken out on my skin sticky. Droplets rolled down the side of my face. My shaking and the pain made it hard to focus, but I managed to make out what it was he held. A tool with a blade designed to carve into wood—or flesh.

"Of course you need to be branded, to show your first owner." He brought the tool close to my belly, and it felt like my belly button touched the back of the seat the way I shrank away from him. "Unless you play 'Tell the Truth.' "

I could have easily visualized Cabot enjoying watching other people inflict pain on their victims, but to do it himself—he was more sadistic than even I had imagined.

My jaw was going to crack if I continued to clench it so tightly.

"One more time." He lightly touched my diamond belly piercing with the instrument. "What is your real name?"

I wasn't about to endanger my family by giving out my real name. My mind shifted to my time in Special Ops, and to RED's intensive training on surviving torture techniques. Pain was a way to control me. Don't allow him to control me. Push away the pain. Meditate. Shift my focus. Repeat a mantra.

My mind darted around like a tiny rubber ball pinging from one wall to another. Think of fun times. Sitting on my back porch watching the Red Sox, and yelling with my neighbors as they sat on theirs and watched the game, too. What was it? Sometime in April? The season was just getting going. How were our guys doing?

Or my family, the last time we'd all gotten together—

I almost shouted as pain snatched me from my "happy

place." There was nothing I could do to stop my body from trembling as he dug the knifepoint of the tool into my flesh on one side of my belly button. "Hmmm." He cocked his head and looked at my belly as he drew a line down.

My tolerance for pain was shot as I struggled to find that place where I couldn't feel what he was doing.

Blood beaded along the cut as he drew a two-inch line fairly deep in my flesh. I strained against the thick leather bindings. I tried to focus on anything but the pain of the cut, and the clamp on my clitoris and the ones on my nipples, but everything in my body was nothing but pain. A world outside of this time—did anything else exist?

Family. Friends. My job. Baseball—

Donovan?

"Shall I continue?" He looked up at me. "Let's go this time with telling me the name of the agency you work for."

How far would he carry this?

He'd never stop.

All I could do was endure.

Cabot looked back at the little bit of blood on my belly, then cut into my flesh again. Blood filled my mouth, too, as I bit the inside of my cheek to keep from screaming.

Really, Steele, what did more pain matter?

I couldn't help but watch him. This time he made two curves against the line.

B.

For Benjamin.

Cabot was carving his initials into my flesh.

He was branding me.

CHAPTER 29

Nick

April 21
Sunday afternoon

"I know you've got what I need." Nick shoved the beefy informant up against the wall in the alleyway. Takamoto and Jensen stood a few feet away from Nick.

"Word's on the street you've been spreading stories," Nick continued. Dickey's head hit the rough brick of the bar on Hanover Street in Charleston. The contents of the paper bag he was holding clunked when it hit the wall. "You'd better get that information out before I gut you."

The contact of Dickey's skull against the brick didn't seem to faze the idiot. Probably too drunk. "Cash. I wanna see it." The informant reeked of whiskey that went well with the stench of vomit, piss, and garbage in the alleyway. His voice squeaked but he sounded determined.

"You'll get your money." Nick put one hand around the big man's throat that was scratchy with stubble. Nick squeezed. Dickey let out a gasp for air. "*If* you give me the information and I let you live."

Dickey glared. Talk about a dumb shit.

Nick let out a low growl and wrapped both hands around Dickey's throat as he thumped the man's head against the brick. Dickey's stringy hair swung across into his pale blue eyes.

"Fuck," Dickey said in a strangled voice. He dropped the paper bag he'd been holding and grabbed both of Nick's wrists. The bag landed with a crash and the sound of glass breaking. "Calm ya livva. I'll tell you what I heard."

Nick backed off, but only a little. Dickey might be a dip-shit loser, but he was a big man, and fast. Nick could take Dickey, but it didn't hurt having Takamoto and Jensen at his back.

"You got it on my dungies." Dickey glared down at the bag now soaked with what smelled like cheap whiskey and at the wet spot on his pant leg. "You gonna pay for that too."

"Dickey, I have no fucking patience left." Nick fisted his hands and was ready to use the big loser as a punching bag.

Dickey hooked his thumbs in his belt loops like he was trying to figure out what to do with his hands now that he didn't have the bag. "Heard it from another guy."

Great. Secondhand information.

"Farther down Hanover," Dickey continued. "Near that real swank place."

Nick went still. The feeling that he was about to get a decent lead prickled his spine. "The Gold Crown?"

"Yeah." Dickey shifted as if he was going to run.

Nick grabbed the collar of the informant's flannel shirt and pressed him against the wall again. "We've had that nightclub under surveillance front and back for a while and haven't seen a goddamned thing."

"That's because you hasn't been inside that place next to it." Dickey's thick alcohol breath was enough to make Nick intoxicated and he pushed away from the bastard.

Nick gave Dickey a skeptical look. "*You* have?"

"Na-ah." Dickey shoved his hands into the front pockets of his stained jeans. Nick and his team had already searched Dickey for weapons so they knew he was clean. "But Jack budged a bulkie roll from the store and was having a drink by a dumpster in the alleyway 'round the corner from that Crown place and next to that craphole."

"Get on with it." Nick gritted his teeth. "My patience is about to snap, Dickey. Your information better be good."

"Jack's no chowdahead." Dickey glanced down the alley toward Hanover Street before looking back at Nick. "Jack said these guys looked like they could rough a guy up. They was talking somethin' about candy."

Candy? But Nick still got that on-fire sensation again. "Get it the hell out."

Dickey pushed his stringy hair away from his ruddy face. "Jack, he said those guys, they talked about women. They said somethinn' about merchandise and girls, like they was the same thing."

Nick had the strangest sensation, as if being near Dickey was like standing too close to a vat of poison. He took a step back. "Are you sure you've got it right?"

Dickey tapped his head with one long finger and grinned, showing his yellowed teeth. "Got me a photographic memory. I know what Jack said he remembered. And Jack himself's no bucka."

"That's what makes Dickey such a good informant," Takamoto said as he came up to Nick's side. "That 'perfect' memory."

Dickey grinned. "And I listen up real well and no one pays no attention to no bazo."

"Yeah, drunks aren't usually as reliable as you, Dickey," Takamoto said.

"Next time don't screw around with me." Nick put deadly meaning in his voice. "You spill your guts right away or I'll do it for you."

"Fuck." Dickey looked at Takamoto. "Where'd you get this guy?"

"We'll req your cash," Nick said. "Right here, same time tomorrow afternoon, you'll get it. An agent will be waiting."

Dickey looked down at the soaked bag now with jagged glass poking through the wet paper that was falling apart. "Don't forget money for the booze."

Nick gave Dickey one last look. "If your info proves to be what we need, I'll make sure you get a bonus."

Dickey cracked another smile, but Nick turned his back on the informant.

No time for anymore of this shit. Nick had to assemble a raid team and he had to do it now.

Nick
April 21
Sunday night

Nick and the rest of the six RED raid teams positioned themselves to the front and the rear of the place near the Golden Crown on First Street. In their black raid gear and with their uncanny abilities to remain virtually invisible the RED teams had no problem remaining unnoticed, regardless of the sheer number of agents.

Even after having been a SEAL, Nick was impressed with RED agents who were equally as well trained, efficient and dangerous, but in larger numbers. RED had more of an advantage when conducting a raid than any other force Nick knew of.

Before Kristin had been kidnapped, Nick hadn't know RED existed. Because of his background in Special Ops, Karen Oxford had tried to recruit him but would never name the organization she worked for, so he refused to have anything to do with it. She'd said with his unique talents he'd make an excellent addition to the division.

Sources had informed him that some kind of covert organization similar to RED operated underground, but it was something no one had been able to prove. And once recruited, no agent would reveal the organization.

When Nick started searching for his sister, Oxford jumped to his mind. She'd told him she was based out of Boston. He'd taken the plain white card with the simple black writing with Karen Oxford's name and phone number.

And called.

A short time later and he was in.

To Nick, most importantly, RED had means to track down Kristin that would make it faster than if he had continued to operate on his own.

And now those resources were about to be put to use to get Lexi back.

Nick's heart thudded so hard it felt like it hit his Kevlar vest. Electricity ran up and down his arms. He was so goddamned charged to make this happen and find Lexi.

Sirens cut through the night in a distant part of Boston. The closer sounds of traffic only slightly muffled the noise and music coming from the Crown. From his hiding place in a doorway of a closed nearby shop, Nick caught the scent of alcohol along with smoke from the patrons who'd come outside for a cigarette.

The crowd was a little thinner on a Sunday than it would be on a Friday or Saturday, but the nightclub was still doing a good piece of business.

Nick spoke into his comm and all teams reported in.

Yellow team was in place, covering the back exit and the green team had the front. Snipers were positioned on the rooftops of nearby buildings.

Blue team would secure the upstairs. Orange team and Red team would head straight for the lower level.

Nick and his own private squad would be searching for Lexi. He had a feeling she was in there—but his gut told him she wasn't going to be easy to locate.

"On my count." Nick's adrenaline rocketed. "Three . . . two . . . one! *Go, go, go!*"

"Police!" Blue team leader shouted as they charged into the building.

A few men were sitting in the front room of the place. They bolted for the back door only to be brought up short by the Yellow team blocking their way. In moments agents had the men slammed face first into the wall, unarmed and cuffed.

Blue team, which had the most number of agents for one team, started searching and cuffing each person.

While Blue team was doing their thing, Red and Orange teams, as well Nick's special unit, charged in with Nick in the lead.

He spotted an armed man who was smart enough to have his hands flat against the wall while an agent disarmed then cuffed him. Where the man had been stationed, there was a real good chance he'd been guarding the entrance to where Lexi and the other women were being hidden.

Nick motioned to his teams to follow. The way Cabot operated, he sure didn't expect their luck would hold for the lower level.

It had been all of three minutes from the time RED busted in the front and rear doors, and Nick's teams located the black door next to the cuffed bouncer. Nick would definitely lay money on that door leading to the operation below.

Shots were fired. Sounded like AK-47s. RED agents returned fire.

Behind them continued the insanity but Nick let it fade into background noise.

As Nick and Takamoto crouched to either side of the black-painted door, screams could also be heard through it. Faint, and probably from the lower level.

Five minutes. Had to get in to find Lexi.

Nick nodded to the shielded agents holding the battering ram and gave the signal for "Go!"

The heavy wood door held with the first crash, but the battering ram made a good-sized hole. The agents rammed the door again even as shots from the other side of the door started peppering the wood.

The door gave and slammed against the wall.

One of the agents with the battering ram dropped, blood bubbling from his throat where the bullet had pierced beneath his shield and above his Kevlar vest.

Shit. One of the other agents pulled the injured man aside.

Nick, still crouched, and took a quick look inside. Lit by a large fluorescent lamp was a black-painted room. On the opposite side of the room a hallway headed to the left and stairs led down.

Two desks and a stack of crates were around the room. A quick count—looked like six fuckers were firing at the door from behind their cover.

Nick held up six fingers to Takamoto who gave a sharp nod and relayed it to the teams.

Agents stood to the sides of the doorway with Nick and

Takamoto who were crouched. Nick made a hand signal to Takamoto and raised his fingers.

One. Two. Three.

At the same time, keeping low, Nick and Takamoto rounded the doorway just enough to unload a few bullets. Nick took out one of his targets, dead center in his forehead. The other target dived and cried out when Nick's bullet hit him in the shoulder.

The doorframe cracked and splintered as the men in the room fired back. The sound of gunfire was followed by shouts of pain or heavy thuds.

A couple of agents were down by the time the six men inside the room had been eliminated.

They weren't taking any fucking prisoners.

Ten minutes.

"Clear!" an agent shouted after he and three other agents examined the room, checking behind and under the desks and a stack of crates.

No doubt at all the stairs went straight to the girls and assholes downstairs. Nick motioned for Red and Orange teams to take the stairs.

Nick hesitated only a fraction of a moment before running in the direction of the black-painted hallway that was also lit with fluorescent lights.

That long, dark path just might lead to Lexi.

CHAPTER 30

He is so going to die

April 21
Sunday evening, screw it

My heart jackhammered. He was carving his initials into me. I'd have Benjamin Cabot's initials on my body.

Oh, God.

Blood spotted the B. He reached for a white cloth from the tray and dabbed the blood from his handiwork, and nodded as if in appreciation.

"Let's move on." Cabot set the now red-spotted cloth aside. "You might as well tell me who you work for."

"And you might as well kill me if that's what you have in mind." I had to force a breath because it was so difficult to speak with still-healing ribs and those clamps and the searing pain in the fresh cuts. "Nothing you can do to me will get me to give you any kind of information."

"Kill you? I have too many plans for that." He gave a casual kind of smile. "If you cooperate, I stop. I'll allow your arms and ribs to fully heal, along with any other injuries, before putting you up on the private auction block." It burned as he traced his finger along the B he had cut into my flesh. "One man will own you, and use you in any way he wants."

The crows were back, pecking at my flesh this time. Being someone's sex slave—unimaginable. I'd never let it happen.

I looked up at the black ceiling and its lone fluorescent bulb, and gritted my teeth to keep from saying a word.

"Look at me." Cabot jabbed the tip of the carving tool into the flesh on the other side of my belly button. He went back to work without a flicker of anger or any other emotion on his face. Except, perhaps, pleasure?

Fire licked at my belly as he carved.

C.

When he finished he didn't even stop to ask me another question. Instead he reached for the salt.

No!

Cabot poured a good amount of salt in his palm before setting the container aside.

Again he smiled at me before he rubbed salt into the initials he'd carved into my belly.

If I'd thought my belly was on fire before, it was nothing to how it felt now.

Again he didn't pause to ask me any more questions. Instead, he picked up the bottle of black liquid, stuck a syringe in through a tiny opening, and filled it.

The ache in my chest increased as my breathing came so hard and fast that I was close to hyperventilating. Maybe I would pass out.

Cabot brought the syringe to my belly and I caught the scent of ink before he started injecting the fluid along the lines of the cuts.

Ink.

"This is very permanent," he said after he finished filling in one cut. "A specially designed ink that not even laser surgery will remove, especially from cuts so deep."

"No." I couldn't hold the words back and I hated myself for begging. "Don't."

He paused as he finished the straight line of the B, the smile of enjoyment on his face. How I wanted to crush his skull. "Does this mean you're ready to tell me everything?"

My ears felt muffled and I could barely hear. My whole body was numb. It seemed like my head wasn't my own as I shook it.

"Never," I whispered.

A hardened expression, then that smile again. "Now that I know how much this bothers you, perhaps I will cover you with my initials in every place imaginable."

I'd committed one of the worst mistakes of my life. Broken a cardinal rule. I let him know one punishment that would hurt me psychologically as well as physically. I couldn't even think about being sold. I could only think of one thing at a time, and right now it was the thought of being tattooed with Benjamin Cabot's initials.

I slumped as he finished filling the B and C with the dye. The initials stood out clear and black against my fair skin, to either side of my piercing.

"You've given me an excellent idea." He set aside the syringe and wiped away what ink had dripped down my belly with the bloody cloth. "I will have a cattle brand made with my initials so that I can properly take care of you. You're nothing more than chattel now, so a cattle brand will be perfect."

The image and the sensations were too incredibly vivid—an iron brand, red-hot and searing, burning away my flesh everywhere he branded me with his initials.

Cabot picked up a packet with a sterilized pad in it and cleaned his fingers. He opened up another packet and wiped it across the initials before he taped a large gauze pad over them and wound the tape around my waist, back, and the pad several times, until it was bandaged almost as much as my ribs. "Can't have you picking at it."

He patted the cuts. I was beyond flinching from the pain. "As far as gathering information from you," he said, "that was the proverbial exercise in futility. At least for today."

Cabot removed the clamps from my clit and nipples, and I slumped in relief even though the pain seemed worse. I'd numbed in those places, and now blood was rushing back to them.

He sterilized every tool with alcohol and the antiseptic scent carried to me. When he was finished cleansing what he had used, he carried the tray to the cabinet and put it all away.

He locked the cabinet again.

Cabot returned to me. He drew a Sig Sauer out of his pocket and held it on me as he reached for the buckle of the strap over my cast. "Make any movements and I'll end this with a bullet in your brain." He kept his eyes on me as he unstrapped my feet and arms.

I purposefully made my movements slow and awkward, like it was difficult to stand. My anger made it easy.

Cabot glanced at the tank of water. "I think a little electrotherapy might be good for you."

Bring it on. I've been through worse.

Just no more initials. Please, no.

The thought of what Cabot had done to me, and what he said he had planned, sent adrenaline rushing back into my limbs, and more of the pain and exhaustion slipped away.

And then I saw it from the corner of my eye. Sticking out of the side of the torture chair. A two-inch nail. Someone probably kept it there to use on their slaves or "victims."

It wouldn't do to let Cabot see the fire and rage in my eyes or on my face. For a woman with murder foremost in her mind, I kept my expression as calm as possible. I moved just enough to the right that I knew he wouldn't be able to see the nail that was within grabbing distance.

The devil scowled. "There are only two choices for the kind of bitch you are. You can be taught as many lessons as needed until you break." The Sig was still pointed directly at me. "Or you can be put out of *my* misery."

"That's original," was the first thing that shot through my head, but I managed to clamp my teeth shut and keep from saying it out loud. Good me.

He tilted his head and examined the gun.

At the same time I reached behind me and prayed he wouldn't see me grasp the nail. It made a small squeaking sound as I jerked it out, but Cabot didn't seem to hear. The nail felt small in my fist, but with the strength of my anger it could have been a needle and I'd still damage him.

Oh, I was going to damage him.

"What should I do, Alexi?" His voice was low, soft, serious. "Would it pain you to see a girl die because you refuse to talk? Alyona for example. With all that you have cost me, does a girl's life matter? Should I kill Alyona while you watch?"

My hearted throbbed and throbbed. No. Noooo.

He was within two feet. Gun gripped in one of his fists. "It's important for me to find out who you work for and how much they know. One girl's life is nothing compared to that information."

Please, don't.

"Your cooperation in everything I ask of you." The barrel of the Sig was now within inches of my chest. "Everything you know about the organization you work for. How much they know about my operation. Everything."

I looked him square in the eyes, my voice level. "Fuck. You."

I twisted up my arm with its rock-hard cast and knocked the Sig from his hand.

A clank and a skittering sound as it landed on the concrete floor and skimmed across the room.

Gun. History.

The motion of my solid cast hitting his hand caused him to twist. I missed his groin but rammed the nail into his gut.

Damn. Why couldn't I get the SOB in his balls?

Cabot howled. Fury and pain raged in his eyes as he drove his fist toward my face.

Pure adrenaline surged through me as I dropped to my knees.

His fist skimmed my hair.

Missing me threw him off balance.

I went for his legs with my free arm.

My much shorter height made it necessary to push up as I drove my shoulder into his closest hip.

His knee buckled against my hand as I slammed my fist into the back of his opposite knee.

One moment Cabot was up. The next he'd landed hard on his back on the floor.

His head thunked against the concrete loud enough for me to hear.

His shout rang out in the room.

I rolled away from him and was on my feet in an instant.

He started to push himself up.

My balance was solid as I braced one foot beneath me. I rammed the other toward his face.

Cabot caught my foot in his hands.

He jerked.

My healing ribs didn't feel like they were healing anymore as pain ripped through my chest when I slammed onto my back.

No time for little things like catching my breath. Or pain.

Cabot dropped down, driving his knee toward my belly.

Oh crap.

I rolled right.

His knee missed me but his full weight hit me as he landed on my back.

I shouted as he pinned me to the concrete on my belly and my cast.

No pain. No pain. No pain.

Mastery over pain.

Uh-huh.

I hooked my leg back, rocking him.

He didn't have a chance to get a good hold on me.

My opposite knee met my elbow as I brought it up. I rocked to both knees. Kept my knees and elbows in tight.

With my good hand I grabbed one of his wrists. My cast made fair leverage as I pushed up.

I flipped him onto his back.

"You bitch," he said as we both rolled to our feet and we stood and faced each other. "This is going to end."

"You bet it is." I gave him my best taunting smile and put a good dose of mockery in my voice. "And you're going to be on the losing team, limp dick."

If fire could spring from someone's hair, I swear it did from his. "I'm through screwing with you."

I laughed. "Your dick would shrivel if you tried."

I'd never seen such an interesting shade of red as the color his face turned. "You're dead."

"Where's your help?" I rocked on the balls of my feet while weighing my options. Blood had spread in a huge circle on his beige Armani slacks and white shirt, from where I'd literally nailed him. "If you remember, you have to have two men hold me while you knock me around. Or shoot me. Can't do it yourself, loser, can you?"

Instead of going for me, he dove for where the gun had slid.

"Slimy coward." I bolted after him. "An injured five-foot-four woman with a cast too much for you?"

I flung myself on his back in my version of a petite woman tackling an almost-six-foot man just as he almost touched the gun.

He went down on his chest with a thud and a shout.

Cabot's fingers hit the Sig hard enough that the gun moved a few inches from his fingers.

Before he could move, I slammed my cast against the back of his head and my opposite hand against his jaw.

The satisfaction of the connection of my knuckles against skin and bone could only last so long.

Damn. That blow with the cast should have knocked him out.

Cabot tried to shove me off as he went for the Sig.

I did him one better.

I played leapfrog off his back and propelled myself toward the gun.

My hands hit the handgun too hard. The Sig skidded straight under the edge of the St. Andrew's cross's platform.

"Cabot!" Danny shouted from the doorway as I rolled away from Cabot. "It's a raid. We've got to get you out of here."

A raid! RED was here! It had to be.

Cabot took one moment to look at me. A former prize that he now wanted to destroy.

Before he made up his mind on what he was going to do, I dove for cover. Pain spiked the shoulder that had been dislocated as I landed behind a metal spanking bench with cabinet drawers beneath it.

Should protect me from bullets. No way to grab me fast and easy.

And I had the distinct impression they were in a hurry.

My cast slipped a little as I maneuvered enough to see them around the corner of the bench.

"Come on!" Danny yelled at Cabot. "The bitch isn't that important."

For one brief moment, Cabot's gaze met mine. His face was bruised and bloody. The stain on his belly was growing. "There will be a next time. And I'll blow your goddamned brains all over Boston."

"Language, Cabot." I smiled, just to piss him off. Maybe hold him back so the good guys would get to us in time. "And watch your clichés. You're full of them."

Danny grabbed Cabot's arm and jerked him from the room right as Cabot started toward me.

Cabot let Danny hurry him out the door.

Damned if I was going to let him escape.

Gun within reach. I pushed myself toward the Sig under the St. Andrew's cross.

My grip was solid as I grasped it in my left hand.

I scrambled to my feet and bolted across the room.

The door shut behind them.

A distinct click echoed through the room.

"No way." I reached the door and jerked the handle. About fifteen times. "Oh, no way!" I shouted at all the unfortunately inanimate dungeon equipment.

I aimed the Sig at the lock. Two shots and it was history.

"Come back, you slimy coward, Benjamin Cabot," I shouted as I rushed out.

And stumbled into a group of men all dressed in black. All carrying very illegal guns. Wearing ski masks. And not wearing standard RED raid gear.

Uh . . . crap?

A man shoved his way through the group.

Before I knew what had happened, his big arms enveloped me and he hugged me tight enough to just about crack my ribs again.

No need to see his face to know whose arms I was in. His

scent alone told me it was Donovan. Nothing ever smelled so wonderful. Ever.

He lessened his grip on me just enough to push up his helmet and for me to look up at his intense features. "Goddamnit, Lexi," he said, right before he kissed me.

"Ultimately a hero is a man who would argue with the gods, and so awakens devils to contest his vision."

Norman Mailer (1923–2007)

CHAPTER 31

A knight in black armor

April 21
Sunday. Seriously, who gives a crap when. . .

Where that man learned how to kiss, I'd like to know. I'd give whoever it was a trophy.

Melt? Me melting? His taste, his scent, the feel of his arms around me and his mouth moving over mine again—

Lexi Steele had never felt so safe, so cared for. With that one kiss a sense of strength and healing flowed through my body that made the nightmare at Cabot's hand a brief blur. If only for that tiny moment in time.

My cast was pressed between our bodies, but I did wrap my good arm around his waist. So strong and sturdy. Something good after everything being so bad.

When he finally raised his head, I wondered if I'd ever catch my breath.

"You can come to my rescue any time." At least my mouth still worked.

He brushed my scraggly hair away from my cheek, which probably had smears of dried blood on it. "By the Sig in your hand and that battle cry, I bet you did a good job of just about nailing him yourself."

"Oh!" Speaking of nailing. I raised my head and started to pull away from Donovan. "We've got to get—"

All those big men with the big guns were gone. The guys must be Donovan's "special, special" recovery specialists. From what I briefly got to see of them, they looked special, all right.

"My boys are already on Cabot's tracks." He brushed his lips over mine. "Right now we need to get you out of here."

Okay. I could go for that.

Enough was enough.

I glanced down at the Sig, then met his eyes. "When your guys catch Cabot, I still get to rip his nuts off."

Donovan looked so sexy when the corner of his mouth quirked like he was trying to hold back a smile. I loved the way he did that. "I'll give Cabot a two-second lead so you'll have a little sport."

I did smile. "I'm great with moving targets."

He shrugged out of his raid jacket and put it around my shoulders. It almost hit my knees. "I think it's time to go home. After we get you checked out at RED's infirmary."

Yeah. Home. Where I'd scrub myself until my skin was raw.

He guided me along one of those long black hallways. "Did you leave a trail of bread crumbs?" I asked.

"Probably should have."

But it was only moments before we walked out of the building, Donovan with his arms around my shoulders like he was supporting me. Or caring for me.

The cheers that rose up to meet us just about knocked me silly. "Steele is back," "Knew she'd kick ass," "Never had a doubt."

Damnit. I didn't choke up over mushy stuff.

Agent after agent slapped me on the back and some even dared to hug the unhuggable Lexi Steele. Okay, so I'd let them get away with it.

April 22
Monday afternoon

"This couch is heaven," I told Donovan as my body sank into the comfortable cushions.

"How are you feeling?" He sat in the chair closest to the couch.

"My arm itches like crazy." But the cast's plaster was fresh and new and bright white. "I am so friggin' glad to be home," I said. "Staying overnight and then the whole friggin' day today in RED's infirmary was about to drive me out of my mind." It would have been even better to be in my own home at the trip, but I had to admit that having someone take care of me while I healed would be nice. Especially when that someone was Donovan.

He frowned. "You should have stayed longer. One night and one day isn't enough."

"But then I'd miss all the mind-exploding sex," I said with the naughtiest grin I could muster.

"No sex for you until you're better." He leaned forward, his forearms on his thighs. "And don't try begging. It's not going to work." His expression was only half serious, but I knew the serious side planned to keep me from tackling him.

Oh, yeah?

"If Oxford hadn't insisted that I stay in the freaking infirmary, we could already be having wild monkey sex," I said.

I swear Donovan almost laughed. "Wild monkey sex, huh?"

"But oh, no," I said with a good dose of sarcasm. "She even made me debrief with the nut crew today. At least the therapist was a chick in slacks instead of some cigar-smoking freak with a beard. Not that I'll be talking to the psycho-logist again. I'll do my 'therapy' with my Glock."

Donovan's mouth was lifting at the corner. I was almost getting a smile out of him! "I'm still stuck on the monkey sex part," he said.

The big oaf had hung around the infirmary to make sure I didn't leave before I was officially released. He limped a little from the bullet wound, but because the bullet had gone through soft tissue in his thigh, not muscle or bone, he said he was down to being sore.

Georgina had come to see me today, and it had been so good to see her bossy self.

"Bet Zane raised hell when he found out I'd been kidnapped and no one had told him." I shifted my cast on my belly. "He sure looked like he was holding back when he stopped by to see me."

Donovan shook his head. "Yeah. I'd say he was pretty pissed nobody had notified him."

I could just picture Zane losing it. "I bet the 'it's part of the job' rhetoric didn't go over real well with him. Or 'you're in a different department,' and 'it was a highly secretive op.' "

"Uh, yeah," Donovan said. "Zane wasn't a good boy when it came to talking to Oxford. She threatened to get him fired from RED, and to kick his butt out the door, personally."

I snorted. "She could do it, too. Both."

"I believe it."

"But now I'm back." Back from hell to the insane life that I loved.

The sigh that left me was pure relief that I was out of that place where Cabot had held me prisoner, and that I wasn't being drugged every day. I tilted my head against the couch and closed my eyes.

And frowned. Tension made my temples ache.

"What's wrong, Steele?"

I opened my eyes and looked at Donovan. "That bastard escaped, that's what." No one knew where Cabot had gone, or how he'd gotten away.

Donovan rubbed his jaw, looking both pissed and tired. "We thought we had everything covered, but the sonofabitch managed to pull one up on us again."

"The best part," I said, "is that Alyona and two other girls were rescued before the next auction."

The seriousness in Donovan's eyes mesmerized me. "The best part was finding you."

I couldn't think of anything to say.

Donovan didn't give me a chance, anyway. "I'm going to check on dinner. It's just about ready."

Donovan's expression and his words stayed in my mind as I heard a few noises coming from the kitchen.

I closed my eyes again, and images of more girls being auctioned off started rolling through my mind, just like they had been every time I was alone. What if Cabot had other girls he'd already kidnapped, kept in different areas before the next auction?

Picture the good, Steele. Not the bad. For now.

Before you have to face every last demon.

The demons that still haunt your dreams every night.

Forget demons. Drink in that heavenly smell rolling from the kitchen.

Mmmm. Food. Real food. Prepared by the best cook I'd ever met.

And the best lay I'd ever had.

While Donovan stayed in my infirmary room he had brushed his lips over mine. No deep, coma-inducing kisses.

My arm was healing just fine beneath that lovely new cast. As much punishment as my ribs had taken, I was surprised that they weren't worse, too. But the doc said they weren't perfect but still perfectly okay. My face ached from bruises, thanks to Cabot's fists, but I wasn't about to complain.

As far as the tattoo of the Devil's initials—I'd get that taken care of as soon as possible. Even if the doctor said they couldn't be lasered away . . . I'd figure something out.

For now I kept them hidden behind a huge gauze bandage that was behind enough waterproof first-aid tape that I could leave it on while I showered.

I didn't want to see Cabot's brand. I didn't want to acknowledge it. As soon as my flesh healed where he'd cut me, I'd take care of it. *Somehow.* Right now the flesh had been sliced too deep and the ink injected just as far.

The small things in my life seemed even more important now, and I wanted them back. What I wouldn't give to head to Foley with Marty and the other guys, and hit a few out of the park. And kick back on my own couch, drinking Guinness with Georgina and naming all the attributes of the hottest agents at RED. Seemed like just about every agent RED hired was hot. A requirement, I'd lay bets.

But most of all, my mind traveled to the bigger, more important things. Being with my family again. Mammy, Daddy, my sister, and my brothers.

Zane was the only one in my family who knew what had happened, and it would stay that way.

I glanced at my cast and wondered how long I should wait before I went to see them. With Cabot still out there, I couldn't put my family in danger. From the crazed look in Cabot's eyes when Danny dragged him from the room, I knew Cabot might try to find me.

Donovan entered Kristin's living room carrying a tray, and I breathed deep and couldn't help a smile. Despite the number of missions I'd been on, I'd never appreciated the good things in life so much as I did after this experience.

Like real food.

He set the tray on the coffee table. Two plates piled with roast beef, baked potatoes, fresh corn—off the cob—warm cornbread, and a couple of bottles of Guinness.

The sigh that left me was one of pure pleasure. "You're worth having around, Donovan," I said as he set up a wooden TV tray table in front of me, so that I wouldn't have to try to hold my plate with my cast while eating. I'd bet he went out and bought the tray before I came home from the infirmary.

Donovan sat maybe a foot away from me on the couch and picked up his own plate. "How'd the debriefing go?" he asked as I was letting a piece of the most incredible cornbread melt in my mouth.

The cornbread nearly caught in my throat as I swallowed. "Honestly?" I studied my plate and punched the baked potato with my fork. "It was one of the hardest things I've ever had to do."

"I'm sorry." His voice was serious, and I met his eyes. "I shouldn't have asked you now."

"It's okay." I gripped my fork tight as he held my gaze. He had the most beautiful blue eyes that made a twisty sensation in my belly. The good kind of twist. "Sooner or later I have to talk about it." I groaned. "And they actually think I'll be spilling my guts to that shrink they assigned me to."

"That's a good thing, Steele." He peppered his baked potato with a hand grinder. "You're going to need to get it all out."

"I guess," I said, and he set the grinder down and looked at me again. "Have you ever seen a shrink for anything you've been through?"

He shrugged and turned back to his plate. "Yeah."

"You'll have to tell me, sometime," I said, but he stuffed a big piece of roast beef into his mouth.

My stomach growled. Okay, I was going to have a piece of that roast beef before I died.

Pure bliss. I made orgasmic sounds as I ate. "You are amazing." My mouth was working double-time as I caught his gaze. "You're as good a cook as you are in bed."

Those blue eyes didn't even blink as he looked at me. "I know there are quite a few things that smart-ass mouth of yours excels at."

My body went on immediate overload. The ache between my thighs was instant.

"Eating." Where the heat in my cheeks came from, when *I* started the whole thing, I don't know. I stabbed another piece of roast beef. "My mouth's real good at that."

"Uh-huh." From the corner of my eye I was sure I saw that almost-smile again.

Everything was heaven. Even if I hadn't spent time in captivity drinking only broth, I would have been in a puddle at Donovan's feet just over this dinner.

The charged silence while we ate had my entire body prickling. Those inches between us might as well have not been there at all. With every bite I took, I could swear my body brushed his. That his hand was on my thigh. Moving higher. And higher.

Unfortunately, it was all wishful fantasizing because Donovan kept his hands to himself.

The cushions threatened to swallow me again when I sagged back after stuffing myself.

"Hey, where are all the pillows?" I asked. Lots had been scattered throughout the room on the couch, the settee, and the chairs the last time I was here.

Donovan looked almost sheepish. "I've got to pick up some new ones."

If I wasn't so tired I would have laughed. "You abused them, didn't you?" I pictured him pummeling the crap out of every pillow in Kristin's living room while I was gone. "At least you didn't kill the walls."

"Gotta get this mess cleaned up," he said without looking at me.

"Let me help, since you cooked," I said, even though I wasn't sure my body would agree to me getting up off my butt.

"Uh-uh." Donovan leaned down and caught me by surprise when he scooped me into his arms. "It's bed for you."

"Mmmm. I snuggled against him as he carried me to the guest room. How did he smell so freaking good? "In a hurry tonight? Works for me."

He settled me on the edge of the bed. "Steele, you never slow down."

I clenched my fists in his soft blue T-shirt. "Right now I don't want it slow at all."

Donovan shook his head. "You need rest. Not sex."

"It's the other way around."

What a tight ass he had as he walked to my duffel and pulled out the long Red Sox T-shirt I usually slept in.

A sigh made my chest rise and fall. "Not going to give in, are you?"

"Nope." He brought the T-shirt to me.

I raised my cast. "You're gonna help me into that shirt, right?"

"You need rest." He tossed me the shirt and I caught it with my good hand. "And I doubt you'll behave."

"That's because behaving's no fun." I looked down at my shirt and back up at him. "Don't trust me, Donovan?"

"Never." Still he came toward me and knelt to help me out of my shirt. He was so careful and so slow that there was plenty of time for that burn inside of me to grow until I was ready to tackle him. The air didn't feel cool at all when my shirt was off. I hadn't worn a bra because all Donovan had brought to the infirmary were my jeans, panties, and a loose T-shirt.

"You had that planned all along." My voice was husky as

I spoke. "Forgetting to grab a bra when you got the rest of my stuff."

An electrical sensation traveled straight between my thighs as he skimmed his fingers over my belly when he went for the button of my jeans.

Bye-bye, sleepiness. Hello, horniness.

"Stand," he said, his voice low and rough.

Yeah, I was going to be a regular electrical transformer and explode by the time he finished with me.

Damn, he was good. It didn't take him long to unfasten my jeans and slide them over my hips straight to the floor. I kicked them out of the way, totally ready for Donovan to take me into his arms. He stepped around me and pulled the covers aside.

Straight to the bed, fine by me. Who was on top or bottom, I didn't care.

He helped me lie on my back while he knelt between my thighs. "Does your lower half hurt?"

I grinned. "Not at all."

Donovan slowly pulled down my underwear and tossed it on the floor. "I missed this," he said as he started lowering himself.

"Me, too—"

I gasped as he slid his hands under my ass and put his mouth on me. He licked and sucked while he thrust his fingers inside of me. He teased me, though. Licked around my clit, bringing me to the brink of orgasm and then drawing away.

"Damnit, Donovan. I'm so close." I reached down with my good hand and held the back of his head. "Stop teasing me and make me come. Please."

He sucked my clit and it was like the world exploded. My hips bucked against his face as he drew out every last bit of strength from me.

Donovan rose up over me, and I tasted my own musk when he kissed me. "Relaxed now?" he said against my lips.

"Oh, yeah." I looped my good arm around his neck. "I haven't been this relaxed since the last night we spent in bed."

"Good." He kissed me again before climbing off the bed

and grabbing my Red Sox T-shirt. "That was for you." Before I even had a chance to say anything, he snatched up my nightshirt and brought it over my head.

"What—" The T-shirt muffled me and I sputtered, not able to get a word out until he had my cast through one sleeve, my good arm through the other, and the neckline dropped over my head.

He pushed me backward onto the mattress. "Sleep."

"But—"

"When you're better," he said in a low and hungry tone, "I'm going to fuck you good and hard."

My glare should have poked him all over, like a million little needles. "You are such a tease."

"And you need your rest." He tucked me in, like I was a defiant child, as I narrowed my gaze at him. "As well as some time to recover," he added.

"You know I'll get even."

"I'm sure you will." He brushed his lips over mine, making me sigh and melting some of the irritation at being sent to bed without the rest of my treat.

Him. Inside me.

Donovan switched off the light, then left the room. I was so relaxed from my orgasm that I think I was asleep before the door closed behind him.

April 23
Tuesday, early, early morning

Nameless, faceless people. I shoot, shoot, shoot.

I'm strapped to a chair. I smell the sweat and stink of the Cuban prison. A man slugs me. I see stars, and then the man starts to unzip his pants.

Randolph. Dead. Her face white as she floats face up in the harbor, her throat slashed, her eyes and mouth open in a scream no one will ever hear.

Kristin. I can see her. But she's so far away. Must get to her!

Fire sears my skin, my entire being, as Cabot presses the brand inside my thigh. I scream, then scream louder as he pulls the hot metal from my skin.

The pain goes on forever as I struggle against the bonds on the St. Andrew's Cross. He's going to take that horrid metal and brand every bit of my naked flesh.

B. C. Benjamin Cabot.

His property.

"No!" I scream over and over again as he heats the metal again in red-hot coals. An orange-red glow from the flaming brand lights the devil's features as he raises it and brings it toward the inside of my other thigh.

Cabot jabs the brand at me like a fencer going in for the kill. He presses the hot metal so hard and so long against my flesh that I know he's going to burn it away, through to the bone.

I'll never stop screaming. I'll never be able to escape. I'll be his property forever.

"No, no, no." The word comes out over and over again before I start begging. "Please, no. Please, stop!"

He laughs. His eyes gleam red, matching the red glow of the coals. He brings the brand up to my breast—

"Lexi!" A male voice shouted at me.

In total darkness, a heavy body pinned me down against something soft. Still I fought, and the man gave a loud "oof" sound when I rammed my elbow into his belly. His shin was hard against my heel and he said, "Lexi!" before holding me tighter.

"No!" I shouted. "Not the brand! I won't let you do it again!"

I fought and screamed with everything I had. For some reason my right arm wouldn't move, but my left elbow worked real well.

"Lexi! Stop." The male voice gave another grunt of pain as I rose and slammed the back of my head into his forehead.

"No," I screamed again. "Get it away. Get it away!"

The man practically growled, "It's Donovan, Lexi. Donovan. Wake up. You're having a nightmare. Wake up."

I still struggled, but my movements were more feeble as my mind started to clear.

Donovan. His scent. The hardness of his body. The way he held me so tight, but trying not to hurt me.

The mattress was soft beneath me as my whole body went limp. Reality crept to my consciousness. I was away from Cabot. He couldn't brand me.

Again.

I pressed my hand to the bandage over my belly button. His initials seemed to burn as hot as the brand that had burned me in my dream.

When I swallowed my throat hurt, probably from screaming.

"Hey." Donovan's voice, softer now as he let up his tight grip on me. "It's going to be all right. It was just a nightmare."

"His brand is there. It's never going to be okay," I whispered.

"We'll make it okay." He pressed his lips to my temple and gave me a soft kiss. "But we'll talk about it in the morning."

"Hold me. Please."

"I'm not going anywhere." Donovan wrapped his arm around my waist and spooned himself against my back. "I'll hold onto you while you sleep. You're safe."

"Thank you," I whispered before I eventually slipped into a dreamless sleep, secure that for the rest of the night Donovan would keep the demons away.

CHAPTER 32

Kristin

April 23
Tuesday

"Now that you're broken in," Michaels said with a smile, once the chain was affixed to a jumbo-sized hook installed in the floor, "I'll let you have free range in the kitchen and dining nook. With the collar and chain on at all times, of course."

Kristin thought of knives. Kitchens usually meant knives.

He chuckled as if he could read her mind. "I've taken out anything lethal. Just in case you get any kind of strange urges that involve pain for me or death for you."

Kristin blinked. Suicide? That was something that had never come to her mind. She always held tight to the belief that Nick would find her.

She was a psychology major and a realist. She knew she wasn't going to get out of this mentally intact. It would take loads of therapy, but one day Michaels would be dead or in prison, and she'd be fine. She might not want to have sex for the rest of her life. But kill herself?

Michaels looked her naked body up and down. "Beautiful, as always."

Every time he did that—appraised her like a prized mare and complimented her—her skin crawled and she wanted to scream. Or cry. Or both.

"Fix my breakfast." Michaels waved toward the fridge and stove. "I don't have much time. My first class is in an hour." He strode away through the swinging doors that were a good ten feet from the end of her chain.

Classes. The semester was nearly over and here she was.

Kristin wasn't in the mood for the thin belt Michaels had used on her when he was ticked that she hadn't done what he said. She had to make this fast.

She looked around a large kitchen filled with cherrywood cabinets, a granite island, and stainless-steel appliances. Unlike Nick, her cooking skills were so-so, but she could get by. She headed for the pantry. The obviously expensive tile had an uneven texture beneath her bare feet.

Windows. What about the windows?

There were plenty.

All shuttered. And her chain didn't reach that far.

For a moment she could only stare at another bit of freedom, so close, but just out of her reach.

Something hard lodged in her chest. She wanted to throw one thing after another at those windows and shatter them all.

But that wouldn't do any good if she wasn't close enough to them to scream for help, and wasn't able to get herself out of this collar with its freaking heavy, thick chain.

Still—she would keep them in mind.

Kristin pulled her long hair back and twisted it into a knot so that it would stay out of her face.

After searching through the fridge and pantry—the entire time looking for anything that could be used as a lethal weapon—she found pancake mix, frozen sausage links, and eggs.

She scavenged through the utensil drawer. All plastic utensils, like spatulas and spaghetti spoons. Pretty useless if she wanted to inflict any damage.

But in one corner in the back was something Michaels didn't think would matter—or he didn't see.

A small, flat, metal punch can opener. The punch opener was about three inches long, with a triangular point on one end and a bottle cap opener on the other.

Kristin looked over her shoulder, her heart racing. It wasn't much, but maybe she could use it to pick at the leather collar, under the strap. If she only had someplace to hide it on her body. The only thing she had on was the half-inch thick, inch-wide leather collar, and it wasn't big enough. The collar was made of a material that was soft and didn't chafe her, and he didn't seem to think she needed balm beneath it.

But she still couldn't hide the can opener there. Instead she'd find someplace he'd never look. She had to get his breakfast done or she'd end up with strap marks from that belt. She ducked under the sink—the idiot had actually left stove cleaner, another thing to think about. She tucked the can opener so far back in the cabinet that she was positive it would never be seen. For good measure she pushed the spray stove cleaner back, too.

Now cook. Fast.

While she made breakfast, the normally delicious smells made her stomach cramp, but she wouldn't throw up.

She had puked on Michaels the first time he'd had her suck him in the bedroom and forced her to swallow. All these weeks later and she swore she could still feel his fists. Who'd have thought a man with zero muscle tone could pack the kind of punch he did?

She flipped a pancake. Food was something she didn't care about anymore. She just ate because she had to. Not just because Michaels insisted, but she had to be ready and well for the first opportunity she had . . .

Whatever that might be.

What was it that Michaels had said? Now that he'd broken her. It had been only a couple of days since he'd let three other professors have her at once, and she wanted to throw up at the memory, and roll up into a ball and stay that way forever.

The green fluid Michaels had shot her up with had made her dazed, but also made her respond sexually to the men, as if she enjoyed it. The whole thing was like something had taken her over and she'd been on the inside watching out. The way she had responded made her feel like she needed to be scrubbed inside and out, and never stop.

She didn't want to remember but the images of herself and the men wouldn't go away, and a tear tried to escape from the corner of her eye.

Grease splattered her naked breasts while the sausages popped and sizzled, and she yelped from the sting. The burn was welcome as it took her away from thinking about things she wanted to forget.

Kristin stared at the pan. A hot pan. It was lightweight, cheap—he probably thought she couldn't hurt him with the single pan he'd left in the kitchen.

Her heart beat faster, like it had when she found the punch opener and the oven cleaner. Somehow she could use these things. She just needed a plan. A good plan.

She flipped the last pancake. She'd get away, yes. But even when she was far away from this monster, she knew she could never forget everything he'd done to her. Everything about him was branded into her permanently.

Michaels walked into the room just as she finished putting out a paper plate and plastic spoon for him. He sure wasn't taking any chances by giving her only plastic spoons.

The collar didn't chafe her but she hated it. Hated everything it represented. She tugged at the leather collar before she picked up the plastic tray of pancakes, sausage links, and fried eggs that she had prepared for *Michaels*. Not professor. Not Professor Michaels. He was nothing.

The chain jangled as she moved from the stove to the kitchen table. No ordinary chain. It weighed her down, not only physically but mentally. It was so large it would take an elephant to break away from it. A tractor might be able to move the hook he'd had installed.

When she reached the table with the tray, Michaels looked up at her and smiled. "Breakfast smells wonderful."

I hope you choke on it.

Kristin had a hard time keeping her lips from trembling as she forced a smile in return, like she was expected to, as well as responding with "Thank you, Professor."

Kristin carefully used the plastic spatula to move four pancakes, six sausage links, and three fried eggs to his plate. Maybe he would die of clogged arteries.

"I'm in the mood for a little something extra this morning

with breakfast." He studied her naked body again, hunger in his small eyes.

Blood seemed to drain from her scalp, through her body, and all the way into the floor.

Oh no. Oh, God, no.

Michaels pointed down. "On your hands and knees."

Kristin trembled so hard the chain links rattled as they scraped against the floor when she obeyed. This was something he'd never made her do before. Another degrading act that sent acid washing through her.

The horror filling her was like someone was taking knives to her body as she watched him unfasten his slacks and release his erection.

Maybe death was better.

"Crawl." He indicated to her to come to him by crooking his finger. "And suck."

Kristin couldn't have stopped it if she wanted to. Right now she welcomed it. That acid she'd felt in her chest bolted up her throat. Her stomach heaved and she threw up all over his cold tile floor.

She felt his kick to her belly before she realized he'd moved.

CHAPTER 33

Nick

April 23
Tuesday afternoon

As they settled down in what Lexi called Nick's "war room," Lexi swiveled on a chair beside him and held her cast to her belly. He was so damned thankful they'd found her, he wanted to hold her and not let her go.

He met her green eyes as she said, "Thank you for finding me."

Nick grabbed her chair and pulled it toward him, the rollers making it easy for him to reach her. He captured her small chin in one of his hands. "How could I let down the best partner I've ever had?"

She grinned. "You just missed the sex."

He almost laughed. "There is that."

One of his cell phones rang and he released her to draw the phone out of its clip, then set it next to a monitor as Lexi rolled her chair back a little.

He pushed the speakerphone button, his eyes still on Lexi. "Donovan," he said.

"Is this Nick Donovan?" a young woman's voice said over the speakerphone. "Kristin's brother?"

Nick's attention snapped fully from Lexi to the cell. "Yeah. Who's this?"

"Carlene." The girl hesitated. "You asked me some questions about Kristin weeks ago, after she disappeared. I was with her that night." Her voice sounded hopeful as she added, "Have you found her?"

Nick rubbed his temples with his thumb and forefinger and he sighed. It was just a friend asking after his sister. "No," his tone was sharp. He sighed again and said in a calmer voice, "We're still looking for leads."

"I wish we would never have talked her into going to the club." Carlene sounded bitter. "She had a paper due for her abnormal psych class. Professor Michaels is a real dickhead."

"I've got your number." Nick was already turning his attention to the surveillance monitors. "I'll let you know when we find her."

"Wait." The girl rushed to get her words out. "I'm on my cell phone and late for class because I just heard a conversation that I think might be important. What I overheard, well, the whole thing didn't sound right." Carlene paused for only a moment. "One of the agents with you mentioned sex slave stuff—that right now there's a huge market for it in Boston and women were being kidnapped from clubs."

Carlene had Nick's full attention again. "Go on." He gritted his teeth, trying to remain calm, but the sex slave reference wasn't making it easy.

Carlene started talking faster, "I'd dropped my backpack by a faculty lounge in the psych building—you know, WJ Hall."

"I interviewed Kristin's teachers there after she disappeared," Nick said. "Along with as many students as I could track down."

"This was creepy and strange," Carlene said and Nick had the urge to tell her to hurry. "Okay, so I dropped my backpack. It's a Louis Vuitton and I'd been in a hurry and hadn't latched it right, so my books fell out." She took a deep, audible breath. "Anyway, I heard voices. Men's voices. I wasn't paying attention until they said something that freaked me out."

A sensation like flames licking his skin raced down Nick's spine. "Go on."

"I heard one man say he wished he had a student who'd drop out of school just to, uh, well . . ." she cleared her throat. "What he said was a student to drop out to 'fuck' any time he wanted to."

Nick stood, his back completely rigid as he stared at the phone, those flames along his back turning into pinpricks of fire. "What else?" he asked.

"A couple of other men were talking, too." The girl started to sound a little frightened. "One man said something about how hot the student was last night. They couldn't believe how excited the cute little blond slut was to have three men, uh, screw her, all at the same time. That she liked doing it while—I didn't catch a name—watched."

Nick dropped back into his chair and his stomach churned. He braced his elbows on his knees and held his head in his hands, his mind suddenly swimming. His voice was hoarse as he raised his head and said to Carlene, "Did any of the men add to that?"

"I don't think—" Carlene paused for a moment. "Wait. They said that the 'professor'—so it was one of them—told the men the girl seemed kinda out of it because she liked to do a little coke before she got it on. One man laughed and said fine by him. He'd sure like to find a piece of ass like that himself."

"Anything else?" Nick was finding it hard to talk. "Are you sure you didn't catch any names? Recognize any voices?"

"No. The psych department is huge and I've only studied under a few of the professors there."

"What happened next?" If it was his sister—goddamn fucking sonofabitch. Then what she was going through was unthinkable. He'd gut every fucker who'd touched her.

The line crackled with a little static. "One of them sounded closer to the door when he talked so I grabbed everything I'd dropped and got out of there."

"That was good." Nick took deep, measured breaths as he continued to bend his head and brace his elbows on his knees. "You sure no one had any idea you heard them?"

"Positive," Carlene said. "A class let out the same time I scooted around the corner so I was sort of in the middle of them before any of the professors could have come out of the lounge."

"Thank you, Carlene," Nick said and he couldn't have helped holding back the pain in his voice if he'd tried.

The floating sensation in his head made this lead seem surreal. It could be nothing, but it could be everything. "Let me know if you hear anything else," Nick said.

"Absolutely." Carlene sounded like she was swallowing down a lump in her throat. "Find her. Please."

"I'll find her." Nick looked at Lexi and his expression said, "And the sonsofbitches who took her will pay."

After Carlene said good-bye, Nick pushed the speaker's off button and he met Lexi's eyes.

"Something about this isn't right, Nick," Lexi said. "Could the blond student the men had been talking about be Kristin? Whoever bought her could have shot her up with that designer drug, Lascivious. The man could have made her do anything he wanted her to do."

"Fuck!" Nick clenched his fists and slammed them onto his thighs. Rage burned within him like before. "We're going to find that fucker and I'm going to blow the sonofabitch's balls away. Before I kill him.

"It might not be her," he continued. "But the whole thing is too big of a coincidence." Nick reached for his RED-issued cell phone. "I'm calling everyone we can get on this." He opened his cell so hard it was a wonder he didn't snap it. "I'm going to find who this sick bastard is and see if he's got my sister."

Nick

April 24th

Wednesday early morning

"Damnit." Nick's strides were long as Lexi tried to keep up with him from the parking garage elevator of RED's HQ, into the lobby. He scanned his fingerprints, and walked into the elevators with Lexi at his side. "You should be resting," he said as he narrowed his eyes at ber.

Lexi had insisted on going with Nick to work even though she was supposed to be on leave. "You couldn't hold me back no matter how hard you tried." And he'd tried. The only thing he didn't do was rat her out to Oxford.

Tuesday, yesterday, after the call from Carlene, Nick had immediately called Oxford on her cell. With her clear go-ahead it hadn't taken Nick long to put together a plan and set up a K-Team—K for Kristin—via phone with the best special agents available to start on the Harvard op.

When Nick and Lexi stepped off the elevator on the fifth floor, they passed Special Agent Rani Ogitani who gestured to Lexi's cast and said, "Aren't you supposed to be home resting up, Steele?"

She rolled her eyes. "Not you, too, Rani."

"Hope for your sake Oxford doesn't see you." Agent Ogitani shook her head before going down the stairs to the command center.

"Same here," Lexi muttered. Nick turned away from Ogitani. Oxford would be all over them both if she found out Lexi was here.

As soon as they got to Conference Room Four, Nick notified his team to meet them in the conference room. It was only a matter of moments after he and Lexi were seated at the conference table when Takamoto, Jensen, Smithe, and Karl Weiss made it to the room.

It was obvious Lexi didn't want to attract too much attention since she wasn't even supposed to be there. She stayed clear on the far end of the table away from the head of the table. Nick was at the head of the table where he'd be leading the strategy session.

Still, all four agents who came into the room greeted Lexi in one way or another. Takamoto asked if he could sign her cast as he gave a wink. Smithe took one look at her face, grinned, and told her she looked like shit. Weiss shook his head and made a smart-ass remark about the size of her cast. And Jensen told her that she should get herself back home.

Nick was too wired to park his ass when his team assembled around the conference table. He still had a slight limp from the bullet wound, but he didn't really notice it.

He leaned over the touchpad mounted into the table, just

long enough to pull up a vertical holographic grid map. The map of Harvard Square and Harvard's main psych building hovered over the center of the conference room table.

Nick held his anger in check—barely—as he laid out all the info he'd gathered from Kristin's friend. He clenched his jaw. What the girl had said wasn't pretty. And if it was Kristin—

The thought left him cold.

"Weiss." Nick directed his attention to the sandy-haired agent who had a knack for appearing to be anywhere between his thirties to his fifties. "I want you on the inside today. Do what it takes to pass yourself off as a psych professor. Early fifties but acting like you're fifteen years younger.

"Our target area is currently the floor where the girl heard the conversation." Nick ran his hand over his stubble. "Let it slip you're into kink if you think you've found a mark. As soon as you leave this conference room get to that building. RED already has you on the roster using your undercover name, Karl Zimmer."

"Harvard, eh?" Weiss, who was actually in his early thirties, grinned. "Haaah-vaaahhhd. Never thought I'd pass onto those hallowed grounds."

"Jensen." Nick didn't feel a damned bit of amusement. He moved his gaze to Jensen and met her eyes as he stepped closer to the table.

The redhead looked expectant. Nick said, "You'll play the pretty co-ed who likes to have sex with professors in exchange for good grades. Weiss will tell the mark you've made excellent grades with him. We've got you registered as Brittany Jacobs and we'll give you a list of classes that you're going to attend, starting today."

Jensen winced. "Brittany?"

Nick braced his hands on the conference table as he continued to speak to Jensen. "You and Weiss will have to act the part if our plan falls into place." He looked at Weiss. "I want it clear Weiss is a perv."

"Won't be hard." Smithe snorted a laugh. "Perfect assignment for Weiss."

"Bite me." Weiss made an obscene gesture with his hand at Smithe, but Weiss was grinning.

"You've got it, Donovan," Jensen said as she ignored Smithe and Weiss. "Ready to start when you give the go-ahead."

"Takamoto, how's the surveillance?" Nick turned to the agent.

"After you called last night, I got a hold of every agent I could find and we did our thing," Takamoto said. "When everyone was out of the building last night, we took over. We've got that whole floor wired from faculty lounges to offices and restrooms."

Takamoto went on, "I've got a thorough, fast team and we've got some new kick-ass gadgets from the RED research and development team that Martinez provided us with. Excellent equipment that's going to allow us greater surveillance with less manpower in all areas."

"Good." Nick gave a sharp nod. "Keep on it."

Nick turned to Smithe. "Smithe, stay on those surveillance vids and the Internet, and keep working on tracking down that van and any nightclub that Benjamin Cabot might be tied to."

"We've been searching ownership records for every nightclub as fast as we can." Smithe looked frustrated. "But there are hundreds and so far we can't trace any of them back to Cabot. Not even the Champagne Slipper, if you can believe that."

"The clubs held by foreign investors are probably the ones we want to keep our eyes on," Nick said.

"My thoughts, too," Smithe said. "However, that doesn't narrow the field down a whole lot."

"It sure doesn't." Nick shoved his hand through his hair. "In the meantime I'm going to snag a few more agents and continue to work every other angle we can come up with."

Nick rolled his shoulders, trying to ease the tension between his shoulder blades. "Maybe we've missed something that will match up between the other girls' disappearances and Kristin's."

"Besides the fact they vanished while at nightclubs and we have all twelve of those nightclubs under surveillance," Jensen said.

"We know the nightclub Kristin was taken from was used twice." Nick scowled and balled his fists on the conference room table. "Maybe we'll get lucky and the idiots will go back to one of the others."

Nick pushed himself away from the table and turned to Smithe. "Anything else on the Internet?"

"Rollins has come up with a few new chat rooms that we've been tracking down," Smithe said, "but nothing that relates to the one we believe was associated with your sister."

Nick slammed his fist on the table. "Let's do it."

CHAPTER 34

Don't call me chick

April 24
Wednesday late afternoon

The grid that Donovan currently had up in his war room at Kristin's was huge. It was a detailed map of the Harvard psychology hall. I had an antsy feeling all over and I had a hard time sitting still in my chair.

Donovan frowned at a monitor showing a series of transcripts from some of Harvard's professors and students. We'd recorded these today while Jensen and Weiss went in and did their thing.

From the fact that we knew Kristin was in the Boston area, that she had attended Harvard, and from what Carlene had said, my bet was on the Harvard lead, too.

In the meantime, we were all following every other damned lead we hit. Internet chat rooms, snitches, surveillance tapes—

So far everything led to nothing.

The doorbell rang.

I frowned at Donovan.

"It's probably the guys." Donovan's eyes looked so tired.

The doorbell's ring was more insistent and I stood. "The special, special specialists?"

Donovan started to get up, but I reached the door first. "I'll go see if it's your special, special guys."

A little amusement crossed his features, and I turned and headed for the front door.

The doorbell rang again. I yanked the door open.

A huge man was on the other side. And I mean *huge*.

His intense black eyes and a deadly air about him that said he'd kill a person without thinking twice about it had my heart pounding and blood pumping.

I stepped one foot back, just enough to anchor myself, and my whole body went on guard as I took a loose-limbed stance.

"Who are you?" I asked.

He gave an amused aren't-you-a-cute-little-thing look. A thick braid brushed his back as he looked over his shoulder and at the same time braced one hand on the door frame. His huge biceps flexed, as did the Bengal tiger tattooed there. "Some chick is here, guys. She's pretty hot, but I think she's got a temper."

Speaking of hot and a temper, heat flushed beneath my skin and I ground my teeth before speaking. "First of all, I'm not some chick. Second of all, I don't appreciate being talked about like I'm not here."

The man looked back at me and narrowed his black eyes. I narrowed mine.

"Tiger, the five-four agent with the attitude of a six-seven linebacker is my partner," came Donovan's voice from his war room. "You can let them in, Steele."

Them? The guy was so huge I hadn't seen the men behind him until I peeked around his arm.

"Jeez," I muttered before letting by all that steely muscle and testosterone.

"Oh, yeah," the first guy said. "That's the naked chick we found."

"Don't. Call. Me. Chick," I shouted at his backside. The naked part I ignored.

The tiredness in my bones totally fled when I came face-to-face with another man who had "killer" written all over him. The soreness of my body was just an afterthought as I stepped back and two more huge men passed by. One of them had an earring and winked at me.

I just stared at their backsides for a moment before I shut the door and followed them into Donovan's war room.

The four huge men crowded the relatively small space. The guy called Tiger was the closest to me. Including Donovan, I was in the Land of the Giant Testosterone Factories. My brothers were big guys—with the exception of my twelve-year-old brother—but this. . . . I felt like a peg about to be pounded by five huge hammers.

Donovan stood and with one hand rubbed his eyes, which looked as tired as I'd felt before I'd come face-to-face with Tiger.

Donovan braced his hand on the back of the chair he'd been sitting in and looked from me to the men surrounding me. I saw another flash of amusement. "These guys worked Special Ops with me when I went back into the service, and you might say we've kept in touch."

I hadn't realized Donovan had gone back into the service. I had wondered what he'd done after Kristin turned eighteen, but we just never had a chance to have another heart-to-heart.

"Guys, this is Special Agent Lexi Steele," Donovan said, "and you'd better play nice because she was a sniper in the Army Special Forces, and a trained assassin."

The guys looked interested, if not disbelieving, as they looked down at little ole me. Jeez, these guys were all anywhere from ten to twelve inches taller than me.

All four of the Special Ops guys were even more powerfully built than Donovan, a couple of them more muscle-bound than the others. I wouldn't call Donovan muscle-bound, but he was damned muscular, and if there was the tiniest bit of fat on him I'd kiss that tight ass of his.

So what if I'd like to bite that ass anyway?

I kept my expression clear as I looked from man to man to man to man. Tiger moved so close to me my skin prickled.

Donovan gestured to the guy beside me. "Tiger Manning." Then he named off the other three guys as he pointed to them. "Aaron Lloyd, Mike Freeman, and Eric Harrison."

The men came up to me one at a time and we shook hands, each guy making me feel as small as a child as they took my hand in their big grips.

I went for the casual you-don't-scare-me-one-damned-bit approach as I was introduced to the guys. "Hi, Lloyd," I said as he gave my hand a firm squeeze. Aaron Lloyd had a hawk's amber eyes—totally amazing eyes.

Mike Freeman was next. "Didn't know Donovan had such a sexy partner," Freeman said in a slow, deep, Southern drawl that could curl a girl's toes.

"Didn't know Donovan had such oafs for friends," I said with a sugar-sweet smile as he released my hand and he grinned.

"We usually call Freeman 'Tank,' " Donovan said.

Yeah, the man with the blond crew cut, barbed-wire tattoo around his biceps on one arm, and a big stocky build *did* look like a friggin' tank.

Next, Eric Harrison took my hand in the firmest grip yet. He had an even more vicious air to him than Tiger had, if that was possible. It was in his grin, and in his brown eyes as he looked at me.

"Harrison," I said as I assessed him, taking in his long brown ponytail and gold earring. He was the one who'd winked at me.

I made myself shake Tiger Manning's hand and he gave me a wicked, wicked grin. Jerk. "Manning," I greeted him before I removed my hand from his grip.

By this time we were all crowded into the small room, me at the center. "Bet you guys are a real kick at a keg party," I said, and Freeman laughed while the others grinned.

I braced my hands on my hips. "So what's the deal?"

Donovan gestured to the other chairs. "Have a seat, guys." I swear it was a wonder those chairs didn't bust beneath their power-packed bodies.

I took my seat close to Donovan. So what if I'd rather be closer to him?

He started laying everything out to the guys, all our plans for tracking down the professors at Harvard who were involved in the "sex with a student dropout."

"We'll take care of that at RED." Donovan didn't notice my stunned expression because he'd named our agency.

"What I need you guys to keep working on is to find that soon-to-be-dead sonofabitch Cabot. We'll keep in close contact, and I'll call you in if we think we've found Kristin."

The guys talked a little more and I mentally took full measure of each man. Speaking of, these guys were mean sonsofbitches, every one of them. I calculated what I thought their biggest weaknesses were, just for the hell of it. Wasn't easy, and I knew it wasn't necessary. If Donovan could trust them, then I would.

I glanced at Tiger Manning. Didn't mean I had to like them.

April 24
Wednesday evening

The sheaf of papers I'd printed out, of notes from the Harvard team, almost slipped from the fingers of my good hand when I picked them up, and I had to tighten my grip.

After the "special special team" left, Donovan and I spent all of our time doing everything we could to search for Kristin. We couldn't find her fast enough. Already she'd been missing far too long.

The ache in my heart was like an anchor weighing me down. I hurt for both of them. Especially Kristin. If it was the last thing I did, I was going to help Donovan find his sister.

Okay, one of the last two things I did. I was going to help find Kristin, but I was going to avenge Randolph's death by gunning for Cabot, too. Even if I had to chase him around the world.

Why did every breath I take in seem to hurt? It wasn't from my broken ribs.

The back of my eyes ached. I closed them and tried to slow my breathing. It wasn't going to do anyone a bit of good if I lost control because of what was happening to Kristin.

Breathe in. Breathe out. Open your eyes.

My gaze rested on Donovan. So serious. So intense.

The words on the Harvard notes blurred. My focus was nonexistent and my brain started misfiring. A loud growl sounded in the room, and it took me a moment to realize it was my stomach making all that noise.

Donovan looked away from what he'd been studying and pushed his chair back from his desk. He swiped his hand down his stubbled face. "I'll fix dinner."

"You so know how to sweet-talk me." I managed a tired smile as we stood.

Talk about a long day. It had started with the early morning meeting with the team penetrating the school, work at RED, then more work at Donovan's, then meeting Donovan's "friends," and then more time on reviewing the first day's notes from the Harvard op. It was hard to believe Carlene's call was only last night.

Donovan caught me by the shoulders before I could leave the room. "Why don't you listen to me and rest? You don't need to be doing this."

I kept my gaze on him. "I'm going to help you find Kristin. Try and stop me."

CHAPTER 35

Skip the strawberries and pass the whipped cream

April 24
Wednesday late evening

After the long friggin' day, I needed a warm, relaxing bath while Donovan fixed us dinner. I still had to keep my bandages and cast out of the water, so it was never easy. I refused to look at the bandage on my belly that covered what hurt me more than anything.

When my skin started to wrinkle from being in the water so long, I got out, towel-dried my body and hair, and got a good look at my face in the mirror. Three days hadn't given the bruises a lot of time to heal, so looking sexy for Donovan wasn't on the menu. But who cared? I had to have him.

I *needed* him. I needed that intimacy with him, and I was sure he did too.

With a little maneuvering, I managed to pull on a pair of stretchy jogging shorts and a clean top with no bra. Hey, why screw with the thing while wearing a damned cast?

I dried my hair some more. I felt refreshed, not worn out from spending the day looking at maps and charts and surveillance vids.

A little more energized, I walked down the hall and headed to the kitchen, following the most heavenly smells.

I went through the kitchen door and saw Dixie with her silver bowl of Fancy Feast. "You spoil her, you know."

Donovan looked up from where he was making some

kind of Chinese dish in a wok. Yummy. Donovan. Oh, and the food, too.

When he caught my gaze all I could concentrate on were his lips.

Those lips. I so wanted to feel them on mine, to taste him like when he had found me.

"I need to help," I said as I moved toward him.

He raised his eyebrows, and his expression was most definitely suspicious.

When I was within inches of him, I would have tried to put my arms around him to pull him toward me for that kiss I wanted so badly, but I'd likely hit him upside the head with my cast and knock him out. Instead I leaned close to him and tipped my head back, inviting him. "You're awfully unfair, you know," I said.

Donovan gave me an amused look. "Oh?"

"You give me the most amazing kisses and mind-blowing orgasms, but you act like I'll crumble if you go any farther."

He settled his hands low on my hips and his mouth crooked in that sexy way. "Maybe I'm afraid I'll crumble."

"Let's find out," I said.

And he kissed me.

Heaven.

His taste, the way his tongue explored my mouth, the way his lips moved over mine—I could seriously get addicted. Fine by me if we stayed here forever. He gently nipped at my lower lip and I gave a sigh of pleasure.

That kiss was doing serious things to my body. Nipples at attention, and lord did I ache between my thighs.

Donovan drew away and I sighed, still in total bliss as I said, "This is worth missing dinner for."

Cast be damned. I just about crawled right up him when he ran his finger over the curve of my ear. "You are not missing dinner."

His T-shirt felt soft and warm as I clutched it in my good fist. "Pretty please?"

"No."

"How about dessert?" I said. "I don't mind missing dessert."

That cute little quirk again. "What if it involves strawberries and whipped cream?"

"As long as I'm wearing it."

A full-fledged grin. I got a grin out of him!

He traced his finger down my collarbone and stopped at the swell of my breast. "I have the strangest desire to skip dinner, too."

"Oh, I love it. Straight for dessert."

"No." He tugged at a lock of my hair. "I bet your mother would think you've been starved to death if she got a good look at you now. After a week of only broth—Steele, you're too thin."

I raised my shirt just enough to show my bandages. "You can't see my ribs anyway. So who'll notice?" I dropped my shirt again and pressed against him.

He brought his fingers up and brushed his knuckles along my cheekbone. "Look at me, honey. The exhaustion and the fact you haven't had decent meals for awhile—it's right in those pretty green eyes of yours."

"Then feed me." I crossed my arm and my cast in front of me, and gave him a pretend glare. "And I demand dessert. Strawberries. With lots and lots of whipped cream." I tipped my head to the side. "On second thought, skip the strawberries."

He pressed his lips tight to mine. "Maybe," he said when he released me.

I looked down at the hard line of his erection and met his eyes. "Uh-huh."

April 24
Wednesday evening

My system was haywire and I could barely think, much less concentrate on dinner.

The moment Donovan set his empty plate on the coffee table, I tackled him, knocking him back on the couch so that I straddled his thighs. I was real careful not to sit on the part of his body that was still healing from the bullet wound.

A grin. Ha! I got a grin again when I tackled him!

As he settled his hands on my hips, I pushed his T-shirt up and ran my palms over his taut abs. Such warm skin and hard muscle—I wanted to kiss and lick and taste every square inch. Not enough time. Had to have him. Now. "Time for dessert, Donovan."

"What about the whipped cream?" The look in his eyes was absolutely wicked.

"Can't wait that long." I pushed his shirt higher up and settled myself over his erection. He felt so big. "I want you inside me right this minute."

Donovan cupped the back of my head with one of his hands, brought my mouth to his, and spoke against my lips. "Don't you think it might help if we weren't wearing clothes?"

"Damn," I murmured before he brought me down hard, kissing me with the same intensity as he had when he'd found me a few nights ago.

Mmmm, delicious. The Guinness he'd had with dinner mingled with this new taste that I didn't think I could get enough of. No describing the flavor, it was uniquely Donovan.

My tongue met his again and again as I braced my good hand on one shoulder. He sure didn't seem to mind my cast pressing against his other.

I groaned into his mouth as his hands moved from my hips and slipped beneath the oversized T-shirt, up my belly, and settled on my breasts. Smart me. No bra.

Had my nipples ever been so tight, ached so much to be touched? Licked? Sucked?

Whoa. Dizzy. His kiss actually made my world spin. I rocked on his erection as he squeezed my nipples and I felt how hard he was between my thighs. Unfortunately there was the tiny matter of his jeans and my shorts between his cock and my achy, achy parts. I wanted to feel his length, his hardness, to have every inch of him inside me.

I gasped when he took his lips from mine and adjusted me so that he could lick one nipple before running his tongue over the other.

"Donovan—" I started to say something, but my mind blanked when he gently bit my nipple. How many times could a woman cry "Oh, my God!" when with a man like Donovan?

I was on my way to finding out.

My shorts were completely damp between my thighs as I squirmed against him. Couldn't take much more.

What was I going to say? Yeah. "Clothes." I moaned with the next nip of his teeth. "Off."

He adjusted me so that he could skim his lips along the curve of my ear. Shivers along my spine. "How loose are those shorts?" A growl. I swear he said it in a low, husky growl that reverberated through me.

Shorts? Loose?

Yes, oh yes. "Loose enough."

His jeans roughened the insides of my thighs as I scooted down just enough to unbutton his jeans. Small problem of the cast.

He did the honors.

What an honor. The sheer size of him was going to feel so good again. Oh, yeah.

The need to taste him first was so strong that I wrapped my fingers around his cock and slid my lips down it. I heard the catch in his breath as I flicked my tongue and tasted the salt of his skin and the bit of semen on the head of his erection. He gave a loud groan and clenched his hands in my hair as I sucked hard.

I looked up at him and his jaw was tight as our eyes met.

"Got to fuck you." He sounded like it was costing him just to talk. "Be inside you."

I raised my head enough to say, "Oh, yeah. Talk dirty. I love it."

He pushed his erection into my mouth before he released my hair with one hand. I flicked my tongue and sucked his cock as he reached beneath him and drew out a packet.

The moment he got that packet open, he tossed it aside and made me stop sucking him so that he could roll the condom down his erection.

Donovan drew me up so that I was directly over him. His hand brushed the curls on my mound as he pulled the crotch of my shorts aside.

"Christ, Lexi," he said. "I'm going to take you hard and I'm not going to stop until you come."

He brought me down so fast that I didn't expect it. The moment he drove his cock into me I gasped and almost shouted.

So thick, long, and hard. My eyes nearly watered as he reached deep inside me. His grasp on my hips tightened as he raised and lowered me in time to every one of his thrusts.

He hadn't been kidding.

I'd never felt anything like this. I clenched my fist in his T-shirt as I hung on for the ride. Trying to keep my eyes from crossing wasn't easy as my climax came rushing toward me like a subway train that had decided it wasn't stopping for anything. No brakes.

Donovan didn't slow his pace, but from the tenseness on his features and the way he clenched his jaw I'd bet he was as close to coming as I was.

When our eyes met and the intensity of his passion hit me, my orgasm slammed into me. I just about screamed. But my cry was almost that loud.

I didn't close my eyes because I wanted to see his face, while my whole body trembled with sensations I couldn't begin to do justice to explaining. A whoosh of heat and the feeling that every nerve ending was on complete fire.

My core contracted as he continued to thrust. Then he gave a shout, with a few final thrusts, and I spasmed even more, my channel gripping his cock as he throbbed inside me. I swear I felt every pulse, like it was in my veins.

Whoa. Muscles wouldn't be supporting me much longer after that orgasm. Or orgasms. Mine and his.

He drew me to him just in time or I would have hit his chest hard.

Donovan held me tight, the side of my head to his heart as we both breathed hard and unevenly. His heartbeat was as crazy as mine.

When I could finally catch my breath, and some of my strength came back, I rose and met his eyes. "Let's try it with whipped cream now."

CHAPTER 36

Professors and pricks

April 26
Friday noon

At RED HQ, Donovan stood with his arms crossing his chest while we stared at the wall monitors covering every restroom, faculty lounge, and all the professors' offices—including their private bathrooms.

The quick research we'd done by interviewing certain staff members had pointed out professors worthy of being checked out, and Weiss had been hot on their tails the past two days, three if you count today.

The old farts with the sticks up their butts, who practically needed walkers or had canes, we weren't bothering with. Yet.

Right now twenty different locations had been cued up on the single giant screen. Each place had more than one camera angle and was monitored by an agent with earphones as the agent listened to conversation in their assigned area.

"I want to scrape this damned cast off," I grumbled to no one while wishing I could itch my arm. The throb that had been in my dislocated shoulder was almost gone—it had been almost two weeks since Danny yanked my arm out of its socket. My face was looking better and my chest didn't hurt so much.

"This is boring as hell," one of the newer agents said.

I gave a low laugh. "Welcome to the world of surveillance."

Yeah, it was boring as hell, all right. A yawn threatened to escape me during our constant surveillance of the monitors while we followed Weiss and Jensen throughout the day.

We were into our third day of the Harvard K-Team op and it felt like we were gradually closing in.

Right now Donovan studied one of the monitors as we watched Weiss. The agent casually walked behind Galsband, a professor who was one of our prime suspects, into a faculty lounge.

Our sources had said Galsband had been forward with several of his female students, more so than most of the other professors. Then we'd seen it happen for ourselves.

No one had ever complained about sexual harassment against Galsband, which was interesting. Probably had something to do with grades—threats perhaps. Who'd believe the word of a young grad student over a well-respected professor?

The scowl that hurt my face gave me a headache. I wanted to spit the sour taste out of my mouth, a taste that increased just at the thought of what the man had done already, right before our eyes. On film in brilliant color. Over the course of just this one day, two female students—at different times—agreed to have dinner with Galsband this weekend. Then there were the arrangements he'd made with a student on Wednesday, and one on Thursday.

Afterward, the professor had stroked his dick through his slacks and given a grin that sent frissons of disgust through me. The man had to be sixty, and the coeds barely twenty.

Donovan and I changed the frequency of our earphones to pick up sound in the lounge Weiss had gone into.

Another reason they'd picked Galsband was his low, frequent conversations with Professors Grumman, Allen, and Michaels. Nothing overt had been said other than Michaels's casual mention of a "poker game" at his house on Friday.

Tonight.

What interested us most was the way the men said the words and the looks they gave each other that included sly grins and innuendos. Reading expressions was something I'd always been good at, and I'd lay bets that it wasn't a poker game the professors were planning.

Which meant Weiss and Jensen had some work to do.

Those professors had it good at Harvard. Rich-looking furniture and an air of wealth.

When Weiss walked into the faculty lounge, Galsband glanced over his shoulder and gave a brief nod to him before reaching into a fridge for a bottle of Perrier.

"Professor Galsband, isn't it?" Weiss said as he bypassed the professor to grab his own bottle.

The professor's hair was trimmed neatly, his sophisticated graying hair on each side of his head like friggin' silver bat wings. He twisted the cap off his bottle and tossed the cap into a waste can. "I met you earlier with, who was it? Allan and Grumman, I believe."

Weiss took a swig of his bottle and swallowed before nodding. "Name is Zimmer."

"That's right." Galsband had a self-important tone to his voice. "What is it you teach?"

Weiss gave a smug grin. "What I'm best at is doing a little tutoring on the side with a few coeds. If you know what I mean."

Galsband raised his eyebrows. "Really, Professor."

Weiss shrugged, but kept what you'd definitely call a lecherous smile on his face. "A bennie that comes along with the job."

"Indeed." Galsband looked like he was suppressing a smile of his own. "I must be getting to class now."

"I'm between classes. Time to do a little 'tutoring.'" Weiss tossed his empty bottle into a garbage bin. "Cute little redhead . . ." He winked and headed out of the lounge.

For a moment Galsband stared at the door after it swung closed behind Weiss. His mouth curved into a smile and he tossed his own green bottle away. "Benefits, most certainly," he said aloud before heading out of the door. The camera switched and the RED agents watched as Galsband walked to his class.

"Jensen, Weiss, you're on," one of the agents said into a microphone. Both Jensen and Weiss were wired.

Weiss glanced up at one of the hall cameras a RED agent

switched to. "Ready and willing," Weiss said as he walked toward Galsband's office.

"Can't wait," Jensen said from around the corner, with an expression that meant she'd rather be doing anything than what they'd planned.

Jensen had done a great job of making herself look like a hot little coed, with a very padded bra that would put Georgina's balloon boobs to shame. Weiss had pulled off the fifty look well when he added some silver to his hair and a pair of older-guy glasses.

Once they met at Galsband's office, Weiss tried to twist the knob. He glanced at the camera as he spoke. "Locked."

"Watch the monitors, HQ." Jensen pushed Weiss out of the way at the same time she pulled a small kit from her Gucci backpack. Part of the game—a pack meant to carry books at the same time it showed she had some money.

"Students coming around right corner into the hallway," the monitoring agent said through her earpiece.

At once Jensen straightened, slung her pack over her shoulder, and she and Weiss appeared to be engaged in an animated conversation about one of her classes, speaking in German to, hopefully, avoid most students understanding them if they overheard.

Weiss and Jensen had to wait until one professor and three more students passed before Jensen could go after the lock.

In seconds Jensen had the door open, her lock pick stuffed in her backpack, and she and Weiss slipped into Galsband's office.

"Well, well," I said, and Donovan looked over his shoulder at me. "Might as well be a library in a mansion." Rosewood desk, shelves, and padded chairs. A collection of brass telescopes in glass cases that also contained other items gleamed in the lighting.

Donovan went back to staring at the monitors. Forty friggin' minutes passed by. I spent the time wishing my arm would stop itching under my cast, and doing my best to make sure Oxford didn't catch me there.

While I was waiting, I scanned information on our prime suspects on a screen a few feet away from the monitors.

Donovan stayed put and watched the other monitors as Weiss and Jensen spent their time going through Galsband's drawers, looking for anything that might give them a lead to Kristin's case.

"Galsband headed your way," one agent finally said into her comm, to Weiss and Jensen. "ETA ninety seconds."

The two agents took their positions close to the door, Jensen on her knees in front of Weiss's crotch, her back to the camera and the door.

"Oh, joy," she muttered, sounding sarcastic as Weiss unfastened his slacks. Then I thought I heard her whisper, "Oh, my," in a much different tone, and I almost sniggered.

"Galsband, five seconds to destination," the monitoring agent said.

"Here goes," Jensen said as Weiss put his hands in her hair.

She started bobbing her head as if she was going down on Weiss, while she made sounds of pleasure. Damn that looked hot. The two of them were a little more realistic than I would have expected. I could swear I saw her mouth *really* on Weiss's cock and that look on his face *really was* one of a man being sucked off.

Weiss watched Jensen as he clenched her hair. "That's it, baby," he said in a hoarse voice as the door opened. Weiss didn't look up, as if he hadn't heard anything.

In the next moment Weiss made a loud groan and pumped his hips a few more times as if he had orgasmed.

Personally, I think he really did. Into Jensen's mouth.

"Damn, baby," Weiss said without looking up. "You get an 'A+' for effort and style. Not to mention the best blow job I've ever had."

Galsband cleared his throat. *"Professor Zimmer."*

Weiss looked up while Jensen gave a very well-done gasp. Weiss's zipper was still hidden by Jensen's head and Weiss did a credible job of adjusting himself and fastening his pants without letting us see anything.

"Sorry, Galsband." Weiss said as he drew Jensen to her feet. "Didn't realize this was your office. Mine is practically underwater, and we grabbed the closest place." He smiled down at Jensen. "Brittany couldn't wait."

By the combination of the bulge in Galsband's slacks and the austere expression on his face, it was clear the professor was struggling between being turned on and angry. "How did you get in here?"

Weiss shrugged as Jensen stood and turned. Her eyes were heavy-lidded as she licked her lips and met Jensen's gaze. "It was the first unlocked door we could find," she said in a sultry voice as she looked Galsband up and down, and licked her lips again.

Weiss glanced at Jensen and grinned as she leaned back against him. He slid his palms up to cup her now huge breasts, and rubbed his thumbs over her enhanced, distended nipples. "If you have a little time, Brittany just told me she'd love some front and backdoor action at the same time, if you know what I mean."

Jeez, Jensen and Weiss would have made a believer out of me. Galsband's throat worked as he swallowed, his stare fixed on what Weiss was doing to Jensen's breasts. "I have a student coming in." He sounded as if he was having a difficult time speaking.

"A girl?" Weiss moved his hands up and down Jensen's body. I had a feeling she was going to kill him once they were alone, since most of RED's agents on the K-Team were watching. "Brittany might like some girl-on-girl action." He brushed his lips over her ear before he raised his head and spoke loud enough to be heard. "Wouldn't you, baby?"

Jensen couldn't have done a better job of acting like the idea made her hot, as if it really did turn her on. "Never tried it," she said in a low, husky voice. "But I have fantasized sucking on a woman's breasts while being screwed. And tied up—the idea of all that BDSM bondage stuff really turns me on."

Oh, honey, you don't know what you're talking about.

But that seemed to do the trick. The bulge in Galsband's pants was big enough to rip a hole through the material. If the professor led RED to Kristin, Jensen just might cut his dick off while Donovan took care of the man who'd kidnapped Kristin.

Galsband cleared his throat again. "There's a private get-together tonight that you might enjoy."

Bingo.

Donovan narrowed his eyes at the monitor as he watched.

Jensen licked her lower lip with the tip of her tongue. "I'm free tonight."

"Ah. Yes." Galsband walked around his desk. "I must talk with the gentleman holding the discreet party to see if we might invite you." He looked up at Weiss. "Both of you, of course, as my personal guests."

"Sounds intriguing." Weiss leaned down and tilted Jensen's face up to give her a brief kiss. "Especially if it involves another woman."

"Another student." Galsband smiled, and the pit of my stomach twisted. "She enjoys the company of a few men at the same time. I will speak with the host."

So much for that poker game.

"Delicious," Jensen said, her eyes on Galsband. She looked up at Weiss. "I have to get to class." She glanced at the professor again. "Call my cell if we're going to play tonight."

Weiss squeezed Jensen's breasts again, and Donovan thought she'd elbow him if he didn't stop. "Talk with you later, baby."

She reached up and kissed him before moving to the desk and sitting on the edge of it. Her short skirt slid up her thighs, almost to her crotch. Jensen was probably hotter than any of the agents watching the show had realized.

"Hope to see you later." She leaned across the desk and brushed her lips over Galsband's before she slid off his desk, gave Weiss a sexy smile, and walked out of his office.

I glanced at the monitor image of Jensen in the corridor after the door closed behind her. She started making gagging motions, pointing her finger down her throat and doubling over like she was going to throw up.

She glanced toward the hidden camera and mumbled into her comm, "I am so going to kill you, Donovan."

Most of the agents around Donovan laughed. He looked like he almost did, too, but he was mostly focused on Weiss and the professor.

"Got a pen and paper?" Weiss asked the professor, who was still staring at the door. "Galsband?"

The man's throat worked, his Adam's apple bobbing. "Yes," he said with a distracted expression. "Pen. Paper." He picked up an expensive pen and pushed it, along with a pad of cream-colored paper, across his desk.

Weiss took the pen and scrawled his undercover name and a number across it. "That's my cell, if Brittany and I can join you tonight."

Galsband looked like he was starting to get himself under control again. He gave a curt nod. "By late this afternoon I will let you know, one way or another."

Weiss winked and made his way out the door.

When it closed behind him, he glanced at the camera and brought his elbow down in a "Yes!" movement.

Donovan shook his head and I smiled.

The rest of the day we monitored Galsband, but he didn't make any calls or meet up with anyone until late in the afternoon. When he was alone in a hallway, he drew out his cell phone and dialed a number. Unfortunately the camera couldn't get a shot of the number pad to see what he was dialing.

Galsband also wasn't standing close to the nearest microphone, and a man with a floor waxer was pushing the thing around a corner. "Isolate and amplify," Donovan said to the agent monitoring that corridor.

It was almost impossible to catch any of the conversation.

All they caught was "student," "tonight," "girl action," and "hot."

Donovan's jaw tensed.

But when he snapped the phone shut, Galsband grinned. He drew a piece of paper from his pocket. The one with Agent Weiss's phone number on it. My heart rate picked up.

Galsband headed out the front doors of the psychology building and began dialing the number.

Weiss's line, which we had already tapped, came through loud and clear.

"The professor said you and Ms. Brittany may join us as my guests tonight. He believes his student will be pleased to meet your young lady."

"Great," Weiss said. "What's the address?"

"Why don't I have my driver pick you and your student up at seven?" Galsband said.

"Christ," Donovan said, and I knew exactly what he meant. Weiss probably didn't live in digs worthy of a wealthy professor.

Weiss paused only a moment before he said, "Brittany and I plan to meet for a drink at six at the Glass House. Why don't we have our drink, then meet you at seven just outside the nightclub." He lowered his voice. "You think she was hot this afternoon. Wait until you see her after a couple of rum and Cokes. She'll be all over both of us before we even make it to Professor—?"

"Ah, there's my driver." Galsband cut in. "I will see you at the Glass House at seven sharp."

"You bet."

Galsband clicked off, and it looked like Donovan wanted to bang his head against a console.

Donovan swiped his hand down his face. "All right. Can't get to the location beforehand with no address." He paced the floor as he spoke to his agents. "So we'll put a tail on Galsband after he picks up Weiss and Jensen. We'll have the raid teams on standby."

"Will do," Takamoto said. "Everyone will be ready and all over that place as soon as we have the address." He braced his hands on the back of a chair. "Who do you want to tail the car?"

"I'll take it." Donovan stopped pacing. "Along with my special unit."

"Color me surprised," Smithe said, and several of the

agents laughed. "Those are some scary dudes. I'm intrigued that Oxford let you bring in outsiders."

I could see the wheels whirling in Donovan's head. He was already planning the operation in his mind at the same time he said, "If you knew what those guys are capable of, you wouldn't be so surprised."

April 26
Friday evening

"Goddamnit, Lexi." Donovan glared at me as he strapped on his raid belt and his scary team secured all of their weapons. We stood in Kristin's living room. "You're not coming. Christ, you're on leave as it is."

"Forced leave." I scowled and crossed my arm and cast over my chest. I bet I made an interesting picture. "I'll drive to the Glass House myself and follow Weiss."

Donovan closed his eyes and looked like he was counting to ten. He opened them and met my eyes. "We'll handle it, Steele." He gestured to the four men who were now watching Donovan and me with obvious interest and amusement. "We've got enough cars following him that we don't need one more that just might catch their attention."

"He wouldn't even notice twelve cars following him. You know Weiss and Jensen are going to keep him occupied," I said.

"Not if Jensen can help it," Donovan said under his breath. "She's ready to kill Weiss as it is, and I can't afford to be an agent down."

"Looked to me like she was having some serious fun." That almost got a smile out of him, but he did a good job of holding it back. "As is obvious to every single one of you mountains, I'm small enough to stick just about anywhere."

"She's got you there," Harrison said with a grin.

"Donovan raised his hands. "Get your stuff together. It's five-thirty and we've got to get down to the Glass House."

I moved my overshirt aside to show my Glock. "All set," I said.

CHAPTER 37

Kristin

April 26
Friday

A "get-together" tonight.

Kristin's whole body trembled. Michaels had just gone upstairs to get ready for his little get-together, while she stood in the kitchen wearing the collar hooked to the chain.

And a girl. A few minutes ago Michaels said she was going to have sex with another student while the men watched.

No way. She never cursed, but one thing came loud and clear to her mind.

No goddamned way.

She tried to control her breathing.

The plan that came to her mind was simple but vicious. Not only was she going to get out of this before he shot her up with that green liquid again, but she was going to make him pay for every last thing he'd done to her.

Got to hurry before he comes down. Kristin rushed to the cabinet under the sink. She had to stretch her arm and feel around, but she finally found it. The punch can opener.

In the fluorescent kitchen lighting the sharp, triangular point glinted. She grabbed a dish towel from a drawer and put it on the counter over the punch opener. She crouched below the sink again and reached back for the oven cleaner Michaels had left beneath the sink. Idiot. But lucky for her.

Kristin glanced around the kitchen. Where could she put it where he wouldn't see it when he came into the kitchen?

The fridge. She opened the huge stainless-steel fridge and shoved plastic containers—no glass, of course—of mustard, ketchup, and other condiments aside to make room for the spray can, putting it closest to the door opening.

Just as she got it settled, she grabbed the single frying pan from beneath the stove, put it on one of the electric burners, and turned the heat on "High." Then she opened the fridge door again, right next to the stove.

"Ready, slut?"

Kristin jumped at the sound of Michaels's voice. Her heart beat like it was going to come up her throat as she held the fridge door open and cool air chilled her naked body.

Michaels was smiling. Grinning.

Sick bastard.

In one hand he held a syringe full of the green liquid. "Never thought I'd get to get in on some girl-on-girl action. Tonight will be a treat for me and my guests." He stopped just outside the reach of her chain. "You're going to get a taste of pussy while you're being screwed."

Kristin's stomach heaved. No. Can't throw up. She gripped the can of oven cleaner and put her finger on the spray button.

Michaels looked at the open fridge. "Close the door before all of the canapés get warm."

Stall him. Make him come closer.

"Please don't make me do that." She tried to keep her hand steady on the oven cleaner. "Please don't make me be with another girl—or those other men. I promise I'll do anything for you."

Michaels's scowl twisted his heavy features. "I said shut the goddamned door."

Her hand shook so badly she didn't know if she'd be able to hold it steady enough.

She would. This was going to end.

"Please," she said, putting all the begging she could into her voice.

"I don't want to mark you before tonight," he said as he strode toward her, and raised the hand that wasn't holding the syringe when he was a few inches away. "But if you refuse to listen to me, so help me I'm going to slap the—"

Kristin jerked the can of oven cleaner out of the fridge and squeezed the button, aiming for his face.

White foam shot from the canister, directly into those eyes she hated so much.

Michaels screamed and dropped the syringe.

The doorbell chimed.

Kristin didn't stop spraying, and his face was nearly covered with the foam. Fumes from the spray attacked her as she said, "You lousy, slimy, scum—"

"Bitch!" He lunged for her.

Kristin tried to back up but her foot slipped in the foam that had plopped onto the tile.

Michaels grabbed her throat, knocking her against the counter.

The can slipped from her hand and rattled as it rolled over the tile floor.

"You are mine to kill." The foam blinded him, but he had found her throat when he lunged for her. "I paid for you!"

His fingers were above her leather collar, and she gasped when he squeezed, his fingers so tight he was digging them into her throat.

Kristin grabbed his wrists with her hands, but his grip was too tight.

Her vision started to blur. She couldn't breathe. Her mind started to shut down as he squeezed harder.

She wasn't sure the chimes she heard in the distance were in her mind or real.

The opener.

She released one of his wrists and started slapping the counter with her palm, even as she felt the world fading.

The opener.

Got to . . . got to . . .

Even as her sight dimmed, her fingers found the cloth covering the punch opener.

Down. He was going down.

She yanked the cloth aside and grasped the opener.

Through her blurry vision, and even as weak as she was, she found the strength to do what she'd planned.

Kristin rammed the triangular point of the punch opener into one of his eyeballs and yanked as hard as she could.

She ripped his eyeball from its socket.

Michaels screamed and released her as his hands went to his eye, where blood poured from the socket.

He screamed as he held one hand to his empty socket and went for her with his other hand. "I'll kill you, I'll kill you! Fucking bitch, I'll kill you!"

Breath rasped through her sore throat to her lungs, giving her just enough strength to switch hands with the opener.

She jabbed the opener into his other eyeball and ripped it out.

"You'll never look at another woman's body again," she shouted as he held his hands to his empty eye sockets and thrashed around. "Never!" she shouted.

"Fucking bitch!" He moved like he had no control over his body and yelled between coherent words. "Dear God. Oh, God." He reached for her, his hands waving in nothing but air as he tried to reach for her. "I'll kill you! I'll kill you! You can't get away and I'll kill you!"

Kristin was having a hard time focusing after nearly being strangled to death, and from all the oven cleaner fumes. But she had the presence of mind to grab the now red-hot empty frying pan, and with a two-handed grip slammed it into his face.

He screamed as the pan burned his flesh and knocked it out of her hand. "You bitch! I'll kill you!" he kept shouting over and over as he floundered and went for her again.

Her strength was nearly gone, but she managed to bring her knee to her breast, plant her foot on his chest, and shove with everything she had.

Michaels fell back and slid across the bloody, foamy floor.

"Kristin!"

Nick, was that Nick?

She slowly slid down the cabinets, her legs starting to give out as well as her sight.

But she had just enough left to see her brother's face. The steel-hard look in his gaze as he pointed a gun at Michaels's groin.

In her haze Kristin almost tipped sideways as she watched, fascinated. She heard a shot, and Michaels screamed even louder and seemed to froth at the mouth.

Then Nick coolly raised the gun and shot the hysterical man between his already sightless eyes.

"I knew you'd find me." Kristin smiled at Nick before everything went dark.

CHAPTER 38

A long road ahead

April 27
Saturday afternoon

Donovan gripped my hand as tight as I was holding onto his when Dr. Shastri came into the room. The doors made shushing sounds as they opened, then closed behind her. Donovan and I had been in the waiting room at the medical center ever since last night, when we found Kristin.

I glanced up at Donovan. I'd seen him intense, focused, angry, and in a killing rage.

I'd never seen him scared.

My cast was hard against my belly, which seemed to twist as I pressed the cast to it.

We got to our feet as the doctor walked closer. Donovan held onto me as if I was his lifeline.

Dr. Shastri was lovely, with dark skin and dark eyes, her hair pulled back tight. She sat on one of the mauve and sea-foam green chairs, the cushion barely giving under her slight weight. The medical center didn't have a hospital's antiseptic smell. At least not in the waiting room—it smelled like paint, dust, and mothballs.

As the doctor waited for us to sit back down, Donovan seemed frozen. I tugged a little on his hand and we sat together.

Donovan's words came out gruff. Hoarse. "How is—" His throat worked. "Is my sister all right?"

"She will be." The doctor gave a gentle smile. I placed her accent as close to Kashmir, in northern India, where I had once worked an op. "But it will take time. You need to understand that."

"How—what—" Donovan sucked in his breath and he looked like the Donovan I knew, not the frightened boy I'd seen while we waited for news. "Please explain everything," he said with a more solid tone to his voice.

"The near strangulation is the worst of Kristin's physical injuries." Dr. Shastri folded her hands in her lap. "The fumes she breathed in from the oven cleaner fortunately did not damage her lungs. However, she does have a few bruises and some mild abrasions from what was probably a whip."

The killing rage was back on Donovan's face, his skin drawn tight over his cheekbones. At the same time, fear for his sister never left his eyes.

"She's been tested for illnesses and diseases, and everything has come back normal so far," Dr. Shastri said.

Those words brought home the fact that Kristin had been sexually abused, and my stomach lurched. It was possible I would end up with two casts if Donovan squeezed my hand any tighter than he was now.

"What now?" Donovan sounded like he had to force the words.

"From what I understand of your background, Mr. Donovan," Dr. Shastri said in her light accent, "I am certain you are aware of what will be the more difficult part of Kristin's healing. The psychological trauma."

Donovan didn't move, didn't respond.

"The extent of this trauma we will not know until she has had a complete mental health assessment," Dr. Shastri said. "At the very least she will be seen by a psychiatrist, a psychologist, and a social worker. She will be prescribed what she most needs based on that assessment.

"Her recovery will involve therapy," she continued. "Not only with a social worker, but the psychiatrist may prescribe medications. As I said, it will depend on her assessment."

Donovan pulled my hand into his lap, and I don't think he even realized it. "When can she come home?"

Dr. Shastri's brown eyes moved from Donovan's to mine,

before she looked at Donovan again. "She will most likely need some in-patient time. How long that will be, it is too soon to tell."

"I don't want her to wake up alone." Donovan looked toward the doors the doctor had come through. "I need to be there for her."

"You may stay with Kristin when you are able to." The doctor had a focused expression, while maintaining an air of soothing calm with her gentle accent. "So that you know, she will never be alone. She will always have a sitter in the room, and we have been assured a guard will always be stationed outside the door. She will be extremely well cared for."

Dr. Shastri stood. "She's resting and may not wake, but you are welcome to spend time with her."

Donovan held onto me as we followed the doctor. I honestly don't think he even realized he hadn't released his grip on me since the doctor came into the waiting room.

For a long time we stood by Kristin's bed. Her bruised, swollen throat, her tortured expression, even in sleep, all those tubes and monitors . . .

"She needs you," I whispered to Donovan, and he released my hand.

Donovan was wholly focused on Kristin when he took her hand in his, and he held it for hours. His voice was husky as he told her how much he loved her.

Then he started talking about how he was waiting for her to come home; about how that old lady had willed him a snotty calico named Dixie; how it was around Boston; memories of things they'd done as kids. Just stuff you would think inane coming from a man like Donovan.

But there was love in every word he spoke, and in the single tear that made its way down his cheek.

CHAPTER 39

It's time

May 10
Friday night

"That feels sooooo good." I fell into Donovan's massage like my friend Tara would fall into a vat of dark chocolate if you gave her the chance.

It was two weeks after the end of Kristin's captivity. Killing Professor Michaels hadn't been enough to satisfy his need for revenge, and he was looking for Cabot harder than ever.

And I was searching just as hard for that sonofabitch whose initials were still carved into my flesh beneath the bandage I wouldn't take off.

The night Donovan rescued her, the Big Men had put a bullet in every professor there. They hadn't killed the men, even though it would have been pretty damned satisfying if he had.

RED covered everything, of course. The agency even found ways to get Harvard to terminate the professors' employment. They'd never work at another major university again.

The carpet in Kristin's living room was soft beneath me as I sat with my back against the couch, between Donovan's knees, while he sat on the couch and massaged my neck and shoulders. The news was just white noise as my head lulled back. I was in ecstasy. His massages were almost as good as the sex.

Well, not quite.

He stopped massaging and his fingers pressed into my shoulders.

"Ow. That hurts." I tipped my head further to look up at him and saw his gaze fixed straight ahead on the TV, his jaw set.

What had been white noise came into focus as the reporter's words sank into my consciousness.

". . . vanished from this local nightclub." The reporter had just the right amount of concern in her voice. "Eyewitnesses believe the young woman was taken by the same man seen abducting other women. What you will see next is an artist's rendering of the suspect."

A white page now filled the screen with a drawing that closely resembled a familiar face. "Danny," I said, and Donovan's hands tightened on me more. It hurt enough that I shrugged out of his hold. "He's one of the men who helped kidnap me, and helped Cabot to escape."

Donovan growled, "He's a dead man."

The reporter continued. "The suspects appear to abduct women from different nightclubs throughout the area, and Boston has hundreds of nightclubs." Then the reporter gave a particularly solemn look. "The Boston Police Department is asking your help in finding the individuals responsible for abducting these young women. If you have any information that might provide any leads, please call . . ."

The TV clicked off, and I saw Donovan set the remote on the end table.

"So much for RED's control over the media and the BPD on this one," I said with a groan. "Senator Shelton's going to be ticked, big-time."

Donovan grunted and started massaging my shoulders again. Rubbing his thumbs at just the right pressure points.

Screw the news.

I sighed in bliss. "Want to talk about when you went back into Navy Special Ops?"

Donovan didn't say anything, but didn't stop the orgasmic massage, for which I was very much pleased.

"It's a long story, Steele." His massage became a little rougher as he added, "And it's not a good one."

"Ease up a bit, Donovan." I tilted my head back so I could see his face, and he stopped the massage and rested his hands on my shoulders. I met his blue eyes. "You can tell me. After all, I totally spilled my guts to you."

"Not totally." He kissed me on the forehead, and his wonderful male scent had an instant effect on me, sending a tingling sensation throughout my body. "One of these days I'll tell you," he said, and I heard the truth in his voice. "Just not now."

Donovan drew me up into his lap, turning me enough so that we were looking at each other. He gave a quirky smile.

"I'm going to miss having you every night when I go home tomorrow," I said softly.

His smile faded and he brushed my hair from my face. "Stay awhile longer."

I touched his stubbled jaw. "It's time, Donovan."

He said nothing, then kissed me before he took me to the floor and slid off my jeans. He kept his clothes on, just pausing long enough to unfasten his jeans and sheathe his erection.

Oh, God. Donovan's cock was inside me, filling me, stretching me before I could catch my breath. It never failed to amaze me how good he felt as he thrust.

Every time with him was wild and passionate, like he couldn't take me hard enough or fast enough.

It curled my toes when I met him with my upward thrusts and felt him hit my G-spot.

He pushed my shirt up and sucked my nipples. "Yeah, like that." I clenched my fingers in his hair. "More. Please suck them more."

Donovan stopped with his groin pressed tight against mine. "What do you want, Agent Steele?"

I whimpered. "I want you to fuck me so hard I'll scream loud enough to shake the walls." Donovan loved it when I begged and talked dirty to him. And he made me beg. "Please, Donovan."

The way he drove in and out of me, pistoning his hips, I don't think he could have stopped if he tried. His clothing felt so good against my naked flesh as he rubbed me in all the right places.

My orgasm was so fabulous that I did cry out, and the walls did seem to rock. Donovan groaned his release, his cock pulsing inside me.

I remained lying on the floor, looking up at him as he tossed the spent condom into a wastebasket. I was amazed at how big his cock still was.

Even more amazing was that he stripped out of his clothing, sheathed his cock again, and was inside me in seconds.

He fucked me like he had to release every demon inside him to be whole again.

And I welcomed him.

May 11
Saturday morning

The itching going on under my cast was going to drive me out of my friggin' mind as I packed. Cast would be off in a week. *Could. Not. Wait.* What a long four weeks since Cabot had broken my arm.

My fillings were going to fall out if I didn't stop grinding my teeth every time I thought of that SOB. How much time since he'd gotten away? Too long. The leads we had managed to turn up went absolutely nowhere. And it was pissing me off, big-time.

But we did know an auction was going down soon.

Tick tock.

My Red Sox nightshirt went into my case first, followed by the shorts, jeans, bikini panties, and everything else.

Home sounded so good. My own bed, my own kitchen, my own mess.

Pecan Sandies and Mountain Dew, here I come.

It had been two weeks since the end of Kristin's captivity. She would be returning home from the medical center tomorrow and I didn't want to be in the way.

At least it looked like she was going to come through better than a lot of women would. Mentally scarred, but she was tough, a lot like her brother. She was a realist, and a graduate student in psychology. She knew she couldn't escape unscathed, and the trauma would take her a long time to get past. And she might never fully heal mentally.

There was no denying the fact, though, that everything had changed for her. To know what to expect wasn't the same as actually living it.

I don't think Donovan could have been happier that she would be back, or more scared to have her coming home—like she might break in his care.

Like I said, since Kristin was returning, I didn't want to be in the way when she got home.

And I missed my own place.

Dixie peered into the room, gave a loud meow, and turned away with her head in the air. I wasn't sure if she approved or disapproved of my leaving.

Just as I gathered all my stuff together—and had proudly done it one-handed—the front door opened and closed with a loud thump. Then heavy footsteps thudded down the hallway and to the door.

Donovan came to me and wrapped his arms around me. "Stay a little while longer," he said for the tenth time.

"You don't have to say it's because you'll miss our fabulous sex," I said.

"Lexi—"

I leaned into him and wrapped my good arm around him. "I just need to be home, okay?"

"Lexi—"

"Take me home."

He heaved a deep sigh that I felt all the way through my body. "I'll carry your stuff."

May 19
Sunday afternoon

The peeling skin on my formerly broken forearm flaked off as I scratched. Okay, gross, but it friggin' itched. It was so good to have that cast off that I'd take the itching any day.

Besides, it was my place and I had a vacuum cleaner. Somewhere.

A week after I'd left Donovan's, I'd settled into my old routine. It felt good. Still, I missed seeing the big jerk every day—and the awesome frequent sex.

I almost dropped the bowl of freshly nuked popcorn and two bottles of Guinness when someone banged on my front door. The Red Sox pregame blared from my little TV on the back balcony.

Damnit. I was all set to kick back and enjoy some time with a bunch of my neighbors who'd be on their balconies, too.

Ugh. This had better be good.

I set the popcorn and Guinness on the coffee table and kicked aside a pair of socks I'd stripped out of the night before.

When I got an eyeful through my peephole of who was on the other side, I grinned. Yeah, it was good all right. Real good.

The chain rattled as I slid it across, and the bolt clicked when I unlocked it. The knob turned before I even had a chance to do it myself and Donovan pushed the door open.

Somehow he managed to slam the door shut and grab me for a hard kiss at the same time. I climbed him, wrapping my thighs around his hips, and held onto his broad shoulders with my palms. He grasped my butt cheeks with his large hands and held me tight to him.

"Mmmm." I tipped my head back as he moved his lips along my jawline. "I like," I said as his erection pressed between my thighs.

"Floor or bedroom?" Donovan said in a throaty growl as he worked his lips down my throat to the gap in my Red Sox jersey.

"Balcony."

That got his attention.

He raised his head and met my gaze.

"Hey, I don't want to miss the game." I brought my lips to his ear. "We're going to kick some Yankee butt."

Donovan quirked his mouth in that adorable way. Although I'm not so sure he'd like the word "adorable" associated with him.

A very naughty glint was in his eyes. "The Red Sox won't even score."

"Blasphemy!" I slugged his biceps and slid down his body until I was standing again. "You know how to live dangerously, Agent Donovan."

He brought me tight again for a hard kiss, but I placed my palms on his chest and shoved him back. Not an easy feat when my lips wanted to stay glued to him.

I headed toward the coffee table. "Twenty-five on the Sox."

"You're on," he said, and slapped my backside when I bent over to pick up the bowl of popcorn and Guinness.

A bottle chilled my palm and I shoved it into his hands when I turned around. "Make yourself useful."

"I can think of lots of ways to make myself useful." He had a wicked expression that almost made me want to forget the baseball game and play a little catch with Donovan.

"Forget it." That was not so easy to say. I walked past him and headed toward the balcony. "There are more important things, you know."

"Why tease ourselves, Steele?" He grabbed one of my ass cheeks with his hand as we crossed the threshold onto my balcony. "The Yanks are going to win anyway."

"This popcorn and that Guinness are going to look so good all over your clothes." I raised the bowl as I faced him and glared.

He lifted his free hand in a gesture of surrender. "We'll just wait until you're forking over that twenty-five."

I narrowed my eyes and increased my glare, but he pulled up a chair in front of the small TV on my balcony and kicked back, with his ankles crossed and his fingers laced behind his head.

The seat next to him was the most comfortable so I had to sit in it, of course.

Mmmm, smelled so good out here. A clean breeze, grilled hot dogs, sun-dried laundry.

My neighbors were already shouting at their screens.

"Heya, Lex," Jerry yelled across the alleyway, through the laundry hanging on the clotheslines between us.

A couple of other neighbors shouted to me, too, and I yelled back at them. The wood railing was rough under my palms as I leaned over the balcony, looked down at the first level, and waved at Marty. When I sat again, I glanced at Donovan, who looked both intrigued and a little amused.

I kicked his shin.

Forget Donovan. Time for the game.

Yeah, nothing like watching "the boys" on a Sunday afternoon and shouting at every good or bad play along with my neighbors across and down the back alleyway. Wasn't long before popcorn was all over my balcony from jumping up with every wicked good play the Sox made. Donovan and I downed a couple of bottles of Guinness each.

Halfway through the game my voice was hoarse from yelling at the umps, who'd made a ridiculous number of bad calls as far as us Red Sox fans were concerned.

During the seventh-inning stretch I wanted to punch Donovan again for looking so smug with the home game at zero-two, Yankees.

"I could rat you out, you know." I leaned close enough to catch the masculine, spicy scent that made me want to climb all over him again. And stay there. "I'd have Jerry and the rest here in seconds if they found out you're a Yankees fan."

Donovan grabbed my waist and pulled me onto his lap, knocking my chair onto the balcony with a loud thump. He cupped the back of my head and kissed me.

Mmmm. What game?

Something vibrated between us. Ooh, that felt good.

He moved his lips from mine, but didn't take his gaze off my mouth as he fumbled between us before drawing out his cell phone.

"Donovan." The irritation in his voice made me smile. He obviously liked being interrupted about as much as I did.

Uh-oh. His expression and his voice hardened. "Steele

and I will be there in fifteen minutes. Have all teams ready, but don't make a move till we get there. Unless necessary."

My heartbeat picked up. Something big was going down, no doubt about it.

Donovan snapped his phone shut and stuffed it back into its clip on his belt. He rose and set me on my feet. "The van came back to the Diamond Castle and made a 'pickup.' I'll fill you in on the way."

First thing, Donovan called each member of his special special team while he locked up. I snatched my always-ready duffel with my raid gear and weapons. After we got into the SUV and took off I strapped on my Kevlar vest and armed myself in every way possible.

CHAPTER 40

It's all in the thighs

May 19
Sunday evening

"A suite in the financial district?" I almost laughed, even though it wasn't a damned bit funny. "Only the best for Cabot. It's got him written all over it."

Donovan and I were hidden in the darkness as we looked up at an office building on Franklin Street, in Boston's financial district. Donovan's special team was around us somewhere—who knew. Ghosts and Shadows.

The ten-story building across the street housed multiple businesses—law firms, insurance agencies, investment offices, real estate brokerages, software companies . . . and sex slave auctions?

Takamoto spoke over the comm. "The surveillance team that's been staking out the Glass House spotted the van when it drove up behind the nightclub."

The comm was clear, with no static as he continued. "One of the suspects was seen taking the woman from the nightclub, and our agents picked up some of the conversation. The men mentioned bringing the woman directly to the auction tonight rather than to a hold. Anxious buyers."

Hearing Takamoto's words brought back all of the sexual and mental abuse Kristin had been through after being auctioned by men like these. It would be so easy to put a bullet between the eyes of every single bastard involved in the slave ring.

And bitch. I hoped that woman we'd overheard at the

Glass House auction was here because, if she gave me an excuse, I'd take her out, too.

I had to find out who killed Randolph and make them pay.

"The van drove directly to this office building and parked in the lowest level of the garage," Takamoto went on in a professional tone. "Van has different plates, but when we checked it out, the dents, scratches, and all other markings on it are identical."

"Just received verification," Donovan said into his RED comm. "My men went on recon ten minutes after notification. Top floor is completely dark from the outside but activity inside behind heavy drapes. One naked, bound victim spotted."

Donovan had a sharp bite to his tone, but satisfaction. "We're going to take out every sonofabitch involved."

Takamoto said, "Ready at your word."

All teams checked in. Green Team was in position on top of the building. Yellow Team covered every fire escape and door shown on the building schematics pulled up on the computer systems in RED's surveillance van. Orange team had the parking garage. Blue Team was all over the stairwells and elevators. We'd brought in Purple Team to make sure air ducts and any other possible escape routes shown on the schematic were covered.

Donovan and I, along with Red Team—which was the largest team—were taking the tenth floor. Donovan's men were there already since they'd gone ahead for recon.

The agents' boots barely made a shuffling sound as we jogged across the tile to the doors leading to the stairs. Blue team had already secured the night guard. Red Team jogged up the stairs to the top floor, not a hitch in our steps.

Blood surged in my veins, kicked up by the adrenaline pumping through my body. I wasn't even winded when we reached the tenth floor. One agent checked the hallway outside the door to the stairs, then gave us the "clear" signal.

Cabot, be here, because your ass is *mine*.

Still didn't know where Donovan's men were, but they were around, no doubt about it.

The stairwell had led us to a hallway that took us directly to a luxurious reception area. By the large gold-lettered script across the glass behind the desk, this operation had a modeling agency as a cover. Well, what do you know.

A modeling agency specializing in private auctions.

Only that part wasn't mentioned.

It was dark in the reception area, but dim light filtered through curtains behind the glass doors to either side of the enormous half-moon desk. Donovan and half the Red Team took the right door while I led the other half of the team to the left.

My heart beat harder, but not from fear. It beat from the desire to hurt these people, like they hurt the women who they enslaved. Like they'd hurt Randolph.

Plush carpeting muffled our footsteps as we moved. I held my Glock in both hands. Steady. Not a tremor.

The glass door felt weighted against my shoulder as I pushed the door open. Whisper-silent. Nothing but the best for Cabot.

There was not a single doubt in my mind that this was his operation.

Once we were in, we could hear the voices that traveled through an enormous area that would probably have been filled with offices and other rooms if it were a real agency. Instead, four separate sets of heavy curtains hung to the floor from huge round hoops. Each hoop was the size of a room, attached to metal chains secured in the ceiling. Thick-linked chains dangled from heavy hooks attached to the ceiling in the very center of each circle.

The chains were moving. Some swinging, some turning, twisting.

Male voices came from behind each of the curtained-off areas. My gut seared as I realized each man was listing a woman's attributes aloud, the words echoing as if they were speaking by microphone.

Then came the computerized voices, just like what Kristin had described.

The hot tingle under my skin grew as hard as pinpricks as I heard the computerized voices saying, "five thousand," "eight," "I'll go ten."

They were bidding.

The sonsofbitches were bidding.

My jaw hurt from clenching it so hard.

But those assholes bidding would be taken care of. RED had traps for those signals and was able to trace them back to the source to bust all of these creeps.

The female voice we'd heard at the Glass House said, "Going once, going twice . . . this little beauty is *sold* to roughman300."

Oh, I was so going to hurt that woman.

As soon as we cleared the door, Red Team slipped around the four sets of curtains in pairs. Jensen was with me.

Someone pushed the curtain in front of me open, the metal rings scraping along the hoop.

"Police!" I shouted when the first man spotted me. "Hands up!"

He reached for his weapon as he started to dive to the side. I nailed the SOB right in the heart.

Shouts of "Police!" echoed throughout the room, followed by gunshots, screams, and cries of "help."

Our agents systematically worked through the chaos. If a man had a gun and was pointing it at anyone—take no prisoners, baby.

If a man or woman wasn't shooting and had their hands up, they'd be taken in for questioning. We didn't fuck around with anyone firing at us.

Three other agents and I circled one of the curtained-off areas. I inclined my head and Jensen nodded. I held my Glock in both hands and peered around the curtain where I'd heard that woman's voice at the end of an auction—

As soon as I peered around the edge of the curtain, a woman aimed her gun directly at me. In that flash I saw two men were behind her, along with a naked woman hanging from a chain.

I jerked and dropped to the side as the men and woman shot through the curtain. From my position I held up three fingers to indicate three shooters.

Jensen nodded. The moment the shots stopped, we swung around the sides of the curtain.

In an instant I had my weapon on the woman, and put a bullet into her forehead before she could shoot at me again.

The men dropped as Jensen nailed one in the heart and someone else got the third one in his chest, then shot him in the head for good measure.

Inside the circular curtained area were the three dead criminals, along with computer and photography equipment. A naked woman dangled from a hook at the center of the round area.

I kept low as I worked my way between the sets of curtains. Not even five minutes had passed since we entered the room. I saw Danny shoving Cabot through a door—where a door shouldn't be.

"Oh, hell no," I shouted, and bolted for Cabot. "You are so not getting out of this, you slimy, sick bastard."

Danny tried to push Cabot ahead, but Cabot looked over his shoulder and his gaze met mine. So much hatred filled his eyes, but I could match him and up him a hundred percent, and then some.

Only a few feet away.

I'd have Cabot this time.

I glanced at Danny to see him pointing his gun at me as I charged toward Cabot. I hit the floor and could almost feel the bullet whiz over my head.

Then Danny shouted, and his knees gave out as blood started seeping through his clothing from his chest.

Someone had my back.

"Cabot's *mine*," I shouted, "I'll take care of him!"

Cabot glanced at Danny before he turned to head through the door into a hidden passageway. That pause, when he looked first at me, then Danny, cost Cabot.

With my version of a battle cry, I dove.

Grabbed both of Cabot's legs.

Using my whole body weight, I slammed into the backs of his knees.

Cabot flipped over my shoulder onto his back.

His cologne hit me thick and heavy, along with the scent of his fear.

He gave a loud shout when he hit the floor.

I was on my feet before he had fully drawn his gun.

A simple roundhouse kick disarmed him.

His gun flew across the room. Wouldn't be reaching that puppy. He'd never have the chance.

I grasped my Glock with both hands and pointed it at his forehead. "You don't deserve to die so easily."

The clicks of other RED agents' guns echoed in the room.

"Back off." I didn't even look at the agents before I flung my own gun as far as I could. "This is personal."

My knee connected with his gut and he gave a cry of pain.

But he grasped my fist and twisted it.

I rolled with the movement to keep him from injuring my arm. Again.

I flipped and landed on one knee on the opposite side of him.

Yanked my fist from his grasp.

Grabbed his wrist and turned his arm in a hundred-and-eighty-degree angle, and bone snapped.

He screamed, but he still had some fight in him. I could end this easy, but I so wanted to hurt him first.

I was out for blood.

He held his broken arm to his chest as he tried to get up.

I beat him to it.

Drew my knee up to my chest.

Drove my leg down.

My foot connected with his face.

He screamed again.

Through my shoe I felt the satisfying crunch of his nose breaking. My heel had slammed into his eye, too.

Blood poured from his nose onto his white shirt. His eye was already swelling shut.

Again he tried to get up.

I jammed my shoe against his collarbone, and his screams grew louder as it broke.

He tried to get up, but I wasn't about to let him.

This man was so going to feel pain.

I dropped, driving my knee onto his forearm, and heard another satisfying crack.

At the same time I jammed one fist into his throat, and his screams became strangled.

"There, you sonofabitch," I gasped. "And I don't have any goons helping me."

He was rolling side to side, whimpering and crying.

Mercy for this sick bastard?

No. Fucking. Way.

I pushed myself to my feet.

With all the power I had, I drove my heel down and into his balls.

Cabot started throwing up as he tried to scream and curl into a fetal position.

I came down on his broken collarbone with all my weight.

Gripped his neck between my thighs and squeezed.

I grasped his chin and the back of his head.

Twisted.

Cabot's neck crunched.

Snapped.

His body went limp.

Silence.

I suppose I should have felt a huge amount of satisfaction from killing the man who had ruined so many lives. But he'd gotten off too easy, no matter how much pain I had cost him in his final few minutes of life.

"Three minutes" I heard one agent break the silence with a laugh. "Hand over the twenty."

"Thought it would take her five," said another. "But anyone should know better than to underestimate Steele."

I kicked away from Cabot, hitting his head with my shoe, shoving his dead, staring eyes away from me.

As I stood, the only emotion I felt was total and complete disgust for the dead man at my feet.

My hands were wet with blood from his nose, my clothes smeared with his vomit. I wiped my palms on Cabot's slacks and turned away to take deep breaths of air that didn't stink of his cologne.

I whirled on a group of three prisoners RED agents had cuffed. "Who killed the undercover female agent, Stella Richards?" I asked, using Randolph's undercover name.

At first no one said anything, but I came at them with death in my eyes and every man's face went white. They knew I meant business after seeing me take down Cabot.

I was about to jam my boot into one man's balls when he yelled and pointed behind me. "Danny. Danny Caserta. He raped then killed the bit—the woman."

Fury seared my body. I kicked his balls. "That's for starting to call her a bitch."

As that man was screaming and crying, I walked to where Danny was still propped up against the wall. He'd been handcuffed while I went after Cabot. Danny Caserta scowled at me even as blood spread across his shirt. Guess he wasn't too injured after all.

"Death is too good for you, too." I pulled out the knife sheathed in my belt. "But I'm going to let you die the same way you killed our agent."

"That bitch got what she deserved." His look was that of a man who knew he was dead no matter what he said. "She screamed while I fucked her, and cried right before I slit her throat."

Rage blinded me.

"This is for Randolph." I reached Danny, grabbed him by his hair, and jerked him down at the same time I rammed my thigh into his face, and *he* screamed. Then with a little twist and a hard yank I tore off his ear and tossed it aside. Danny started to act freaked-out, the psychological impact of having his ear torn off slamming into him, bringing home the fact that he was a dead man.

I grabbed Danny by the hair, slammed his head against the wall, and slit his throat.

Blood gurgled from his mouth, and in seconds his sightless eyes stared ahead.

When I raised my gaze I met Donovan's, and he looked like he was trying to hold back a grin. The four Big Men on his special special team *were* grinning, and looked like they'd never seen a better show.

"Shit, Donovan," Tiger Manning said. "You weren't kidding about that little thing."

I focused my scowl on Manning and he put his palms facing me in a stop signal even as he laughed. "No way I'm taking you on right now, girl."

"Steele suits you," Lloyd said with a grin.

Harrison looked at Donovan. "I've never seen anything like her."

Tank shook his head as I glared at the four of them. He said in his deep Southern drawl, "I ain't sayin' nothin'."

I brushed my hair out of my eyes with the back of one hand and blew out a deep breath. It was then that I noticed my heart was still racing, adrenaline still pumping. Felt like I could take down one of those Big Men right now.

"Hey, Takamoto." I braced both hands on my hips. "Red Sox over Yanks, right?"

"Hold on." Takamoto pulled out his phone, pressing a couple of keys and obviously accessing the Internet. "Yup. Sox, four-two."

"Ha." My lips twisted into a smug smile as I looked at Donovan and held out my hand. "Pay up, Donovan."

CHAPTER 41

Atonement

May 20
Monday morning

Cabot was history.

As a good number of the agents gathered in the big lecture hall, I popped a couple of Excedrin tablets and chased them down with a swig from a plastic bottle of water.

The headache must be from the emotional rollercoaster I'd been on ever since things went bad with Cabot. At least now I had some closure.

When the agents were seated in the hall, I sat on the edge of a table on the platform at the front. "Agent Randolph's killer was taken down last night."

All of the agents' satisfaction was evident, but it was hard on each of us because, at the same time, we all mourned our loss. There was no bringing back Randolph.

"Benjamin Cabot is no longer a problem, nor will he ever be a problem again." Donovan leaned against the same table as he looked at me. "Thanks in great part to Steele."

I raised my bottle in a gesture like I was toasting the clapping agents while a few, who'd been there, made comments like "Should have been there," "Steele kicked major ass," "That sonofabitch got what he deserved."

"Cabot's operations are going to tumble like rocks in a landslide," I said. I could hear the roar of those rocks now. "The guys we didn't eliminate are spilling a lot of what we need to know about Cabot's Boston-based ops."

Thanks to a little persuasion, and truth serum that didn't

give them the same reaction as Schilling, who probably wouldn't live much longer. Scumbag.

An old lady named Grace, who'd been hiding behind a makeup cart, was being particularly informative. Without any special techniques.

"As some of you know, from Cabot's hard drive we found out who the so-called 'ringleader,' is." Donovan crossed his arms over his broad chest. "For those of you who don't, the man's name is Anders Hagstedt."

I set the bottle of water on the table beside me. "Hagstedt's base of operations is unknown, so far. However we do know that he has numerous individuals like Cabot who run sex slave rings or other forms of human trafficking."

I clenched my jaw before I added, "We're going to find Hagstedt and take him down."

May 25
Saturday noon

I felt like I could run a mile as I hurried around my apartment to straighten up before Donovan came over.

Okay, so I'd sorta missed staying with Mr. Neat-Freak-Fabulous-Cook-and-Best-Sex-of-My-Life.

But I had my own life and I'd needed to get back to it.

Unfortunately, when he'd come over last weekend that had been interrupted, but all's well that ends well.

The Hefty bag in my hand slipped when I chucked an empty pizza box from last night into it. Got a better grip and tossed empty Guinness and Mountain Dew bottles, Pecan Sandies packages, paper plates, along with other crap. Well, I had to pick up every now and then.

Like when I cleaned up that garbage, Cabot.

A knock at the door—that sounded a lot like Donovan's—reverberated in the room.

I grinned, tossed the bag of garbage near the kitchen, and headed toward the front door.

A skirt would be real convenient right now, or loose shorts. My jeans felt almost too tight as I headed toward the living room. Could've been Donovan's cooking from when I'd been staying with him, but I didn't think that was the reason why they seemed so snug. I could strip pretty fast, though.

"Heya," I said when I opened the front door and looked at the hot man standing in the doorway.

Donovan grabbed me with one arm, and kissed me hard and fiercely as he kicked the door shut behind him.

I tried to get closer to him when I realized something was between us and digging into my chest. And it smelled incredibly good.

"Food!" I drew away, and he gave me a quirky smile as I took the big casserole pan from him. "Whatever it is, I'm going to die if I don't eat it soon."

He followed me into the kitchen. "Sour-cream-and-chicken enchiladas."

"Oh, yeah. You lived out in the Southwest before you came to Boston." I was already grabbing paper plates out of a cabinet, and plastic forks from a drawer.

"I'll make you tacos someday." Donovan was taking aluminum foil off the top of the casserole pan. I smiled at him. "Like I said, Steele, the way to you is through your stomach."

I pinched his butt. "And the sex. Don't forget the sex."

Every time I ate something Donovan fixed I was in sheer heaven. "This is so good. One of the things I miss most about staying with you is the food."

"And the sex," he repeated for me.

"Uh-huh." I took another bite, and sighed when I finished. "Can I keep the leftovers?"

He just gave his quirky smile.

But then he looked serious. "How are your nightmares?"

I shrugged. "Not as frequent."

He reached up with a paper napkin and wiped the corner of my mouth.

"Maybe saving Kristin and the girls we could, and bringing down Cabot's operation . . ." I said quietly. "Maybe somehow that helped atone for my sins." At least partially.

"Lexi." He so rarely used my first name that I knew he had something important to say. "You did what you had to. They didn't give you a choice."

"Yeah, they did." I sighed. "I don't think I'll entirely be free of the guilt." I shuddered at the thought of the alternative. Being mutilated and chopped into pieces, and forced to live that way day after day . . . "I wasn't strong enough for the other option. Even now I think I would have done the same."

"In reality you were only given one choice." His tone was firm. "Don't beat yourself up over it anymore."

I won't say it was okay because at least those people had quick, painless deaths. But it was true that I'd made the only choice I could make. For me.

"Never being able to see my family and friends again, and the fact that they would never know what happened to me," I said. "That would have been a form of torture and death for them, too." So in some ways, saving my own life had saved others from pain and anguish.

I still didn't think I'd ever be able to cry again. After that first assassination, every tear left me and had never come back.

"It doesn't make it all okay," I said, "but I have to live with it. And accept it."

May 25
Saturday afternoon

Air cooled my chest as I pulled my tank top away from my sticky skin. A beautiful day, but on the warm and humid side. Donovan had run a quick errand—probably to get more condoms.

I smiled. Food and sex with Donovan—and not in that order.

As moist as my skin was getting sitting outside, you probably couldn't tell I'd taken a shower after our last bout of hard countertop sex. We had the hardest time making it to the bedrooms.

The white steps beneath my backside and legs had that bumpy/smooth feeling from someone having painted over older wooden steps without sanding them first. The odor of paint was strong, but I still smelled the neighbor's freshly mowed grass and the white blooms of the purple sandcherry shrubs to the side of our egg yolk–colored triple decker.

My cheeks warmed in the sunshine as I tipped my head up and closed my eyes. Donovan would be back soon.

He drove up in his black Explorer a few minutes later.

Donovan got out of the SUV carrying a notebook.

I cocked my head. "Watcha got there?"

He sat on the steps next to me and opened the notebook. Inside were pictures of tattoos. "We're going to take care of it."

"It," referring to Cabot's initials, which neither of us talked about. I just kept a bandage over it, not even looking when I changed the bandage.

My stomach did a flip-flop. "We can have a tattoo put over it?"

He flipped open to a page with Chinese symbols on it.

My gaze met Donovan's. "The Chinese symbol for dragon."

"A symbol of power, mystery and intelligence," Donovan said, then smiled. "As well as bloodthirsty and fire-breathing."

I liked it when he gave me a full smile. It was so rare.

I returned his smile. "Let's do it."

May 25
Saturday afternoon

Donovan helped me sit up on my elbows and glanced at my belly. "Take a look."

For weeks I hadn't looked at my bare belly, and my heart rate picked up. What if it didn't cover the initials?

When I looked down, it didn't really register at first.

No sign of those horrid devil's initials. Not a single sign.

I couldn't stop staring at the new tattoo on my belly, around my diamond piercing. The tatt covered about the same area the initials had—but it was like the B and C had totally vanished.

A little skip in my heart came out of nowhere.

"I can't believe they're gone." It wasn't registering yet. "Really gone. Like they'd never been there at all."

"It's something to give you only good thoughts whenever you see it." Donovan's expression was soft when I looked at him. He brushed some of my hair from my face and behind my ear. Then he smiled in that sexy way I liked so much. "And to remind me to watch out so I don't get my ass fried when you're breathing fire."

Damn. An ache behind my eyes. I sat up, wrapped my arms around Donovan's waist, and pressed my cheek to his chest. "Thank you."

CHAPTER 42

Family and friends are everything

June 22
Saturday afternoon

The power in my swing sent that ball straight out of Foley to win the game. Grand slam, baby. My family, Donovan, Kristin, and some of my cousins cheered as I made the round, and my mother and two of my brothers touched home plate.

My other cousins were on the losing side, but they only shouted with good-natured jeering.

Donovan slapped me on the butt as soon I stepped onto home plate. "Good job, Steele."

I laughed. "Despite the fact you're on the losing team? Just like the Skanks," I added with a wink. "Oops, I meant the Yanks."

He gave me a harder pat on the butt.

Warmth centered in my chest as I looked at my family. Including Mammy and Daddy we made a team of nine—with the exception of my brother, who'd had to ship out again not long after that dinner with the whole family together.

My parents, who were in their early sixties, were wicked good at softball. Mammy could catch a pop-up fly and hit a line drive with the best of them. Daddy was home run king.

Donovan and I walked to where Kristin was sitting with her back to a tree. She looked melancholy, but happy to be with us.

I looked at Kristin. "It's been about seven weeks now." It seemed like the days had gone by fast since the end of her ordeal, but I imagined they hadn't passed quickly enough for her.

"She's a long way from being healed," Donovan said with a sigh. "But she's tough."

I'd warned my brothers off from flirting with her. She was still skittish around men and probably would be for a very long time. So they treated her like one of our many cousins, aunts, and uncles who were at the park for our annual beginning-of-summer baseball game.

Yesterday had been the first day of summer and, with the heat and humidity, I could really feel it.

Sunshine warmed my skin, and I ran my fingers over my diamond belly button piercing and dragon tatt. I'd taken to wearing crop tops when I wasn't on duty so that my tattoo showed.

It felt good to look at it. Only fond memories came when I did—somehow that dragon tatt, that gesture from a friend, washed away every bit of what had been done to me.

Mammy handed out corned beef and cheese sandwiches while my aunts gave out whatever they'd brought. Donovan's thigh brushed mine as he sat between me and Kristin. Since he'd found her, he didn't seem to let her too far out of sight.

"So you're staying for a while?" I asked, before biting into my sandwich. Yum.

He finished chewing his bite and glanced at his sister before looking back at me. "I'm taking Oxford up on her offer and staying with RED."

Okay, so I felt absurdly pleased. More great sex!

"Are you going to live with Kristin?"

"Just a little while longer. Until she's better, and not scared to be alone." He crossed his legs at his ankles. "There's a brownstone not too far from her place that I'm looking into buying. I'd like to move her in and let her have one of the floors so that we'll be close, but she'll still have her own place."

"A whole brownstone?" I widened my eyes. "Not just an apartment in one?"

He shrugged.

"Christ, you have to have a little money tucked away somewhere," I said, and tossed aside a sliver of an onion onto the pile of garbage we were going to clean up. Ewww. Since when did Mammy put onions in our corned beef sandwiches? "Any of the Big Men hanging around Boston?"

"Doubt it." Donovan took a swig from a bottle of lemonade. "Those guys have been freelancing forever. Not sure any one of them would like any kind of tether."

I cocked my head to the side. "Do you think you'll feel tethered?"

He took another bite of his sandwich and seemed to consider my words for a moment as he chewed. He swallowed. "Not the way RED operates. Oxford doesn't manage with a leash."

"True." Thoughts of what I'd done three months ago came to mind and I gave a rueful smile. "Unless you beat the crap out of your ex-boyfriend's truck."

Donovan snorted then laughed. "*That* won't be a problem for me."

At the realization of what he meant I laughed so hard my stomach hurt.

"Still paying the car company Gary owes for the damage to their merchandise?" Donovan asked.

I jerked my thumb toward one of my cousins. "Lucky for me Dean owns a body shop and did the repairs for cheap. Nothing like having a big, loving family. The car company resold that piece of crap, and I'm down to owing them just a few hundred more."

He nodded and looked at his sister, who was talking with one of my female cousins. He turned back to me. "Even though Kristin's the only family I have, I wouldn't change a thing." His expression darkened. "Except the last few months. If I could take them back—I'd do anything."

I sighed. "It doesn't make up for a damned thing that Kristin went through, but at least Cabot's personal slave auctions are history."

"There are more Cabots out there for us to find and take down." Donovan wiped his hands on a paper napkin before reaching for another plastic-wrapped sandwich. "Your mother makes a mean corned beef."

"You should try her shepherd's pie." I glanced at my mother. "Nummy."

"Oxford intends to pair you and me up on the next operation," Donovan said, drawing my attention back to him. "Eventually *Operation Cinderella* will go international. You up for it?"

"Ha." I smiled and rubbed my Chinese dragon tattoo. "We'll just see if *you're* up to it."

Donovan's mouth had that quirky little smile. "I've requisitioned fireproof gear to work with my fire-breathing dragon of a partner."

FOR CHEYENNE'S READERS

Be sure to go to http://cheyennemccray.com to sign up for her PRIVATE book announcement list and get FREE EXCLUSIVE Cheyenne McCray goodies. Please feel free to e-mail her at chey@cheyennemccray.com. She would love to hear from you.

Keep reading for a sneak peek at
Cheyenne McCray's debut urban fantasy novel

DEMONS NOT INCLUDED

Coming Summer 2009 from St. Martin's Paperbacks

Olivia, T, and I arrived at almost the same time in the Upper East Side Manhattan neighborhood where the NYPD officer's family had been murdered. We parked a distance from the home—couldn't get any closer due to the large number of emergency vehicles.

At least four police cruisers, three ambulances, a fire truck, and two unmarked vehicles had arrived at the scene. Standing outside the fringes of the crime-scene tape and police barricades were neighbors, most still in their bathrobes.

Everyone and everything was motionless. Frozen.

Thanks to a Soothsayer's power to control air and the minute water particles in it, the moment an onlooker happened by, that person instantly "froze," too. The Soothsayer also would use an air spell to put a glamour over the entire block.

Of course, the spells excluded paranorms.

A strange scent came from the house, and I grimaced as Olivia, T, and I walked toward the scene. Burned flesh and the additional sickly sweet scent of burned sugar.

I'd seen dead bodies before. Lots of them. But with each step I took, my back and arms felt tighter. I had to bite my bottom lip to hold back a powerful retch.

There was more here than dead bodies. Something else. Something . . .

Evil?

I shivered as I walked. Tried to remind myself that there was no such division as good and evil. Only dark and light, and all the shades in between—but that was my Drow mind talking. The human part of me definitely wanted to scream and run away from this place.

Crime-scene tape remained as motionless as the people. We made it to the front door of the home after dodging our way through motionless NYPD officers, an FDNY response unit, paramedics, and on past crime-scene investigators, including a photographer and a sketch artist. Our Soothsayer would have to take care of them later when she wiped their memories of the paranormal parts of the crimes.

The lurch of my heart was no less painful than the churning in the pit of my belly when I saw four body bags outside the home, two of the bags small.

The moment I entered the home, the stench hit me even harder—along with a sick, slithering feeling of something wrong, something unnatural and more terrible than I could put into words.

The smells and sensations were absurdly followed by the Soothsayer's gardenia scent, along with a hint of vanilla candles that must have been lit when the humans were attacked.

Olivia came up beside me. "Here comes Tinkerbell."

Great, the Soothsayer standing away from a chalk outline was Lulu, and she flexed her fingers at the sight of me and Olivia.

I was so not in the mood to be frozen. But I'm sure Lulu wasn't in the mood to be tracked down afterward and face my fist.

All Soothsayers were shapeshifters, and Lulu's form was a Manx cat with a bobbed tail. Funny as hell, but she still should have been a rat instead.

When Lulu saw T, her manner changed completely and she turned her petite nose away from Olivia and me.

Olivia smirked when she met my gaze. "Oh, brother."

Lulu smiled and practically drifted over to T like the air carried her on a royal carpet. The beautiful beyond beautiful

Soothsayer wore her hair in golden ringlets and had on a frilly, long iridescent dress (give me a break) that made her look like a Disney fairy princess.

"I'm Lulu." She actually fluttered her eyelashes. "Who might you be?"

I tried not to roll my eyes. Honestly. But I couldn't help it.

Score one for T because he didn't fall all over himself to introduce himself. He gave a simple nod. "Torin."

Lulu raised her chin and immediately had a miffed expression. No doubt because T hadn't referred to her as "my lady" and bowed or showed any other formalities to please her enormous ego.

I looked around what was apparently the living room. Experts had been dusting for fingerprints while other police officers were obviously looking for clues.

And there was Adam, frozen in a crouch, his back to me, his muscles tight, radiating a bleak, gut-tearing energy I had never felt from him before.

Immediately my heart started pounding, from excitement at the sight of him, and from worry. I left T and Olivia behind and went to Adam and crouched beside him.

He wouldn't know I was there until I touched him, but I could see pain in those gorgeous blue eyes that made my chest ache.

His expression told me everything I needed to know.

These were his people, a cop's family. He was taking this as personally as I took the death of a fellow Tracker. Seeing these innocent people slaughtered was as bad for Adam as it was for me watching Demons demolish what was left of Jon.

I braced one knee on the polished wood floor and I touched the sleeve of Adam's worn leather bomber jacket, unfreezing him. "Adam," I whispered, overcome by his sadness.

"This blue looks like fresh paint—" Adam stopped and glanced at me. "Nyx."

He seemed both pleased to see me, yet angry at what had happened. I gave him a sad smile.

Adam moved his gaze to the man on the other side of him,

who was still frozen. "Christ, I wish your Soothsayers wouldn't do this freezing sh—crap. It makes everything harder."

When he shifted his weight from one knee to the other, I caught his leather, coffee, and masculine scent, and wanted to wrap my arms around him. I leaned closer so that I could breathe more of him in, and hoped that he might take comfort from my presence.

He looked around and saw Lulu, who had her hands on her hips. Humans were the lowest of creatures as far as she was concerned.

"Oh, lighten up," Olivia said, moving away from T and intercepting Lulu before she could fire any smart remarks—or nasty spells—in Adam's direction. "Finding lipstick on your teeth is about the only thing worse than being sent on paranormal cases involving humans, isn't it, *Lu-lu*?"

Olivia emphasized the name as she pushed aside her Mets jacket to rest her hand near her Sig.

The slogan on Olivia's navy blue T-shirt said it all:

People like you are the reason
people like me need medication.

Lulu's voice snapped like one of those firecrackers kids tossed around during the human Fourth of July celebration. "Hurry and do *whatever* so that I might leave this Goddess-forsaken place."

She looked away, her nose in the air, and Adam and I glanced at each other, both of us trying to hide a laugh.

While Olivia started her part of the investigation, T came up and crouched on the other side of me. I worked to keep my attention fully on Adam to let him know I was there for him, that I understood how bad this kind of thing felt.

A few moments later, I felt T's awareness turn to Adam, too, and Adam's turned to T.

They did that male sizing-up thing, and Adam's tension seemed to rise. I almost rolled my eyes for the second time since coming to the liaison officer's home.

"Boyd." Adam got to his feet and held out his hand to T.

"Torin." With a slight nod, T stood at the same time I

did, then he reached across me and shook hands with Adam.

"Definitely a paranormal crime," Adam said to me after he and T released their grips. "You won't believe some of the shit we found." He gestured toward what I knew wasn't paint, but blue blood. "This isn't the half of it. Think it could be those Demons you were telling me about?"

I took a good look around me. "I don't think that underling Demons could possibly do this."

"Why not?" Adam said.

"After fighting the underling Demons for a while, I just can't picture it." The total destruction of the home was almost overwhelming. "The power it would have taken to do this is like a cyclone was contained within this house."

"Could be the major or master Demons Rodán told you about." Olivia gripped her electro-pad in one hand. "No one knows what they're capable of. Yet."

I made an absentminded sound of acknowledgment as I caught sight of more blue spots. They were on a carpet that lay over a portion of the wood floor. "The Demons do have blue blood and there are more scattered droplets." I pointed. "Right there."

"Not paint, huh?" Adam said as we walked toward the spots of blue that hadn't fully dried.

"It's possible the major Demons or master Demon also have that same color of blood," T said.

"Did your Proctor tell you anything?" Adam cleared his throat. "Do you think Officer Crisman was, uh, eaten or something?"

T's expression turned amused. I ignored him. Adam had a valid question, and it was way past obvious that this was a big deal for him.

"It *is* possible but we really don't know," I said. "Hopefully we'll find more clues than this blue stuff."

Somewhere in my purse was my electro-pad where I kept my notes on every case. I dug through my purse and came up with it. Adam watched me as I jotted down a few notes with the stylus.

I looked up at Adam. My human half didn't like to ask these kinds of questions. "Were the bodies mutilated?"

It was obvious to me that Adam was trying to keep his professional cop-cool. "Their faces are—hell, I don't know what you'd call it. Mutilated and burned off would be the closest thing I can come up with."

"Goddess." I glanced at T, who frowned. I moved my gaze back to Adam's. "That's definitely not underling Demon behavior."

T shook his head in a slight movement, his frown deepening. "Impossible."

"So you think we're probably dealing with another type of Demon or Demons," Adam said.

"Right now the only thing I know for sure is that a Tracker and a human law enforcement officer were attacked the same night, in the same vicinity," I said. I didn't want to ask, but I had to. "May I see one of the bodies?"

Adam studied me. "They're pretty bad."

"I need to get a look at them." I rubbed my fingers lightly over my Drow collar, which always gave me a burst of strength and confidence when I needed it. "Olivia and I need to." I glanced at T. "Oh, and him, too."

T scowled.

Adam started toward the body bags. "I know you've seen some pretty crappy things, Nyx, but this—like I said, it's bad."

"Stop babying her," Olivia said as she came toward us with her electro-pad and stylus gripped tight. "She needs toughening up."

As if.

Adam nodded, and I walked beside him to the largest of the bags. "From the ID he was carrying, apparently this is the grandfather."

He inched down the zipper. A very much human gag reflex came over me as I breathed in the even stronger smell of burned sugar and flesh.

And saw the face—or what was left of the man's face.

It wasn't like the flesh had been seared. No part of the skull was exposed. Instead it was like something had taken a big stomp and flattened the flesh so that the face was like a wax blob and not human.

A shock went through my elemental energies, nearly stealing my ability to breathe. The haze in my mind was like I'd drained nearly all of my powers.

"Holy shit," Olivia said.

T grunted.

My Drow half was screaming for me to draw blades at the side of it. I could hardly keep my own cool.

"Do you need to leave?" T said in an arrogant tone.

"Go fuck yourself," I said in a voice so harsh it didn't sound like my own. The words weren't even my own. They were deeper, more primal, as each sensation hit me.

"Nyx." Olivia's voice came through the haze in my mind. "What are you sensing?"

"I don't know." I swallowed down the desire to vomit, scream, and run like I've never run before.

Adam said, "I think we'd better get you out of here." The concern in his voice was unmistakable and protective. It was so different from T's asinine tone.

Even though I felt my energies draining, I forced myself to study the face. I had to be professional. But all I wanted to do was flee.

Calm down. *Calm down, Nyx.*

I scanned the horrific image. It took a moment, but then I made it out. A pattern had been "stamped" into the flesh.

"What the hell is that?" Olivia said, but like Adam maintained her professional cop-cool.

My gaze traced the strange lines and whirls. I couldn't speak.

T stood. "Let's see the others."

I looked at Adam, and even though all of my muscles felt weak, I managed to talk. "Believe me, it's the last thing I want to do."

He paused. Nodded. "Okay," he said quietly.

Olivia, T, and I checked the other bodies, and each time the human half of me wanted to throw up. Only my Drow half kept me from losing it.

Each face had the same symbol distorting the darkened flesh. A sort of cone or funnel. The symbol was like nothing I'd ever seen.

Pretending that the horrible images I was looking at were just on wax dummies and not on real people, I used my electro-pad to photograph the faces.

Just in case the symbol wouldn't photograph well, or the Demon had put some kind of sick spell on the faces, I used the stylus on a blank screen to copy the pattern. My artistry isn't the best and I could barely keep my hand from shaking as I did it, but I managed a fair rendering.

I started to get up, but what T did next brought me to a complete halt. With slow purpose, he moved his hand over the face of the fourth victim. The nightmarish look of the face vanished and was replaced by what looked like a sleeping child. The bad energy vanished around the child's body.

Oh, my Goddess. I held my hand to my mouth. As I looked at that small angelic-looking girl, I would have cried if I could. Whatever T had done made it all the more real.

"Maybe he'll be useful after all," Olivia said.

I watched as T did the same to the other three faces so that they looked normal and human, and peaceful with their eyes closed.

Even the odor of charred flesh had vanished. Only the smell of burned sugar remained. I no longer felt a hint of the darkness remaining in the bodies, and my own energy started to flow back into me.

I stared at T for a moment when he was finished. "How did you do that?"

He studied the room. "We should start looking for clues."

Adam and I exchanged looks.

"Thank you," Adam said to T. "It would have been pretty damned bad for their extended families to see them that way."

I nodded. It was hard enough having the images burned into my own mind.

People were still frozen around us, and we had to dodge police officers and others as we searched for any kind of clue. I walked slowly around the house, checking each room and looking around furniture.

Then I found it.

"Hey." I stared at the same image that had been on the faces, but it was much clearer on the wood floor of the dining room. It looked like it had been lasered into the wood, then painted with blood. Smelled like it, too. "Get over here."

They reached my side at almost the same time. Adam whistled through his teeth as T and Olivia crouched beside the symbol. I took a few pictures with my electro-pad.

I lowered myself so that one of my knees was on the floor while I used my thigh to brace the pad on so that I could do my best to sketch the symbol again, this time a lot more clearly and with more detail—or at least the best I could with my limited artistic talents.

The symbol started with a flat, bumpy surface, then spiraled down, like a cone, but was jagged and uneven in what looked like layers.

"What does this thing mean?" Adam said as he crouched beside me so that all four of us were down, examining the strange symbol.

"Not sure." I shook my head. "I'll have to check with my Proctor to see if he has any ideas. Derek, James's partner, is an occult expert. I'll scan and email the image to Derek right away."

I could see Olivia's mind working overtime as she appraised the symbol. "We'll do an Internet search to see if we come up with a match."

"We can check a few symbol books, too," I said. "I have some, and Rodán has a good-sized library. Then there's always the public library."

"Sure." Olivia smirked. "Good ol' New York Public Library. I'm sure it's up to date on the latest Demons that escape through well-guarded Demon Gates."

T's voice came from the other side of me. "We have more on our hands than random acts by a rogue Demon."

A chill ran through me even though I'd been thinking the same thing. All I could do was nod.

Adam's expression went from his usual calm to furious. "I'm going to get this fucking sonofabitch who did this to the kids, whatever it is."

The fire in his eyes and the fact he'd forgotten to watch his language in front of me like he normally did gave me a pretty good idea of just how angry he was, how angry he'd keep being until we shut down the creature or creatures who'd committed these atrocities.

"I think this Demon is taunting us with this clue," I said as I shut off my electro-pad and stuffed it into my purse.

T's strong features seemed strangely impassive. "It wants to let us know what it can do. And maybe that it can't be stopped."

With her brows narrowed and her lips twisted into a frown, Olivia got to her feet. "We'll find the sicko, whatever this Demon is, and it won't have time to wish it could go home to mommy."

Adam had clear meaning in his eyes when he met my gaze. "I'm not letting the sonofabitch get away with this."

He had so much courage and determination to fight whatever paranormal creature was evil and involved humans. And he was a mere human himself.

He'd helped me solve paranormal crimes against humans, but I'd never given him the chance to eliminate the threats. With my Drow abilities, I always managed to slip away from him and take care of business myself at night. Vampires, Brownies, a rogue Werepack, Metamorphs. Because all of the cases had been so easy for me and Olivia to eliminate, there had been no need for additional backup—human or paranorm.

Not to mention I hadn't been ready for Adam to see the other half of me. The dark half. The half that came out only when the sun slipped away and darkness took hold.

But soon, I told myself. It was time to let him see all of me.

Each time I'd taken care of a paranormal crime myself, Adam made it clear he wasn't happy about it and that he should be with me taking down whatever being had committed the crime. But he really had no idea what he was asking. He was a brave human, and I didn't want him to get hurt.

This time I wasn't sure I could stop him from avenging these deaths. And if I tried, he would probably never forgive me. But we were dealing with a Demon. What looked like a powerful Demon. A master Demon.

A gut feeling told me this Demon was playing with us and that a timer had started to count down.

Tick. Tick. Tick.

The Demon had given us a bizarre symbol that we had to decipher.

Before we ran out of time.